Making
Love to
the Minor
Poets of
Chicago

Making Love to the Minor Poets of Chicago

A NOVEL

James Conrad

ST. MARTIN'S PRESS
 NEW YORK

The characters and many of the events in this book are fictitious. Any similarity to real persons, living or dead, is coincidental and not intended by the author.

THOMAS DUNNE BOOKS
An imprint of St. Martin's Press.

Designed by Michelle McMillian

Library of Congress Cataloging-in-Publication Data

Conrad, James.
    Making love to the minor poets of Chicago / by James Conrad.—1st ed.
       p. cm.
    ISBN 0-312-20472-8
    1. Poets, American—Illinois—Chicago—Fiction. 2. Radioactive waste
disposal—Nevada—Fiction. 3. Epic poetry—Authorship—Fiction. 4. Chicago
(Ill.)—Fiction. I. Title.

PS3553.O5183 M34 2000
813'.54—dc21
                                                              99-055719

First Edition: March 2000

10 9 8 7 6 5 4 3 2 1

For my parents,
Phyllis and Harold Conrad,
Alison and Mike,
and especially Paul,
and Jenny, of course

ACKNOWLEDGMENTS

I must give thanks to my agent Neeti Madan at Sterling Lord and my editor Melissa Jacobs at Thomas Dunne Books for believing in this in the first place and for putting in so much time, energy, and care along the way.

I must also specifically acknowledge some people whose support in various stages of this book made it possible for me to see it through to the end: Anne-Christine d'Adesky, Cindy Chastain, Elizabeth Cohen, Carol Ebbecke, Steven Fuhrmann, Sarah Pettit, and Guillermo Zalamea Jr.

Finally, a great debt is owed to Alison Sloane Gaylin, who took the time to find every last mistake and who knows a few things herself about poets in love in Chicago.

PART 1

Nuclear Winter

"The poetry and mystery of the mountains are lost to those who make themselves familiar with their details, not the less because such familiarity may have useful results. In this world things are beautiful only because they are not quite seen, or not perfectly understood. Poetry is precious chiefly because it suggests more than it declares. Look in there, through that valley, where you just see the distant little peak at the end. Are you not dreaming of the unknown beautiful world that exists up there;—beautiful, as heaven is beautiful, because you know nothing of the reality? If you make your way back up there and back to-morrow, and find out all about it, do you mean to say that it will be as beautiful to you when you come back?"

"Yes;—I think it would," said Alice.

—Anthony Trollope,
Can You Forgive Her?

1

THE CLIFF DWELLERS' CLUB

The teacher-student relationship will forever remain just that: the one who knows and the one who learns. Though friendships and love affairs test these limits, they are truly tests; and the one who used to grade the papers, pass or fail the student, and bestow honors when so inclined will always settle back into that disposition, while the ex-student-turned-friend will always feel overcome with a sense of inadequacy and desire for approval. Usually such students will achieve a sense of equality, if not superiority, to their adolescent instructors, but, as in any family, they will fall back into their amateur role when in the presence of the one who first taught what was not known. Resident Poet Joanne Mueller and poetry mogul Vivian Reape were anything but an exception to this rule. When Joanne first met Vivian, in the 1970s at the University of Missouri in Columbia, it was across a desk where Vivian sat on one side and Joanne nervously stood, too afraid to ask if she could be seated. In the course of twelve years, their relationship had barely progressed from that dynamic.

It was a humid September afternoon in Vivian's un-air-conditioned office on the third floor of the University of Missouri English department, and Joanne still vividly remembered how the simple cotton dress she wore had hung on her like a damp sheet in an airless laundry. Vivian, if pressed, could probably offer no memory of the sounds and smells of that late Missouri summer, for Joanne was merely one of fifty students hoping for admittance into her exclusive poetry class, a market Vivian proudly owned as there was no other class available in the three-state region where a student could read and write poetry for university credit. In front of Vivian was a smattering of sentimental and formless verse Joanne had pulled from various scrapbooks, letters, and journals as an offering to the statuesque instructor—statuesque, because Vivian barely moved. She was an overweight woman in her late forties on the third floor of a tower somewhere in the middle of a prairie, suffering from what was hoped to be the last heat wave of the season. She had learned to sit perfectly still in her high-backed chair, occasionally fanning herself with an academic journal or reaching for her tall glass of iced tea, which a department secretary obediently refilled every hour. The environment only added to Vivian's appearance of queenly nonchalance to the slight girl who stood across from her, nervously shifting her weight from foot to foot.

But Vivian was very interested and pleased by what she saw. The empty vessel politely asking to be filled is perhaps the most common source of all mankind's greatest endeavors, and twenty-year-old Joanne Mueller could not have been more empty or polite. The bad poetry in front of her was actually her best attribute in the eyes of a teacher not exactly looking to *teach* but to *impress*; to form without argument a new generation of poetry, written and read, and, most importantly, overseen, by Vivian Reape herself. Vivian was the end of the line of the now extinct breed of creative writing instructors who taught how to write without writing themselves. She used to write, all through her twenties, but her classically formed sonnets and rigid elegies were more in tribute to the old masters and thought to be an unnecessary footnote to the scores of anthologies that had remained in print for centuries. It was an assessment Vivian herself had made as she began to focus more on the academic faculty games that had started her on her cross-country tour of campuses, remaining just long enough at each one to establish the right relationships with the right heads and upcoming heads of the appropriate departments. Not to mention that Vivian's poetry was as unfashionable and impractical as dry-clean-only wool in an era of polyester. The confessional and beat poets of the sixties had seized center stage, daring not only to publish in the respectable journals once reserved for the dry intellectual musings of Vivian and her like, but to actually sell books. The apparent fashion for this kind of poetry, which had forever exiled Vivian from the poetry shelf to that of criticism (should a bookstore actually have one), inspired her quest for whatever powers the art of letters had to offer; and many universities, anxious to explore this new market for creative writing but afraid of turning their departments over to suicidal hippies who wrote about their own orgasms, found in Vivian a safe compromise, a compromise she would successfully exploit all the way to being named head of the National Institute of Poetry a decade later.

For Joanne Mueller, a small-town girl from Missouri, all underlying political intrigue was lost, and she desperately promised to work very hard, read every book referred to in class, and put all other competing course work second to Vivian's great adventure. It appeared to be the chance of a lifetime, and a lifetime was what Joanne committed. Long after Vivian had moved on from her year of shaking hands in the heartland, Joanne stayed in constant touch, sending her poems, revisions of poems, revisions of revisions of poems, until it was subtly suggested to her that she should send them on to Vivian's "dear" colleague Mr. So-and-So at *IQ: Indiana Quarterly,* or Mrs. So-and-So at the *Allentown Review,* and ultimately, to Mr. Daniel Kirby at *Poem,* the seventy-five-year-old poetry magazine based in Chicago. All of these initial submissions were accepted long before Joanne ever wrote out her self-addressed, stamped envelopes, just as her interview for a poetry residence at Lake Bluff College near Chicago ten years later was hardly an interview at all but a polite tea where Joanne and Douglas Skidmore, the ten-year chairman of the English department, spent an hour discussing the virtues of Vivian Reape, newly appointed head of NIP, the National Institute of Poetry.

After eight years teaching poetry at Lake Bluff College, Joanne had most definitely become a member of the club. And she was reminded of this privilege as she was escorted to the penthouse of Chicago's Root Tower and into the Cliff Dwellers' Club, a hundred-year-old gentlemen's-agreement private fraternity for the city's architects, authors, and painters and their philistine keepers. How Vivian Reape, who as far as Joanne knew rarely came to this midwestern Paris, was able to secure a table in such society Joanne could not imagine. In fact, she was cruelly reminded that it was she, Joanne, who should be treating her old mentor to such hospitality and not the other way around. Joanne had never even heard of the Cliff Dwellers' existence until a message had appeared in her department mailbox slot "inviting" her to meet Vivian there promptly at seven that evening. Edith, the ancient secretary of the department, was kind enough to enlighten Joanne as to its importance.

"Frank Lloyd Wright used to belong," Edith said, while Joanne puzzled over the note. "What I'd give for such an evening as you have before you."

Edith Hall *was* Chicago to Joanne. Chicago with all its ashes-to-glory history, a history Edith had worked alongside of, never gaining access to the prizes of the lakeshore, but an ardent admirer of such castles nonetheless. From Joanne's first day at the college Edith had been all too happy to take the girl from Missouri under her wing and tell her all she'd need to know about the overemphasized surroundings she had landed in. A kind of keeper for Sister Carrie.

"Dress up, dear," Edith whispered. Joanne smiled appreciatively, cramming the note, which carefully bore the precise address and cross streets (courtesy of Edith) into her pocket.

When Joanne entered the club at 6:55, dressed in her only suit, a gray pin-striped coat and knee-length skirt she had paid too much for on a trip to New York nearly five years before, she had her name checked off the last of the lists and was graciously led in. She looked down as she walked by the other tables, smoothing her skirt with her hands and admiring how well expensive clothes lasted, or perhaps how someone with little money took such extra care of the few costly items they possessed. Later that night she would wrap this suit up again like a wedding dress. Now she tried to remind herself to walk in it as if it were one, proud and radiant. When she looked up, she was struck dumb by the skyline surrounding the room. The January sun had been dispersed by the million glass stars up and down the magnificent towers along the lakefront, precisely lit grids of man's triumph over prairie, walls that only the select were allowed to look over, as she did now. It was only the voice of Vivian Reape that could instantly pull her back down from this uppermost tree limb, like the dreaded falconer himself, keeping her firmly planted on his thick leather glove.

"Joanne, how lovely you look!" Vivian exclaimed, making no move to rise as Joanne approached the table. Vivian had already secured the best of the two seats, the one with the most expanse of skyline before her and enough of the room facing her should she need to see or be seen.

"Vivian, it was so kind of you to invite me," Joanne said, a pathetic attempt at being the first to announce her own deficiencies in social spheres, a midwestern pride that someone like Vivian Reape could only compare to that of a Willa Cather heroine.

"Well, I'll confess, I'm only able to invite you due to the good graces of various faculty at the University of Chicago." Vivian leaned over the elaborately laid-out table while she said this, as if her words could possibly get them evicted. "A few years back when I was out here presenting various grants and endowments to the

7

university's linguistics department, we came here for a late dinner, and Professor Gray, a brilliant man, noted how I took to the magnificence of the room and its views and managed to squire me an honorary membership. I'm only in Chicago every five years or so, and this rather exclusive nest realizes that various artistic dignitaries from the East may come through every few years or so, and thus, without crowding the true local membership, they can distinguish the club all the more with us passing luminaries."

Joanne was amazed by this statement. Though it contained the usual amount of self-congratulation common to a Vivian Reape sermon, its very presentation offered a kind of humility in the face of Joanne's five-year-old pin-striped suit. Joanne for the first time realized the strangeness of the occasion. Indeed, why would Vivian waste a night at the palace with a lowly ex-student who taught at a midwestern city's *other* university?

"I'm sure, my dear," Vivian continued, "that you will belong to all of this someday. And I can only hope that when you do, and when my gracious absentee membership comes up for renewal, you will remember our night here and vote favorably for your old friend."

Of course, Joanne incredulously realized as she agreed to the martini Vivian ordered for her, Vivian needed something from *her*, but what? What could Joanne possibly be connected to that in any way could tempt Vivian to lift her up to such heights? Joanne started to relax, convinced that the question wouldn't be answered until well into the main course, or, perhaps, would even be held off for after-dinner coffee, a civility even this poor girl from Missouri had picked up from Edith Wharton novels.

They talked of local authors and magazines, the shrinking of art budgets, and the difficulties in selecting candidates for the various programs that Joanne applied for and Vivian judged. Vivian even asked about her home life, though Joanne could not remember whether Vivian knew of her impending divorce and was certain she did not know all the reasons behind it. Again Vivian praised

8

Joanne's suit, and by the end of the second martini Joanne found herself joking that she was glad Vivian liked it as it was the only thing Vivian had probably ever seen her in over the past five years. Vivian roared at this admission, though she quickly caught herself and landed with a hand on Joanne's. "My dear, you work very hard, and that is what I notice, not one or even one thousand pretty suits." Joanne accepted these motherly words with a slight smile and blush, and racked her brain for a time when she had ever seen Vivian dressed in the same suit twice.

By the time their steaks arrived, Vivian was pointing out various local intellectuals, names Joanne was glad she knew, though she was mortified because she could not recognize their faces. The only famous face Joanne found was the *Herald*'s film critic, who had made a name for himself with the first movie review television show and was known nationwide. Cruising comfortably on martinis, Joanne started then stopped herself from pointing him out to Vivian's critical eye.

It was at this point that Vivian's face took on its more serious lines. Her eyes seemed to dim as she looked out the window, not with the appreciation that had gained her entrance into the club, but in distraction, as she began collecting her thoughts, moving in for the attack. The magnitude of what Vivian was about to say became clear to Joanne, who felt her own appetite falling, wishing she had skipped that second martini as she pushed her wineglass a little farther out of reach.

"I don't suppose you've ever been to Nevada?" Vivian finally said, shifting her gaze from the office towers outside to her companion across from her.

"Nevada?" Joanne almost laughed. "Yes, of course I've been there."

"I don't mean Vegas, my dear."

"Oh, of course not," Joanne replied, setting down her knife and fork and grabbing for the wineglass.

"I'm talking about Yucca Mountain, a very old and sacred site for various Native American tribes. You have heard of Yucca Mountain? Recently?"

Joanne stared blankly back at her old teacher, who studied her like a pitcher having just thrown the ball. Only Joanne was never given the bat. "I'm sorry, I'm afraid I haven't."

"Oh Joanne, *really*. There's no need to be shy about your husband's success. Unless what I'm asking has already been entrusted to someone else."

"Jon? Jon's success?" Joanne set the nearly empty glass down. "Vivian, I'm afraid Jon and I have been separated for over a year. Why I haven't spoken to him in months."

Vivian's hand massaged the front of her neck, a gesture Joanne remembered as one of disappointment. Grave disappointment.

"I'm sorry to hear of your troubles. Of course I wish you had confided in me earlier," Vivian neatly replied. So as not to have dragged you all the way up to the Cliff Dwellers' Club for nothing, Joanne translated. The waiter approached, offering more wine, and Vivian quickly shifted them to coffee. Business had begun.

"Your husband has recently enjoyed a most extraordinary success. Do not be ashamed. Though I've never married, I've witnessed various marital behaviors for a lot longer than you have, and this is nothing to be ashamed of." Joanne could only stare down at the sugar she poured in her coffee. "The important thing here is your husband's success. I only wish I had had the privilege of seeing some of his art, something you were able to inspire and nurture in your many years together. Ten years, I believe?" Joanne looked up and nodded. "You haven't signed any papers yet, have you?"

"Look, Vivian, I'm not comfortable talking about this with people. I'm surprised by this 'success' you keep referring to as I haven't seen him work on his paintings for years."

Vivian laughed. "Well, work is only part of the equation here. Isn't his uncle some kind of nuclear diplomat?"

"Vivian, please, what exactly is going on?"

10

"The Nuclear Waste Depository Plant at the base of Yucca Mountain, dear. Or, more for our purposes, the 'Doomsday designs' recently commissioned by the federal government. One of the reasons I'm here in Chicago is to meet with friends of friends who head the scientific panels planning this site."

"What could any of this possibly have to do with Jon?"

"He's been selected as the official painter. Along with an architect, a sculptor, a landscape designer, and a composer, he has been chosen to create the images that will warn people away from the site thousands of years from now. You see, they plan to deposit a vast quantity of nuclear waste and warheads into the base of this poor mountain and seal it up for, hopefully, the ten thousand years it will take for the plutonium to break down and no longer be so toxic. Now obviously our present-day civilization cannot very well look into a crystal ball and know just what kind of people may stumble upon this site. What nationality, what language, what form of intelligence. Why they might not even be humans as we know them. So they've formed this team of artists to create modern-day cave paintings, if you will, that can convey the danger lurking behind the locked doors. Doors that may very well have withered away by the time someone stumbles upon them a thousand years from now. This is the greatest of artistic achievements, Joanne. To literally be the creative mind that, through architecture, sculpture, plant life, and paintings, will warn of the immense danger that awaits the poor innocent who arrives on the scene. A danger that could completely destroy any civilization there exists to destroy."

"My Jon?" was the only thing Joanne could say to this.

"I think we need some brandy," Vivian replied, again placing her hand on Joanne's and motioning for a waiter.

"But Jon hasn't worked in years. In fact, he's back at school, a community college, starting all over from what I can tell."

"Don't forget who his uncle is, darling. You see, I am in agreement with you. This entire project, one with the very lives of millions of people thousands of years from now in its hands, and one with an immense amount of federal dollars behind it, is being thrown together by bureaucrats and scientists who have, perhaps, less knowledge of the arts than anyone. Now apparently your husband has a particular interest in aboriginal art?" Joanne nodded, not taking her lips off the rim of her brandy glass. "Well, they're smart enough to realize the need for artists who have some grasp upon the past in order to create the road signs for the future. Other than that, I'd say the scientists are looking for the easiest way to placate public opinion by involving elements of the artistic community whose reputation is a bit more, shall we say, liberal. Now they don't want to risk all their work and funds by involving some high-profile art world ego or Marxist radical, so why not bestow the honor on someone who hasn't even painted in years and would certainly be willing to work just for the money and opportunity within whatever parameters they establish? So, they hand it to a relative of someone big in Washington to guarantee their control: like an inheritance, keep it in the family."

Joanne smiled at this and quickly thought about those "papers" Vivian had alluded to earlier. Papers she hadn't signed, hadn't even had drawn up, though Joanne was now certain she'd find them in her mailbox this evening.

"Joanne, look at us, a couple of girls sitting in the boys' club enjoying the view." Vivan beamed and sat back, taking in the entire room and skyline at once, like someone tasting a wine in one gulp and deciding to take the rest of the bottle.

"I don't follow you."

"What has been left out?" Vivian continued. "What very important element has been left out of this historic plan? What very important element, which you and I live in service to?"

Joanne was flabbergasted by the question. Vivian Reape and Joanne Mueller arm and arm in something? Her head seemed to spin from this very remote possibility.

"Poetry," Vivian finally said, flatly and with an edge of impatience. "Don't you see? Language, and not just any particular language, but language with form, metaphor, imagery. Language that can defy the odds of time, politics, and fashion. What is lacking is the *Beowulf* of the next century. The words, which may not be the easiest to be initially understood, but with the proper study and appreciation can warn of the impending doom behind the doors breaking down behind them."

"Are you proposing they etch some poem onto the side of an entire mountain as a way of protecting people thousands of years from now?"

Joanne regretted the question the moment she finished it. As a student of Vivian's, she had never been one who asked how or why, and she was amazed, upon looking up, to find Vivian beaming at her, perhaps appreciating the challenge.

"What city are we in, Joanne?"

This, Joanne knew, was a question not to be answered.

"Any fool can say Chicago, locate it on a map, memorize its area code, zip codes, thoroughfares, and interstates. But a city is not made up of just that, is it? What if I answered the question with the 'City of the big shoulders,' would that still answer the question correctly? Look out there." Vivian waved at the skyline, which Joanne had to slightly crook her neck to take in completely. "Do you see that phrase written out in the lights of those magnificent skyscrapers? Of course not. But it *is* there, isn't it? Doesn't that purely poetic line stay with you every time you catch yourself considering the place you call your home, its buildings, its people, its heart? No, dear, we shall not be scarring up some mountain with a poem, but there will be a poem, and it will be written, read, taught, memorized, anthologized, criticized until it survives beyond the resources of paper or computers. Narrative endures. Rhymed right, it stays forever in the mind, passed on as truth or myth and repeated from tribe to tribe. Oh, Joanne, don't you see, we have work to do, great work to do."

Vivian fell back in her chair again after this speech, a speech

Joanne knew was still being practiced and developed for all the future committees and subcommittees, brochures, acceptance speeches, critical magazine articles, and Nobel Prize–winning progress reports. They stared at each other over the rumpled remains of the once-white tablecloth, empty brandy snifters, and cold coffees. High up in a room of mastery, they looked for the other to make something happen. And Joanne was intimately aware of who she was and who she'd never be; the logrolling, back-scratching and -stabbing, plotting, and powerful head of half a dozen academies. A new kind of admiration crept into Joanne's heart for her old teacher. An admiration for a woman who knew how to seize the controls; and if the controls didn't exist, how to create them. It was exactly like writing a poem, this creation of a need when no one had even noticed something lacking. The founding of a great new company. The invention of the wheel and its patent all at once.

"Jon left me for another woman. A young student. His own."

"Fight back."

"Sue him for divorce?"

"No, sue her. Get him back."

"You don't need him, Vivian, any more than I do. You have the friends of friends on nuclear panels. Go to them."

"I have, and they won't. Half of them think the mountain will just blow up anyway. And none of them are particularly eager to give away any future funds to a bunch of long-haired artists."

"Art for nukes? Have you really thought this through?"

"Apparently your husband has."

"My husband would be crazy to turn down any dime handed to him."

"And you'd be crazy not to take half."

Joanne's instinct was to stand up and say thank you and good night. But as she turned away, she was struck dumb again by the skyline flickering around her. On clear days it was said that you could see all the way to Wisconsin, Iowa, and Indiana from rooms such as this. Joanne would be lucky to maneuver herself through the crowd and to the rail on the public observation deck of the Sears Tower. As always, Vivian Reape was right. Right in all the wrong ways, but still right. Vivian sat across from her looking as if the feast had included Joanne herself and it had been exceptional. Joanne felt slightly exceptional as well and sick at the same time.

"I'll see what I can do," she finally managed, struggling to remain seated.

"Good. Now I really must be going. One more thing, dear. You're looking good in the selection for the Traveling Degan Scholarship. I'd start paging through some travel magazines if I were you. But enough with the short stories; dialogue was never your specialty. And enough with the slang in your poems. Stick to formal; it's what you do best."

2

WHERE'S "I'M OVER HERE"?

The next day Joanne Mueller paused outside the door of Douglas Skidmore's office at Lake Bluff College and listened to the party going on inside celebrating his birthday. Though she was expected to attend and was always careful to fulfill all her obligations to the man who had hired her nearly ten years ago, she had barely slept after her dinner with Vivian and had impatiently gone through the motions of her workday without the usual wit and enthusiasm that made her so popular as a teacher. In fact, she hadn't felt this out of sorts in the hallways of the English department since she had left her husband last spring, and with that she decided her absence at the chairman's party would be far more agreeable than her presence in her current state of mind. But as she turned to leave, she saw four students approaching at the end of the hall, two of them current students in her poetry workshop. She quickly went into the faculty party, realizing it would be much easier to spend half an hour listening to a colleague's dull theories than stand in the hall for ten minutes inspiring a much younger, hungry mind.

Joanne felt more like rock-star-in-residence than poet-in-residence at Lake Bluff College, just thirty minutes north of the Chicago metropolitan border. With the right mix of self-help and self-promotion, her creative writing classes were all the rage, closing in preregistration before registration officially started and selling out office hours like any hot road show. Students with appointments lined the hallway for hours. For a woman in her early thirties with long hair going solidly gray and a life made up of her work, the school's work, and her students' work, such popularity could make an ordinary day bearable, as she flirted with accolades from students on the one hand and the jealous scorn of the competing faculty on the other. "Surely there must be something wrong with her teaching skills," Prof. Helen Drake was frequently heard to complain. No student, it would seem, should enjoy learning to such a degree. "Unless nothing is essentially being taught."

Such accusations became dangerous when these peers were the ones making up tenure committees, review committees, budgetary committees, and even holiday party committees, and Joanne usually tried to walk her thin line gracefully between setting campus registration records and keeping in good standing with her more dour colleagues, though even she couldn't help laughing when her fiction class was denied extra funding for a Christmas party, and it turned into a three-hundred-person affair at a student's apartment. A live band had taken over around midnight, and the campus police were unable to shut the party down until nearly 4:00 A.M. Joanne, fortunately, had left the event shortly after the band started and was not among the nearly fifty students arrested, including one stray philosophy professor charged with possession of narcotics.

For the most part, Joanne's ascension to the top of the teaching charts had been a calm, admirable affair. So what exactly occurred in her classroom that at one point induced Prof. Helen Drake to speculate that Joanne condoned the use of hallucinatory drugs? Was it a kind of coolness that hadn't been properly made use of since the late sixties, when professors led student strikes and took their classes to gardens for lectures? For Joanne, a child of that era though a stranger to such practices with her bland background at the University of Missouri at Columbia, such actions would appear far too blatant as appeals for approval. She was dealing with eighteen-, nineteen-, and twenty-year-olds, and she merely put herself in their shoes and taught them about love. *Truth* and *love*: two words she'd once written on a page as her only notes for a two-hour workshop; two principles that were endlessly diagrammed and researched throughout the many halls of Lake Bluff College, but not in quite the same way as in Joanne's classroom. She sent her students back to their dorm rooms, apartments, work-study cafeteria jobs, and parents' vacation homes to find such principles in themselves. And she demanded they bring them all back and lay them on the table for the entire class to dissect. It was common for students of Joanne's to cry. It was also common for them to shout. Anger became part of the process, such as when Debi confessed to having an alcoholic father and Bill announced he was a homosexual. It was at this point, Joanne believed, that the real writing could begin; and whether or not its quality improved, its passion certainly leapt in volume as she found that students would spend more time at least staring into a book if it could be confused with a mirror.

For all of the domestic and emotional angst she dragged out of her fifteen-student workshops (one in beginning poetry, one in advanced, and a middle-level workshop in fiction), Joanne revealed next to nothing about herself. And the students never asked. Speculation and gossip as to Ms. Mueller's personal life were a favorite pastime at more than one table in the Cage, the cafeteria in the student union. The discussions were usually prompted by a new publication of one of Joanne's own poems or short stories. She would never point out her accomplishments to her classes, but would always be found out by her current and past students, who pored over the contents pages in every literary magazine the campus store and Lake Bluff's own literary newsstand, the Book Bar, carried. When "Where's 'I'm Over Here'?" appeared in *The North American,* this single story scandalized the entire school—student fans and faculty detractors alike.

"Where's 'I'm Over Here'?" like all of Joanne's fiction (six published stories in all and rumors of work on a novel) and like most of her poetry (which was far more coded and open for interpretation), begged to be read as pure autobiography. Published after the start of her separation from her artist husband, Jon, and presumably written shortly after his legendary leaving of Lake Bluff's acclaimed poet-in-residence, "Where's 'I'm Over Here'?" is a first-person narrative alternating between a woman with a philandering husband and the much younger woman with whom the husband consorts. The title is taken from the story's opening scene, in which the wife unexpectedly arrives home early from an academic conference (yes, the protagonist is a college professor at a small midwestern school) to what she thinks is an empty house when she hears her husband shouting, "I'm over here," from their bedroom while a younger woman, fumbling in the dark upstairs hallway, replies, "Where's 'I'm over here'?" The academic wife, unnamed through the perfect anonymity of the first-person narrative, stays downstairs on the living room couch in the dark, listening to the ensuing lovemaking and recalling all the past moments of her life when she'd felt betrayed. In her monologues, the other woman, the much younger other woman, recounts the times in her life when she has betrayed other people. The story eventually dabbles in the meaning of the husband in each woman's life, and each woman's search for her true self, as its title not-so-subtly suggests. The other woman eventually leaves without the knowledge that the wife has come home, and the wife ascends the staircase to—confront the husband? Pack a bag and leave? Get in bed with him and pretend nothing happened? Such questions, of course, are left with the reader, and the epiphany is perfected.

Epiphany was, like *truth* and *love,* another of Joanne's key words. Most of her students thought she'd invented it, while her colleagues acknowledged that she had shrewdly cashed in on it. Defined as a revelation of meaning, *epiphany* had been bandied about the long corridors of writing and criticism for years. When Joanne championed it in her short stories in the late 1980s, she did it with an innovation that was deceptively incongruous to the word's meaning. It was her own signature style. She removed the climax from the climax, the answer from the answer, the resolution from the resolution.

Simply put, Joanne would write the end of her story before writing the story, and then filter this ending as "clues" throughout the scenes and poetic ruminations, and usually end on an exceptionally quiet note. In "Where's 'I'm Over Here'?" the betrayed wife climbs the stairs in the way she's always climbed them, only noticing that she's ascending to sleep as day rises. All key plot points are left for the reader or critic to go back and seek within the emotional flourishes throughout the scenes preceding. What made Joanne exceptionally good at this style was her ability to tackle it with confidence. She was capable of engulfing the reader with an underlying belief that the writer, presumed to be the "I," knows for a fact what happens once the ink stops on the page. Her imitators would feebly construct such scenarios without this commanding style, and would usually leave editors and instructors annoyed at such vague and self-important nonstory lines.

Vague was a word Resident Poet Joanne Mueller avoided. Other avoided words were *autobiography, minimalism,* and the all-encompassing *What happens?* From her poetic training, she took the fiction world by surprise attack, and in one short year made more money publishing half a dozen short stories than she had ever accumulated in ten years of publishing poems. Her prestigious *North American* appearance was the invisible feather in her hat. Her students raved, and her audience instantly grew to students all across the country, young and old, who harped on the "literary mystery" of her worlds and were completely enamored by the strength of such an elusive voice. Her peers at Lake Bluff College, however, were thrown into a completely jealous rage.

"What's the literary mystery?" Prof. Helen Drake was overheard to say. "Her husband left her for a younger woman. Perhaps I should be putting out a short story every time I can't find a good parking space at the supermarket." Though it is not known whether this, or any similar comments, ever reached Joanne's ears, she was savvy to the spoils success brought her and immediately turned up the volume in praising the work of her fellow poets and fiction writers in residence, an accomplishment that was truly worthy of the strength of her elusive voice.

A sorrier lot of the blind leading the blind could not have been found on any midwestern campus. In some ways it was such overall dull company that helped create the extreme of Joanne's success in teaching. Her fellow warriors of words were Alex Dupree, the other poet-in-residence, and two fiction instructors. Of the three, Alex was the most interesting. Openly gay, Alex was a true heir to Vivian Reape's American formalism, as well as an heir to the Dupree fortune, from which it was rumored he had already received millions. He specialized in Greek and Latin, and his poems, at times, were exact excavations of lost forms and subject matters. Heady stuff indeed, though virtually assured of never breaking the pop poetry charts. In response to his own academic career overriding his publishing (colleges, academies, and institutions liked Mr. Dupree, as any such brand name could lead to many possible monetary rewards), Alex came out of the closet and sensationalized his verse with glimpses of beautiful native boys attending to the gay-man-on-holiday, as well as the typical go-back-to-her, one-night-stand poems, where the narrator's sexual encounter completely outstrips any possible relationship with a woman that his recent partner may have experienced beforehand. Though these "gay poems" were a bit of an embarrassment to the faculty of Lake Bluff College, not to mention the Dupree family and foundation, the homosexual themes in such a safe formalist environment were an easy way for more-conservative literary journals and prize boards to acknowledge a gay poet and avoid being labeled homophobic. And if that didn't work, a few chips being called in would always smooth the edges, a resort Joanne knew about all too well.

Alex Dupree was in his midthirties, balding, and cursed with large lips and small eyes. He stood tall at six foot two, and kept himself in great gay shape with a steady gym membership as well as racquetball and jogging. His address was what most impressed his colleagues—Lake Point Tower at East Grand Avenue on what appeared to be a peninsula at the base of Lake Michigan. This dark glass condominium, with three curved wings gracefully extending out of a single center column, was one of the seven wonders of Lake Shore Drive, and to have an apartment in it was on a scale with owning a town house on one of the most prestigious blocks of Manhattan's Upper East Side. The rumor was that Alex's family partly owned the building, and he was unique in owning an entire corner of one wing, close to the top, with views of the lake *and* skyline. As much as the Lake Bluff English department complained of Joanne and her rowdy fan club, they saved just enough envy for Alex and his privileged life. "I can just see him trying to decide whether to write a poem on man or nature," Prof. Helen Drake once said. "So he turns his head to the left and stares at the city, then he turns his head to the right and stares at Lake Michigan and the near shores of Canada, and then he shuts his eyes and decides not to bother writing a poem at all."

Both resident poets, Joanne Mueller and Alex Dupree, called Chicago, not Lake Bluff, home, though Joanne lived thirty stories down and a half a dozen city blocks in from the lake, and if she turned her head to the right, she'd see the building across the street, and if she turned her head to the left, she'd see the fire escape of the building behind her. The two of them, however, could almost be called confidants, considering the bitter distance the rest of the faculty—who mostly resided in the Lake Bluff area—kept from them. But what did they really think of each other? Alex was very jealous of Joanne's popularity with students and especially of the appearance of her name on the contents page of *The North American*. Joanne was very envious of a man who lived in a castle without any anxieties about health care, rent, or raises. With each other, though, and, more important, in front of the rest of the faculty, they were truly brother and sister. Alex covered classes for Joanne during the first month of her separation (Joanne had confided her troubles to him and only him in the third-floor faculty lounge); and had Alex not leaked his knowledge of Joanne's personal troubles, her students would probably have revolted, instead of forcing themselves to work with him for the sake of Ms. Mueller. On Joanne's part, she was the first and, for a few months, the only member of the faculty to openly congratulate Alex on the publication of his first gay poems, which she had found out about while waiting in line at the Book Bar behind some snickering students, who were reading between the lines of his single-spaced verse in *Rose Is a Rose*, a well-known lesbian and gay literary quarterly. Joanne promptly reached her hand between the two childish sophomores, pulled the quarterly out of their hands, and stared ahead of them icily until reaching the front of the line, where she bought the journal herself. This story, of course, was one of Lake Bluff's most famous Joanne Mueller legends, and the rumors persisted that she personally had the students removed from the creative writing division, and that one of them eventually transferred (true) and that the other was secretly gay and hanged himself in a shower stall (not quite true—there was a suicide attempt, but the closeted young man went on to graduate with honors in premed).

With such camaraderie between Lake Bluff's resident poets, the question remained, why didn't they really like each other? One important insight into their relationship was the fact that they were both career poets-in-residence. On the one hand, they were savvy enough to appear supportive of each other as two adults surrounded by ambitious teenagers, but on the other hand, they couldn't help acting just like two ambitious teenagers when it came to competing for bragging rights in publishing and prizes, as well as being rivals for the attentions of their boss, Douglas Skidmore. But beyond career jealousy and monetary envy, they simply had nothing in common. Where Joanne was a striking, graying beauty, Alex was a goofy-looking man with a receding hairline that he was investigating concealing with expensive repair work. Where Joanne was emaciated to the point of looking bulimic, Alex was over-pumped from serious gym hours with his own personal trainer. While Joanne taught love, Alex had long stopped believing in such possibilities.

But it was in Vivian Reape that the two had found their most serious grounds for friendship and rivalry. Both had been star students of hers during her cross-country campaign to take the helm of poetry in America, and both had been smart enough to see that she would succeed and had always kept themselves high in her favor. In fact, it was Alex who had warned Joanne of Vivian's most recent arrival. Both poets had presumed that her wanting to dine with Joanne could only mean some type of scolding for the way she was conducting her classes, the amount of time she was now spending on her fiction, or both. And while Alex secretly delighted in this probable wrist-slapping, Joanne now secretly wondered about the Yucca Mountain Doomsday Project and all the possibilities it held. Perhaps an apartment in Lake Point Towers? Perhaps the floor above Alex Dupree?

Prof. Helen Drake, who was not privy to any type of relationship with someone as famous as Vivian Reape and consequently knew nothing of either scenario, was nosy enough to notice the playacting between these supposed two musketeers-in-residence and cornered them at the wine and cheese at Douglas Skidmore's birthday celebration, asking, "Why don't you two Lake Bluff exiles car pool, for heaven's sake?"

This potentially quality-of-life-upsetting suggestion was immediately resolved by both of them. First Alex said, "I really don't see how that would do, as my work on various charity, historical, and corporate boards sends me all across the metropolitan area each day I leave Lake Bluff."

"And besides," Joanne pointed out, "my commute alone is truly the time when I come upon all of my epiphanies."

Joanne's forty-five-minute anti–rush hour commute (north out of the city to Lake Bluff each morning while nearly all other residents of the state of Illinois went south into the city and vice versa at the end of the day) was, depending on the outcome of her career, her modern-day "room of her own." While both Alex and Helen would have liked to laugh out loud at this silly woman's reference to her art, a copy of that week's *North American* (the one in which Joanne graced the contents page) in the hands of Douglas Skidmore made them both bite their all-too-sharp tongues. Alex, in fact, sort of looked like he'd changed his mind about the car pool in favor of possibly finding out just where these damned epiphanies came from anyway.

Joanne's epiphanies came from the city, a literal primer in modern and postmodern architecture, which slowly gave way, as Joanne rounded Sheridan Road and entered the suburb of Evanston, to grand old houses with lawns that looked almost like New England, which gave way, as Joanne curved west, to the famous plains now growing gray strip malls and dull housing developments, and which finally gave way, as Joanne made a sharp right, to the rolling hills and nearly untouched countryside of Lake Bluff. They came from all of the words she had ever read and heard, often brought back to her by some simplistic ballad on the lousy car radio she kept on at all times. They came from remembered dreams and forgotten ambitions. First loves and adult disappointments. As she made this long, winding drive twice each day (a much quicker route was available on Chicago's famous string of freeways), Joanne could clear out all of her students' words, all of her committees, proposals, and fellow writers' blurbs, and even her own personal language of impending divorce, challenging career, and single woman nearing forty, and let in something other. And that other was what she built stories and poems out of, not necessarily a creation, but more a strange mixture of everything she knew and what she still longed to find out.

On the morning after her dinner with Vivian, as Joanne pulled onto Lake Shore Drive and drove along the wall of condominiums pressed up against the magnificent shoreline, she found herself thinking about Nevada and the way Yucca Mountain must, like these condominiums, invite the eye to imagine various possibilities of power and success. For years Joanne and Vivian had been quite a successful team of their own. Vivian would call on Joanne to read at a particular seminar, teach at a weekend retreat, or write a poem to fulfill the requirements of a certain grant or anthology— assignments not unlike the ones she gave to her own students— which Joanne would complete and complete well. In ways Vivian acted like Joanne's agent, something poets lacked, and Joanne was careful to remind herself to be grateful for this. But Vivian was paid as well, and with the absence of any formal contract and agreed-upon percentage in terms of a fee, Joanne was always suspicious when her check arrived in the mail, usually funneled through the National Institute of Poetry itself. As much as Joanne longed to outgrow this relationship and set up shop on her own, she was dependent all the more on those checks from NIP now that she was entirely supporting herself, and was wary of ever crossing anyone as powerful as Vivian in this field.

But the Yucca Mountain concept was different. For once, Vivian wasn't the one who held all the power in setting up the framework in which Joanne was to write. Joanne herself was the one with the connection Vivian needed, and though it was something as mundane as a relation to her estranged husband, Joanne couldn't help enjoying the feeling of their roles shifting for once and all of the bounty that went with it—dinner at the Cliff Dwellers' Club instead of a five-minute phone conversation, for instance.

Vivian herself should be the one to write the poem, Joanne fantasized, as she turned off Lake Shore Drive that morning and the steely gray glass skyscrapers gave way to what they had been reflecting: the steely gray sky. For the rest of her drive to Lake Bluff, she amused herself with the thought of being the one to critique and edit, attend all the dinners and meetings with the heads of departments and officials from the government, cash the check in full, and decide just what percentage Vivian deserved for her labor. But ultimately it was Joanne's name and not Vivian's that would appear on the poem; and like the waste they planned to store in that mountain, no one would really remember the names of who had put it there ten thousand years from now, but perhaps only the name of the one who'd warned them about it. Vivian also hadn't written a poem in twenty years, and she wasn't likely to start now with something as high profile as this, Joanne realized. Besides, had Vivian ever experienced the hopeless effort and joy of having to climb a mountain?

3

THE ANGEL OF LAKE BLUFF

Sink Lewis was not one of the major poets of the English language, the twentieth century, or even the American Midwest, but he was one of the major minor poets of Chicago by the turn of the century. Sink was short for Sinclair, a name that had not been used in his presence since his first birthday. His mother had fallen in love with his father in a high school English class while reading the required novel *Main Street* by Sinclair Lewis; he'd left her on Sink's first birthday, leading her to eradicate any memory of him from her life, including her son's full name. Lewis, her maiden name, she left unscathed.

Sink was one of Joanne Mueller's more famous discoveries. In an approaching decade when "angels" were to become the dominant image of a civilization facing a new millennium after a century of wars, disease, and civil unrest, "angelic" wasn't a bad adjective to be known by, and it was the most popular adjective used to describe Sink.

Sink was blessed with a perfectly smooth and naturally shaped body, which he never exercised and often terrorized with large doses of nicotine, alcohol, designer drugs, and junk food. His hair was blond and silky, kept short on the sides to highlight his boyishness and long on top so that he was usually noticed pushing its golden strands out of his eyes and behind his ears. His eyes were the most unpolluted of blues, and the bones of his face were so perfectly sculpted (high on the cheeks, broad on the chin, straight at the brow) that it was classically trained Alex Dupree himself who first took notice of the creature, long before Sink ever came upon Sandburg Hall, where all the resident writers and wanna-be resident writers congregated each weekday for two semesters a year and a six-week summer program.

Shortly after Alex's initial sighting and right before Joanne's famous discovery came William Dunning's quiet study of Sink's powers, as he sat just across and down the table from Sink three days a week for Joanne's beginning poetry workshop that fall of 1988. William sat next to his friend Diane Whitestone, the two of them (as well as the majority of the class) representing sophomores lucky enough to pull low registration numbers, which they had used to gain entrance to this sold-out course. William had known Diane since his freshman year, and though Sink lived in the same dormitory as Diane, neither she nor William could claim any prior relationship to this future minor poet of Chicago. Actually, when Joanne went around the room asking for their names, where they were from, and why they wanted to take her class, friends like William and Diane had no idea just how little they really knew each other and how much Joanne would convince them to expose within her safety net of sonnets, couplets, and quatrains.

"My name is Sink Lewis. I'm from Toledo, Ohio, and I wanted to take your class because everyone else wanted to take it so I wanted to find out why." As was often the case in Sink's life, this rather bold admission brought smiles from around the table and none brighter than William Dunning's and Joanne's. While William made a note about Sink's incredible honesty, Joanne, who knew something about his type, made a note to be careful what kind of questions she asked him as he was obviously prone to answer them.

Sink had been raised on attention. As the only child of a single mother, he was already guaranteed a certain focus, but it was more his father's similar background that assured him an attentive up-bringing by his mother, who blamed her ex-husband's own single child/single parent status for his mistrust of the world in general and his inability to communicate his feelings. Sink's mother had made it her mission that he would not turn out the same way, and encouraged every talent and trick the boy happened upon. The result, on the one hand, was a total concentration of ego; but mixed with a middle-class background in Toledo, Ohio, a person-ality developed that was always seeking approval while presenting a confidence that appeared to have no need for it.

In high school Sink had found his way to an actual stage in the high school gymnasium, where he heartily took on the rather small male lead in *Hello, Dolly!* (though he couldn't really sing—he'd have played Dolly Levi herself if the midwestern elders had per-mitted it) and was then cast as the lead in *Death of a Salesman.* In this he so impressed the school's drama teacher that the pro-duction was taken around the state to compete in various high school festivals (many of which Sink won) and ultimately paved his way out of Toledo to the big city. Well, thirty minutes north of it. Though Sink always appeared to possess a superior intelli-gence, his problem was his own popularity, and he much preferred his high marks to come from friends and lovers rather than from teachers and standardized tests.

At Lake Bluff he had pursued acting in the relatively small, though appropriately prestigious, theater department, and, despite his expressed desire to study with Joanne because everyone else did too, Sink had actually been encouraged by his drama professors to study dance, music, and writing as a way of thoroughly preparing for the many-faceted world of theater. Dance had proved to be somewhat successful, while music was an overall disaster (forcing one music professor to declare Sink completely tone-deaf—though he won points for effort), and now, three seats down from famed writer-teacher Joanne Mueller, Sink had no idea what lay ahead for him in the world of letters, a sort of one-man show for an extremely small audience. But he immediately liked the smile he was able to bring to Joanne's serious face, and resolved to focus all his attention on her in order to acquire all of hers on him.

Getting what he wanted was Sink's specialty, and the wider the net he cast, the more of the world he gained. In a country obsessed with sexual roles and rules, Sink existed well past all the boundaries. Sexuality was, so to speak, merely another specialty. From a young age he had, like most people, been attracted to both men and women. But instead of growing out of it, he grew into it, developing flirtatious talents to accommodate both sexes, gay and straight, in order to keep every option open in a world he was just beginning to get around in. For Sink, opportunity existed in other people, and though such a philosophy comes off more like a business transaction, for Sink, opportunity included the physical, emotional, artistic, as well as the monetary. For example, Sink's affair with the boy next door when he was fifteen gave him an ally at school, where the boy was a star receiver on the football team. His affair with June Lindstrom at age seventeen also gave him emotional support by getting him linked to one of the most popular girls in his school, who ultimately proved to be his trophy date for the prom. His nonsexual love affair with his high school drama teacher made it possible for him to secure the lead in *Death of a Salesman,* which ultimately got him out of Toledo and into Lake Bluff with a substantial scholarship. But within all of this, it seemed to him there must be a true sexuality made up of all the roles and rules that ran the world around him, some kind of identity he would fall into and remain in for his adult life.

William, across and down the table from Renaissance man Sink Lewis, had already found his place in this adult world, comfortably settling into his position as a gay man—a rather easy role to take at a young age in a liberal arts college. While the spoils of age and the rigidity of suburban society were far from his mind, William positioned himself just so he could keep one eye on Sink and the other on Joanne for the full hour of class time. William had already noticed Sink's homosexual tendency and believed that any mixed signals involving women were only a leftover, closeted defense mechanism. What William didn't know was if and when he could manage to attract Sink for himself, a conquest that became more and more out of reach as Sink's personality seemed to win the approval of more and more of the class each week. And besides, Diane seemed equally smitten, which, in William's wishful opinion, only meant that Sink was certainly gay as he was confident of Diane's attraction to himself as well.

What effect did Joanne's creed of truth and love have on this developing triangle of sophomores? Joanne had patiently waited out the first month of class before lowering her sermon upon them, possibly to ensure she had their full trust in what she was about to ask of them. It is no small task to require a group of fifteen students to begin the process of exposing their own personal demons for the entire class to critique. And in counterbalance to this often painful truth telling, she was asking them to imagine that most elusive of truths, love, and to try and describe what none of them might ever achieve. Since her separation, Joanne herself now paused whenever she reached for that word, and her life seemed to blow up in contradictions because she now had to question what she'd always been so sure about. She reminded herself that she was relatively young, though every time she glanced in a mirror she was more and more struck by each graying hair, every wrinkle spreading like roots from her eyes and mouth, and the permanent red puffiness below her eyes (which in the past had represented a morning after a particularly long night but was now a solemn reminder of one endless night). That fall's class was her first attempt at teaching what she herself felt completely betrayed by, and if any of her students were aware of her personal crisis, they were not reminded of it that afternoon as she asked them to look deeply into themselves.

"These two words, 'truth' and 'love,' may sound like clichés. I'd expect all of you to pick up on that. But we've decided that the world is our subject matter, and a cliché is nothing more than something heard so often that its commonplace ideals are cynically held up to ridicule. But ignoring them, ignoring the truth of feeling, the love we wake up wanting every morning and the compassion we always have to remind ourselves to show the people around us, will never negate the truth of the clichés. In fact, it would be like you were leading your life by negating them. In other words, you're still ruled by them."

Outside the second-floor window of Joanne's classroom in Sandburg Hall, the day was ending sooner than the previous day, and as shadows engulfed the leaf-strewn campus around them, Joanne called her fifteen students inside, farther inside, to let the brutal midwestern winter arrive and fill their hours with the light from reading lamps and the glow of computer monitors. "Practice writing while you read; confront your own mysteries while you write. Your work in this class should be less of a therapy session and more of a detective novel. The first five truths you will each admit to me about yourselves, I can guarantee you, are insignificant. So your assignment tonight is to go home and write six, and may the sixth be the one you don't know now. If you do know it, write seven, eight, twelve, twenty until you find one you don't know. Use complete sentences. Use the first person. Once this is done, we can find the proper forms."

Not all of Joanne's apprentices would succeed in this approach. How can you grade students for not admitting to things they do not even know? But in the three years Joanne had used this method, only one student had dropped out and formally complained, an incident that had brought Joanne's strange approach to the attention of the department but was not enough for it to request her to alter her course, considering the number of creative writing majors who came from her ranks. For those students who never bought into her creed, her sensationalized class was far less dull than, say, Alex Dupree's; his rigorous assignments of classic forms and word origins seemed at best to provide his students with tools but with few ideas as to how to apply them. Other students of hers would realize the point of what she was asking of them years later, while others would think only that they were doing what was asked and find themselves hopelessly staring at blank computer screens once the semester was over.

Joanne always felt confident she could distinguish one student from another. By letting them pour out a grab bag of whatever they considered to be poetry for the first month, she believed she could grade them on the development of their writing once they took on material they had previously been afraid of. To some degree, all of her students achieved this end result. Even if it was one single couplet buried in the more than twenty poems she required of them, she'd find it, circle it, read it aloud to the class, and send the student out into the world armed with those ten perfect metrical feet.

"When you say 'truth,' " Sink asked, as most of the class, including Joanne, had expected him to, "do you mean, like my first romantic experience was with someone twice my age?"

Various erotic images flooded the students' minds as they laughed, gasped, or feigned a serious expression at Sink's blunt confession, while Joanne let herself shift rather uncomfortably in her chair, realizing she was the only one in the room close to twice the boy's age.

"You can make that number one on your list. And keep going, not now but tonight, until you reach one that you never imagined writing down and turning in. These lists, by the way, are not to be passed around to the class. I'll read aloud a dozen of them anonymously just so you all can feel like you're in good company. The truths will later reemerge in your poetry, coded with metaphors and rhyme, and only I will know your starting points, which, by then, will probably have shifted to even deeper meanings once you use the proper forms to pursue the proper subject."

Friends Diane and William felt appropriately challenged and clear about the assignment that lay ahead of them. Perhaps a little too clear. Both were already editing the five known truths about themselves that they would put down and were eager to decide upon the one "unknown" among those they already knew. Will knew he couldn't put "I'm gay" as his self-revelation, though he would surely include it in the five preceding. He actually debated writing "I love Sink Lewis," in a definitely sophomoric fantasy that the great Joanne Mueller would choose it as one of the dozen truths she'd read aloud, and Sink would look directly across and down the table at William and smile ever so knowingly.

Sink left the classroom the moment Joanne looked at her watch and announced the hour. He rushed past Joanne, who was fending off various requests for office hour appointments (she was booked for the next two weeks); passed William, who was waiting for a chance to get more recommended readings, as he had already burned through the initial list Joanne had given the class; and passed Diane, who stayed in her seat in front of her open notebook, already lost in the strange assignment Joanne had handed them. When Sink stepped out of Sandburg Hall, he was struck by the darkness. It was only five o'clock. He quickly turned in the opposite direction of his dormitory and walked out to the lake, Lake Bluff itself, which encompassed the southern boundary of the campus, a lake about a dozen city blocks large, with lighted sidewalks to attract bikers, joggers, and solitary walkers like himself. He buttoned up his black denim jacket as he neared the lake, feeling the cool northwestern wind coming off it, and wondered how many couples were desperate enough to brave the chill and go down into the darker pockets of the shoreline to make love without the threat of roommates. In his first year at Lake Bluff, Sink had made the trip down to the shoreline with three different students, one male, two female; and though one of the women had graduated, the other two might as well have, considering how little Sink now saw of either of them since their initial encounters months ago. He went to the exact spot of the best of these three affairs, a large, flat rock right at the shoreline at the base of a large weeping willow tree, which provided such a good curtained canopy that Sink and the man he had come here with had laughed that they could be removing each other's clothes in broad daylight if need be. By the end of their lovemaking, both of them were somewhat embarrassed, and though they walked back to campus together discussing weekend parties they could find each other at, neither of them did, and they now only nodded at each other when they passed in the cafeteria or student union.

Sink wondered what the guy was really like. He was in a fraternity, often had an arm around a girl who appeared to be more than a friend, planned to major in math, and wanted to get to the conference championships as first baseman on the college baseball team. At one point, while they wrestled each other on the hard, cold surface of the rock, they started to kiss rather passionately, and Sink opened his eyes to find this frat boy staring directly back at him. It was as if one of them should say something, something perfectly innocent but emotional too, something that may have been said a million times before but suddenly seemed true, and their saying it could almost sound like another language that had been practiced for years but was finally understood, not in the words, but in the idea behind the words. Instead, the distant feet of a jogger made them both look quickly toward the nearest spot of sidewalk where the footfalls arrived and went by. They may have laughed in relief once the runner was gone, or was it relief that the strange emotion that had suddenly engulfed them had been interrupted? Sink couldn't exactly remember which transaction took place before their bodies returned to purely physical desires.

Now, alone, Sink stared across the lake at the orange glow of the hidden Chicago skyline spreading out into the night, which always seemed to him like a ghost of the historic fire that had once

36

completely stopped and started the city all over again. He reached into his backpack and took out a notebook and pen. Quickly, like any math equation he was eager to write down an answer for and be done with, he wrote his name, Joanne Mueller's name, and the next day's date at the top. And instead of writing twenty things, or even five, Sink wrote, "I've never been in love," and shoved the notebook back into his bag. After walking a few steps, he pulled the notebook back out, tore out the page he had just written, and again wrote his name, Joanne Mueller's name, the next day's date, and "I've never been to Las Vegas." Balling up the earlier draft and dropping it into a nearby trash can, Sink ran back to his dormitory, hoping to catch up with some friends who would most likely be heading out to the campus pizza parlor for a Chicago deep-dish and pitchers of beer for which they never had to show identification.

4

VIVIAN'S PROGRESS

Vivian Reape's wake-up call came promptly at 5:00 A.M, but she had already beaten it by twenty minutes, waking from a dream of Joanne Mueller's mysterious, estranged husband. In her dream Jon Sullivan was a handsome man, slightly disheveled, with an unkempt day or two of beard, and unruly blond hair, which he combed with his fingers. He was also tall with broad shoulders, she imagined, most likely from a farm, the best kind of gym for developing a strong work ethic and practical good sense—not to mention broad shoulders and forearms. *Giants in the Earth,* Willa Cather heroes, and hard and uncontrollable flat landscapes right out of, well, Laura Ingalls Wilder were the best images Vivian could refer to at such an early hour. It was not a sexual dream. Vivian did not dream in such carnal moods, or at least managed not to remember those impulses when she woke up at 4:40 A.M in a strange city.

And what a strange city to wake up to. After dealing with the woman from the hotel desk (who sounded more asleep than Vivian was), she'd walked to the curtained window and peered out at the early stream of car lights that flowed right to the front door of the Drake Hotel, proudly perched at the southern turn of Lake Shore Drive. As far as she could see into the dark winter morning, towers of condominiums lined the Drive, right out of Miami Beach without the heat or ocean, or even the edges of Manhattan without the history or danger. Chicago seemed like an overgrown child, play-acting, demanding to be treated like an adult when its very naïveté was its most attractive feature. Vivian noted this comparison, ready to use it in one of her next critical essays on a Chicago-based writer. Perhaps Joanne. If Joanne didn't drop the fiction, Vivian would have to write something up and publish it to help her see why she should.

Joanne reminded Vivian of Jon. Naturally, Joanne had kept her maiden name, which had made it all the more difficult for Vivian to find her way into the Yucca Mountain Project in the first place. In her dream Vivian and Jon had been driving through the endless deserts of Nevada in a comfortably large American car with tinted glass and a steady blast of air-conditioning. His art was in the trunk, and the nuclear waste facility was expecting it. Vivian had dutifully accompanied him on this great day, and though Vivian had never even seen any art from the hand of Jon Sullivan (well, how many people had?), she was sure it was an intricate study of primal cave sketches, done with rich southwestern colors—stone turquoise, clay red. In Vivian's hand was a leather-bound note-book, a sort of worn, western leather, dried from the hard sun and dust. She had just opened it to read aloud to Jon when she woke up in Chicago. Yes, thought Vivian, turning away from the cur-tained window, it was time to start work.

Next to the small writing table along the wall was a large carton of books, courtesy of the University of Chicago's library. The one-cup automatic-drip coffeemaker had finished its steam huffing, and Vivian thankfully poured out her coffee. She appreciated the plastic minibrewer, as she hated to be bothered with the trials of room service, which never seemed to be open early enough and always mixed up half her order no matter how many times she had them repeat it back to her. As she blew on the hot surface of her coffee, she set up a second filter and poured in more mineral water so another cup would be waiting when she finished her first. The mineral water seemed an extravagance—was definitely an extravagance at three dollars a bottle from the hotel minibar—but she smiled at the thought of the University of Chicago nuclear scientists, who had so rudely rejected her interest in bringing on a poet for their Yucca Mountain Project, having to make do with one or two fewer test tubes or computer disks because of her extravagant strain on the university's funds. Besides, weren't hotel bars meant for expense accounts in the first place?

At the desk she pulled out a fresh tablet of paper, which she had carefully selected at a stationery store a few days earlier: virgin white, college ruled, legal size. She had selected it as one would choose a dog from the pound, with her heart and a faint reserve of practicality. She also pulled out a new pencil from a box of twelve and quickly sharpened it with the miniature, battery-operated sharpener she had also purchased (all from the same stationery store, all chosen without regard for price, and all expensed to the University of Chicago as supplies for this trip). Once the pencil was sharp and the legal pad set out, Vivian sighed, listening for a moment to the hollow gusts of Canadian air, which gathered speed coming down Lake Michigan and slammed into the hotel and condos like runaway trains. The old hotel slightly creaked and groaned from the endless assault, and Vivian turned away from the still virgin legal pad and reached down beside her to the carton of books.

She first glanced at the packing slip, an agreement between her and the University of Chicago that all seventeen books she had requested were enclosed, and that all seventeen books would be returned undamaged within a week's time. Vivian crumpled the form and dropped it in the empty wastebasket by her side. She had two more lectures and a half a dozen more meetings in Hyde Park before returning to Boston. She'd decide then what she would or wouldn't return of the old, worn volumes that had been messengered to her the day before.

Turning her full attention to the box, she started pulling out the books, stacking them chronologically on the floor around her. There were only a few titles, but many editions. From Old English to the beginning of the fifteenth century: two editions of *Beowulf,* three editions of *The Canterbury Tales,* and one edition (partially edited by Vivian herself; thus no need for a second opinion) of *Sir Gawain and the Green Knight.* From the sixteenth century: two editions of *The Faerie Queene* (what else was there?). From the seventeenth century: four editions of *Paradise Lost* (it endlessly amused Vivian that no one had seemed to get it right, something she meant to get to at some point in her career), one volume of the selected works of Ben Jonson (to encourage her, she felt), and three editions of *The Pilgrim's Progress.* Finally, the Restoration, her old friend and comforter, but only one title from all the work in that rich era, a single copy ("Just send the handiest one," she had told the grudgingly helpful librarian over the phone the morning before) of Swift's *Gulliver's Travels*—a truly inspirational afterthought on which she had prided herself, though she now set it the farthest from her reach, realizing there was something a bit too modern about the work.

Her preparations complete, Vivian again glanced at the blank tablet on her desktop and listened for the wind. She wished it was daylight as she felt so out of place at this early hour, alone in a strange city. Slightly distracted, she poured her second cup of coffee (her last, until lunch), closed her eyes, and stretched out her left leg over the piles of books around her. Like some odd office aerobic, she moved her leg to the left, right, left, right, until another gale of north wind struck the hotel, generating a low moan from what seemed like the very masonry of the building's foundation, and her foot in its red wool sock came down with full gravity onto the carpet. She opened her eyes, a bit disappointed. Just below her

41

foot was her old friend Ben Jonson, and to the left (surely the closest) were the two editions of *The Faerie Queene*. But directly in front of her toes, like the shadow of a sundial, waited the imposing stack of Bunyan's *Pilgrim's Progress*, and she nearly leapt at the top edition.

"As I walked through the wilderness of this world, I lighted on a certain place where was a Den, and I laid me down in that place to sleep and, as I slept, I dreamed a dream." On cue, Vivian looked up from the page and toward the unmade king-size bed she had left over an hour ago. She made her way to it, propped up all four pillows, burrowed herself back under the blankets, and kept reading. Though she had gone to the trouble of making out the list of books, harassed a half-dozen administrators at the University of Chicago's English department for proper clearance (which included use of a next-day messenger service), carefully gone over the list of editions with the tiresome librarian, and had the box brought up to her room by a bellboy (which, of course, required a tip), Vivian had always known she'd only wanted Christian from *Pilgrim's Progress*; and even though she already had all three of these editions carefully alphabetized and written off in her own library back home in Boston, she needed him now like any impatient lover. Vivian didn't sleep and didn't dream, but read; and despite all of the mixed emotions one feels when rereading a book turned to at so many different times and places in one's life, she managed to ignore all the signposts for such sentimentality and pay attention to her larger concern, which was more "How to create a poem" than "Why."

The phone startled her out of her reading, and she answered it on the first ring.

"Ms. Vivian Reape?"

"Yes," Vivian answered, with a note of irritation to remind the caller of the early hour he was intruding upon her.

"Oh, god, I didn't really think they'd just connect me and that you'd answer. I hope I didn't wake you."

"Who is this?" Vivian demanded, glancing at her watch and seeing it was after ten. Four hours had gone by since she had started reading.

"You don't know me, I'm afraid. I mean, I was in the lecture hall where you spoke, I'm a student, you see, at the university. I'm—"

"Yes?" Vivian put in, with well-acted impatience. She was beginning to feel flattered.

"I'm a poet, Ms. Reape."

The first step, wasn't it, Vivian thought, *admitting the disease?* She set the book to her side, charmed by the voice of the young male caller, who must have been choking on the silence between them.

"I see. And what is your name?" Vivian had softened her tone, and the boy's voice seemed to burst through the line in relief.

"As I said, you don't know me. I have yet to publish so you couldn't have read me, but my name—my name? Oh, god, my name is Peter. Peter Brooks. I'm an English major at the University of Chicago, and I take as many poetry classes, both reading and writing, as I can possibly find, though you know there's only limited emphasis on creative writing in the English department, not a major, so you can imagine how pleased I was when you came for the week to discuss the importance of form, something the few writing instructors here don't seem to feel is too important."

"All poetry is form, Peter. Some forms are just richer than, well, than what most poets are using these days."

"Yes, yes, I see that."

Again there was a silence, as if her correcting him had sprung a leak in his sudden enthusiasm. Vivian realized she had a lunch date in an hour and had yet to dress. She wound things up.

"Look, Peter, I'll be back at the university on Monday. Why not meet me for a cup of coffee, say three-thirty? The Green Café? You know where that is?"

43

"Of course I do, and of course I will. Oh, thank you, Ms. Reape, that would be most helpful for me, I had only hoped to—"

"Fine, Monday at three-thirty. Good-bye."

Vivian smiled to herself after hanging up on the boy and went to the desk to make a note in her calendar. While she was doing so, the whiteness of her new tablet caught the corner of her eye and filled her with a sense of loss, a momentary lapse of energy. She quickly jumped into the shower to shake herself out of it.

Downstairs in the main restaurant, purposely ten minutes late, Vivian made her way right past the hostess, confident her lunch date would be waiting, which he was. Daniel Kirby rose to greet her as she arrived at the table, extending his hand, which she promptly pushed away. Instead she kissed his cheek, surprising them both with this rather youthful, girlish gesture towards an old professional friend.

"Why, Vivian, I see you're well."

"Quite, oh, quite. And you seem well too, successful and well." Vivian referred to Daniel's magazine, *Poem,* which he had edited now for twelve years, keeping it the leading journal devoted to poetry, though its circulation had fallen, as had that of all the other poetry journals, so it was a somewhat bitter success that Daniel looked so well from.

"I must say I was very pleased when I received your call yesterday that not only were you in town but that you *absolutely* had to see me. Why it must have been—"

"Three years ago this spring. We were both at the National Institute of Poetry's annual awards, handing out the checks. We managed to miss each other at the next two, though I hope that won't be the case this spring. Right now, my schedule seems clear for it."

"As does mine," Daniel replied, and they both, a little nervously, looked down at their menus. Daniel was Vivian's age, and though his head had lost most of its gray hair and his face seemed to have fallen into deeper wrinkles around the mouth, forehead, and eyes, to Vivian he looked fresh and slightly vigorous, as most people do when coming in from subzero temperatures. She quickly found something to order and almost laughed, remembering her foot moving over the stacks of books in her hotel room a few hours earlier. Again, the choosing was not important to her; her objective was quite clear.

"So, Vivian, what brings you to Chicago. A new discovery? Another theory?"

They both laughed at this usual excuse for why she would call him, often to promote a new poet she had nurtured, desiring to see herself thanked in a biographical note on the last page of *Poem*, or to rant and rave about some current fashion of verse until Daniel would finally ask her to put it down in an essay he would publish, which would generate bags of angry responses and, finally, a half-dozen carefully chosen words of support (usually from the very poets whom Vivian had started off in *Poem* over the past twelve years). Daniel had obviously grown used to the particular dynamic of their relationship. Whenever the year's circulation figures came in below the previous year's, he would call Vivian to bemoan the poor state of American letters, and she would promptly send a few praising notes about Daniel's fledgling periodical to the various board members who donated to the cause, as well as locate a new grant to bestow upon the magazine, which had already seen its paper stock thinned three times in the last five years and its page count reduced from seventy-five an issue to less than fifty.

"As a matter of fact, a young man did call me up this morning looking for guidance. From the University of Chicago, where I'm lecturing this week."

"I see," Daniel replied, still trying to decipher the meaning of Vivian's flushed cheeks. He admired her expensively tailored suit, which was in fact the same one she had worn when dining with Joanne a few nights earlier. Vivian had figured that only Joanne had seen her in it in Chicago, and that Joanne was not very likely to be lunching in the main dining room of the Drake Hotel on a cold Thursday in January. A waiter appeared and took their order.

Surprising herself again, Vivian wasted no time and got right to it. She knew well that one should usually trade pleasantries before and during the meal and get to business only when the cigarettes have been lit and the coffee poured. Daniel was a smoker, a habit she detested, and she'd expect him to wait until then.

"How would you like exclusive rights to the most important poem of the next century? Exclusive first periodical rights, I should clarify."

Daniel smiled at this, interested in the idea but leery of the price and all the other possible baggage that usually came with a request from Vivian.

Vivian went on. "You could call it a *Beowulf* of the twentieth century, but it's much more important. This is a poem designed to actually save lives. Save civilization. Our very planet as we know it." Daniel stopped smiling and stared back with his full attention, his left hand starting to feel around his pockets in nervous instinct. Vivian knew she was blushing and talking so fast that she was conveying information that probably wasn't wise to pass on at this time. But something very old and dormant was stirring within her, something she hadn't felt, or at least paid attention to, for years, or at least as long as she'd known Daniel Kirby, or as long as anyone who was anyone in the field had known her name. There was a way the brilliant sunlight hit the iced snowbanks outside the window that seemed to blind her, and the brightness made her giddy and feel the newness of the year like someone suddenly spoken to by God. She took a deep breath to pursue this new-found joy.

"You should know that the poem in question is an extremely long one, like in the old days when poetry satisfied the way novels do now. You'll have to think in terms of devoting a single issue to it, or publishing installments of it in every issue for a full year. But the world will wait in anticipation for it. You can count on newspapers and television announcing it, alerting people as to where they can find your magazine. You'll have to be prepared to reprint, lines will form, waiting lists, unruly mobs!"

"Vivian, really," Daniel finally interrupted, completely caught up in the glory she related, but also trying to calm her from destroying this beautiful picture with too much hyperbole. "Who? Who is this poet in your pocket?"

Vivian smiled and leaned back in her velvet chair. "Oh, Daniel. My pockets are finally emptied. The poet is myself, the one who just kissed you."

5

LAYOVER

William Dunning searched for poetry. This search seemed more difficult than usual. He found himself unable to sleep in the studio apartment of a United Airlines flight attendant he had picked up at Water Tower Place. Impossible, really. William wrestled with an impending loneliness, lying awake beside Wayne, who was fifteen years older, hailed originally from Miami, hated Chicago, and didn't have a single book shelved or stacked anywhere in his one-room, overpriced, hotel-room-like studio apartment. The apartment, in fact, was the worst part. It was located on one of those solitary blocks of Chicago that had been razed in order to build clean, cubic condos and upper-income apartments, boasting perfectly manicured curbs and sidewalks, while surrounding it city life went on with all its graffiti, mixed incomes, and haphazard architecture. Surely the block had its own privately paid police protection, something not uncommon in the city, for while life in the surrounding neighborhood bloomed with all its overflowing garbage cans, unanswered car alarms, and residents yelling out of apartment windows, passing cars, and shop doors, this block nearly choked on its own sterility. Inside, it looked like Wayne had furnished his room entirely from the nearest Swedish furniture outlet, simply ordering one of everything by catalog. No pets, no smoking, and an occupant who spent more time in the air or on layovers in other cities; Wayne kept the place truly unlivable as it never really was lived in. He had made William promise to spend the night before they had even gotten through the door. William now understood why.

Sitting up on the fold-out bed, William lit a cigarette (something Wayne had grudgingly allowed by providing a paper cup half-filled with water for an ashtray and reminding William that his mouth would taste just like the water in that cup) and concentrated on his loneliness. William had been with his friend Diane at Water Tower Place shopping the after-holiday sales for all the gifts they had not had time to buy during finals week, which had ended a mere three days before Christmas. When he was going up the escalator, Wayne was coming down. Their eye contact was all that was necessary for William to hurry back down and find Wayne patiently waiting near a window display, turning to smile as if they'd already met. He arranged to meet Wayne at a nearby bar in an hour, which would give him enough time to find Diane and beg out of shopping, dinner, a movie, and the long train ride back with her to Lake Bluff. He had felt extremely guilty having lied to her about the liaison, telling her he wanted to wander downtown alone—something poets could actually get away with telling each other—but the guilt he had felt at the time only increased his erotic tension, providing a welcome opportunity for William to distract himself from a heartache he knew was approaching. In truth, William knew the heartache had already arrived, but through proper romantic lenses he had been avoiding it with the constant hope for a message on his answering machine, a personal note in his mailbox, a sudden hand on his shoulder to turn him back from the train impatient to leave the station.

William had always led an optimistic life. As the only child of a high school principal and his wife, who sold real estate part time, William grew up with a mixture of independence and protectiveness, making him daring yet vulnerable, something he hoped experience would eventually resolve. He had always been smart, though he had difficulty in proving talent. He played the piano, wrote poems, drew still lifes, and played baseball. On reflection, he almost felt too spread out and suffered from second-place syndrome by never having learned the focus necessary to excel completely in one chosen field. By the time he did choose it, poetry, he tortured himself by believing his life in Madison, Wisconsin, to be too dull, too safe to harbor the necessary secrets someone like Joanne Mueller would hope to draw out. Indeed, his coming out as a gay man at the young age of eighteen seemed his trump card, and for a while his poetry flourished in gay literary magazines and gained him admittance into the poetry circles of Lake Bluff College. His parents never had much to say about his expectations in poetry and his insistence on being homosexual. There were no violent scenes or attempts to join a contingent in his parade. No matter, William resolved, Lake Bluff was surely his springboard into the rougher streets of Chicago, where experience would chase him down, hold him at knifepoint if necessary, turn off the heat in the winter, and trap him on trains in the summer.

"Chicago," he insisted to people when asked where he lived, which wasn't too often as he rarely had the opportunity to go to places other than Madison, where such inquiries were appropriate. William loved the sound of the word. "Chi-ca-go," he'd say most clearly, dragging out the second syllable to full effect. He had little understanding of someone like Wayne, who talked so dismissively about the city, claiming it as a half-way point between where he had started and the European capitals he was sure to end up in. Wayne had attended a "party" university in Florida, where he had dropped out once securing a job in the airline industry. Wayne claimed to be thirty, but William had found his wallet while he showered and figured his age actually to be thirty-eight. He had short, curly red hair (which William guessed was dyed red and which his driver's license confirmed), a tall, smooth body, and a youthful expression. Wayne was actually rather handsome, William decided, as he looked down at his one-night lover. In sleep, his face seemed more mellowed, and if only, when awake, he'd keep his expressions a little less bright eyed and a little more solemn, he'd fit well into the role of the older lover—mature, wise, and experienced, smiling with a distant nostalgia at the capricious ideas and sexual urges of his younger partner, remembering his own strange blend of confidence and cowardice at that age as he appreciatively made love to the fantasy he had once been.

"Leave the light on; I want to see you," Sink Lewis had said a few weeks earlier, though in retrospect, William now wondered if Sink had actually wished to see himself. Their one-night stand had taken place the night before William left for Madison for his two-week Christmas vacation. Diane had taken him to one of Lake Bluff's famous off-campus parties, which were held on a single block in what was ironically referred to as Lake Bluff's "downtown." Downtown Lake Bluff was an area made up of one department store, a few minimalls, an old hotel, and a string of slightly rundown apartment buildings near the rail station inhabited by students and ex-students experimenting with the bohemian world of artists living in the worst kind of urban squalor. It was a sort of prep school for much larger, more downtrodden, and very expensive neighborhoods in cities like New York and San Francisco. Chicago boasted its own up-and-coming artistic decay in neighborhoods like Wicker Park, Rogers Park, and various blocks of the near West Side. In Lake Bluff, this kind of lifestyle seemed all the more frivolous to the people of the town, due to the large number of low-priced apartments around the campus, some new, others well kept, on tree-lined streets with lawns and gardens. But for

William and Diane, this type of block provided an opportunity to wear black and sit on dirty floors discussing art and politics and still be within walking distance of their dormitories.

The rules of etiquette for such a party were quite clear. No dancing. Though music played at a near deafening level through all the rooms, most of it was undanceable anyway as it shifted wildly from moody punk to kitsch seventies pop, with enough Lou Reed, Clash, and poorly produced demos of small-town rock bands donated by students from their respective small towns. Dancing was for fraternity parties, and for those present who were in a sorority or fraternity (a rather small number); sweatshirts bearing Greek letters or even conversation referring to their Greek activities seemed explicitly forbidden. No ashtrays. Empty beer bottles, windowsills, and even the bare floor were the preferred choices for ashing. No lights. Candles and a few red lightbulbs provided the proper ambiance. No food. A large keg of beer was kept on the fire escape, and the kitchen counter was crammed with various bottles of cheap gin and vodka, with plastic cups next to a ripped open bag of ice in the sink, which was usually covered in cigarette ash. No host or hostess greeted you at the door. In fact, a majority of the people at the party couldn't even say whose apartment they were in. Furniture usually consisted of a rolled-up futon in each room next to carelessly piled boxes and milk crates stuffed with books, clothes, and whatever else a person who would have such a party might own. Sink was seated on the floor leaning back against one of these stained, rolled-up futons, and William, again, fell completely in love.

At a party like this, Sink was a star. He consciously avoided the black uniform, which made William and Diane look like two people intimidated enough to need to dress like everybody else. He wore old blue Levis, which were so extremely torn open at one knee that a good six inches of his leg stuck out bare when he sat cross-legged. For a shirt he wore vintage orange paisley, a pattern just about to make a comeback, and once it did, Sink would continue to wear it, and everyone would already know that he had owned it long before its trendiness made it laughable on anyone else. He seemed made for sitting on a dirty floor, filling the space as one would an easy chair, never tipping his beer when he'd suddenly jolt in laughter, never drawing attention to his cigarette ash, which he managed to secretly flick off to one side, and never looking around with that expectant nervousness that gripped almost everybody at a party. Why should he? Most of the people passing in and out of the room were looking with nervous expectation at him.

His well-known bisexuality also came in handy in a situation like this. Straight people looked, well, straight. The men awkwardly tried to join conversations, oblivious to the women, who couldn't help pulling back into smaller groups, where they whispered about the men as if they were back at their lockers in high school. The gay men and lesbians tended to keep a respectful distance from nearly everyone, as if afraid to stigmatize whatever group they were seen in or to appear wanton with any member of the same sex they so much as brushed up against. Sink, however, brought the best out of everyone. Flirting, praising, listening, questioning, and, most important, allowing enough self-cynicism to make everyone feel more at ease about themselves.

"Will Dunning, one of Mueller's mules, and one of her best," Sink called out, as William and Diane carefully made their way by his group of about six people. Everyone in the group laughed, including William, wondering how much Sink had had to drink or what drug he was on.

"Now Will's a great poet," Sink continued, reaching up to grip the edge of William's black shirt so that he wouldn't move away, as if the thought could even enter William's mind. "He's filled with truth and believes in love. Don't you?" Diane waved to someone across the room and made her way to him, leaving William standing there, so light-headed he was glad for Sink's anchoring him with his hand on his shirt. The loud music made it possible for William to avoid saying anything back to Sink's confident teasing, and Sink soon inched away a bit and by doing so, started pulling William down to sit in the space he had cleared.

"You are a good writer, Will. You have discipline," Sink told him, once William was seated. His bare knee pressed against William's, which was discretely covered in black denim.

"And I admire your writing," William managed, "though I think you have some trouble with the discipline."

Sink laughed. "Do you imagine people reading you hundreds of years from now? Is that what motivates you?"

William could feel himself blush at this directness. Sink placed one of his large, smooth hands on William's knee, the one already pressed up against Sink's, and William couldn't take his eyes off of it, almost afraid to look up into a face that would surely be looking back into his. He glanced around the rest of the group. They were all talking among themselves and watching people coming in and out, strangely oblivious to Sink's intimate movements, or was it too dark to see, too loud to hear, or too common to take notice of? For three months William had sat across and down the table from this man, and now was his chance, the drunken party, the last night before break, the first move by Sink himself. It seemed that everything depended on what he said, and yet he didn't want to choose words so carefully that they would come out souding too well studied. He reached for Sink's beer and drank heartily from it.

"I'm not so sure people will be reading at all a hundred years from now," he finally managed, looking at Sink as he said it, relieved by the thick Milwaukee brew making its way through him.

Sink reached behind him and pulled out a can of Miller, which he opened with one hand, keeping his other on William's leg, casually moving it down onto his calf, which he gently squeezed. Should William put his hand on Sink's? He didn't think there would be any way to do it without noticeably trembling.

"Your eyes are such a light green," Sink said, making it impossible for William to stop from looking back at him. "I can see myself in them."

William's mouth opened to say something, but nothing was there to come out.

"Have you ever been to Las Vegas?" Sink asked.

William stared at him for a moment, thinking he had missed something. "No, I haven't. I've hardly been out of the Midwest. Why?"

"I want to go there. I think gamblers must be a lot like writers. They study forms, spend hours alone trying to get one in a million."

"I don't really think about money," William answered, trying to casually move his hand toward Sink's.

Sink stared at him in a way that looked right through him, no longer looking at what was reflected but at what was possibly showing through. He abruptly removed his hand from William's leg and reached for his cigarettes in his front pocket.

"Gamblers don't necessarily think about money," he told him. "It's the big win, lousy odds. Success making you everyone's friend. Do you want to go home?"

William blanked. To Madison? Leave with Sink? Leave without him? "I live alone," William stammered.

"Well, let's go there." Sink stood up and walked toward the front room, where all the winter coats were piled up in a corner. He didn't say good-bye to anyone, and as William quickly followed behind, he noticed a few people glance at Sink as he walked by, but there were no waves, no attempts to keep either of them there any longer. Diane must be somewhere in that dark crowd, he knew, and by the time he had dug his own coat out of the pile, Sink was already downstairs waiting on the street.

They walked the six blocks to William's dormitory in total silence, giving William time to worry about what was on his bed, on his desk, on his walls, and on his stereo turntable. Everything in his room suddenly seemed uncool or embarrassing, including the room itself, a regular closet under a staircase on the first floor. They managed not to bump into any people in the dorm's hallway, as many of them had already left for vacation, and as for the rest, it was after midnight in Lake Bluff, Illinois, and most residents were already where they'd be for the rest of the night. Before William could even think of what to say or do once the door shut behind them, Sink grabbed him, kissed him, and pulled him down on the bed. William tried to relax once they had established that the light be left on, but the sex was clumsy and quick, and halfway through William realized that it wasn't what he wanted. That is, he wanted Sink, but he wanted a whole night of just touching knees, staying up late to talk about their hometowns, and he now feared that the entire affair was spiraling into an encounter in a rest room. Eventually, they were just two twenty-year-old men, lying on a lumpy, single bed in a dorm room after sex. William felt Sink's desire to leave. He also felt his own desire to leave, not to leave Sink, but to avoid being the one left.

There was a sound of a plane passing overhead, and William wished he was on it, smiling at the fact that he was now with his own flight attendant, though he didn't feel like he was going anywhere in particular. He looked down at Wayne and wondered if Sink had looked down on him that night several weeks before, considering why William tried to make himself attractive in all the wrong ways, ignoring all that was right. He didn't want to remember anymore. Sink's socks hadn't matched: one was an old, worn sweat sock, and the other was forest green wool.

Sink had never called William, as he had said he would. A few nights earlier William had finally broken down and looked him up in the directory and called him. He'd left a message with a roommate, never knowing if it had been passed on. Outside the snow was three inches high on the windowsill, and in the sphere of a streetlight the storm looked like one of those plastic snow globes all shaken up. William started to worry again about Diane getting home alone on that long train ride to Lake Bluff. But William did not know that Diane wasn't alone. And Diane had never been to Las Vegas either.

6

REFORM OR REVOLUTION?

The snow that had started while William and Wayne entered into their doomed affair was the beginning of a severe blizzard for the Chicago metropolitan area, and Joanne stood at her living room window also watching the snow swirl in the perfect sphere of a streetlight, wondering what it reminded her of. But before she could think to compare it to a shaken-up snow globe, she despaired about the number of years she had now spent comparing the world to something else, and she gulped her glass of red wine and craved a cigarette. Joanne had quit smoking two years ago and always regretted it. She had nearly reached the point of starting up again when Jon left, and while her very flesh demanded nicotine in the resulting trauma, her pride refused to allow Jon to think he had caused her to end up back at a pack a day in his absence. She simply found herself hanging out more with her smoking students, fellow professors, and friends to enjoy the occasional drag, and someday, she promised herself, when Jon had been dealt with, she'd actually buy a pack to celebrate.

Joanne walked over to her bookcase and instinctively pulled out her college copy of *The Pilgrim's Progress*. It had occurred to her, on her drive back to the city from campus (among numerous things that occurred to her, such as a new ending for an exceptionally difficult story she was working on, a new title for an old poem she had been thinking of sending around again, and an idea for a novel, which was actually a combination of two previous ideas), that she was going to need some help with her great nuclear ode. On the one hand, the prospect of the poem excited her with all of its grandness and importance (not to mention money), but on the other hand, it scared the hell out of her as she imagined worming her way through Vivian's bitter comments, which would surely blemish the margins. It occurred to her that she should get a leg up on Vivian and do some primary research, for wasn't Vivian always demanding a literary and historical context for the simplest haiku? And wasn't goddamned John Bunyan and his *Pilgrim's Progress* about as deathly and tiring as any literary, historical epic could hope to be? She flipped through the pages, which were dry and coarse, a kind of blue comatose color she'd seen on television hospital dramas. She reread a few underlined passages and remembered the bored girl who had so hopefully drawn those lines, the girl who'd believed a work like this would actually take root somewhere in her and reemerge in a future lecture or critical anecdote. Joanne quickly shoved the book back in its dusty spot. Too obvious, she decided; any freshman would pull this out when faced with an assignment like Joanne's.

What Joanne needed was a leg up. An ace up her sleeve. A duplicate key. If she was going to take this on, this job that didn't really exist yet, with powers of the Vivian Reape persuasion observing her every move, she needed an alternative plan, something she could turn to when the writing buried and confused her. What she needed was Jon. Ever since returning from the Cliff Dwellers' Club two nights before and not finding divorce papers in her mailbox, Joanne had become quietly preoccupied with Jon having inherited this laurel of artistic recognition. As Vivian had hoped,

Joanne fumed that after ten years of her hard work, during which time her husband had abandoned any possibilities of creating an income on which Joanne could, even for a single day, count on, rest on, *write on* (with the exception, naturally, of the one night class where he had shacked up with one of his students), Jon should receive government money—that most precious endorsement, U.S. tax dollars—to pay for him to create art he had given up on years ago. A northern wind suddenly hit Joanne's row house, sending her scurrying to her closet for a sweater to put over the one she wore.

When Joanne had thrown Jon out, it had been an early spring. March bloomed and greened, and by April, air conditioners appeared like anvils precariously tipping from window ledges, ready to pummel an unsuspecting pedestrian to death. Joanne had immediately realized that the house they rented in Lake Bluff, which she paid the full monthly amount on, was far beyond her financial and emotional limits. Horrified at the thought of striking out as a single woman in the suburbs, she quickly secured what seemed to be a dream apartment in Wrigleyville, just a few blocks from Wrigley Field, where the Chicago Cubs played as one of the few remaining outdoor baseball clubs in the country. The apartment was an entire second floor of a four-story walk-up on a well-lit, tree-lined street, with a backyard and garage behind it. The landlord had seemed like a nice enough man, showing her the newly installed window blinds, the track lights in the kitchen, the recently sanded wooden floors and the convenience of a garage in back. She was mortified when the real estate company informed her that because most of her credit for the past ten years was under her husband's name, she would need him to cosign her lease.

With Jon's cooperation, she finally signed a two-year lease, agreeing that it was the best option for not facing a rent increase too soon, and moved in on one of the hottest days the month of April had ever inflicted on the Midwest. The first thing that went wrong was her air conditioner blew out the power. Then one of the hundred-year-old windows crashed down and broke. The track lights never came back on no matter how much money she spent replacing wires and bulbs, and by June a notice had arrived informing her that the nice man who had initially rented her the apartment was no longer within the city limits and that the new real estate corporation taking over had decided Joanne had no right to the garage unless she was willing to pay an additional hundred dollars a month. Joanne, her feminist pride already stung by the string of household disasters, realized she had never bothered to check out the conditions of her lease more carefully before signing anything. So, she promptly moved her car to the street and threw the notice in the trash.

A month after that, Wrigley Field, until that summer the only baseball field left in the league without night games, as requested by nearby residents who did not want to return home from work in the evening to find their parking spaces robbed by baseball fans, had finally been forced by the league to host night games and install lights by August. If Wrigley Field refused to comply, the Cubs would not be allowed to play home games should they make the playoffs due to the amount of advertising dollars that would be lost from not being able to show the games live during prime time. In an instant, the charm of the old ballpark (Joanne could actually hear the national anthem from her shower, which usually ran out of hot water after five minutes) flicked off just as the field's lights flicked on. Joanne survived baseball season through an amazingly complex and ineffectual permit system, offered to the residents by the city, having had her car towed twice, broken into three times, and vomited and urinated upon god only knows how many times by the gangs of beer-drunk Cubbies who roamed the once quiet blocks for hours after each game, win or lose. What had truly suffered, however, were Joanne's epiphanies. On the days when she was held up at school and arrived in the neighborhood bursting with a new poem or fictional scene freshly yanked from the asphalt of Lake Shore Drive, it was all nearly forgotten, at least her enthusiasm was, as she drove around, sometimes for more than an hour, trying to locate the one last parking place on the entire North Side.

Toward the middle of October, the Cubs fell out of the playoffs, and Joanne thought her life could fall back into a kind of domestic routine of schoolwork, creative work, and sound sleep. But on the first below-freezing night, she discovered the final, and perhaps cruelest, eccentricity of her bacheloress pad. Though heat gurgled and spit its way through the apartment's three radiators starting the first of November, the hundred-year-old windows and insulation surrounding them were no match for the wind, which provided an endless source of cute names for the city she called home. When standing in front of one of Joanne's windows during such a bitter, windy night, she felt like there was actually no glass barrier at all. Joanne began the new season going to bed each night wearing socks, gloves, and sweats, her bed propped right against the bickering radiator and a space heater positioned as close as she dared on the chair beside her. She would wake each morning by boiling pots of water on the stove while the oven door stayed open pouring its heat out into her kitchen. What amazed her was how used to it she became, how easily she could adapt. It was only that half hour it took her to fall asleep at night, madly rubbing her limbs on the mattress to absorb the cold that had settled there like an extra bottom sheet, that turned her anger back toward Jon, Jon the artist, with his nuclear relatives and government grant.

A leg up. An ace up her sleeve. A duplicate key.

Joanne hadn't called Jon in three months, yet she was able to dial his number by memory. She had never seen the house this number reached, an apartment in Rogers Park about a fifteen-minute drive north of hers. It was nearly eleven on a Friday night, and if *she* answered, Joanne would hang up. If a machine answered, Joanne would hang up. If Jon answered, Joanne would think of something.

"Hello?"

"Jon. It's Joanne."

"I'd just been thinking about you."

Joanne let this pass. "I'd like to get together and talk. I sort of need your help."

"*My* help? Are you all right?"

Joanne laughed. Jon knew she must be desperate to have said something like that. "I'm fine. Very fine. It's actually a professional matter. No money, nothing like that. It's just a favor."

"For who?"

"For me. Do you remember Vivian Reape?"

"That old bitch? What on earth does she—"

"No, Jon. It's for me. Please. Just this one thing."

There was a pause during which Joanne imagined their entire ten-year relationship passing through his mind in one simple sentence, starting off with something like "Once upon a time" and ending with something like "Child molester!"

"Sure, Jo. You know you can always count on me."

Joanne took a very deep breath at this. "So let's meet. Monday, for dinner?"

"Does this have anything to do with Nevada?"

"Just meet me. Monday at seven, Gianni's on Lincoln. You remember, we used to go there. Oh, and would you come alone?"

This stung just enough to get him off the Nevada track. "Yes. Seven. I'll be there."

Joanne hung up and fell back onto the couch, the very couch she had sat up on all night listening to him and Shelly, the twenty-year-old he'd left her for and now lived with, making love in their bed upstairs. This ordeal had been so significant that *The North American* even published it. What had she been thinking? She didn't have to sit on that couch. She didn't have to stay up all night waiting for some coed to leave just so she could go up there and get in bed and wait another two weeks before confronting him. Joanne actually wondered if she had been looking for that short story. If she had removed herself enough to let life create a fiction so good, so domestic and dramatic, so perfectly unsaid and unre-solved that the sound of Jon and Shelley's voices wouldn't make her crazy but instead provide her with a career opportunity. Joanne shuddered from the wind hitting the house and the aching possi-bility that something so cold and calculating, so entirely beyond her control, could actually be true.

In an instant she was off the couch and in the frozen bedroom, ripping off her two sweaters, blue jeans, long underwear, and wool socks. It was almost midnight, and Joanne couldn't face that sheet of ice, that space heater waiting to set her bed on fire, that terrible half hour before sleep, if it ever came. Before the chill in the room could completely engulf her, she quickly pulled on a clean pair of panties, a pair of somewhat clean jeans that fit her much tighter, a slightly butch but feminine muscle T-shirt, and one of Jon's old cardigans, which she buttoned up, leaving just enough bare chest showing. In the bathroom she doused her face in hot then cold water and brushed her hair back twenty times. She barely paused in the mirror when she had finished, knowing there was nothing left to do should she be unhappy with the reflection.

Keeping the lights on, she threw on her coat and went out. Three blocks, she repeated to herself, as she stepped out into the now blinding snowstorm. Her car was somewhere in the white mountain range of parked cars across the street, and she felt relief that she had the whole weekend to dig it out. Bending forward, she walked headfirst into the wind, taking long strides in the snow that already came up to her ankles. Three blocks. The wonderful part was the quiet. Snow seemed to pad the entire world in such a way that every dropped bottle, every bad muffler, and every hu-man scream of pleasure or pain were muffled by the thick, white blanket covering everything. Just the wind roared past Joanne's ears as she finally reached the apartment house just three blocks west of her own.

She pressed the buzzer of the garden apartment, and the front security door was quickly buzzed open without any intercom conversation. He knew it was her. She'd done this before. By the time she reached the bottom of the half-flight of stairs to his apartment, Walter was already standing at the door, smiling, blocking the entrance, waiting for her to ask to come in.

Walter was a professional socialist. Joanne had met him through friends at a dinner party that fall. He was tall, hairy chested, and bearded, with button-brown eyes that made him seem deceptively warm. What Joanne had found interesting was his politics, a type of Chicago socialism that was a polite veil for communism. Walter supported the Soviet Union. Walter despised the U.S. government and all the citizens who were active in it. Though he mainly worked on unionizing and antiracism, he ran groups teaching Marx, Lenin, and never Trotsky. Walter didn't drink, smoke, eat meat, or laugh too much of the time; but Joanne had had too much to drink at the dinner party, and Walter, who lived three blocks from her, had offered to drive her home.

It had been a foregone conclusion for Joanne that she would sleep with Walter once she had accepted his offer of a ride. The reason she drank so much lately was that she was trying to start up a social life again but without Jon, Jon's friends, and Jon's bad habits to watch over. Walter had proved to be the only single, straight man at the dinner party; and though he had fascinated her with his commitment to socialism, and then insulted her with his theory that poetry was a product of bourgeois culture (he included family farms and all forms of American entertainment in this theory as well), Joanne was tired of spending her thirties as a single woman writing comments on student love poems each night. Besides, he lived three blocks away.

Both Walter and Joanne were in silent agreement on how little the other had to offer beyond sex. But Joanne had discovered one other good thing about Walter the night he took her to his apartment (Joanne had simply gotten in his car, and when he asked for her address, she'd told him to go to his place and she'd find her way from there). Walter's apartment suffered the opposite problem of Joanne's. As a garden apartment right next to the building's central plumbing, Walter's apartment was never colder than seventy-five degrees all winter. In fact, he usually kept a window open so he wouldn't sweat. While at Walter's, Joanne found herself lounging around in her underwear or in nothing at all. Sandwiched between the building's central plumbing and Walter's broad, naked body, Joanne slept better than she had for years.

The sex was satisfying and efficient. They never made plans for dinner or a movie. By the third time Joanne had stayed over, they'd even stopped making plans for her to come. Joanne would just show up (usually after ten), and they'd go straight to bed. On some nights Walter would get back up and work on various projects he had going: an anti-Klan march in Indianapolis, a lecture on Rosa Luxemburg for a college group at the University of Chicago, an article on the Hormel strike for the *Socialist Masses,* a monthly newspaper he coedited. Joanne actually believed Walter was a closeted homosexual. And maybe that was what he was secretly enjoying with her, the illusion of heterosexuality, while she enjoyed the very real presence of his overheated apartment. The idea of it actually balanced the scales for Joanne, and now, in their third month and this the eleventh storm of the winter so far, Joanne coolly walked over to where he stood at the door of his apartment and lightly kissed him on the lips.

"You've been drinking," Walter said, as he stepped out of the door frame to let her pass.

"Only one glass of wine," Joanne replied, surprised, as she would usually remember to brush her teeth if she had had a drink or smoked a cigarette before coming. Walter shook a finger in her face in scolding, then swept his arm grandly by his side to let her know she could enter. *The little match girl could do worse,* Joanne thought, as she nearly leapt into the hothouse inside.

7

LIKE, AS, IS

"Tell me the truth," Diane Whitestone insisted, still young enough to think that after one had slept with a man the truth was something not to be afraid of and readily available upon request. She sat in her desk chair next to the bed, wearing an oversized Los Angeles Lakers T-shirt and cupping a mug of coffee in both hands close to her mouth so she could blow on the hot surface.

"I always tell the truth," Sink Lewis said, telling what he believed to be the truth.

"Joanne Mueller says that's dangerous. She also says that the truth and what you believe to be the truth are really—"

"Two separate things," Sink said, finishing their teacher's truism for her. "Her husband left her for a girl around your age, and that's something not so easy to separate."

This silenced Diane for a moment, and she pulled at the hem of her shirt, which was riding up her bare thigh. Though covered, she realized she had never been this naked in front of a man before without the shield of darkness and sheets. "Well, then?"

Sink sighed and fell back on the pillow, which propped him up against the wall. The sheet fell down to his stomach, revealing his hairless chest of skin so white it seemed to Diane that she could leave her handprint on it if she pressed too hard.

"I don't think your poetry is really about anything," he finally said.

Diane fell in love every time it snowed. A southern California girl who had picked her college more with the help of an atlas than a guidance counselor, she counted snow as one of about a dozen things of which she had always felt deprived. A short list of the other things: an unbroken home, pets (her father, with whom she lived, was allergic to all types of fur), and a more rural and dull upbringing, which she felt, from reading enough biographies of poets, would inspire her mind to create. Though she had graduated close to the top of her high school class, the East Coast had never even crossed her mind as a possibility for higher education as it seemed so far, while the West was too close and the South already overwritten by people who knew it far better than she ever could. Chicago had stood out by the fact that it seemed so overlooked. She had pored over her books, her father's leather-bound first editions, and the stacks in the public library, finding, to her amazement, a city virtually unspoiled by too much description.

The University of Chicago seemed the obvious choice once her intentions were clear, but her visit to the strange, fortresslike campus had been most disappointing. The university was located in Hyde Park on Chicago's South Side, once a neighborhood of the city's upper class. Hyde Park was made up of beautiful, rundown mansions now housing students, faculty, and some remnants of the royalty from the meat packing and lumber dynasties, most of whom had long ago transferred north when the neighborhoods surrounding it went working class at the height of the industrial migration. The University of Chicago was literally walled in by the lower-class, minority neighborhoods that had made Chicago's South Side synonymous with Lyndon Johnson's Great Society housing projects and were now notorious for poverty and gangs. On Diane's first night there, for a weekend admissions department visit, she spent the majority of her time sitting through lectures covering self-defense, not talking to strangers, and never going anywhere alone after dark. By the time they got around to what the school actually offered, she learned there wasn't a major in creative writing, just a concentration, and Diane already felt she had had enough of a *concentration* out in Los Angeles.

The next day she heard about Lake Bluff, a small college, half an hour north of the city, with a creative writing major (and faculty that included poet-in-residence Joanne Mueller, a name Diane actually recognized). Diane wasted no time locating the nearest car rental, and with the help of her father's credit card and her own acute sense of direction and freeway expertise, arrived at the pastoral college in less than an hour. It was a Saturday afternoon in late October, and the town and campus were in the full flames of autumn. Each tree wore a slightly different pigment of red, orange, and yellow, and the unfenced fields and nonbuilt-up shorelines of the lake seemed the stuff movie sets were based on. By the time she stumbled on the Book Bar, the literary center of Lake Bluff, with its friendly cats and definitive section of poetry, Diane had made up her mind and promptly took a room at the only hotel in town for her last night in the Midwest before she would return the next fall for good.

"Diane? Maybe that didn't come out right."

Diane used all of her willpower not to flinch, not to blink, not to move her eyes in the slightest as they stared right back into Sink's. She was aware of moments passing, embarrassing moments where her inability to respond drew the four walls in even tighter around them as each second ticked by. *This is a very adult moment,* she thought, asking a question and having it answered, but she lacked the sophistication to know exactly who to ask who could offer her the answer she wanted. At the same time, she realized, it was like talking to a child. Children will say anything without attempting to dilute their opinions with niceties, and Diane started to laugh.

"I'm sorry," Sink said, sitting forward and reaching a hand out to her. "I'm sure you'll be accepted in the writing major. What do I know? You're great with similes."

This made Diane laugh even harder. She got up and started pulling on clothes. She hadn't showered, and her body felt heavy from all that had passed between the two of them the night before. Like a new layer of skin that made her itch underneath, skin as thick as a sponge, which had somehow absorbed all of the sweat and oil from Sink's body while he slept on top of her all night long.

"I don't want to be 'great with similes,' " Diane replied. "I want metaphor—not such-and-such-as, but such-and-such-is."

She stood at the foot of the bed staring down at him, a little unsure of what she was trying to get at and definitely afraid of asking him anything else. Sink smiled and slid one of his hands beneath the sheet to his crotch. "I was just answering a question," Sink said and ran his toe up her thigh. "Ask me another one."

"Favorite color," Sink asked, and passed her the joint.

"Green."

Outside the window of Diane's dormitory room, the lit buildings of the campus were nearly whited out by the blizzard. Small piles of snow melted slowly by the door into the industrial gray carpeting where they had left their shoes. She couldn't get over the fact that this man from her poetry class was now sitting after midnight on the bed in her dormitory room. Their hair was wet where it had once been beaded with ice, and the room was filled with the sweet, musty odor of damp wool. The marijuana made Diane feel like she was at the very beginning of a poem, a place both familiar enough to understand and strange enough to want to describe.

"Favorite book."

"*Madame Bovary.*"

"Favorite parent."

"I only have one," Diane sort of lied, coughed, and passed back the joint. Her father had raised her since she was thirteen after her mother had run off with another man. Diane wasn't about to go into any of that right now.

"Me, too." Sink paused, but Diane didn't prompt him. She was not only protective about the amount of personal information she'd give out about herself but also the amount she was willing to take in. "Favorite time of day."

"Morning."

Sink made a face. "Favorite month."

"September."

"Favorite city."

"Chicago."

"Favorite part of the body." Sink leaned forward and ran a finger along the knuckles of her hands, which were folded tightly in her lap. The joint, half-smoked, smoldered on a small plate Diane had lifted months ago from the cafeteria. Diane paused. She knew this was the cue for the right answer, that any answer would be the right answer. Whatever she said he would kiss or touch. The whole game was a charade, a fast-food get-to-know-you so-I-can-get-you-in-bed foreplay. What Sink didn't realize was that Diane had already presumed sex by inviting him to her room in the first place and did not really care to spend so much time finding out about each other, as it was actually beginning to turn her off once she started to ponder their differences, the probable course her emotions would take, the amount of months they would be together before one of them inevitably got bored.

"Your mouth," Diane finally answered, deciding it was time to shut him up before she'd just want him to leave.

This startled Sink, but he recovered quickly and clamped his mouth down on hers, hard, his eyes still open and searching hers, a little unsure whether or not she was putting him on.

As they fell back on her bed, Diane shut her eyes and thought of the usual responsibilities that came with these actions, her diaphragm in her desk drawer, the condom in the wallet, which always made her think that instead of a condom, a moist towlette, like the kind they give you in restaurants after barbecued ribs to clean your fingers, mouth, and chin, would emerge from the plastic package. Most likely, Diane would have to pull away at the last possible moment to ask about it or gently remind him with one firm push away at the center of his chest and a glance that bordered on being scolding. But Diane actually wished he wouldn't stop and that she wouldn't either, and life would continue on with a kind of discovery where consequences a month from now, a year, ten years, a whole generation could be affected by this one small pleasure—*It was the worst blizzard in twenty years; we were both so young.* Diane didn't push firmly; she merely stopped kissing him back for a second, let her head tilt just slightly to the right, and Sink instantly reached down for his jeans with one hand while holding her to him with the other, and the storm outside her window seemed a little less severe.

Lake Bluff College offered one class in women's studies, and Diane had enrolled in it. That semester it was taught by a history professor and was called "Women and Discovery." Besides the required readings and oral presentations, each student had to choose one particular famous woman and write a term paper on her particular discovery. Diane chose Marie Curie. Science had always been a subject that had eluded her, and Diane, an overambitious sophomore, couldn't resist the challenge to study what had always seemed impossible.

Diane read very slowly once Marie was set up in her laboratory in Paris. She tried hard to understand the concept of magnetism, the rays she discovered, the properties she named polonium (after her native Poland) and radium (which won her the Nobel Prize); but whenever Diane tried to describe such scientific work, she found herself copying phrases verbatim from the biographies, like a second language, her mind only capable of memorization, unable to really "think" with such foreign words.

After spending weeks worrying about what would happen to her grade-point average, she realized she should just shift the paper's focus from "discovery" to the responsibilities of such invention, and took an incomplete for the class, agreeing to turn the paper in at the end of the holiday recess. She'd analyze all of Curie's recorded knowledge of the potential harmful uses of radium, her admissions of its effects on her own health as well as on that of the other scientists in her lab, the fine line between heroism and ambition, the ultimate power of knowledge and its deadly effects in the hands of mankind. Diane had realized all of this staring out the window from the elevated train, which inched to its last few stops on the northern end of the line. *It was the worst blizzard in twenty years.* When the train announcer told them this would be the last train of the night, all the passengers looked at each other expectantly, thrilled by the adventure they had fallen into and obviously spared the burden of where to park a car.

Diane stared out at the snowed-in intersections the train rumbled over. There were no longer any tire treads, and in some areas the snow had drifted in such a way as to make it impossible to tell where the streets, sidewalks, and small yards separated. The snow sloped over fences, newspaper dispensers, and parked cars, and nothing could be seen more than a few feet from any light. Diane longed to write about this, but couldn't come up with any point of reference. How do you start to describe something you've never seen before? How do you know what it's about? How will it turn out?

"Think we'll make it?" a voice asked from behind her. Diane turned and saw that pretty boy from her poetry workshop, the one with the strange name, Sink, the one her friend William had such a crush on—William, who had left her earlier that day downtown and would hate himself for missing this opportunity.

"It doesn't really matter to me," Diane said. "I'm thinking about getting off at the next stop and walking the ten blocks left."

"Why don't we then?" Sink said and stood up. He seemed barely dressed for such weather, in a loose leather jacket and jeans with a hole at the knee. She had lied about wanting to get off a stop early to walk the rest of the way, but suddenly it seemed like a good idea.

"Is it dangerous?" Diane asked, as they waited for the doors to open onto the deserted platform.

"Let's hope so," Sink said, and led her off the train to the stairs, which were nearly a foot deep in a drift. On the street, she couldn't get over the strange feeling of walking through snow that was completely untouched by any cars or other pedestrians. Sink led her into the center of the street, where the drifts were the lowest and there seemed to be nobody else in the whole city. It was like walking on the moon, she almost said, but decided it would sound too stupid.

"I think you should leave," Diane said, and Sink left. Just like that. He didn't argue with her; he didn't really even say good-bye. He sort of shrugged and threw off the sheet, which made Diane turn away, and when she turned back around a minute later, he was dressed and going to the door.

She imagined that he must think he had terribly offended her by criticizing her writing. She *was* offended, but hated the idea that he thought that. Offended wasn't really the word, though. She had been caught off guard and, at the same time, been a bit drawn to his succinct response. Like he had thought about it before; like he knew she was capable of being better.

Diane spent the rest of her day in bed reading about Marie Curie's last days. The constant work on her famous radium laboratory, the awards and grants, the deterioration of her health, which she kept to herself, the handful of Polish soil a relative dropped on her coffin before it was covered in French dirt.

8

LOVE INC.

Alex Dupree drove his shiny red Mustang convertible out of its well-heated garage beneath Lake Point Towers and into the brilliant sun of a snowbound Saturday afternoon. He had been able to see from his bedroom window that all eight lanes of Lake Shore Drive had been cleared and salted, and as he hopelessly tried to keep his Mustang away from the few other snow-covered cars on the Drive that were making use of speed to blow the snow off their vehicles (and onto Alex's), he plotted a course of major freeways and well-traveled country roads that, like Lake Shore Drive, should also be the first to be cleared, a course that would take him back to Lake Bluff.

Had he forgotten some critical paper in his office on the second floor of Sandburg Hall? Did he have an unavoidable meeting or lecture he had promised to attend? For what could possibly make a man as important as himself drive half an hour to the office on a Saturday after one of the city's worst snowstorms? Lake Shore Drive was about as empty as Alex had ever seen it, and he worried that his trip would be short-lived, for the radio and television had been filled with endless notices of closings and delays for nearly every conceivable service and business in both the city and surrounding suburbs. Surely he should join the rest of the city and enjoy the day, snowbound, without a car to dig out; the convenience of a supermarket in the lobby of his condominium; a fully equipped gym, sauna, and Olympic-size pool next door to it; fifty cable channels to choose from on his remote; and best of all, ten whole rooms of an apartment to wander through with views of the entire city. But this was precisely how he had spent the night before: a one-hour workout with his personal trainer, twenty laps in the pool, followed by a long sauna, a quick trip to the supermarket to pick up a preprepared gourmet meal, some television while he ate, and then six solid hours of wandering from room to room watching the snow come down and feeling like he was going to suffocate in his own luxurious isolation. When he had stood at the windows of his study (which offered the best views of the city), it was as if he could actually hear the sound of people, millions of people, molding their bodies against someone else's as their Friday night plans were sweetly canceled by the unexpected force of the storm.

Alex had woken up that morning with his mind made up. After fifty push-ups and one hundred sit-ups, a careful shave and quick shower, he thoughtfully picked out a clean pair of dungarees, unpleated, to show off his trim waist, a simple Calvin Klein T-shirt to emphasize his full chest, and an old, classic plaid sport coat to highlight his literary inclinations and exceptional good taste. Now, cruising at fifty-five and irritably dodging snow-covered cars, he only hoped for one thing, that the Book Bar in Lake Bluff would be open for business.

Alex was in love. Alex had been in love many times in his life. One could even say Alex's life had been devoted to being in love, falling in love, getting over love, and feeling the absence of love. Perhaps you could say that about any minor poet chosen randomly from a literary journal; but in Alex's case, love was, perhaps, a more elusive and mysterious business. The Dupree family could not simply make a provision of love for Alex in any of the reams of documents he had been cosigning for as long as he could remember. Nor could Dupree Properties hand Alex a deed for love as they had handed him his precious wing of Lake Point Towers six years ago when he had accepted an associate professorship at Lake Bluff College and had called his family to tell them he *must* live in the city. And the Dupree Foundation could certainly not accommodate love in any of their shrewd investments or carefully chosen and well-publicized charities should Alex storm the board of directors and thrust it on the table. From age six, Alex had begun to realize the pricelessness of love when his parents presented him with the kitten he had begged them for, and he promptly discovered that no matter how patiently he sat, how playfully he acted, or how generously he offered food, the cat simply could not stand him.

Besides the obvious cliché lessons of what money could and could not buy, Alex's need for love was unique in a family that had long prided itself on proper marriages with generous rewards in respect to lineage. Alex was gay. He had known he was gay since the third or fourth grade. Realizing there was nothing he could do about being gay, Alex mustered up all of the ingenuity, ambition, and pride that had made it possible for his family to become and remain one of the richest in the American Midwest and decided to *be* gay, to *be* a Dupree, and to *be* a poet, even if it meant shaking the very foundations of the lakefront condominiums, Loop offices, and industrial centers his family had set up for him to inherit.

He had started small. A rumored lesbian aunt in Madison, a hallucinating sister at Berkeley, a half-dozen cousins devoted to various civil rights causes, which all led him to his own father and mother, though his father managed to collapse and die from a heart attack literally the Wednesday before Alex had planned to spend the weekend with them at their summer house in Michigan to break the news. A few months later, he told his mother anyway. Not in a gazebo far north of Chicago in Michigan, but in her bedroom in the family home on Goethe Street, deep in the city, where all the shades were tightly drawn and the silk sheets were pulled up to her chin in the giant mahogany-framed bed, as if heart attacks were contagious and she, unlike her deceased husband, was riding it out.

The timing proved Alex to be as ingenious as any of the colossal Duprees preceding him who had argued their way into getting what they wanted for centuries. His mother cried, looked as if this was to be the final blow, and then turned to him with her most "Oh, you poor thing" expression, and then put everything into her declaration of how terrible Alex must feel having seen his father die without being able to let him know who he really was. Margaret Dupree blamed society (she was a Boston girl; there had been a time in her life when all her friends knew someone gay). She blamed the Great Plains, with its rigid puritans, for forcing Alex to hide what should have been shared between a child and his parents. Though they had never discussed it again in the two years since his father's death, Alex blamed this silence on his endless bachelorhood. Who really wanted to hear someone endlessly announcing he was gay if there was no one in particular for him to be gay with?

Now Alex knew who that lucky lover should be and sped north on the clear interstate with the good news. Alex only knew his name to be Tom (he knew this because he had heard people call it out upon entering or leaving while Alex busied himself in the poetry section, which took up nearly half the store), and he knew Tom was the owner and, presumably, the only full-time employee of the Book Bar. All further information was clouded in conjecture and wishful thinking. For example, Alex presumed Tom to be in his late twenties. He was a brunette and wore his hair slightly past the ear and completely out of control, which endeared him to Alex all the more as he kept his own head nearly shaved in a vain effort to conceal his balding. Tom's body was the most interesting part. He was slender, obviously did not belong to a gym or practice any home weight lifting, but was blessed with midwestern shoulders and legs, "midwestern" because such a build was usually presumed to have come from hard labor on an actual farm at a young age, although such romantic youths rarely lived up to their legends lately. In any case, Tom had apparently been in great shape at one point in his life—star of the high school track team? Camp counselor? Alex naturally waxed poetic imagining the possibilities as he finally turned off the interstate and found himself crawling along a much smaller country road that had barely been plowed for the final ten miles to downtown Lake Bluff.

It was Tom's face Alex had most admired across the store's counter for the past year. A soft, kind face, with large, green eyes and a strange, oversized nose that accentuated a certain kind of masculinity as he argued with salesmen or stood out front in the below-freezing temperatures without a jacket, quickly smoking a cigarette. Alex could only presume Tom was gay. A pink triangle sticker on the cash register (among many other quasiliberal kinds of stickers) and a small, but thorough, gay and lesbian section in the store (including copies of all the free gay and lesbian newspapers and journals) were his only actual pieces of evidence. But Alex, like all gay men and women, was known for his second sense in finding his own. A certain way they'd catch each other's eye, the strange way they'd avoid getting to know each other as if any friendliness could potentially "out" one of them, who wasn't prepared to be out. A type of sensitivity that didn't have anything to do with being creative or emotional (though in most cases, it did), but a kind of overall sensitivity to everything going on about them, sprung from a life spent feeling left out, not included, so that the world would always remain a slightly threatening, foreign place. Of course homosexuals, like everyone else, often allowed their judgment to be impaired by the calling of the heart, but Alex didn't pay attention to this possibility. How could he? He had enough on his mind being ten years older, slightly balding, and a little goofy looking to contend with in trying to woo a potential mate.

As Alex's once shiny and dry, red Mustang snowplowed into the city limits of Lake Bluff, he gave up worrying about keeping it clean as the streets became even smaller and the plowing even more dependent on large quantities of salt dropped to eat up the snow and ice, leaving a virtual canal of slush for cars to speed through. Now, the moment he had been waiting for, the possibility that this entire trip, dirty car and all, had been complete folly should the store not even be open. But it was. Of course it was! How could a store the size of Book Bar afford not to be open on a Saturday, surely its major bread-and-butter day in the dawning of the era of megamalls and superstores.

Alex managed to park the car almost in the middle of a street due to the imposing drifts, and after a quick glance in the rearview mirror (which politely cropped off the top of his head), he got out of the car, cleared his throat, and walked to the store, determined not to stop walking until getting all the way in and then, well, taking it from there. He had not thought of anything to say. He had not thought of a question to ask. Should it come down to it, Alex would buy the required fifty dollars' worth of books in order to use one of his four credit cards, force some kind of conversation with the boy, and include his home number on the charge receipt. Maybe he'd even leave his credit card behind—he could always use the pay phone on the corner to put a hold on the account.

So it was that Alex boldly turned the corner, reached the store, and swung open the old, heavy door, which caused a bell to ring somewhere (or perhaps Alex was just hearing things). Stepping into the store, he found Tom busy behind the register with a customer. Tom quickly glanced up at him, and as he seemed about to smile, the woman he was helping turned around and shouted, "Why Alex Dupree! So good of you to travel such a distance to little Lake Bluff!" as Prof. Helen Drake always tended to shout at him whenever he'd pass her in the hallway or faculty lounge.

Alex's instinct was to turn and flee, but there he stood, looking like a hustler at a poetry reading in his Calvin Klein T-shirt beneath a plaid sport coat. In a moment Helen was upon him.

"I should say it's fate you walked in when you did. I was just debating with the nice young man over there," Helen said, pointing back at Tom, who now leaned his beautiful face on his fists on the counter, smiling at the two old and foolish professors, "whether or not to pick up that damned new Virginia Woolf biography. Yes, I know, *another* Woolf biography. I mean how many times can the poor woman fill her pockets with rocks and throw herself in a river for an entirely new cause and effect? I nearly slipped and cracked my head open on the ice getting over here today, but do I rush home to write a journal entry about it? Do I expect the entire course of Western literature to change because I'm lying on my back in the middle of the street hearing voices? We *all* hear voices. We just aren't meant to hear each other's."

Prof. Helen Drake was Lake Bluff's resident scholar on Virginia Woolf. She had come to the college at the height of the Woolf fashion over twenty years ago when feminists, homosexuals, and drug users championed Woolf, and every major college and university quickly absorbed the few scholars on the subject. Helen's first five years had been a legendary success. Besides her teaching, she had penned three book-length critical studies, was a featured speaker at nearly all Virginia Woolf symposiums, edited *Sheep's Clothing*, a quarterly devoted to the writer, and was the rumored front-runner for the job of completing the also rumored unfinished novel, for which Helen was said to have received a sizable advance from a New York publishing house, which she never returned even after the *New York Times* declared such stories to be a hoax. By that time, Helen had received tenure, and her hectic schedule beyond the classroom had been simultaneously reduced to a few book reviews and endless litigation with the New York publisher wanting their advance back. Professor Drake was, perhaps, the country's official book reviewer of Virginia Woolf biographies, most of which she held up for disdain, as if the emergence of them only meant she had to go through the trouble of reading and reviewing them.

"Why, Alex Dupree, I'd say *you're* hearing voices."

"I'm sorry, Helen," Alex said, at a volume nearly half of what Helen's had been. He politely touched her elbow and steered her away from the front door out of Tom's sight toward the New Age section by the window. "Were you hurt by your fall?"

"Not at all. Woke me up, actually. Now, what in the world are you doing all the way up here? Or didn't you make it home last night?"

Alex could think of no way to lower the high pitch of her voice other than to seize her by the throat, but he managed to laugh nervously instead. "Of course I made it home, was home all night; why I had just stopped by Sandburg Hall to pick up a few papers and thought I'd drop by to catch up on some contemporary poetry."

Helen shook her head accusingly. "Alex, really. The campus won't be plowed out until Monday. Or perhaps you have access to a prize team of Alaskan huskies?"

"A Mustang, Helen. A red, convertible Mustang," Alex replied, saying each word as if it would be the last Helen would hear and looking her intensely in the eye as if to say that the Dupree family lawyers had joined forces with her New York publishing house to throw her back out into the street.

Helen obediently changed the subject. "I presume you've congratulated fellow resident poet Joanne Mueller on her husband's extraordinary success? Not that she's in need of more success, what with 'Where's Here?' or 'I'm Over' or whatever, in *The North American* of all places. To publish such a story about her husband's indiscretions the same month he receives such an extraordinary grant, why, she must have called him right up to say, 'Over here!' or something."

"I'm afraid I haven't heard any of this," Alex replied, momentarily forgetting Tom in order to envy anything of Joanne's, no less something attached to the word *grant*.

"No? Surely the two of you must start confiding more in each other, you both being resident poets, both living in the same city, and both, well, I'm sure there's something else you have in common. It's some kind of nuclear waste art, no, that can't be right. Nuclear waste warning art? What an age we live in. I didn't think Mr. Mueller still dealt in art at all anymore, but it's apparently an extremely gracious grant and from the federal government no less. A kind of nuclear waste genius award? Anyway, I'm sure Joanne will put it all down in some poem or story someday in the pages of *The North American* so we can all understand it."

"Yes. I'm sure she will," Alex managed, wondering if Helen planned to keep him cornered in the New Age section until that time.

"I do believe you've talked me out of it," Helen said, frowning at the gigantic Virginia Woolf biography in her hand. "Perhaps it will go out of print before I finally get to it."

Amazingly, Helen handed Alex the book and started walking to the door.

"I'm afraid you're thirty-five dollars the poorer, Tom," she unfortunately called out as she opened the door, "Mr. Dupree has talked me out of it." She then turned back to Alex, who was hiding behind a tree of endangered species postcards. "As for you, you simply must drop by 'the House of My Own' one of these dangerous, travel advisory days to have a cup of tea." Helen referred to her large, mansionlike house on the shores of Lake Bluff, which she had purchased almost immediately after receiving the advance for the rumored unfinished novel.

"I'll see you Monday," Alex called out, holding open then shutting the door behind her to make sure she was actually gone. He stood there a few minutes watching her carefully cross the street. Though there didn't appear to be a car in sight, Helen dramatically extended her arms out from each side like a school crossing guard as she made her way, testing each step with her toe, and Alex found himself pleading for the salt to hold and get her to the other side. His plans now ruined, Alex debated opening the door back up and running straight to his car, which had surely been towed, when a gentle, but purposeful, tap fell on his shoulder. Alex turned, and it was Tom; there was no one else in the store. But before Alex could speak or even think to speak, Tom did.

"Mr. Dupree? I'm Tom McMann, a coeditor of *Rose Is a Rose*. We had the pleasure of publishing some poems of yours last spring. I have to say what a pleasure it is to finally meet you."

Alex must have said something back, to which Tom must have said something back, but Alex could never remember what, for the world was suddenly couplets—two perfect lines, end stopped, stressed and rhymed.

9

CITY OF DESTRUCTION

" 'Rose is a rose is a rose'," Vivian Reape announced to the somewhat amused and somewhat suspicious University of Chicago Board of Regents early Monday morning in the ornate oak-paneled conference room on the freshly plowed-out Hyde Park campus. She paused for all the dramatic effect a literary critic could hope for with an audience of a dozen elderly men and a few equally stately women. " 'To be or not to be, that is the question.' " Again Vivian paused, and a few of the spectators circling the enormous mahogany table placed in the room's center shifted in their high-backed chairs. " 'Two roads diverged in a wood, and I—I took the road less traveled by, And that has made all the difference.' "

A cough from the opposite end of the table prompted Vivian to get a bit on with it. "We all know these words, we know what words come next, we know the authors and could even name dozens of films, books, and other cultural mediums that have taken these exact words and interpreted them for their own various needs. We could go around the table and each recite a line or two off the tops of our heads, and I can assure you that all of us would be able to recall the meaning and, perhaps, be bored by the familiarity." The room again shifted as the regents, like any freshmen seminar, feared she'd truly ask this of them. With this, Vivian eyed the man opposite her who had coughed earlier, confident she had put him in his place by acknowledging his very boredom with her speech. The man was not unknown to Vivian. He was Prof. Joseph Wright, head of the nuclear science department and the main point man for the entire Yucca Mountain Nuclear Depository Program. He maintained both jealous and complete control of the project, while slowly spending the millions of government dollars behind it on the complex scientific plans and research for this largest of nuclear waste developments, as well as the more human side that included the "Doomsday designs." The concept for the Doomsday designs actually came from Washington, and it was only reluctantly that Wright oversaw the execution of it, believing such cultural artifacts to be more for the people of the twentieth century than for those who would survive them. Science would answer all mysteries, he firmly believed. Art was merely the simpleminded entertainment for those left behind by the rigors of scientific theories and invention. Vivian had already locked horns with Professor Wright by relentlessly inquiring into a poetry grant as part of the art budget. The fund for the Doomsday designs truly had more than enough allotted to it and, in truth, had been set up to encourage a more personal side of the program so as to thwart the environmental lobbyists and sympathizers, who would surely try and stall the project for years in red tape. Still, Joseph Wright would only spend the money when properly bullied by Washington, believing that once the program went into action he could persuade the federal government not to waste valuable funds on such pop culture and reinvest them into the science of the university's nuclear department, his very own office. Vivian, already rebuked by Wright, would not be so easily fooled.

Under the guise of announcing a new National Institute of Poetry fellowship for the university, which would place a full-time poet-in-residence at the school, all expenses paid by NIP, Vivian had been granted twenty minutes of the floor at the monthly board of regents meeting and intended to devote no less than nineteen of those minutes to discussing the Doomsday designs. Having already used up five of those valuable minutes, Vivian proceeded. "We plant time capsules for a reason: art endures. We develop paints, building materials, and microchips for a reason: art endures. We maintain universities for the same reason: art endures. Art not only teaches the passing fads of a generation, but dutifully records the worldly truths and historical lessons of all civilizations like rings in a tree, the tree of knowledge, the very trees we turn into paper to hold our words, our most precious communication, the very way human beings are set above all other creatures, our ability to rationally think and to pass that information along to each other and for generations to come."

She seemed to have them, though only Professor Wright knew what for. "I have the privilege of congratulating your university for its singular role in the Yucca Mountain Nuclear Waste Depository Program. No nuclear science department could compare with the legacy and expertise yours has, and I go along with the federal government in its praise. I must, however, take one singular exception to the historic plans being made for what certainly is the very survival of our planet, and that is the blatant exclusion of perhaps our most valuable asset: words. For without words what good are all the numbers, computer programs, and laboratory studies your university is being so generously rewarded for? I speak to you right now in words, and you will each choose to agree with me or challenge me with words. Both I welcome, for both only prove my point."

Vivian paused again and sipped her water. She eyed Professor Wright, who stared straight back at her. Was he annoyed that Vivian had overstepped his ruthless control of the project by appealing to the regents for what he had already denied her? Professor Wright was a middle-aged man whose entire life had been spent in patient study for this opportunity. He knew very well the global and historic scale of the project he had been handed; and though he now tightly approved every memo and requisition, he realized that eventually the importance of his project would shift it into a more public arena. There would be newspaper editorials and political demonstrations, inquiries from world leaders and jokes on late night talk shows. He had steeled himself to the fact that at some point he'd have to watch his own power handed over to the foolish whims and popular fashions of the media at large. But Vivian had cast the first stone, and no matter what he'd allow and not take personally from here on, Vivian would remain the one enemy, the messenger bearing the bad news, and she would pay for it.

Vivian, meanwhile, continued. "I am aware that a painter, a gardener and an architect have been chosen to carry the burden of protecting the human race a thousand years from now against any danger your science might unintentionally overlook. I only ask you to allow someone to place a few words of warning on that very door. Not literally, of course. I speak of the door to the mind, of cultures and canons that inspire and civilize for generations. And who better to do this than a poet, whose words look backward and forward at once, whose words take on all the knowledge we've acquired since time began and put it into lines as easy to remember, to understand, to pass along from tribe to tribe as 'Mary had a little lamb.' " This drew a few laughs from the suits, and Vivian smiled, confident she still had them. A secretary pointed to her watch, and Vivian recognized it as her two-minute warning to wrap up.

"I come to you as the head of the National Institute of Poetry to bestow a five-year residency of a poet still to be selected to teach your students and inspire your faculty, salary fully paid by our grant. In an age of technology, I wish to bestow on your school a bard whose duty it will be to remind us all of the natural beauty and intellectual importance of art and how it makes this a world we all work toward protecting and developing. Should you accept this gift, I only ask for you to consider your commitment to the power of poetry, which, by accepting my grant, you'd be taking an active role in. I have left my modest proposal with Professor Wright and look forward to hearing from you regarding specific ways a poet can help in the future of our planet. I'll leave you with a few lines that may not be so familiar to you and that I had the pleasure of rereading this snowy weekend, courtesy of your fine university library. The words are John Bunyan's from *The Pilgrim's Progress,* written over three hundred years ago and still filled with enough meaning to be appropriate for our roundtable today: 'Then I saw that there was a way to hell, even from the gates of heaven, as well as from the City of Destruction. So I awoke, and behold it was a dream.' I thank you for your attention."

The room couldn't help but applaud, so simple had been Vivian's proposal, so generous had been her pleas for the good of the university, the good of literature and the good of the world that contained them. Not to applaud would have seemed as arrogant and greedy as each and every regent member feared they would eventually be made out to be, once certain political organizations and liberal newspapers had gotten hold of the fact that their university planned to profit off the burial of highly toxic nuclear waste on Native American land in Nevada. Vivian had cunningly praised them while at the same time reprimanding them for their one singular omission: poetry. And how poetry had softened the blow. How well it had placed the words *destruction, heaven,* and *hell* within the same sentence and left them with an unearned sense of hope. Nobody went so far as to stand, but they all did applaud, including Professor Wright, who did not intend to allow anyone to know of his adversity until everything could be properly played out.

The rest of the day's business was quickly concluded, and Vivian, waiting patiently in a not-so-high-backed chair away from the roundtable, leapt up to work the crowd. The first person to approach her was Rose Gluck, head of the library science department. Rose, Vivian noticed, bore a strange resemblance to Joanne Mueller, as a woman who was also in her thirties, extremely thin, and with shoulder-length, graying hair. But Vivian knew that where Joanne championed truth and love, Rose worshipped research and a type of old-fashioned Marxism. In fact, her Marxism had made her department one of the most controversial on campus, creating a loyal cult of students not unlike Joanne's fan club, though definitely a smaller and more somber bunch, who worked out Marxist theories in regard to the rigors of library management and development—that is, the very way information can be manipulated and cataloged in regard to the more oppressed elements of postindustrial society. That the University of Chicago would allow a woman with her rumored reputation to run one of its most prized departments (one with specific ties to the federal government, including the FBI and CIA) brought up another aspect of Rose that Rose herself would rather forget and Vivian couldn't help remembering. Rose's father, Thomas Gluck, was one of the university's most generous alumni, having achieved great success investing in the Chicago architecture firms that had created the city's celebrated postmodern skyline. Though Thomas Gluck had barely worked a day of his life, he had made a career out of spending his family's money wisely, including large donations to the University of Chicago, which directly benefited his one child, Rose, who, from an early age, had retreated from the family's celebrity lifestyle for a world of books and their respective card catalogs. Vivian barely knew Rose, and only the rumors about her, but the smile on Rose's face made Vivian smile right back in relief as she was admitted to the circle of department heads and regents.

"Ms. Reape, I must say how much I admire your spirit," Rose told her as the two women shook hands. "Nuclear waste, federal grants, sacred Native American ground—yes, Ms. Reape, your spirit in all this is indeed a burst of fresh air." Vivian smiled politely at these remarks, anxious to keep an eye on Joseph Wright and also to look for her chance to meet Dean Griffith, the seventy-year-old chairman of the board. Rose suddenly dropped the volume of her voice, and Vivian had to lean forward to hear what she was now saying. "As a fellow woman who condescends to work within the system, I just wanted to encourage you on your endeavors, and I was glad to hear that our own university library has been able to help you in that regard."

Vivian stopped smiling as she realized she must now return the books. Had this woman guessed that Vivian planned to keep them? Did this woman commit to memory every book lent out of her precious library? Vivian was slightly annoyed, but equally impressed, and with another quick handshake, moved on.

Various heads of departments were making their way out the door, and a few smiled and nodded toward her as they pushed by. But before Vivian could locate the dean, Joseph Wright was in front of her.

"A most excellent speech, Ms. Reape, or should I say recitation?" They both laughed with an underlying coldness, much like that of the snowdrifts pressed up against the windows around them. "I look forward to reading over the proposal you so kindly alluded to leaving on my desk, though you mustn't despair if it takes me a while to get to it; you see, my office is completely buried with this project, and being short a work-study student doesn't help us out with the paperwork—*surely* you understand."

Before Vivian could think of something equally dismisive to say, Dean Griffith approached and shook Vivian's hand with both of his.

"Ah, Bunyan, Ms. Reape. How wonderful it would be to come to this table once a month and hear Bunyan. Wouldn't you say, Wright?" Dean Griffith was a jovial old man, who seemed to grow more and more outrageous each year past the official age of retirement. He maintained a head of white hair and seemed an embodiment of the word *grandfather*. Joseph Wright, who obviously had some trouble appealing to such friendliness, especially that involving matters of poetry, took a step back.

"Dean Griffith, I'm so pleased I could think to quote a writer you revere," Vivian replied, not releasing her grip from his. "May my future appointed poet-in-residence be an expert in Bunyan just for your sake!"

"Perhaps you can get us that Joanne Mueller girl, the one up at Lake Bluff. Damned good story in the latest issue of *The North American*. You know her?"

Seventy-year-old Dean Griffith didn't know what to make of Vivian's face as it first turned a bloodless white and then flushed completely over, as if she had inhaled the color and exhaled it all again at once. But Joseph Wright noticed and made a quick note: *The North American*. Someone in his office must subscribe.

By the time Vivian reached the Green Café at three-thirty, she had managed to go through the full range of emotions Dean Griffith had elicited in her at the mere mention of Joanne's name. Vivian had decided to walk the six blocks across campus to the café hoping the cold weather would sober her bad mood, but the wind had managed to bring most of the plowed snowbanks back down upon the sidewalks, and for a woman of Vivian's bulk, such deep, heavy steps only kept her body temperature high. Around her the white snow covered the lawns, rooftops, streets, and walls, and she was rudely reminded of her beautiful blank tablet on her hotel desk, which had remained blank all weekend as she stayed in bed ordering room service and hibernating with *The Pilgrim's Progress*. She considered hailing a cab and just skipping her coffee date with the eager student who had so brazenly called her at the hotel. Reneging would allow her to finally tackle the very poem she had just made such pains to sell, but she had hopes that the encounter would lift her spirits, and by the time she reached the Green Café, she actually had a plan.

• • •

Peter Brooks was, of course, already there, occupying a prime window booth that he had held for nearly an hour. He excitedly watched Vivian nearly crawl over a dirty snowbank to reach the door of the café, a warm, eccentric vegetarian food and coffeehouse that featured used furniture, folk music, and political pamphlets. Vivian had no trouble finding Peter once she had nearly fallen through the door, for he met her there and immediately helped her with her briefcase and coat.

"Snow removal doesn't mean just shoving it all up on the sidewalks, or does it?" she hissed at Peter, who had barely managed an introduction. "I would think the Midwest would be a little practiced in this, or do they just expect people to remain in their skyscrapers until spring?"

"Ms. Reape, it is such an honor to meet you in person—"

"I'd like a brandy," Vivian told the waitress once she was seated. The waitress, who had half her head shaved and the other half dyed a light green, didn't bother explaining to Vivian that the Green Café didn't serve alcohol and just walked off. Peter quickly went over the menu with her.

"Espresso, cappucino, international coffees, and no brandy? What's wrong with this city today?"

Peter offered to take her elsewhere, but Vivian was not about to go a step farther than a cab door to take her back to the Drake. She ordered coffee and the half-green-haired waitress attempted a joke about finding something to slip into it but was quickly quieted by the look on Vivian's face.

"I brought these along. I'm afraid they're not good, but I wanted to show you how hard I've been working." Peter placed a perfectly clean folder, which was filled with perfectly typed bad poems, in front of Vivian. Trying to smile, Vivian leafed through them. "The Children of Yesterday," "Bathing My Lover," and "Autumn Reflection" were good titles in the sense that they warned Vivian not to bother reading further. But what did this remind her of? The oppressive warmth of a Missouri heat wave as a fair young girl in front of her nervously shifted her weight. Probably not, though her first meeting with Joanne Mueller had been across poems equally as rotten. She found herself warming to the eager, dark-haired boy across from her, who, like a good dog near the table at mealtime, hung upon whatever might fall from her mouth. This was perhaps one of Vivian's favorite situations. She slapped the folder shut so fast it made Peter jump.

"This is fine. Fine. May I take them with me?" Of course she could; she knew they had been typed furiously all weekend toward the goal of her keeping them. "Now I, of course, must spend some time with your work, pinpoint exactly who you should be reading, what forms you should pursue and do daily, like at any good boot camp; and I will, of course, be more than happy to do all of this for you."

Peter sat back stunned.

"What's your time like? Do you work as well as study?" Vivian innocently proceeded, sipping the hot coffee.

"Do I work? Why yes, but don't think I can't handle the writing on top of my classes and work; why I'll stay up all night if I have to, I'll—"

"Work-study? What I mean is do you work toward your tuition through the university?"

Peter was puzzled. "Yes, I'm afraid my family can't afford all the tuition. I'm a slide projectionist for the classics department."

"You mean you project the same sets of slides over and over again each semester?"

"Yes. I'm afraid I nearly fall asleep during the morning classes, though I'm sure the imagery will prove itself to be most valuable for my writing!"

"Look, Peter, the reason I'm asking all this is I could use a little favor. A very simple favor."

"Anything, Ms. Reape, anything." Peter leaned forward again so that the steam from Vivian's coffee rose up to open every pore

93

of his beautifully clear skin. *The empty vessel,* Vivian remembered, and she could hardly wait to proceed.

"Well, I was thinking, since I'm to be writing you rather lengthy instructions on your apprenticeship in poetry, I thought you could write me back with some information on a project I'm, well you could say, I'm consulting upon."

"What do I have to do?"

"Quit the classics department."

"Quit? But—"

"I hear there's an opening in nuclear science."

Peter almost repeated the words *nuclear science* in his most in-credulous of voices, but something in the way Vivian looked di-rectly in his eyes told him not to. In fact, Vivian's eyes seemed to tell him there was a secret little spot, a simple door somewhere deep in a very dense wood, or perhaps on a shore, a perfectly deserted picture-postcard shore with a simple rowboat anchored half on the sand and half in the sea, and Vivian, and only Vivian, would direct him there—and Peter was more than willing to go.

10

THE DOWRY IN THE MAHOGANY CHEST

William Dunning had come to Chicago to become a poet. That he had only made it thirty miles north of the city's limits was a minor technicality to him, a low hurdle toward the skyline he could not quite see from the pastures of Lake Bluff, settling instead for the ominous orange glow the city gave off each night above the dark wood that blocked his view. In fact, William's first "Chicago poem" was inspired by this very image. "Ghosts of the Fire" used this "always-setting southern sun," to quote, of the Chicago lights to evoke the memory of the great fire that had made it possible for the city to become the architecturally planned Mecca it was known as, at the cost of thousands of lives. William's poem was very outsider-looking-in, a young romantic's overexcitement as the train pulled into the station, though William's ticket had run out a few stops too soon and he had taken temporary root in the quiet of this college town, not very unlike the Wisconsin town he had come from. But for William, Lake Bluff tremored from the nearby pulse of Chicago, the Paris of the prairie, the obvious place for his career to be born.

Joanne promptly rejected William's first poem as a classic example of what happens when small town meets big city at a too impressionable age. After a quick lecture forbidding any further "city" poems, especially "subway/elevated illusions," "lake/ocean comparisons," and, most importantly, "skyscraper/masculine, prairie/feminine personifications," William placed himself entirely in his mentor's hands to prepare him to someday write about the city he had dreamed of all his life, now an easy half-hour commuter ride south.

"You know, I too once saw this city as the place for all my dreams to be realized," Oma quietly told William one especially bitter winter night, the Sunday after the Friday blizzard that had stranded him deep in the city's heart in the bed of a flight attendant. "That was fifty years ago. I was twenty-five. Things didn't quite work out that way."

William took a sip of the port they were sharing at her candlelit dining room table, studying the way she seemed to sigh these sentences so that he could describe it later someday in a book he'd surely write about her life, instead of pondering the true weight of the wisdom she was handing him.

The farmhouse they sat in was a twenty-minute walk from the Lake Bluff campus, a walk William had been making for over a year without ever meeting the woman who lived in the simple, white, two-story wooden house. It was Joanne who had inspired this ritual, as Joanne inspired most of anything William did that was not required of him in class or sought out for simple pleasure. In William's class with Joanne, she had confessed her ritual for epiphanies, her long drives to and from Lake Bluff each day, and encouraged her students to take similar excursions for themselves either by foot, bike, or train in order to find the strange mixtures of words deep in their minds from which she could pull out their poems. That very day, had a helicopter flown overhead, the pilot could perhaps have seen all fifteen students heading out in opposite directions on foot, bike, and train in search of the poems Resident

Poet Joanne Mueller was confident they had in them. William often wondered if he was the only one who had kept up the regimen, and had he investigated, he would have found out that he was.

Though William had pretty much failed beginning poetry in the eyes of Joanne and had recently struggled through the second year of the workshop, barely maintaining enough points to keep him in the Lake Bluff creative writing program, he had succeeded by sheer will, surpassing all the other students in the amount of time he put into becoming one of Joanne's great students. William never missed a class, an assignment, a book casually referred to by Joanne in class, and he certainly never missed his coveted thirty minutes' office time once every two weeks. In ways, William may have reminded Joanne of her own ambition at his age, her desire to find the right instructor to drag her out of the sentimental greeting card verse of her college years and instill in her the proper subjects and forms that had rewarded her with the position and fame she now enjoyed. William could not have known how often Joanne had wondered how much better of a writer she could have been had her mentor (Vivian, of course) not only taught her all the proper forms of the trade she wished to learn but also nurtured her emotionally, instead of setting her up as an ally on the midwestern front of Vivian's ongoing battles in art and letters. Other students had noticed Joanne's tolerance of William's often blundering verse, and though many of these students were gifted with simple, clear voices that could produce a few young poems worthy of any of the masters they studied, they lacked the interest and desire to make her class their major, their career and life partner all in one, something William had striven for all his young life.

There was no better evidence of this drive than William's hour-long walk north of campus twice a week. What he returned with, however, was not exactly the stuff of personalized acceptance letters from even the smallest of the small literary magazines. It had been on the morning of the region's latest blizzard—after William had made it back to campus from his rather depressing one-night stand, unable to face the loneliness of his room and the guilt he felt about having deserted his good friend Diane—that he had set off on his walk in hopes of finding a hidden epiphany from the lustful but empty night he had just spent in the city where none of his dreams had yet been realized. He had found Oma instead.

William had been her savior that morning when he took his walk down the middle of the recently plowed country road and passed her house. Oma stood in a simple blue housedress behind the frosted glass of her front storm door. Snow had piled up nearly two feet in front of it with a deep layer of ice that made it impossible for her to open it. "Young man!" she had called out to him a half a dozen times before William was able to see her slight figure through the webs of ice crystallized on the glass. When he had reached her, she was impatiently rattling the metal door frame against the ice and cursing, which was enough to instruct him to find the shovel alongside the house to rescue her. William obediently started digging, going so far as to uncover the large flat stones of her walkway leading from the door to the unplowed driveway, hardly noticing she had disappeared back inside, though beginning to wonder if she'd expect him to shovel out the rather long driveway once he had reached it.

"I've made sandwiches," she suddenly called from the door she could now open. "Don't worry about the rest of it, a plow should be along, and I'm not allowed to drive anyway. Leave your boots at the door."

Sandwiches had amounted to an entire kitchen table covered in what looked like everything she had in her refrigerator. Plates of cold cuts and cheeses, five different jars of jam, three kinds of bread in baskets alongside butter and margarine, milk, orange juice, tomato juice, and cider in various antique glass and porcelain pitchers, all covered the table in front of him, set only for him. Oma sat nearby chain-smoking, while William politely attempted at least one thing from every plate and bowl.

While he ate, Oma informed him of her name, Oma, German

for grandmother, which she said was what everyone had called her for the past twenty years. Her ancestry had been announced to him from the moment she had first called out from behind the frozen storm door in a thick German accent that seemed to throw out English words like fish too small to keep, and William could almost hear the longing in her voice for the much harsher tones of her native tongue. Oma also complained about her lazy grandson, who apparently attended the University of Chicago and was supposed to keep an eye on her now that she was a widow and unable to drive and the rest of her children and grandchildren all lived outside the state. The fact that she was a widow of ten years she had divulged to him with little regret and a quick wave in front of her face when William started to impart a token sympathetic word or two.

The house around her was a cluttered display of antique farm life (though her husband had been a local doctor, the culture of farmlands around them had permeated the home without much resistance). William had never seen anything quite so lived-in as Oma's house, and he felt envious of her thoughtless grandson, who hadn't even called to see how she had weathered the recent storm. The phone did start ringing as William started pushing his plate away. Oma lit her fifth cigarette, making no move to answer it, and let out a loud "A-ha!" as if to say that must be him. She smiled wickedly, glad to worry the grandson by not answering it.

"I've seen you before," Oma said, allowing William to start clearing the table the moment he had offered to. "You walk by here. At one point it was every Tuesday around four. Now it's more erratic."

William had wanted to ask where to put some of the dishes and food he had moved from the table to the crowded kitchen counter but just used his best judgment and was able to find the Tupperware and aluminum foil necessary to clean up the feast he had barely touched.

"I do walk this way about twice a week," he told her. "It's kind of a class assignment, a way of clearing out my head to find certain things." Oma stared at him like he had just told her something offensive. She started to reply but actually put her hand over her mouth.

Once William had finished cleaning up his meal, Oma asked him over for Sunday dinner, and William, strangely flattered, quickly agreed.

"You should know right off that I never loved my husband," Oma told William, though it was far from right off. Dinner had been served promptly at seven when William arrived (pork chops and potatoes), and now it was close to eleven, and, after a bottle of wine over dinner, followed by William again cleaning up the table and even washing some pans, the two of them were on their fourth glass of port and still sitting at the dining room table, which William had wiped clean. Oma had instructed him to cover it with an elegant white tablecloth, which was kept in a drawer nearby.

William lifted his eyebrows in surprise at her statement about her husband, though he had stopped being surprised by the intensely opinionated information she had been giving out about herself all night, information that came in no logical order and covered the seventy years of her life in what seemed to be a deliberately random way.

"He was my one-way ticket out of Europe and my escape from the wonderful and promising life robbed from me in Germany. He was a paramedic coming out of France, and we met near his barracks in London. Actually, I sought him out. You could say I had been searching for an American once the war ended and my father announced we'd be returning to Berlin. I just couldn't face going back, and I could certainly not confront my father with that kind of treason. There were a lot of young women roaming the streets of London at that time looking for men, the few remaining men, to replace the ones who had been lost. You see, every woman in Europe at this point had lost a man in some capacity."

Listening attentively, at least as attentively as a college student who had just consumed three glasses of red wine and four after-dinner drinks could, William studied Oma to try to memorize physical details the way Joanne had encouraged the class to do. Oma was very short, just over five feet, and though she was only seventy-five, she looked much older, most likely a result of the chain-smoking, heavy drinking, and rural living she had done for so many years. Her thin face was a mass of folds and wrinkles, punctuated by her sharp blue eyes, which darted about so quickly that whenever they'd fall on him, William would almost jump up as if called upon in class. The most distinctive feature William could make out was her hair. She wore it up, wound tightly into a single ball at the back of her head, a mixture of gray and white, with hardly any strands escaping at the sides. Oma spoke a lot with her hands, which were small and seemed delicate despite the boniness of her joints and knuckles. Her hands would constantly fly up in front of her face, as if in defense, or toward William whenever he'd say something she heartily agreed with.

Outside, the wind beat at the house from all sides, coming in strong from the surrounding lakes and open fields, gaining a kind of strength as it ran across the open spaces. The old house groaned a little at each gust, and William, starting to worry about his twenty-minute walk back to campus, switched to coffee, which Oma had probably kept warm from the morning as it tasted more like a thick espresso in the fragile Meisen cup he carefully held with both hands.

"Have you been in love yet?" Oma suddenly asked.

"Probably not," William answered, choosing his words carefully, feeling the strange nervousness of his sexuality in the hands of an older person. "I think I might be now, though."

Oma laughed and covered her face, and William wondered if she thought he meant her. "I mean, someone I've known for a while now, well, just recently we, sort of—"

"Why do you write poetry?" Oma interrupted, done with the

subject, though William wasn't so sure the subject had really changed.

"I don't really know," he confessed, looking up at the circles of candlelight on the ceiling, truly stumped by the question. "Perhaps to find truth—truth and love."

Oma's eyes darted to him, and her pencil-thin eyebrows arched up. "Do you see that chest against the wall?" Oma pointed, and William looked, spotting a rather large wooden chest that looked like it was made of mahogany. "After Douglas and I were married in England, you see, we couldn't wait to do it. Neither of us had much money, and there was no way for us to travel affording two separate rooms. My family returned to Berlin before I left for Chicago, but before leaving, they had asked if I'd like them to send on my grandmother's chest, which had contained her dowry fifty years ago: dishes, linens, perfumes, nightgowns. Now my father hadn't spoken to me since I had announced my intention of marrying the American, and my mother, always led by my father's will, had barely said a word to me either. So of course I was thrilled. This seemed a sign that they wanted to reconcile, to actually put together a proper wedding chest for me to take to the strange country that now occupied their own destroyed country. Douglas, naturally, didn't see all of this. He only remarked that he hoped it was filled with money—gold, that is—as the mark wasn't exactly worth the paper it was printed on at that time."

The candles had sunk down into their holders by now, and Oma seemed farther away as the shadows enveloped her. She stared directly at William while she spoke, and William stared back, momentarily forgetting himself as the story went on.

"A few weeks later they wired me an address in Berlin where I could find the trunk. Douglas was furious. I guess we had both imagined they'd send it on to us in Lake Bluff, but I convinced him to go about sending for it and somehow arranging for it to be transported all the way from the rubble of my parents' home to his in America, which had never seen a single bomb blast. You see,

102

Douglas was in love with me at this point, something I used fully to my advantage for as long as it lasted. Well, you can imagine the nearly impossible feat of shipping a hundred-pound mahogany chest all the way out of ravaged Germany, through France and England, and finally to the middle of America. It was nearly a year later—I had already become rather fluent in English, and Douglas was entirely out of love with me—by the time the phone rang and I heard him shouting, 'What? From Berlin? *How much?*' I went racing across the house to him to remind him about my dowry. A day, and I don't know how many dollars, later, it finally arrived. We both could hardly contain our excitement, waiting for the men who heaved it into the house to leave. We were nearly laughing as we clumsily tried getting it open, and I thought how strange this felt, like when we'd first met and courted, our hands fumbling at each other's, that giddy anticipation. Of course it finally flew open, and the laughing stopped. William, it was completely empty."

William gasped, nearly dropping the antique cup in his hands, and Oma broke out in a loud whoop of laughter. William just stared at her for the minute it took her to stop, wondering if it would turn into tears and what he'd do then. But Oma didn't cry; she went on.

"I had never seen Douglas so angry. He actually stood up and kicked it, though of course it didn't budge and his poor toe made everything worse. He went on about how stupid this whole idea had been in the first place, how he had tried then to put a stop to it, and finally, he decided that it had probably been slowly emptied at each border it crossed, all at his expense. Of course, I knew differently. There had never been anything in it in the first place, that the whole enterprise was all my father's way of reminding me of my disloyalty to him, my family, even my country. It's stayed there, against that wall, since the day it arrived forty years ago, nothing in it but my poor mother's very breath."

They were both silent for a moment, and a gust of wind slapped the side of the house.

"So if anybody asked me about 'truth' or 'love,' that's what I'd tell them," Oma concluded, looking down now. The room had grown nearly dark, and William couldn't remember having asked in the first place.

"You know," she said suddenly, jumping up as if remembering William had to go. "You must really meet my grandson someday. All this poetry. The two of you would have a lot in common." In an instant, William was outside, glad to discover the wind at his back as he was nearly carried by it all the way to the campus.

11

LET'S JUST

Every couple has an Italian restaurant, even after they have stopped being a couple and attempted to evolve their relationship into a sort of civil friendship, which tends to be short on civility and far from friendly. Even pop music approves of this cliché, and Resident Poet Joanne Mueller, who tended to confront clichés head-on with great success, found herself wondering why she had gone so far as to suggest Gianni's when she'd impulsively set up her dinner engagement with Jon the Monday night after the blizzard. Like most couples, Jon and Joanne had frequented their Italian restaurant about once a month for the ten years they were together. They found it their first weekend in Chicago. After signing a mortgage for a house in Lake Bluff, they had immediately jumped on the train for the city to celebrate. Gianni's wasn't the best Italian restaurant in Chicago. In fact, despite its fame among wine enthusiasts as having one of the best wine cellars in the city, it didn't come close to making the top ten or twenty Italian restaurants. But this didn't matter to them. A couple wouldn't want their Italian restaurant to be too trendy (it would surely close before the relationship would) or too legendary (you didn't want to have to wait for a table and never become familiar with the staff). What a couple wanted was the celebrity status they'd receive each time they'd come, the same waiter inquiring into the same two or three topics and, after a few months, not bothering with menus as he'd remember the exact meals the two would always order, the owner stopping by the table to pay his respects, and even the cook waving from the kitchen as he sent out the same two entrées cooked, he always believed, exactly how they liked it, though he could never say just how that was as he'd never been told how to cook them in the first place.

Gianni's on Lincoln Avenue, just twenty blocks south of where Joanne now lived since leaving Jon, was a small, twenty-year-old family-run restaurant on the garden level of a busy city block. With the right amount of candlelight, crisp white paper covering the twenty-five tables, and single flowers in empty wine bottles, Gianni's perfected the right kind of quaintness and romance for a couple to call their own. Though they were open for lunch, it really would never have occurred to a couple like Jon and Joanne to come in daylight, as it would look more like a diner than the sacred spot the two would associate with all of the best aspects of their failed ten-year marriage. Though Jon supposedly had found his new mate in twenty-one-year-old Shelly, he hadn't quite felt with her the easy comfort of a martini followed by a bottle of red wine with dinner in the golden orange candlelight of a place like Gianni's, and when Joanne had suggested it, he had instantly felt nostalgic and aroused at the prospect. Joanne, on the other hand, completely regretted her choice of the restaurant for those very same reasons—nostalgia and desire. How could she be instigating such a thing? she agonized, as she walked up and down the restaurant's side streets, having arrived half an hour early. Poetry, she kept repeating to herself, followed automatically by the name Vivian.

Her day at Lake Bluff had hammered it home. It had started off in the faculty lounge with Alex Dupree leaping at her with loud

106

congratulations for Jon's grant and gentle insinuations as to how this must make Joanne feel.

"How much did he get?" he blurted out, right to the point.

Joanne, shocked by how rapidly the news seemed to spread after she had found out about it only three days earlier, shrugged her shoulders, a little surprised at Alex for breaking the midwestern rule of not discussing money.

"You must find out. Why some of that money may rightfully be yours," Alex lectured.

Joanne quickly steered Alex to a remote corner of the lounge away from the curious eyes of the two resident fiction writers and few stray literature professors. "Alex, how in the world did you find out?"

"Helen Drake, I'm afraid. I must admit I was a bit affronted to be caught not knowing anything about this."

"I just found out myself three nights ago."

Alex completed a quick calculation. "Vivian?"

"I really don't want to go into any of this right now. I'm fine about it. And don't worry, I am looking into any legal aspects that could concern me."

"Why in the world would Vivian—"

"A wonderful sight to see," came the unmistakable voice of Prof. Helen Drake, "the two of you in conference. What's the topic? Villanelles? Shakespearean sonnets? Nuclear waste?"

"Actually, I was just leaving. I have class on the hour," Joanne said through her teeth.

"Well, I am so glad to see the two of you catching up. I bumped into Alex this weekend and was troubled to discover that he hadn't heard your great news. Forgive me for enlightening him, though it appears the two of you have sorted it out."

"Yes, Helen, it's all sorted," Joanne replied, growing irritated as the weight of her day, this conversation with Alex and Helen, and her imminent dinner with Jon grew heavier upon her.

"Well, dear, what are Mr. Mueller's plans? Perhaps an exotic trip somewhere, just the two of you, an archeological dig, Love Canal?"

Obviously Helen knew all about Joanne's separation from Jon and was only hoping to gain more particulars about the amount of money involved that could possibly bring the estranged couple back together. Alex also looked over at Joanne expectantly, a little eager to hear the answer to this himself, but Joanne walked past them and out of the faculty lounge smiling, well aware that silence was the only way to confound Helen.

Somehow Joanne made it through the rest of the day and, after an epiphanyless drive back into the city, now waited at a table in Gianni's for Jon, who was late. Jon could afford to be late, for it was Jon who had the twenty-one-year-old lover, Jon who had received the Nobel Prize of federal arts grants, and Jon from whom Joanne needed help.

Joanne wore khakis, which were slightly wrinkled and stained from the five years she had already worn them, and a thick, black sweater that she knew would suit her in the candlelight of the restaurant. The last time she had seen Jon was for coffee in his neighborhood six months earlier to sort out their joint checking account (which, by then, was made up entirely of Joanne's salary) and to sign away their Lake Bluff house, which had finally been sold to the young couple who had rented it shortly after Joanne had moved downtown. The coffee meeting had been quick and businesslike; and though the word "divorce" hadn't been uttered, it had stayed on the tips of their tongues, Joanne remembered, wishing at the same time that she could just pull out a form for him to sign and be done with it. As they had parted outside the diner in the unbreathable August air, Jon had actually attempted to embrace Joanne, while nervously inquiring as to her well-being; but Joanne had firmly placed her palm upon his chest and said, "Let's just—" and nothing more. She'd jumped into her car and avoided Lake Shore Drive, knowing there would be no metaphor to be found to explain the waste she felt sorting out the meager financial remains of her failed marriage.

Now things were a bit more complicated. In a way, Joanne should have felt lucky that she hadn't pressed for a divorce before Jon's coffers had filled, but she couldn't help wishing she had so that the temptation of what she was about to ask of him wouldn't even exist and she could simply wish Vivian well and get back to the work of building her career with her own bare hands. She was tempted to jump up from the table and flee, perhaps take in a subtitled movie at the art house next door, or just drive all the way to Milwaukee and back (something she had done half a dozen times in her life when she was on the verge of giving something up or taking something on that she knew would cause enormous regret should she make the wrong choice). But Joanne remained at the table sipping her vodka and tonic, and finally Jon stomped his way down the short flight of stairs from the street and smiled at her as if he had just signed another mortgage on a house for the two of them.

"I'm sorry—" he said, when he reached the table.

"Don't be."

"You look terrific."

"You, too."

"New haircut?"

"No, just longer than before."

Jon quickly ordered his martini, and the two of them waited quietly for it, both knowing it would get easier with alcohol. Jon did look good, Joanne realized right after saying it. He had the looks of a corporate raider or a suave movie villain who always tempted but never won the heroine, occupying a place in a woman's mind as the man she'd have chosen over the blond hero who seemed too nice to go to bed with. He was tall with slightly long, dark hair, and his broad shoulders were equally matched by broad cheekbones and a good chin. He had been a catch when

Joanne married him ten years earlier, and as Joanne noticed in a few of the women's eyes as he came across the restaurant toward her, he was still a catch for a romantic Italian dinner on a cold Monday night after a blizzard.

Over their menus, while the first round of drinks were quickly replaced by a second, they managed on small talk. Joanne talked of Lake Bluff and even joked about some of the mishaps with her apartment. Jon caught her up on some of his old friends and relatives (most of whom Joanne could care less about, but she appreciated his not mentioning Shelly—they'd get to that). When the waiter came over, he overacted surprise at finally seeing them again after so long, gave them a bottle of wine on the house, and pulled the menus out of their hands, insisting he remembered exactly what they always ordered (fettucine alfredo for Joanne, spaghetti with meatballs for Jon). The waiter's good spirits insinuated he knew all about their separation and presumed this dinner to be the great reunion. After he left, Joanne allowed herself to smile at Jon, who seemed to enjoy the possibilities of the waiter's assumption.

She couldn't put things off much longer. "I hear you are to be congratulated."

Jon sat back from the table, and Joanne knew he expected to be handed legal papers attempting to wrangle half of his grant away from him.

"How did you find out?"

"Our old friend Vivian Reape told me. I don't know how she knew; I guess she just keeps up on such things."

"Well, it's really not that much of a—"

"Jon, it's all right. I'm happy for you. Don't spend it all in one place."

He lifted his left eyebrow at her in wonder, a talent she had always envied, and quickly poured her a glass of the free wine as if to celebrate this admission.

"But this *is* what this is all about, isn't it?"

"I need your help. It has nothing to do with your money, but everything to do with how you got it. How *did* you get it?"

"You probably don't remember my uncle Oscar. You met him only once, at our wedding." There was a dramatic pause at the mention of their wedding, one of the best worst days of both of their lives. "He's big in D.C., working on nuclear power issues for the government. He helped spearhead this whole Yucca Mountain dump and helped develop the art grants in order to answer concerns about burying something as toxic as nuclear waste for the ten thousand years it will take to decompose. He knew I had studied aboriginal cave drawings and called me up with this. I've just lately found out what a huge deal the whole thing is. My god, Vivian Reape sent you. This should be good."

Jon had never met Joanne's mentor, but he had gone through the ten years of Joanne's frustrations and advancements, which Vivian inspired. Vivian was a name he'd heard endlessly from Joanne as she'd share whatever latest outrage Vivian had demanded from her protegée. Joanne felt a little better at Jon's comment, like she could turn to him now about Vivian and that he, of all people, would understand her dilemma.

"It's quite simple. She wants in on this whole thing. She wants a poet to be selected to write the nuclear waste epic for the next century. I'd imagine she wants part of the money to set herself up a kind of board to oversee the poet, who, it seems, would be me. And honestly, Jon, I could use some of that grant money myself. Not your grant money, additional grant money. The teaching takes a lot out of me. I need a little more time, and time's money."

Jon eyed her carefully across the table. Behind him Joanne could see the legs of pedestrians struggling with the sidewalk, which had by now frozen up as the night grew colder. She knew Jon was taking a moment to thoroughly enjoy his position. He could embrace her now, and she would not push him away. Oddly, Joanne regretted not having asked him to bring Shelly. Though it would have put her in the most uncomfortable and embarrassing position she had ever been in, the presence of the twenty-one-year-old would possibly have made Joanne more sympathetic in Jon's eyes, if he could have managed not to enjoy himself too much in the process.

"You want me to speak to my uncle Oscar?" Jon asked slowly, possibly trying not to smile.

"Yes, that is all. Nothing more. If your uncle can't help, that's fine. If he can, well, Vivian will take it from there."

"And just what do I get out of this?"

Joanne was flabbergasted. "Well, Jon, I don't know. Haven't you already gotten everything you could possibly want? I don't think there's anything left." Joanne instantly regretted the sharpness of her words, but she couldn't hold back any longer.

"I don't have you," Jon replied.

"No you don't, and I think the reason for that is named Shelly. Are you done with her?"

Jon paused and looked up at the ceiling like a little boy being reprimanded for doing something he had no intention of stopping. It infuriated Joanne. Whenever they'd fight, Jon would fall into his little boy act, and she'd turn into the hysterical mother.

"No," he finally said, "I'm not quite finished with her."

Joanne wanted to stand up and walk out, just as she had wanted to when she had been with Vivian at the Cliff Dwellers' Club a few nights earlier; and once again she remained seated, soaking in the insult. Had she entered a phase in which all of her dinners would be filled with insults she had to sit through? What exactly had gone so wrong in her life?

"I don't understand. You left me. You left me for another woman. You are still with another woman. What in the world do you want?"

Jon poured them both more wine, settling them in for a story, though Joanne didn't expect it to be one of her own. "I read your story in *The North American* last week. That was what I had meant when I told you I had been thinking about you. You are an extraordinary writer and an extraordinary woman. I felt blessed that I was perhaps the only person in the whole world who knew how that story turned out. That's what I want. I want to remain that person, that single person who knows the endings to your stories. I know what you're up to, and I'll do whatever I can to help, but I want—"

"You want, you want, you want. Jon, this is simple. You left me. You aren't leaving her. Call your uncle or don't call your uncle, let's just—"

"Let's just remember we've had ten years together. Do you remember Sunday mornings in bed with the *Tribune* and the *Sun-Times* and the pot of coffee and donuts and those awful news shows you would watch and how sometimes it would get dark before we'd even get up? Now, with my painting and your writing, well, I can't help thinking we're suited for each other and that we may go through periods of time when I have to, well, step out, but I want to know I can come back. I still love you."

The room around Joanne seemed to suffocate her, and she felt on the verge of tears. She was reminded of the night she had spent on the couch listening to Jon and Shelly. She felt the exact helplessness she had felt then, and again, as she reached for her wineglass instead of her coat and purse, she felt like she was climbing back up those stairs on that terrible morning to join Jon in their bed.

"I already told you I didn't come here for a divorce," Joanne said. The waiter brought their check and instinctively didn't interrupt them. "Will you talk to your uncle?"

"I'll call him in the morning."

"Thank you."

Jon insisted on paying the bill, and Joanne just watched. But as she stood up and put on her coat, she felt the eyes of someone else upon her, and, turning toward the back of the restaurant, she saw Alex Dupree. He was at an equally romantic table sitting across from a younger-looking man who looked vaguely familiar to her.

Gianni's wasn't exactly the kind of place she'd expect to find a man with the sophistication and finances of Alex. She guessed it had something to do with the wine list and, perhaps, his dinner companion, who may not have been as experienced with formal dining. The irony was as sharp as an after-dinner mint on her tongue. While Joanne had come to Gianni's to beg for money, Alex was five tables away acting like he had none to give.

The two poets-in-residence stared at each other for a moment with an equal look of fear, both wishing the other would keep their distance; but this was the Midwest after all, so she made her way over to Alex, who finally smiled at her approach.

Light-headed, Joanne actually leaned down and kissed Alex on the cheek. Alex, also light-headed, clasped her hand in both of his, and the two of them stood in this brother-sister position that would have made Prof. Helen Drake proud. Jon was soon behind her, and Alex's date looked expectantly at Joanne.

"Joanne, this is Tom McMann. You probably recognize him; he runs the Book Bar. Tom, Joanne Mueller." Tom stood up and shook her hand, which Alex had dropped from his own.

Joanne finished the introductions before Alex could stumble over the name of her husband with the suave and villainous good looks. "Alex, Tom, this is Jon Sullivan," and before she could think better or worse of it, "my husband."

Jon's left hand fell on Joanne's shoulder as his right went out to aggressively shake the two gay men's hands. Jon always acted out a more masculine role in the company of gay men, Joanne remembered, just like Jon remembered their Sundays in bed, just like Joanne remembered the meal they had just completed as if it was a foregone conclusion to something she no longer had control over. All three men stared at Joanne, Joanne the woman, poet, and wife, and Joanne felt a desire to stare at herself as well. There was classical music playing in the background. For ten years Joanne had come to this restaurant and had never really noticed the classical music. Vivaldi's *Four Seasons*. It had always been Vivaldi's *Four Seasons*. She was about to mention it aloud.

Book Bar Tom spoke before her. "Joanne Mueller, it's such a pleasure to meet you. I'm quite a fan of your work. I follow all your stories."

Joanne stared at the young man in a way that suggested he had mistaken her for someone else. Tom looked at Alex, who looked at Jon, who touched Joanne's sleeve. She said good night to the three of them and sailed through the restaurant until she was out onto the street. The city blazed around her, and usually, Joanne gained a sense of confidence when she walked its streets, a power deriving from the conviction that that she had left behind her rural upbringing and had mastered an exotic urban environment that demanded a patient heart and hard shell. But suddenly Joanne felt exposed, like there was someone she knew around each corner, driving by in every car, and Chicago seemed transformed into a small town exaggerated in size like a fun house mirror, and she hurried to her car. A light snow still fell on the mountains of snow piled up all around her, and as she put the key in the ignition, she looked up into the great orange dome of the winter sky, hoping it wouldn't last, hoping it would.

12

A ROSE

The birth of a poet involves an odd combination of coincidence and emotion, outside forces forcing their way in at a particularly vulnerable moment; and, should the poet happen to take pen to paper, finger to keyboard, spray paint to wall, a voice that has been trained, retrained, tested, lost, and changed a thousand times before will suddenly find the perfect pitch that had never been achieved no matter how hard the poet previously tried. All newly born poets are minor poets. Most poets die as minor poets. Even more poets never achieve that one perfect pitch and reach minor poethood at all. Outside forces come in all shapes and sizes, though certain ones have proven more valuable than others. What better muse than the failed suicide attempt? The death of a parent or the death of a lover, any lover, who will suddenly become the only lover, the one always loved the most. If a suicide attempt is too extreme, mere thoughts of suicide can suffice. When mixed with a death in the family, there can be no holding back the sonnets and elegies waiting to burst forth. Of course the great poets have not all been created out of the ashes of dramatic incidence. But minor poets are another breed, given life to occupy the day to day of verse, the support staff if you will. How else can the journals, quarterlies, reviews, and monthlies be filled; how else can the very consumerism of poetry be maintained if the readers didn't write or the writers read? How else can the classrooms at Lake Bluff College be filled and the readings at the Book Bar attended and the likes of Vivian Reape given anything to rail against if there is no one to provide the targets? Prodigy or target. These are two ways the minor poet, once born, can succeed.

Diane Whitestone was born at 11:50 A.M. in Orange County Hospital, cesarean, two weeks late and one pound heavier than the average babies brought into the world at this medical establishment. Diane was also born a minor poet in her second-floor dormitory room at Lake Bluff College in Lake Bluff, Illinois, sometime between the hours of midnight and 4:00 A.M. Diane was unique in being both prodigy and target. As for outside forces, Diane was also unique. She did not write of her own vulnerabilities or who died. Nor had she embarked upon something that had never been attempted before; in fact, she was truly falling in line with a string of poetic successes that had emerged on the map of poetry around the time of the sexual revolution. Indeed, Diane's subject was sex. Diane's muse was sex. Diane's voice, style, signature, and thesis were born to be sex.

Sexual verse dates from far before the bawdy lines of Shakespeare, but for Diane, in a small midwestern town ten years from the close of the twentieth century, sex was about as far from all her previously attempted subject matter as snow had been from southern California. Though it had never been something she'd longed for or something she'd missed, large-breasted, long-legged Diane thought sex seemed very clear: sex sells; sex kills. Sex was, well, messy. Diane was no prude. She had certainly had all the sexual urgings of any twenty-one-year-old college girl, but they had stayed low on her list of priorities as she set out for class each day and never even entered her mind as she rolled a fresh piece of typing paper into her fifty-pound IBM electric and began her business of words: her business, which had yet to produce a minor poem, which had barely kept her eligible for the creative writing program until one fateful Tuesday night toward the end of January.

Sink Lewis was and was not her outside force. She didn't return any of his calls (three in two weeks), go anywhere near his room (just down the hall), or attend any party or campus event where she suspected he might be in attendance. But flowers came early for Diane that year—three months early. Roses, daisies, tulips, lilies, orchids, carnations, and half a dozen more she had never seen or heard of, until her room was a literal greenhouse; and after borrowing every conceivable vase and tall glass from rooms nearby, she propped them into coffee mugs and saved paper cups from the student union in order to keep the cut things alive. It started with a simple red rose on the floor outside her door a day after her one-night stand with Sink. She knew it must be him, and though she was instantly embarrassed that someone might have seen it or, worse, seen him put it there, she placed it in a simple vase by her frosted window and found herself looking up at it from her books as she studied into the night. She even found herself sniffing it the next morning, after her hot shower, as she began burying her body in wool to face the winter outside, which had started to look like it would never stop.

A few days later the daisies arrived, a riotous bunch that actually made her laugh when she opened her door and found them, as one would laugh at a litter of kittens. The next day there were carnations, six of them, and each in a different pastel shade. The orchid came in its own plastic coffin and more roses after that, long stemmed, then miniature. For two straight weeks there was a delivery every day. Most of the time she'd find them in the morning, though a few times, after studying late in the library, she'd find them waiting for her like a postcard from some exotic place at the end of a long day. Once she stopped by her room in the

118

middle of the day between classes and found a half-dozen yellow tulips all tightly folded in, waiting for the right amount of warm water to open their petals. She questioned how a college student propped up on scholarships and loans could afford such an expensive enterprise, but she remembered Sink to be someone with a friend on every corner, in every department on campus, at every store in town. He was a master of a kind of modern-day barter system, where favors were exchanged for six-packs and possibly drugs. She never received a note, and she never saw Sink, though by the end of the two weeks she had started walking by his door on her way out of the dormitory and looking over the heads of students and faculty eating lunch at the Cage.

Nearly everyone enjoys being pursued, and Diane had never been pursued. Not many college juniors at Lake Bluff College can say they have been pursued like Diane was pursued those last two bitter cold weeks of January. Her rather sparse, undecorated dormitory room had taken on a new life, with flowers on the windowsill, by her bedside, on every shelf of her bookcase, and even against the walls on the floor. She would come home now to an unmistakable force of fragrance that reminded her of her grandmother's garden in California when she was a child or certain parts of the sidewalk around Lake Bluff on those first precious days of spring. Diane would also wake up to this overabundance of smell, and fall asleep to it each night to the point where she started looking forward to crawling in under the heavy comforter and breathing in all the flowers that made her feel like Snow White.

As the two weeks went by, Diane couldn't exactly hide the bounty she'd accumulated from her few close friends and neighbors. But it was only William Dunning in whom she confided. She felt she couldn't avoid it. She had always been a lousy liar. For the first few days after her night with Sink, she'd simply avoided William until he finally met her after a class, believing she was mad at him for having run off on her in Chicago the Friday before.

Perhaps it was this guilt she had felt when her old friend told her he thought that he had caused her harm that made her confess to what would only hurt him.

"Sink Lewis?" was all William could reply.

"It had nothing to do with what had gone on with the two of you, at least not on my end. I even brought it up. I don't know, it was just very late at night, and I guess I was lonely. I threw him out the next morning, but now there're these flowers."

"Flowers?" William could only continue to repeat the last words she said in the form of a question to keep her talking and keep him from blurting out anything embarrassing.

"I've been receiving flowers in front of my door every morning, no note. I mean, I can't know if it's him, but I can't imagine who else they'd be from."

They were sitting in the Cage over coffee, both of them realizing they were about to skip their next class, though William would probably tell her he would go to his class and then run back to his own single dormitory room, which held only the fragrance of dirty laundry and stale cigarette smoke.

"I had to tell you because I value our friendship. Sink's the same old ass he's ever been; I guess we're both conquests of his now."

"You don't love him?"

Diane heard herself laugh. It unnerved her. "We had a one-night stand, like you did." They stared at each other, knowing the obvious. "Are you okay?"

"I'll be okay, I promise. But I'm late for class." With that William ran off in the direction of his class and then turned and ran back to his dormitory to lie down. Diane also went home and discovered six more tulips in need of water.

Diane told herself she didn't love Sink, though she had started to look for him. She even hoped he'd call again as she felt silly trying to call him, remembering William's story of his unreturned phone call. She found herself to be in a constant good mood as the weeks went by. She studied harder, woke at six in the morning

120

to jog before breakfast (and see what waited for her outside her door). One time, as she left late for a friend's birthday, she grabbed the latest bouquet of flowers she couldn't even identify and made it halfway down the hall before thinking better of it and showed up at the party extremely apologetic and empty-handed.

She didn't write any poetry during this period. In fact, she didn't bother to try. Joanne Meuller's workshop was over, and there wouldn't be another until the next fall. She knew she needed all the practice she could get, but the writing block didn't affect her good spirits as she got further ahead in her classes and felt like she could catch up with her writing once things had settled down. This, too, unnerved her. Settled down, like seeing Sink? Or settled down, like Sink growing bored of pursuing her and perhaps making a joke about it at some terrible party where he was about to pick up a man.

The latter came first. It was a Tuesday morning when Diane woke up at six to jog, and she put off opening her door until she was dressed in all her running gear, thinking she'd leave the flowers in front of her door until she came back, wide-awake from the below-zero weather, all her senses alert. But there was nothing in front of her door when she opened it to go out. After madly running through her twenty-block course and literally jogging up the stairs and around the corner to her door, she found nothing waiting for her. Her two-week good mood sunk down with her on the bed as she lay there trying to catch her breath, and she remembered Sink lying on top of her just two weeks before also trying to catch his. She considered skipping class. She considered skipping breakfast, class, lunch, afternoon classes, and dinner. The worst part was the potential embarrassment: "Oh, the flowers. Well, whoever it was, he just stopped. I guess he lost interest." Or was that the worst part?

Diane suddenly decided they had been stolen—this was a college dormitory, after all. Perhaps they'd come in the afternoon or the evening. Or maybe he was taking a day off; god knows it wasn't like she needed them. In fact, there wasn't much space left in which to put them. Armed with possibilities, Diane made it through her day as usual.

She avoided her room until eleven that night, spending the late afternoon in the Cage with William—who wasn't exactly over it but was valiantly trying—going straight from there to dinner and then to the library, where she forced herself to complete all the week's calculus assignments before nearly running across the campus and up the flight of stairs to her door which—was just her door. No petal, no dandelion, no hint of baby's breath. Her mood grew darker.

She found herself cleaning and reorganizing her room until well after midnight. Finally she crawled into bed; and after a few moments of breathing in the fumes of the floral arrangements on all sides of her, she knew that sleep was not going to be much of a possibility. She wished she hadn't thrown out the second half of the joint Sink had smoked with her as it could have made her dizzy enough to pass out. She even allowed herself to quickly open and shut her door to check for a late delivery, but she knew before she did that nothing would be there.

Diane had been depressed many times in her life. Her absent mother had provided years of steady anger and insecurity, her grandmother had died when she was sixteen, and men, well men never seemed to promise her much of anything, though she couldn't say she had given them much of a chance. Her problems in Joanne's workshop were probably Diane's most recent occasion of sleeplessness, producing a restless frustration that made her want to go to some horrible fraternity party or catch the next flight back to California. Remembering those nights spent unsuccessfully completing sonnets, villanelles, sestinas, and blank verse for her mentor, Joanne Mueller, Diane finally sat down at her typewriter, fed in the ever-threatening blank sheet of typing paper, and started to write.

Diane wrote like she had never written. It wasn't for Joanne, it wasn't for Sink, it wasn't for any college or competition. It started out in paragraphs. Long, rambling, angry paragraphs about men, sex, and, of all things, flowers. The arrogant rose, the bland daisy, the religious tulip, and the tender orchid. The strange customs of cutting and selling them, the politics of growing something that cannot feed the hungry or employ the masses, the dull aesthetics attached to them, and the stink of the water when they were finally thrown out.

Diane had soon filled the page single-spaced, and she tore the sheet out of her typewriter, read it over quickly, and threw it away. More carefully now, she evenly rolled in a fresh sheet of paper and removed herself a bit further from the words. She pushed the flowers into metaphor, gently, but with a frustration that turned them on their heads (she kept the part about the stink of the water when they died). To her surprise, the words came out in perfect iambic pentameter, overflowing line to line with a purpose, half-rhyming before she could even decide on a rhyme scheme. By the time she had filled the page, she had to stand up and pace the short distance from one wall to the next. She didn't look at the time. She didn't think to look out her door anymore.

She sat down again, rolled in another piece of paper, and the horrible flowers turned into a new metaphor, a man's body, Sink's body, with all its soft and angular beauty, but wrapped up in the package of sex, where it assumed a role of dominance, demanding complete worship and submission. This time the lines were shorter, and nearly every word was stressed to the breaking point, and the rhyme scheme was sing-songy, obvious, like a nursery rhyme in hell, and again, she reached the bottom of the page before she even knew what she was trying to get at.

By now Diane had grown tired. All the anger and worry from the day, all the concentration from having filled three sheets of paper with a kind of writing she had never before seen spring from her own fingers, brought her to a kind of melancholy; and she remembered the morning two weeks earlier when she had sat in that very chair with her back to Sink, wishing he'd wake up and leave, wondering why she so wished it. She remembered him asking her to get back into bed, the way the sheet had fallen from his bare chest, and how strange it was to see someone else in the bed she was always in by herself. Would they have had sex again? Or would they have fallen back into a lazy sleep, partially aroused by the proximity of each other's bodies, all alone on a weekend morning suspended by a blizzard. Perhaps her head on his shoulder. Perhaps his head on her breast.

Diane sat down one more time and slowly rolled one more sheet into the typewriter. The sonnet has always been love's most popular expression. The Shakespearean sonnet, fourteen extremely contained, intimate lines, ends with a couplet that restates what had been said in the previous twelve lines. Like love, the Shakespearean sonnet has always remained in the same form; just the words and authors have changed. Diane's sonnet took place in that realm of loss as she imagined what would have happened had she crawled back into bed with Sink, and the kind of sex they'd have had, and whether or not it would have been better than being alone surrounded by dozens of bouquets of flowers. She kept the part about the ugliness of flowers. She also kept the details of Sink's body and added in her own.

Diane's anger had disappeared, replaced with sadness as she wondered what if, though she managed to avoid sentimentality by focusing on the sex and mocking the flowers. When she had finished, she stood up and read it aloud to herself, amazed at the density of each line, how she had managed to pack in so much with so little, and she felt heady about the quality. She quickly sat back down and typed another copy. She had reached a stage of fatigue where she couldn't control what she normally would have controlled; and instead of worrying about the endless possible repercussions, she decided to take advantage of it. So she folded up the poem and put it in an envelope, wrote "Sink Lewis" on the front, and sealed it. She barely remembered getting up, opening her door, and walking the short distance down the deserted hallway to Sink's door, where she quickly slipped the envelope through the thin, dark space at the bottom before running back to her room.

Diane stood in front of her mirror. With the exception of the enormous bags beneath her eyes, she looked the same. The room behind her looked the same. The below-zero wind drifting snow against her window was also the same. The only thing different was her good mood being back, and for a moment, she wondered if she were in love. She started to pull off her clothes, knowing she'd finally be able to sleep; but before climbing into bed, she rolled one more piece of paper into her IBM and carefully typed out another copy of her poem. As she read over what she had written, she noticed how naturally the last six lines turned, as a sonnet is supposed to, turning slightly in perspective, slightly in tone, as if an ulterior motive had slipped in and indirectly challenged the poem's true purpose. And it had. This copy was for Joanne Mueller.

13

A STRANGER

Joanne Mueller had lived in the Chicago area for ten years and still couldn't find an adequate way to describe it. Her celebrated poems, written while in the city, were all inspired by a long girlhood in rural Missouri, and her even more celebrated stories existed in a faceless environment, "the small midwestern college town," framed by the geography of bad relationships instead of the squalor of the oversized metropolis nearby. Since Joanne was a woman with high literary ambitions, her inadequacy to describe the city weighed as heavily on her as the blankets she buried herself under each cold Chicago night.

This flaw in her imagination had become even more apparent as she began thinking about Nevada, a place she had never truly been to, despite a weekend in Las Vegas, and a few random stanzas formed so quickly on the page in front of her about the hot, dry land she imagined waiting out there for her that she longed to go and feel the electric pulse of a foreign environment. Truly, Joanne decided, she had been in the Midwest too long.

When her marriage had fallen apart, someone had suggested

that she should quit Chicago altogether and start out again somewhere completely new, a place she could make solely her own. The idea had insulted her. Why should she be the one to run away, quit a good job, and leave a city where she had worked so hard to learn every shortcut and parking restriction, the best restaurants, and cheapest stores? In her opinion it was Jon who had tried to bring everything down around her, and he should be the one to politely make his exit. Lately, however, as her long drives back and forth between her apartment and Lake Bluff seemed to get lost in irritable thoughts about her dealings with her estranged husband and her involvement with Vivian, the city itself seemed dirtier and less friendly. People seemed to purposely jostle her on crowded sidewalks, and cars rudely cut in front of her as she drove. She felt like she had forgotten a crucial step in an elaborate dance and was doing her best to keep up and not get trampled by the younger, more ambitious people sharing the stage with her. And whenever she stepped outside of the city, she found herself staring more and more across the flat plains stretching to the horizon, land so flat that she couldn't imagine what possible force could ever create a mountain from it, just as there seemed to be no possibility of a tremor in her own mind to push up the poem she had to write.

Before she could consider leaving, however, there were many things for her to settle in the city she couldn't describe; and as she lay in Walter's warm bed four blocks away from her own cold apartment, she knew that the first issue was the man who had let her into this very room at midnight seven hours earlier. She had come straight here from the Italian restaurant, parking across the street from her apartment, and, unable to face being alone with her conflicting thoughts about her husband's strange return to her life, run the four blocks to Walter's, nearly pulling him down on the floor of the hallway before he was finally able to maneuver her to his bed.

Alone there now, Joanne was able to see her own motives more clearly. Jon had asked for her presence in his life as the price for a simple phone call to get her a grant; and after wordlessly agreeing, she had made wild love with another man. In truth, Jon no longer threatened her emotionally as he had for the ten long years of their marriage. In fact, she couldn't have asked for a better teacher in deceit. She'd stay in his life. If pressed, she'd even tell him she still loved him. Her own spiritual and physical world would stay her own secret, just as Jon's had been. Perhaps he was right, Joanne thought, sitting up and pulling on the first of her sweaters, maybe they were made for each other.

Joanne sat down at Walter's desk, which was completely covered in books, papers, folders, and magazines, found a blank sheet of paper, and began her "Dear Walter" letter. Though she had decided upon a course of independence involving her rekindled relationship with Jon, a kind of emotional double life, Joanne had also decided to break off with Walter shortly before he left for work that morning. After they had made love, he had sat beside her, brushing her hair out of her face, and she could tell he had something on his mind before he said it, and though it had seemed a simple request, she knew by the bashful way he asked that it meant something much more. Walter had asked if she'd like to go with him that night to his Tuesday meeting of the Independent Revolutionary Socialists. Immediately Joanne answered that she'd think about it and leave him a message. In the way he instantly pulled his hand away from the side of her face, she knew he had gotten the message. Joanne actually had no problem with the idea of attending a political meeting; the writer in her actually longed for the opportunity of gaining some insight into the political mechanisms that had historically empowered the city around her. But she sensed a different kind of intimacy from Walter the moment he said it, asking her to join him in something that was obviously a major part of his life, and she was instantly sad knowing they had somehow lost the innocence of their relationship at that moment. Joanne didn't see how she could ever just show up at his door again late at night and make love to his body with all the uncomplicated passion they had enjoyed all winter. As duplicitous as she felt capable of being, she did not feel ready to take on the more complex aspects of having a lover. "Dear Walter," she began writing, already a little less sad feeling the pen in her hand moving over the paper. The act of writing was like an old friend to her, whom she could always rely on in moments of loss. "I'm sorry to have to tell you . . ."

Later that afternoon, Joanne had all but forgotten the theatrics of her morning, when Edith, the department's secretary, interrupted her beginning poetry class to tell her she had a call. "A woman named Amy Briggs of a Scientific Analysis Data Corporation in New York. She said it was urgent," Edith whispered just loud enough for the class to hear. Joanne reacted swiftly and calmly, as she always did when she was scared to death.

"Take out your notebooks," she told the class. "For ten minutes I want you to write, and write without letting your pen leave the page. Write whatever is going through your minds, and don't worry if the sentences are complete or the grammar correct. I'll be back in ten minutes, and we'll find a single phrase in your raw writing and create a poem for tomorrow." She paused for breath, and the class stared back at her. Edith waited at the door. "Is there anything in what I just said that you don't understand?" Joanne demanded with a rare note of irritation in her voice. The fifteen students quickly pulled out notebooks and began to write. "Good. You ought to be able to fill about five full pages by the time I get back."

Edith and Joanne walked quickly down the hall to the English department office. "Every call from New York is urgent," Edith was saying, and Joanne recognized the bait but remained silent. "I have her on my line in the corner; you can have some privacy."

"Thank you, Edith, I appreciate your help," Joanne efficiently responded when they had reached the office. She pressed the one blinking light on Edith's phone.

"Ms. Mueller?"

"Joanne, please."

"Amy Briggs. Our company has been contracted by the federal government to analyze the proposed nuclear waste depository site for Yucca Mountain. I assume you are familiar with this project?" There was a note of resentment in her voice, indicating to Joanne that her presence was not exactly welcome and the phone call obligatory.

"Yes I am, Ms. Briggs; that is, I am familiar with Yucca Mountain, but not with your company."

"There wouldn't be any reason for you to be familiar with Scientific Analysis Data as we haven't released reports yet, though we were on the verge of completing one before we were instructed to contact you."

"Who instructed you?"

Ms. Briggs ignored the question. "Time is of the essence, Ms. Mueller. The Department of Energy would like to see a preliminary report in Washington by the end of the month. At this stage you can waive your involvement so we can proceed as planned. I'll just need a letter addressed to me stating that. You can overnight the letter to me, on our account, of course—"

"What's the second alternative, Ms. Briggs?" Joanne interrupted, attempting to match her tone to that of Ms. Briggs, who had obviously already decided just what Joanne Mueller's role in this situation should be.

There was a pause, and Joanne could hear Amy Briggs muttering to someone else. Though she couldn't make out any words, she didn't need them to guess the trouble she was causing.

"Ms. Mueller, your second alternative is to be in New York Friday night, I'd say for three or four days, to go over our data regarding site design and message conveyance. At that point you can also contribute any notes of your own in terms of language. I should warn you that at this stage we've pretty much ruled out oral tradition in favor of literary. Will you have a problem with that?"

Confused, Joanne thought it best to concede something, as opposed to admitting to her own noncomprehension. Besides, wasn't literary tradition what she specialized in anyway? "I have no problem with that," Joanne said, then quickly added, "at this point, that is. I'd like to go over your findings for ruling it out, however."

Amy Briggs sighed heavily into the phone. "I will overnight you plane tickets, an itinerary, and hotel information. We are affiliated with New York University. I can put you up in a campus apartment or the Gramercy Park Hotel. Have you ever been to Manhattan, Ms. Mueller?"

"Yes, Ms. Briggs. The Gramercy Park Hotel will be fine."

"I can overnight tickets to Lake Bluff College, or would you prefer your residence?"

"The college will be fine. You said time is of the essence, so I think you should also include any preliminary reports your corporation has produced or worked from."

Again Amy Briggs sighed. "Of course, Ms. Mueller. I feel I must remind you, however, that all data at this point are confidential. Our work is for the federal government. You will be briefed further on this when you get here."

"I understand."

"Is there anything else?"

Joanne thought for a moment. Edith was the only other person in the office, and she was a few feet away replacing a toner cartridge in the Xerox machine, which, undoubtedly, didn't need replacing.

"Have you also been instructed to contact Vivian Reape?"

"I am to call her after I'm done with you. I presume she will not waive involvement in our work at this point?"

Joanne laughed as she imagined Amy Briggs taking on Vivian. "I would never presume anything of Vivian Reape, Ms. Briggs. I look forward to our meeting next Monday."

Edith—unable to draw any further information out of Joanne besides the fact that she needed to take a few days off, which would
require her speaking with Douglas Skidmore immediately after
class—was efficient in conveying the urgency of the New York
phone call to the head of the department, who arranged to see
Joanne immediately.

"Well, my dear," Douglas Skidmore said in welcome, rising from
behind his monstrous mahogany desk when she entered, something
he had failed to do ten years earlier when she had nervously approached him asking for a job Vivian had already secured for her.
"First *The North American,* now New York. Are we to lose you?"

Joanne quickly sat down, surprised by her lack of nervousness.
"You mean do I have a job interview? No. Though it is a job, but
one that will only enhance my job here, not take away from it."

"Though it *is* taking you away from us," Douglas continued,
teasing her.

"I'm afraid I'm not permitted to speak of it."

"Nonsense. This has to do with your husband's recent project,
perhaps the same project? Art for nuclear waste in the gallery of
Yucca Mountain?"

Joanne's nerves returned at the mention of her husband's name,
as if Douglas had opened a window directly behind her, letting in
the bitter wind chill. He was still standing, with his hands clasped
behind him. *Why must all department heads become father figures?*
Joanne wondered. Though she had only worked for one, she imagined they must all be of this variety.

"You are right on all accounts, Douglas. My ambition precedes
me."

"*Ambition?*" Douglas nearly laughed. "*The North American*
was ambition and well done, let me remind you. Our generation,
our nuclear generation, if you will, bears some responsibilities,
don't you think?"

Joanne nodded, eager for him to do the talking.

"I fought in World War II, Joanne, the Pacific. I have three children and four grandchildren. What we told ourselves when we worked the ships that sunk other ships was that we were doing it all for our families, our inheritors. A better world, Joanne. I am a simple old man, you see?"

"You're saying we bear responsibility."

"I'm saying that this environment, this planet, this waste we've generated in our haste to project ourselves ahead of others, is your world war, not mine. I've fought my battles." He sat down at this admission, momentarily fatigued by the memory of it.

"My time off then won't be a problem?" Joanne asked carefully.

"Of course not. Alex Dupree can cover your classes. He could use the workload."

"Thank you, Douglas. I'll report to you as soon as I am able," Joanne said, rising and turning to the door.

"Joanne, do you believe we should have dropped the bomb on Hiroshima?"

Joanne was dumbstruck by the question. It was like she was interviewing for her job again, only this time Vivian hadn't prepared the way.

"Millions of American lives would have been lost," Joanne said slowly, as if reciting a creed she had been taught long ago. "Japanese lives, too."

"*And* Nagasaki?" He eyed her like he'd revealed the trick part of the question, the riddle he had spent his own life trying to solve. Joanne smiled.

"I guess it wasn't *my* world war, Douglas."

"Nor yours, mine," he concluded.

Joanne made it through the rest of her day in a nervous excitement that made her students and fellow faculty notice her with a kind of curious awe. In class she critiqued and inspired, while in the faculty room she laughed and small talked with such newly discovered energy that when her day ended at four, she felt her body slightly collapse within the bucket seat of her car. By the time she turned the corner onto her street, she noticed a darkness slightly shadowing her block that reminded her of the strange vision she had had that morning as she'd returned home from Walter's.

When she had rounded her corner that morning, she had noticed a parked car ahead with the dome light on and a single passenger sitting in the driver's seat. Joanne walked a little more slowly up the sidewalk as she stared at the back of the stranger's head, fully illuminated by the inside car light across the street from her, not far from her apartment building. There was no one else walking or driving by, and the rare quiet of a city street surprised her as always, though she was not afraid. It appeared to be a woman with shoulder-length hair, and as Joanne got closer, she kept expecting her to get out of the car or to start it and drive off. But she just sat there, seeming to stare straight ahead, from what Joanne could make out from behind. When Joanne reached the front steps of her building, she stopped and looked again at the woman; only this time Joanne noticed the car more as the daylight had increased just enough for her to see that the woman was sitting in Joanne's blue Honda, just fifty feet away, where Joanne had parked it the night before. Her mind seemed blank as she crossed the street and walked toward her car. There was a moment in which the van behind her Honda blocked her view, and when she finally came up to her car and placed her hand on the handle, Joanne saw that no one was there. The dome light was still on, illuminating the empty car, and the door was locked.

Quickly glancing up and down the still deserted street, Joanne found her keys, opened the car, and got in. She reached down and turned off the inside light, which she must have accidentally turned on when she got home the night before. At this her ever-practical mind kicked in, and she sighed, realizing that with extreme cold and the car light left on all night her battery would surely be dead. She put the key in the ignition, and the Honda started right up.

134

But instead of feeling relieved that she had been spared the time and expense of calling the corner gas station for a jump, Joanne felt a chill run through her that was not the chill of a cold car. In fact, the seat was warm, like someone had just been sitting in it. Joanne jumped out of the car so fast she almost forgot to turn it off first before quickly running inside.

Now, ten hours later and with a glass of wine in her hand instead of hot coffee, Joanne stood at her front window and watched the darkness slowly erase her car from the quiet, windy block. Going over the experience again, she felt not exactly afraid, but alone. Her apartment was becoming colder with each wind gust slapping the window in front of her, and she found herself wondering if any of the things she had set out to do and had done in the past few days were actually toward any good in terms of the lifeless room she now stood in, accompanied only by her red wine. When the phone suddenly rang, she didn't take the time to decide whether she wished it were Jon or wished it were Walter or even some strange voice as unexpected as the back of the woman's head she had walked toward that morning, feeling more drawn to her than defensive, which was what Joanne finally realized as she picked up the receiver and said hello.

"Joanne? Vivian. Congratulations are truly in order! Though I must immediately say, we have won the battle, not the war. Oh, Joanne, there is so much to do!"

14

ONE HUNDRED YEARS AFTER
THE ANARCHISTS WERE HUNG

"The question put to the floor is whether or not to take up arms to defend workers' rights in the face of police brutality on the picket lines," Walter Steward told the thirty-one present members of the Chicago chapter of Independent Revolutionary Socialists meeting on the second floor of Parson's Pub on the West Side on a bitterly cold Tuesday night. Rose Gluck recrossed her legs and stifled a yawn. The question is *still* whether or not, she nearly mouthed down into her lap, where she was refolding her pair of leather gloves. As if a show of hands could alter the destiny of union disputes across the land. Rose pictured hordes of reporters rushing for phones to alert their front page editors of the decision, families of law-enforcement officials and strikers clutching their children to their chests as television shows were preempted by the result of the vote, Warren Beatty and Diane Keaton picking out their free Christmas tree in front of the occupied Winter Palace and pushing their way home through jubilant Muscovites to make love beneath the simple candles and ribbons they'd adorn it with. When Rose finally looked back up, her thirty comrades were staring at her as if she had actually broken out in a round of the "International" during her imaginings.

Before Rose could even come up with an excuse as to why she hadn't heard what had obviously been asked of her, Walter saved her, as he had saved her earlier before the start of the meeting. This time he politely restated the question, kindly filling in additional information that might help her, such as who had asked it of her in the first place.

"Lydia inquired as to what your position is in terms of the possible arming and self-defense of workers when faced with a brutal police force allowing scabs to work their jobs when they are on strike," he said warmly, like it was perfectly natural for someone not to hear a question directly asked of them in a small room above a bar surrounded by thirty attentive people.

Lydia, Rose thought. Lydia, who a moment ago had been smiling wildly in Rose's direction, now glanced back at Walter with annoyance. Rose quickly answered before embarrassing herself further.

"Strategically, I believe that any action on the part of the striker to take up arms against an officer, no matter how brutal, will risk losing the sympathy of the public once the forces of the police and conservative media distort his self-defense into gross offense. Obviously, this will only hurry a victory for the bosses."

Lydia was immediately on her feet. "So, Rose, you advance a theory of pity to end the suffering of the working class?"

Rose looked down hard at her gloves, which were now gripped in her bare hands. She felt the sides of her face get hot.

"That's unfair, Lydia," Rose heard Walter say, and without raising her head too far, she glanced up at him. "You asked Rose for her opinion, and she gave it to you. If you would like to give yours, please do so. If not, allow somebody else to give theirs."

Lydia fell back hard on her metal folding chair and waved her hand in front of her face to say the subject wasn't worth her opinion, and the discussion moved on, away from Rose, who again smoothed her gloves back down on her jeans. *There,* she mouthed, *he did it again.*

This was Rose's first weekly Tuesday meeting of the Independent Revolutionary Socialists in the two months, exactly two months, since her arrest with half a dozen fellow comrades for refusing to leave a speech by a U.S.-sponsored Nicaraguan Contra at the University of Chicago, where she taught library science. The incident had caused far more controversy than Rose had ever imagined it would. In truth, Rose was by now very well versed in how certain actions can drain public sympathy from obvious underdogs, for in her case six lonely chanters sat in an auditorium filled with campus conservatives and frat boys waving flags for Ronald Reagan's secret war against the Sandinista government. Rose had nearly lost her job once the campus and city newspapers had spun the incident into an attempt to "suppress the freedom of speech" of one campus organization (the University of Chicago Eagle Club, campus membership 342) by another (the Independent Revolutionary Socialists, campus membership 9). Through the pull of her powerful father, one of the school's most generous alumni, Rose was spared a campus tribunal, where anything short of an apology would have definitely cost her her job. She was placed on university probation, while her comrades, with the exception of one University of Chicago student who was also placed on probation, walked free, the university deciding that not dropping charges could only create the possibility of liberal sympathies turning back to the underdogs. For her month of probation, Rose had agreed with her father not to have contact with her socialist group, a promise she'd added another month to, perhaps as a way of thanking him without ever having to utter the actual words. In truth, Rose was horrified by the witch-hunt that had turned her overnight into one of academia's greatest foes. Suddenly, she was someone who had denied her own school freedom of speech. She was further humiliated by her wealthy father stepping in to save her, something she was sure was not lost upon any of her fellow faculty or socialist friends, so it hadn't been a hard decision to avoid the group for an additional month. Just walking in the door of Parson's Pub a half hour earlier had taken nearly all of her courage, and Lydia seemed to have been waiting at the top of the stairs for her.

"Rose, long time no see." Lydia was a pretty woman of medium height, with long, frizzy brown hair, which she was constantly pulling back into a ponytail, only to dramatically undo it moments later. From her vantage point at the top of the stairs where she calmly rolled a single long lock of hair around one of her fingers, she towered over Rose.

"Hello, Lydia. How's Walter?" Rose replied, attempting to change the subject with her own subtle sarcasm. Lydia had arrived at the Independent Revolutionary Socialists by way of Walter's bed some six months earlier. In fact, many members came and went by way of many of the men's mattresses, most dropping their newfound socialist commitment once the relationship ended, and a few staying on to eventually prove their politics to the more skeptical members. Rose had always been a skeptic of the "one-nighters," as Lydia's kind was referred to, and Lydia had picked up on this early on.

"I guess you wouldn't have known, being off on your sabbatical, or probation, or whatever the deal was you struck, but Walter and I broke up over a month ago."

Rose stood dumbly in the shine of Lydia's smile as if discovering the six chambers of her gun weren't loaded after all. Then, in the small room, partially blocked by Lydia's wide hair, Rose noticed Walter, or noticed Walter notice her. He was talking with a small group of fellow members when his eyes caught hers, and his head jerked up suddenly smiling, not with his mouth, but with a kind of excitement in his eyes that had instantly become large. Rose fought an instinct to look behind her, because she had known Walter for years and though they had always been friendly, she had never seen this kind of look from him before, a stare she couldn't help but hold onto as if it were his hand pulling her to him. *She felt like somebody else.* Walter started walking toward her, and Rose finally looked down, nervous, like there was something she was afraid of letting onto in front of his ex-lover, who had already turned to see Walter's approach. But when Rose glanced up again, Walter was not looking at Lydia, but staring hard at her.

"It's good to see you back," Walter said, and his eyes became more of a squint as if he were confused, like something had moved him all the way across the room and once he'd gotten there he couldn't completely remember what it was. Rose managed to smile, and Lydia looked suspiciously back and forth between them. "Well, come in. We're about to start."

Rose motioned for Lydia to go before her, and once both of their backs were turned, she glanced quickly behind her. No one was there.

The meeting was now concluding with committee reports and upcoming actions. Workers at Gould Meats in Milwaukee had been on strike because the company had announced layoffs and an overall 10 percent salary cut. Recently the company had begun to bring in replacement workers, and a contingent from the Independent Revolutionary Socialists was going up for the weekend to help rally the workers faced with scabs. Walter announced he was going, and Rose noticed he looked quickly in her direction after raising his hand; but Rose kept her own hands pressed down on her jeans once she saw Lydia's hand go up after Walter's.

Local college and university drives were the final topic of the two-hour meeting, and Rose felt the muscles in her neck tighten when it was announced that a volunteer was needed for the University of Chicago as well as two volunteers for tiny Lake Bluff College, which had somehow been forgotten for the school year so far. The reason a volunteer was needed for the University of Chicago was because Rose had privately told Carl Engstrom, one of the chapter heads, that she could no longer perform the job of leafleting and selling newspapers on the campus due to the incident she had just come out of with her employer. A member who lived on the South Side quickly volunteered, and Rose relaxed again.

"Now for Lake Bluff," Carl said, and a few people laughed at this suburban school, which could hardly be included with the more industrial parts of the Chicago metropolitan region. "Come on, everyone, it's not so far away. This is the time of life when very important political minds are born. Just an hour a week, anyone?"

Rose saw Lydia's hand go up, and her neck instantly tensed again. "Why doesn't Rose go; she's experienced with students. Besides, she has a comfortable car." A few people smiled and looked in Rose's direction as she tried to suppress a blush spreading across her cheeks.

"I'll do it with her," came Walter's voice. Rose couldn't help but beam at him for this latest protective gesture, and then cast a quick glance at Lydia. But before Rose could begin pulling her long wool coat around her and leave, Lydia's hand was up again like any problem weed that isn't removed completely by the root.

"I must voice my frustration," she began, growing taller as she spoke and pushing back her wild hair over her head. "After an hour of discussion, we have come to no answer as to the self-defense of the Milwaukee workers we hope to support this weekend. Conflicting calls for heroic defense and cowardly pity make our effort seem futile. I'd hope an organization like ours could provide confident answers to questions these men and women must have regarding the protection of their jobs as they are brutally forced back from the gates by police and company bullies hoping to dismantle their movement from within."

A few members nodded and clapped their support for what Lydia had said, while Rose stared at Walter, whose arm slowly went up just as Rose knew it would.

"If I may attempt to address this," he said, standing up to face the entire room. Rose had first met Walter when she'd joined five years earlier, and she'd be lying to herself if she said she had never felt an attraction to him. Almost every woman in the room was attracted to him. He was tall with a well-kept body, had a well-defined face, which always appeared kindly, and was thoroughly committed to the politics at hand in ways that were extremely well thought out and expressed. But Walter always had a woman at his side, some of whom became members and most of whom just disappeared without explanation. Walter's women were always beautiful, though in a variety of ways. Sherry was tall and blonde, while Lydia was shorter and brunette; Cindy was packaged in one of the most perfect bodies that had ever walked a picket line, while Barbara was built like a boy, and black. What all of Walter's women shared was a sense of confidence and ambition in both their social and professional lives. They were all quick to read most of the socialist books and essays from which the group had extrapolated its particular philosophies, and all of them had no qualms about shooting up their hands to question anything they didn't understand or agree with, no matter how many times longer-term members had already explained and argued nearly all these points. That Rose felt more confused than flattered by Walter's sudden attention was hardly surprising; she tended to speak only when spoken to, take a step back when a man stepped toward her, and hunch down around herself in the most unflattering positions whenever her name came up. Ironically, Rose was known to be the most difficult and opinionated member of her family and the school faculty, for when the company was made up of those whose respect she did not desire, Rose unleashed herself with an irritable fury. She was even able to look at Walter now as he made his way around the front of the group of thirty folding chairs.

"I'd like to remind the room of the tragedy that occurred in this city one hundred years ago, in which seven of our greatest socialist and anarchic leaders and organizers were horribly murdered by this country's judicial system. I'm sure the Haymarket bombing is an event we all know well, but I'll repeat its history because I can't help feeling it remains one of our most valuable sources on this very issue. At a peaceful demonstration of workers calling for a national strike for an eight-hour workday, a bomb was thrown into a contingent of police officers intending to disperse the crowd with probable violence. Three police officers were killed, and seven leaders of various unions and political groups were eventually hanged as coconspirators for the crime. Though most of these men were not even present when the bomb was thrown, they were charged with instilling the idea of violence against the state, even when it was the very same state that was suppressing man's fundamental right to congregate peaceably. I believe the issue of violence in terms of revolutionary change will never be resolved. The Haymarket incident turned socialism and anarchy into dirty words among a large number of this country's populace; and the jailings, raids, and hangings set our movement back in significant ways. The workers of this country, however, were eventually granted an eight-hour workday. Historical change comes in all forms, both peaceable and violent. Some change is carefully planned and executed, while most is the result of chance events and coincidence. I don't feel that our group can attempt a single answer to this complex question; and as for traveling to Milwaukee this weekend to join workers on subzero picket lines, I feel that it is not our right to put a weapon in their hands and face the responsibility of their suffering lives ending in a more tragic consequence. Our job there is to support and advise whatever possible situations they find themselves in. We should all hope for peaceful resolutions in their favor and stand by them in the face of all brutalities and defeats that may occur." Walter sat down.

No one stirred in the room, and even Lydia looked at him with more interest than contempt. Rose started to feel the effects of his attention come over her like alcohol, that sudden feeling of tipsiness coupled with an optimistic self-confidence. While those in the room began to get up, pull on coats, and talk quietly among themselves, Rose remained very still, staring at the spot Walter had just stood in, a spot of dusty floor that had always seemed like an empty one in Rose's life, though he now seemed to have always been standing there. She finally stood up, folded her coat neatly over her arm, and started walking slowly toward the door, knowing and not knowing she was giving him another chance to come to her, which he did, and this time she lifted her face completely toward his.

"It's good you're back, Rose," he said, looking at her again like he wasn't sure who the woman was he kept pursuing.

"You already said that," Rose replied like a joke, something rare for her.

"I hope you're coming this weekend?"

"Oh," Rose felt her nervousness returning and concentrated on keeping her back straight and her eyes on his. "I really don't know. It's only two days from now."

"Please come," he said, and lightly put his hand on the arm that held her coat in front of her now like a crutch. "There's room in my car. We're meeting on the corner of Sheffield and Belmont at eight o'clock, Friday. Please. I want you to."

Do you have a comfortable car? Rose wanted to ask, but just smiled. Walter squeezed her arm one last time before removing it, knowing she'd come; and Rose quickly turned away from him, making it to the door without looking back.

Before she was halfway down the stairs and could even begin to overanalyze what had just occurred, she heard her name called from behind, but this time by Carl Engstrom, who came down to her once she had turned.

"Rose, I was wondering if you could tell me anything about Prof. Joseph Wright at your university," he whispered to her.

"Wright?" Rose asked.

"Yes, in nuclear science."

Rose paused, remembering Carl's special interest in ecosocialism, a rather recent sect of the older socialist groups, who had always distanced themselves from environmentalists, believing they put animals and the natural world on a higher plane than the needs of the common man and woman. Recently the more established, hard-line socialist groups had begun to give an ear to the concepts of Third World toxins and pollution caused by large companies looking to escape the United States's costly regulations by destroying the water and resources of less developed countries, and Carl was their own expert in this developing ideology.

"What is it you need to know?" Rose asked carefully, reminding herself of the humiliating probation she had just completed and the suspicious stares most of the faculty gave her as she walked across campus.

"I'm particularly interested in the recent government grants given to his department regarding long-term storage of nuclear waste in Yucca Mountain. Have you heard about this?"

"Vaguely," Rose lied.

They stared at each other for a minute, and Rose knew Carl realized her reluctance to discuss the politics of her university on her first night back with the same group that had put her position there in such jeopardy.

"I'm late right now. Why don't I find out a little more about Wright's program, and we can talk later?"

"It's good to have you back, Rose," Carl said, and touched her arm like Walter just had, only this time the coat, which she still held, felt less like a crutch and more like a shield, the man touching her didn't make her feel like some witty, confident woman come alive in an exotic environment, and when she finally stepped outside on the sidewalk, she wasn't at all surprised to see the world around her still empty and covered with snow.

15

THE ART OF BUSINESS

The only way to fight capitalism is with capitalism, Tom McMann resolved after more than fifteen years of inner political debate. He glanced nervously around his bookstore, worried he had said this aloud. But it was noon on a Wednesday, and the emptiness of the small store did little to argue a second point of view. Tom had enjoyed many political points of view in his twenty-nine years of life, and as much as he hated seeing himself join the cliché of radical leftist college graduates falling prey to the tentacles of a right-wing, less government, less taxation, profit-driven lifestyle, he couldn't exactly just lie down and die in front of the small headline on the back page of that day's *Lake Bluff Star,* announcing the invasion of Book Inc., the nationwide chain superstore, on the innocent shores of his small campus town.

According to the article, Book Inc. had just purchased the majestic but abandoned Steven's Department Store, which had lost its own lease on life five years earlier when the Lake Bluff Mall had razed what was once a thriving downtown business center. Though the Lake Bluff Mall had spared Book Bar (students, teachers, and small-town literary types weren't tempted to spend their book-buying hours in a decadent mall with teenage gangs), Book Inc. was a much shrewder competitor. For the past two years, Tom had followed the chain's pillaging of small stores by opening its three-level stores right next to them, complete with wooden bookcases, Oriental rugs, comfortable couches, and an endless inventory of titles on nearly every subject, which were continually marked down in sales, something no small store could ever afford to compete with. On top of all this was a coffee bar, usually located on an upper floor overlooking the main floor. Book Inc. provided what was essentially a town square in late-twentieth-century America: a trendy, overpriced coffeehouse offering little more than a caffeine- and sugar-laced sustenance in an atmosphere of endless merchandise. So vast was their inventory that it was not uncommon to see an espresso-sipping woman reading the New Testament next to a cheesecake-eating man studying Marx's *Communist Manifesto*.

Or so the book trades so lovingly made example of. Lovingly, because superstores like Book Inc. were the first noticeable boom in the book industry since the Hollywood "novelization," the concept of writing the book *after* making the movie. According to the *Lake Bluff Star*, Book Inc. sent undercover scouts to small towns all across the country to rate the popularity and quantity of small bookstores and coffeehouses. Instead of looking for towns in need of books, they'd piggyback on areas thriving with bookstores and promptly steal away the market these stores had spent years creating. All of this was quoted by a man in Michigan who had seen his store closed in two short months when Book Inc. descended directly across the street from him. The ever-objective *Lake Bluff Star* quoted a representative of Book Inc. to follow up this accusation: "There will always be a place for the small bookstore in America. Book Inc. only hopes to provide an inventory not available from such smaller operations. We exist because people want us to exist."

Tom slammed the paper down on the counter. He walked

through the small, cluttered shop to the front door and cracked it open just enough to blow cigarette smoke out without letting too much of the cold in. He had been doing this for eight years, even after Mrs. Peterson had passed away, deciding it was better for business to keep the business nonsmoking, especially since it was now Tom's business.

Eight years earlier, when Tom had been a heady student of the Lake Bluff creative writing program, he began what seemed the budding poet's dream career, a part-time job in the local literary/leftist bookstore. Working three days a week for the minimum of minimum wage, he quickly learned that the hours he had imagined himself comfortably seated behind the counter reading books for free or composing his verse in the inspired company of hundreds of published authors were to be entirely taken up with boxes, opening boxes and sealing boxes. Like most small stores, Book Bar had no back room. "You're in the back," Mrs. Peterson loved to reply to a customer inquiring if they by chance had a copy of a certain book in the back. Daily, the UPS man and mailman unloaded cartons of books needing to be inventoried and shelved, while Tom endlessly gathered up returns to inventory, box, and send out. For twenty years Mrs. Peterson had maintained a business bank account with just enough profit to live on and pay Tom by refilling a box of new books with old books and waiting for checks to cross in the mail.

Still, Tom loved the job. Mrs. Peterson, nearly seventy when Tom first started work at her store, immediately fell into the role of absent mother (Tom's own mother having died when he was ten), and Tom enjoyed the role of surrogate son to a woman who had married but had never had a child. A year after Tom graduated from Lake Bluff (supplementing his meager store hours with a terrible, but well-paying, waiting job), Mrs. Peterson died, and Tom closed the store for a week in mourning. After he reopened the store to very good business (the community seemed to offer condolences with their charge cards in hand), two men in lawyer uniforms arrived to inform him that according to Mrs. Peterson's will, Tom was the beneficiary of a five-year lease, the entire inventory of the store, and a bank account in the amount of eighteen hundred dollars. Tom frowned at the documents they handed him, instead of smiling at the rare legalese of good fortune.

Once-budding minor poet Tom McMann had suffered the post-graduation slump in his writing as he found himself more exhausted from a dinner shift at the restaurant than he ever felt writing critical papers past midnight. In the week following Mrs. Peterson's death, Tom had decided it was a sign to move out of the Midwest after a quarter of a century of calling it home (Tom hailed from a small town outside of Detroit). He had always dreamed of the ocean, and having seen it only twice, he decided to reduce his belongings to one suitcase and take a bus to San Francisco. There, with the help of a few college friends, he could return to his career serving food, but at least he'd be doing it in a radically different environment, an environment, perhaps, with the possibility of love.

One of the lawyers, the better-looking of the two, was quick to point out that Tom could simply sell off his inventory, break his lease, and make off with what looked to be around five thousand dollars. But as a trained romantic poet, Tom had learned to read between the lines of even the most dry legal documents and find the sentimental clause inside. To sell the store, even to donate the money, would mean erasing the legacy of a woman who had given him the only thing she had. It was one of the first hot days of the summer when Tom followed the two suits out the door and lit his cigarette. He had never felt more alone. He could feel himself age in ten-year bursts as he watched elevated commuter trains roar by at the end of the block, and when the UPS man pulled up with a backlog of deliveries from the week the store was closed, Tom accepted the clipboard handed to him and signed his name.

Six years of sixty-hour workweeks had gone by, and Tom still lived in his one-bedroom rental, did not own a car, and had barely been able to increase the initial balance in the store's bank account by more than a thousand dollars. As for poetry, the closest Tom came to it was when he unpacked the books for the store's well-stocked poetry section, which wasted more space than it ever paid out. As for love, Tom liked to think it was long out of print, and with the exception of a few month-or-so-long, more-physical-than-emotional relationships, Tom found himself alone at night after the store had closed, preoccupied with visions of checks passing in the mail. True, Alex Dupree had entered his life a few weeks ago, but Tom found it hard to believe that he was going to wake up one morning passionately in love with the goofy-looking academic poet, no matter how hard Alex willed it to happen. Tom worried about what attracted him to Alex: money, money, and more money. His envy of Alex's apartment, job, and relative peace of mind, which made it possible for him to turn out his formally impeccable, self-absorbed verse, had begun to make Tom wish he'd hurry up and wake up in love. Besides, it had been so long since Tom *had* been in love what would it hurt if he misread the signals a little.

But all this was far from Tom's mind as he tossed his cigarette in the street and gave his empty store a sad once-over as he imagined the crowded three stories of Steven's Department Store filled with every book imaginable for every potential customer county-wide. And then he thought of Alex again. But before he could complete the connection, the door pressed open at his back, and he jumped around to find Richard Miller, the salesman for Small World Books, representing a dozen small publishers of contemporary literature that, like Tom's store, earned just enough to pay the bills.

"You won't believe where I just was," Richard said in way of greeting, pushing his black suitcase of catalogs and advance reading copies into the store in front of him.

"Steven's Department Store getting the order of your lifetime?"

Richard gave the store the same quick once-over Tom just had and, finding it empty, stepped up to him, put his still-gloved hands on Tom's sides, and kissed him gently on his cheek. The cold cigarette smell from Richard's wool coat reminded Tom of his father, which, in turn, reminded him of his own overly burdened adulthood. He and Richard were the best kind of casual lovers. Richard lived in Minneapolis and came through Chicago twice a year for sales calls. Tom forced himself not to think about how many other twenty-nine-year-old failed poets Richard sold books to in the five-state region.

"You'll make it; they're a bunch of idiots," Richard consoled him, as Tom pulled away and walked back to the counter, always feeling the need to keep the counter between them when they transacted business.

"Idiots with an empire. I should be such an idiot."

Richard paused, and Tom could see him saying something in his mind before deciding to say it aloud. Richard was older, late thirties, with slightly receding hair on an otherwise handsome face. There was either a wife or lover back in Minneapolis, something Tom had never pursued too far, preferring just to enjoy their bi-annual encounters with a quiet dream that one day some strange circumstance would put them in the same city, where they'd fall passionately in love with each other. Of course one of them would have to escape the wage slavery of the book industry and embark upon an incredible career to pay the bills for their house, cars, and vacations.

"You've always said you wished you could just wake up and find the store gone."

Without much thought, Tom took it the wrong way. "I didn't say I hoped to wake up completely bankrupt, owing vendors thousands of dollars, the latest local business failure."

"I'm sorry. In Minnesota we're required to look on the bright side."

Tom let him off the hook.

"Do you want to do this today?" Richard said, pointing back

at his black suitcase. Tom instantly knew that Richard was the one who didn't want to do it today, most likely exhausted from a stressful morning selling every backlist he had to Book Inc. "I'm still in town tomorrow."

"Tomorrow would be good," Tom agreed, unable to imagine going through all fifty of Richard's catalogs right now to place his measly twenty-title order.

"I'll come by tonight?" Richard reached an ungloved hand across the counter, lightly running his index finger in circles on the top of Tom's hand.

"No," Tom said. They both looked at each other confused. "I have a friend in town. I'm sorry. It was last minute." Lies like this always seemed funny to Tom when both parties were aware it was a lie. "I just don't think it would be a good idea tonight, okay?"

Richard pulled his leather glove back on his hand.

"I haven't met someone," Tom answered without Richard's asking. "This whole Book Inc. deal has me really messed up. I just don't think I'd be good company."

Richard reached both hands back across the counter and clasped Tom's. "I'm at the Holiday Inn downtown. Call me if you change your mind, or just call to talk. Noon tomorrow?"

"You know where to find me."

Tom watched Richard leave, his body unrecognizable from the heavy wool coat over a heavy sweater and sport coat, a deep red scarf wrapped tightly around his neck, with earmuffs clamped on top, temporarily forgotten from the ears like a pair of glasses left on the top of the head. His body bent down as he walked into the crisp wind and passed by the store's window with a slight nod in Tom's direction. It had been six months since Tom had last seen Richard's body, but he remembered it well. Tom was attracted to the slight flab of Richard's waist, something he worried men would never find attractive on himself, as he neared an age where his own lack of consistent exercise would certainly show itself in those exact spots. Tom believed the two of them stayed slender from a shared concern about money, about whether or not the business they were in would actually be in business the next year, a future not padded with retirement accounts, real estate, or stocks.

Tom remembered Alex Dupree's body of precise angles and definitions. He hadn't exactly seen Alex's body, but had briefly felt it in an extremely awkward encounter in the front seat of Alex's Mustang parked outside of Tom's apartment building the night he had been introduced to Joanne Mueller. Tom was slightly drunk from the expensive wine they had had at dinner on top of feeling light-headed from meeting a writer he had admired for so long. That Alex wasn't this writer was unfortunate, but the fact of his personal relationship to her allowed Tom to be pulled into his arms after safely informing Alex that he couldn't come up as Tom had the ever-useful "friend in town." After a rather sloppy kiss and jerky caress (Tom accidentally jammed his elbow on the dashboard, ending their love-making much sooner than Alex had hoped), Tom tried again to say good-bye.

"You should spend a weekend with me at my place," Alex dared, grabbing onto Tom's hand with both of his. "There's an Olympic-size pool that hardly anyone uses and a fantastic gym—I could show you around."

"Are you telling me I could use some hours in a gym?" Tom asked, smiling. Not exactly insulted.

"Of course not," Alex quickly answered. "You know I think you have a wonderful body, but why not improve? It's what my father always said: the things to improve in yourself are the things that are already pretty good."

Alex was nervous again. Tom could see the rapid way his eyes darted around the car as he spoke, almost afraid of letting them stay too long on Tom, perhaps in fear of forgetting what he was saying should he allow himself to stare at the young man he was saying it to. Tom politely reminded Alex that he worked on weekends but promised to call him later that week.

Later that week Tom still hadn't called, and as he stepped back out of the store, he made a mental note to do so. Outside, the sidewalk was empty of pedestrians, a product of the combination of a severe wind chill and the Lake Bluff Mall. He quickly walked to the empty store next to his. Peering through the dirty glass just above the FOR RENT sign that had been there since the Native American art gallery had closed a year ago, Tom surveyed the large, bright room. The floors were wooden like his own store's and the ceilings covered with an antique tin in need of a few repairs. The best thing about the store was its corner location, allowing it to have floor-to-ceiling windows on two sides, which even on a gray winter day allowed enough light in to make the dusty place seem cheerful. Wrapping his arms tightly around his chest and stomping his feet in place, Tom made some quick calculations.

Half the wall could come down between the two stores, creating an opening into the Book Bar right about where the New Age section was. This would keep the bookstore's cash register where it was, right at the entrance to the addition. This was important because in what was once the Native American art gallery, there would be a coffee bar with small tables and chairs lining all the windows. Tom imagined the windows steamed up on a cold winter day like this, college students and local housewives or house husbands filling the tables, waving in their friends passing by. By having customers enter through the bookstore, Tom could sell them books to read or pretend to read as they waited for their milk to be steamed or their espressos to cool. A bitter winter day like this would be the perfect time for business by providing a place for people to escape the inevitable isolation of the season. Book Inc. wasn't the only one who could smell opportunity in a town like this, and Tom started to imagine Book Bars popping up all over the country: college towns, liberal cities, Haight/Ashbury, Cambridge.

Tom had little over twenty-five hundred dollars in the store's savings account. The money in the checking account would barely cover billing by the first of March. The store's accounts were

Tom's, but there was no house to mortgage, no car to sell, and definitely no cash stuffed under the mattress. A loan was the only option, and Tom not only had no idea how to go about getting one, he doubted the feasibility of a bank handing money over for a venture such as this on a street they had only been foreclosing for the past three years. Surely Alex could help. Not give Tom the money. He could never accept something as simple as that, he resolved, remembering Alex's hands groping inside Tom's coat, the bitterly cold touch of his fingertips on Tom's warm chest, but Alex certainly knew people in banks. A good word here, an introduction there, a reference?

The slam of his store's front door quickly pulled him out of his scheme, and he hurried back inside. When he got in, he saw a young man and woman at the poetry section and recognized them as customers who would come in about once a week, spend about an hour looking over books, and rarely make a purchase. Tom forced himself to say hello and quickly went back behind the counter. The woman was pretty and wore a deep blue ski coat over a long cardigan and jeans. The man was even prettier, with silky blond hair (no hat) and underdressed in an old leather bomber jacket. Tom guessed they were both students, recalling the days when he too would thoughtlessly underdress in the winter, rarely paying attention to the natural elements in a world that seemed to revolve around much more important matters. Now Tom's life was all weather forecasts. Snowstorms and windchills meant anywhere from five hundred dollars to one thousand dollars less in daily receipts, not to mention having to shovel the sidewalk and pay the heating bill.

As Tom started organizing invoices, he felt the glances of the young man, whom he had presumed to be the boyfriend of the woman he was with. Tom had long ago sworn off college students, but the slight flirtation picked up his mood and made his body shift beneath the three layers of clothes that had been his only companion for the past three months. Before he could think better

155

of it, he picked up the phone and left a message at the Holiday Inn downtown for Richard that he'd come by around eight that night. Alex could wait until the morning. Book Bar/Coffee Bar could wait until the morning, too. It wasn't like he couldn't be a day late to be turned down for a loan.

"Excuse me, I'm Diane," the young woman in the ski jacket said, approaching the counter. "That's my friend Sink." She indicated the pretty boy behind her, who leapt up at his name, always glad to hear it. "I'm a student at Lake Bluff College, and we've, well, I've recently decided to stay at Lake Bluff for the summer and was wondering if you had any job openings."

Tom could only smile at the pretty woman and her possibly homosexual boyfriend in front of him. It was so much like that day eight years ago when he had stood in front of Mrs. Peterson. A slender volume of poetry was held tightly in Diane's hand, and Tom knew she intended to purchase it as a sign of her commitment to the store, just as Tom had bought three books the day Mrs. Peterson had given him the job. Tom waited a few moments before answering, taking in the budding poetess and her boyfriend, who probably wrote poetry too, unless his role was chiefly to inspire poetry in the people he met. Before answering, Tom recalled the lazy afternoons Diane presumed she'd spend behind the counter of Book Bar, reading great poets and writing great poems, and when he did finally speak, he consciously had to keep the words from coming out too fast, as he pictured her beautiful brown hair curling out at the sides and sticking to her face as she steamed milk in one hand and poured cup after cup of coffee with the other.

16

THE BUSINESS OF ART

"Are you listening to me?" Shelly asked, blowing up at a long blonde strand of hair pulled down by the steam from the stove.

As far as muses go, Jon Sullivan had been unlucky in love. There had been one love, one depressed inspiration of his rather modestly endowed body of work, but that one love, or nonmuse, had certainly transformed herself in a variety of ways to tempt the lonely visions out of his soul and onto the canvas before him. That muse, Joanne Mueller, had started out as a romantic girlfriend, slipped easily into devoted wife, ventured out to become a selfless bread-winner, and returned home a selfish success. At least that's how Jon diagrammed it. He drew the line at jealousy—weren't visual art and literary art two very different schools at the same university? He even went so far as to fondly remember the months he had spent hoping to seduce Joanne's own muse, sitting at her desk, sketch pad in hand, the moment she left for class, drinking from her coffee cup, switching sides of the bed, even forcing her to sit at the kitchen table with him while she wrote and he sketched, which only resulted in a half-dozen bad charcoals of Joanne filling page after page.

After ten years he felt he had no other choice. He had quit painting altogether in their last three years of marriage, and when a young blonde in his class at Edgewater Community College oh-so-accidentally brushed her breast against his arm as he leaned over her to add some red to her sunflower's yellow, he felt something stir in him that had been dormant for too long. A sleeping giant stretching. A soft whisper that he could do it, *he could do it.* The young girl, Shelly, could not be put off; in fact, she must be pursued; and when spring came early that year, Jon found himself opening windows, dusting surfaces, and feeling, for the first time in a long time, that youthful force of anything being possible. Naturally, the youthful force in question had, by then, submitted to his advances; and when Joanne threw Jon out and he arrived at his mistress's door, Shelly recognized what was once only possible as having its own potential heavy permanence, but the wind off the lake came through the window behind her smelling warm and sweet, and she took his bag and gave him a key.

"What did you just say?" Jon Sullivan looked over the top of his newspaper at Shelly for the first time in their conversation. She stood with her back to him at the stove, frantically combining ingredients for an Alfredo sauce. Nine months had passed since the door had been shut behind him, nine months in which his new muse had spoken only sexually, sometimes as much as three times a day, three days in a row. Just when he felt he had mistaken the calling of his young mistress and began to once again long for the more mature world of Joanne, the Yucca Mountain Project had literally fallen out of the sky, and he and Shelly had moved from her cramped first-floor one-bedroom to truly loftier digs, the second to top floor of the tallest building in Rogers Park. Shelly had insisted on staying in Rogers Park as her waitressing job was there. Despite the neighborhood, consisting of recent graduates and old Polish couples, their twelfth-floor apartment allowed Jon an unobstructed southern view of the Chicago skyline and an equally broad eastern view of the lake. The view of the city represented something Jon needed to reach, like a secondary shoreline. Though when he looked left, at the blackness of Lake Michigan, he felt even more challenged, by what lay beyond it: New York, Europe, everything but the Midwest.

"I said I can't get the fucking cheese to separate," Shelly replied. She wore a green flannel shirt and panties, still young enough to make such sloppiness sexy.

"Before that." Jon slammed the newspaper down on the small kitchen table and walked over to her. "That part about the Aztecs."

"The Aztec lines? I said that about ten minutes ago."

"Well, say it again."

Jon said this with a tone of irritation that had lately crept up in a lot of their conversations. So recently had this new tone appeared that Shelly looked back at him slightly hurt, the pores of her smooth face wide open from the heat of the stove. Jon stared back at her, impatient.

"I said those aerial shots of the mountains you showed me re-minded me of the Aztec lines I learned about in high school. I guess the way the sun caught the colors and sort of made a pattern. The Aztecs made these long rows of rocks that colored the earth, or was it the other way around? In school we used to think they were messages to spaceships, which is why I remember them, I guess."

Jon moved his hand toward Shelly's face, causing her to jump slightly, and swept back the stray wisp of hair that was falling down again. She looked at him appreciatively, and he leaned over and kissed her on the forehead as a father would kiss his daughter. Running his hand down her narrow back, he rested his fingers at the base of her buttocks, just where her panties held everything in.

"The sun didn't make those lines, sweetie, a color Xerox did." He lightly slapped her butt and walked out of the cramped kitchen into the not-so-cramped bedroom next to it, which he used as a

159

studio. Shelly had suggested he take the larger bedroom for his studio when they'd moved in six months ago, and Jon hadn't argued with this, as he had always planned on taking it. It was the one room Jon and Shelly hadn't made love in. When he shut the door, as he did now, Shelly was not supposed to disturb him, for any reason. When it was open, she could call down the short hallway for him, which she rarely did. The room was the only corner room, with a view of both the lake and the city, containing a daybed, a drafting table, a bookshelf filled with every possible book he could think of for inspiration, and a cabinet filled with every possible tool to carry out such inspirations. Since they had moved into this new apartment, Jon had done nothing in the room but fill space. When the Yucca Mountain Project showed up, he'd felt relieved at having achieved something for nothing and planned on executing whatever came to him in the shortest time possible.

"Something aboriginal," he had been advised. "Didn't you specialize in it?"

When Joanne called and mentioned a name as large as Vivian Reape, followed by two reporters calling, one a Leslie Meyer from *ArtTalk,* a prestigious monthly out of New York, Jon had begun to see both the career opportunity and profound humiliation facing him as the project gained notoriety. A lot of people would actually pay attention to this work, people who had never heard of him before, people who would never hear of him again, and if he didn't create something great, all they'd write about would be his uncle who'd gotten him the job. His strange deal with Joanne was based, in fact, on this new fear. Joanne knew a lot about grants such as this; she knew how to fulfill the obligation and make new friends along the way. Perhaps the two of them could even collaborate on something. Surely her mind had already assessed just what was appropriate, what would impress, what it all meant.

"How about starting with the entire history of civilization up to this point," she'd sarcastically suggested when he called her a few days after their dinner, prodding her for help. He laughed, like she was joking, and she didn't laugh with him. Well, he decided, perhaps she'd have to go through all of civilization and just give him the highlights.

Jon was suddenly aware of a gentle tapping at the door. It was slowly getting louder, and he wondered how long Shelly had been at this. When he flung open the door, she stepped all the way back to the wall and looked toward the living room.

"They're here. I just buzzed them in."

She was still dressed only in her flannel shirt and panties, and visibly torn between getting back to the kitchen where dinner had probably exploded over every available surface or running to the bedroom and getting dressed. Jon didn't think about how he hadn't done a thing to help her. He could only see that rather childish desire to please as she pulled down at her flannel shirt as if the guests could already see her. He thought how Joanne would have had everything under control at this point, including himself; and despite the fact that this dinner *was* important, that his career had never been so much on the line, and how a trophy wife like Joanne would have relieved him of a lot of the pressure of entertaining, he felt a raging attraction to the young girl in front of him to the point of wanting to make love to her right there against the wall while the guests waited outside the door.

"Turn everything off in the kitchen and get dressed, then come out and meet everyone, and then you can go back and finish dinner," Jon said, kissing her gently and working a hand up her shirt; but a knock at the door sent her out from under him like a cat, and he walked slowly to the living room, giving her time to make it from the kitchen to the bedroom, though part of him would have liked to have opened the door in time for his old friend to see this young girl fly across the living room with her flannel shirt flapping above her perfect rear end.

The old friend Jon so wished to impress was artist Raymond Black (not his real name, but even Jon had acquiesced to call him this) and his "companion," the art dealer Anneliese Lange. Jon and

Raymond had gone to school together in St. Louis. After Jon and Joanne had been in Chicago for a few years, he started receiving invitations to shows that included some of Raymond's work, and at first Jon had gone, attempting not to show any rivalry with his old friend. But as the amount of Raymond's work increased, soon coupled with Anneliese Lange's name (one of the most important dealers in the Midwest, with a direct line to New York), Jon allowed himself to drop out of Raymond's life. If Raymond had even noticed the loss of his old friend, he surely had enough new friends to keep him occupied. Jon hadn't seen or spoken to Raymond in over two years; and when Jon had called him a week earlier to invite him and Anneliese over for dinner (Shelly's idea; she had been thrilled at the prospect of meeting one of Jon's old friends, no less an artist as famous as Raymond Black), Raymond had enthusiastically agreed.

"Oh, Jon, how did we let it get so long? What a wonderful invitation, and I know Anneliese is just dying to hear all about this nuclear bomb thing you're doing."

Jon hadn't bothered to correct him. As for Anneliese, Jon felt a small pleasure in knowing that she had heard about the grant, and, good dealer that she was, had perhaps thought about calling him up herself to set up a dinner, just to keep herself in contention for any possible kickbacks his career could suddenly have to offer. Anneliese was an intensely skinny woman who chain-smoked to such a degree that she resembled a cigarette. She wore her black hair short and spiky and kept her makeup severe, an attempt, Jon felt, to overemphasize her already strange face (small forehead, no chin, flat nose). Her relationship with Raymond had always been a mystery. They had lived together for the last five years and had not married. By being successful, they had both been rumored to be gay, rumored to be bi, and rumored to be asexual. But Jon guessed Raymond was straight, having seen him with women in college, and was certain Anneliese was as well, having slept with her nearly ten years ago himself trying to get her to represent him

162

when he first arrived in Chicago. What Jon wasn't sure of was what each of them knew of what he knew of each of them, but details like that had never bothered him, and once Shelly was safely in the bedroom, he eagerly opened the door.

In the chorus of greetings, Jon almost didn't notice the third person with them, a woman who was definitely employed by the arts, as she could have been Anneliese's twin: black hair in a straight bob; severe makeup, which seemed to overemphasize a beautiful face, just as Anneliese's worked in the opposite way; and a rail-thin body entirely covered in shades of black.

"You won't think we're too awful bringing an old friend who was very interested in coming. Jon Sullivan, Leslie Meyer."

Bewildered, Jon gripped her black-gloved hand firmly and re-membered why her name had brought an instant flush to his face.

"She's editor-at-large for *ArtTalk* and apparently wants to pro-file you."

"I feel like I'm intruding, Mr. Sullivan. I didn't realize until we were in the elevator that they hadn't told you I was—"

"Nonsense, Leslie." Anneliese made her way into the living room and looked around it as if inspecting an installation she was both interested in and repelled by simultaneously. She dropped her coat on the sofa, a habit of knowing it would be taken care of. "I told you, it's all very midwestern to just show up with people when invited for dinner."

"It is?" Jon asked, worried less about the dinner than he was about Leslie Meyer beginning her interview without notice. He was immediately conscious of his clothes, a three-button shirt of long underwear material, a burgundy cardigan, and tight jeans. *Oh, god,* he thought, *what is Shelly putting on?*

"Has everyone just forgotten about me?" said a rather exasper-ated Raymond Black, who was still standing outside the door. Ray-mond had gained considerable weight around his middle, and his hair had thinned far back to the top of his head. He looked well fed, well rested, and well pampered, and Jon hated himself for envying this unsightly image of success. But before he could decide on the proper words to say, Anneliese's voice cackled from behind him. "Jon, please, who is this creature?"

Shelly stood in the bedroom door wearing a knee-length, flower-print dress that was possibly older than she was under an old corduroy sport coat of his. Her hair was loosely pulled back so it slightly billowed around her face, which was completely clean of makeup. Anneliese was holding an unlit cigarette to her thin lips and pacing from side to side, looking her up and down as though Jon had cast Shelly that day. He couldn't decide whether he loved or hated how she looked standing there with her hands tightly gripped together in front of her.

"Well, it's certainly not Joanne," Raymond roared from behind. Jon quickly moved over to Shelly and led her into the room.

"Shelly, this is Anneliese and Raymond. And this is Leslie Meyer, from *ArtTalk*. Remember, the woman who called last week?"

Shelly just stared at Leslie.

"She's staying for dinner," Jon said slowly, rubbing his hand on her back, afraid she might suddenly burst into tears.

"I just hate this," Leslie said, stopping in the middle of taking off her long black cape.

"Oh, for god's sake, I'll just pick at a salad; surely there's enough," Anneliese replied, walking over to Leslie and pulling off her cape and dropping it on top of her coat on the couch.

"Salad?" Shelly asked, turning to Jon.

"Dinner isn't quite done yet anyway; why don't I get you drinks," Jon said, pushing Shelly in front of him toward the kitchen.

"I hope you have vodka," Raymond yelled from behind them as they went down the hall.

They didn't say a word to each other as Jon quickly grabbed four glasses, an ice bucket, and a bottle of Absolut he had remembered to put in the freezer only an hour before. Shelly stared down at her sauce, now cold, on the stove top. When he got back to the living room, Leslie and Anneliese were sitting on the couch, Raymond in the chair to the right, and all three of their coats on the only chair left. "Raymond, why don't you do the honors while I just get rid of these," Jon said, and quickly hauled the coats to the bedroom.

"She's adorable," Anneliese announced when he reentered. "I expected a bookish girl. I guess I was thinking of Joanne, back when the two of you first got here."

"Are you and Joanne Mueller divorced?" Leslie asked, always the reporter.

All three of them looked hard at Jon, who quickly grabbed the glass of vodka Raymond held out for him.

"Let's not go into all that now," Jon replied, in a slightly low voice, causing Anneliese to overdramatically clamp a hand to her mouth and nod toward the kitchen.

"Fabulous story in *The North American*. Leslie and I read it together on the plane," Anneliese whispered, so fiercely that her words came out louder than her normal speaking voice. She lit her cigarette and just dropped the match on the coffee table as there was no ashtray. Jon didn't have the energy to explain that they probably didn't have one.

Leslie turned the conversation toward a discussion of Raymond's first New York show, which had been at a small SoHo gallery Anneliese had invested in, while the four of them went through the first round of vodka. Jon relaxed as he listened to sounds from the kitchen, and Anneliese managed to smoke her entire cigarette without seeming to ash. Jon quickly pulled it from her long bony fingers and threw it out the window.

"Do you miss the smell of a woman's cigarette?" Anneliese asked, pulling another one from her large, black canvas bag, which seemed to only hold about three things.

"I should check on Shelly," Jon said.

"What's for dinner?" Leslie asked, and Jon realized she was a woman with a particular diet.

"Fettuccini Alfredo, I believe."

"Oh no, I told you, Anneliese. I'm afraid I'm allergic to all dairy. I *really* shouldn't have come."

"Nonsense," Anneliese replied. "Tell Shelly just to whip up a light olive oil with some basil leaves and garlic to put over Leslie's noodles. And make mine with extra black pepper."

When Jon turned to go, he saw Shelly in the doorway, obviously having heard all of Leslie Meyer's diet.

"There you are. We were just about to bother you again," Anneliese called out. Raymond stood up when he saw Shelly. Jon and Anneliese both noticed.

"Do you know if the pasta has egg in it?" Leslie asked, and Shelly started to laugh. She stood in the doorway with one hand over her eyes and laughed while everyone looked around at each other except for Jon, who stared at her, hard.

"It's fine," she tried to say between her laughter. "Everything's just fine."

"Dinner's ready?" Jon asked, incredulously.

"No, I mean—get your coats. We're going out."

"Oh dear, we won't find a cab in this neighborhood, and our car won't be on call for at least another hour," Anneliese said, smiling at the domestic incident she had just caused.

"We can walk. I made a reservation at a restaurant just a few blocks away."

"A restaurant? *In Rogers Park?*" Anneliese exclaimed, the smile instantly slapped from her face.

"Earthly Delight?" Jon asked, though he already knew it was the vegetarian, folk restaurant where Shelly waitressed four days a week.

In less than half an hour the five of them were jammed around what seemed like a table for two, surrounded by recent graduates

166

and not-so-recent graduates with long hair and beards, talking loudly over a bluegrass band that had just started a set. After the initial shock that the place didn't serve hard liquor, they settled into three carafes of wine. Shelly sat next to Raymond, who was enraptured by her rapture over his work, while Jon was sandwiched between Anneliese and Leslie, who both told him exactly why they loved New York. Shelly continually got up, out of habit, to help with getting the food, clearing the table, and endlessly refilling the carafes of wine. Each time she stood, Raymond stood, until Anneliese had turned her chair so obviously away from Raymond that the smoke from her cigarettes enveloped Jon's whole head. Leslie had stopped inquiring into Jon, his work, or his personal life. Jon wondered if it was because she was embarrassed by the trouble her presence had caused earlier or she just hated the health food cafeteria they were in so intensely that she wanted to hurry and get it over with. But just as Jon had started to despair that his chance to appear in *ArtTalk* was as ruined as Shelly's Alfredo sauce, Leslie pushed away her half-finished nondairy entrée and dove back in.

"Your grant is impressive, perhaps one of the largest federal arts grants in recent years."

"How much did they throw at you?" Raymond yelled from his end of the table, causing Shelly to burst into laughter. Anneliese occupied herself by digging through the three items in her canvas bag, looking like she was about to crawl inside. Raymond seemed extremely drunk, which made Jon worry about what would fall out of him next.

"Generous," Jon admitted, wondering if he would be expected to pick up the tab. "But not nearly as much as everyone thinks."

"And what did you have to do to get that—what?—uncle or something to hand this over to you?" The table froze. Jon looked into Raymond's eyes, feeling as though a wild animal had just bit him. Leslie and Anneliese looked down at the table, not so much because they were offended by the comment but in fear that Raymond would continue and expose everything he knew about whatever friends, lovers, relatives, or roommates who had contributed to their own careers.

"Well, I'll tell you, Raymond," Jon calmly replied, "at least I didn't have to sleep with him."

Raymond led the explosion of laughter that followed, and Anneliese seemed like she wouldn't be able to stop. Finally, Leslie picked the conversation up again.

"You must have some sort of idea of what you're going to do. Something in its early stages you're developing? Oh, hell, can't you give me something?"

Jon had dreaded this moment all night, the job interview. Though he already had the job, it was what he would do with it that really mattered. He'd burn through the grant in five years, tops. Then what? Ridicule from *ArtTalk,* or, worse, no mention at all? He needed Joanne right now, Joanne who knew how to coach critics and praise herself with just enough self-deprecation that people who hadn't even heard of her believed in her. Jon swallowed the last of the wine in his glass and remembered what he had gone into his studio to write down earlier that night, before Shelly had knocked, before Leslie Meyer had even showed up.

"You know about the Aztec lines?" Jon asked, with as much authority as possible, hoping they did or wouldn't dare admit they didn't, as he didn't really know any more than what Shelley had told him earlier. "I'm seeing this project in need of something on that scale, something to be seen for miles, to last for centuries, to inspire the kind of awe that can protect man from the danger lying beneath, the danger of mankind himself."

There was a silence at their small table. Shelly looked across at him a little drunkenly, while Raymond, Anneliese, and Leslie just stared, each waiting for someone else to speak.

"They were used to send messages to other planets," Shelly finally said, and Raymond started to laugh. Anneliese squinted her eyes and was about to speak, but Leslie did first.

"I think that's brilliant," she said, with so much emphasis that Jon worried she might be joking. "I leave for New York on Friday. When can we talk again?"

"Before you make too many plans," Anneliese said, pulling out her daybook from her canvas bag, "Jon and I need to set up a lunch. Is tomorrow asking too much?"

Jon smiled at Shelly and slipped his foot out of his shoe. Leaning far back in his chair, he could just stretch his foot into Shelly's lap, under her dress. Raymond was gesticulating madly at her, most likely explaining his first New York show, who would be coming, who he knew, while Jon sat back with his toes comfortably wedged between Shelly's thighs listening to Anneliese Lange and Leslie Meyer argue over the check.

17

JOANNE CHECKS HER MESSAGES

For whatever reason, when she traveled, Joanne Mueller would notice the most minute gestures and details, like how the rain had hit the wing of the plane as it taxied from the runway at New York's LaGuardia—nearly perfect ninety-degree angles, long gray lines cutting across a gray horizon. Remembering these details made her sad. More likely her mood had been affected by all the long and, at times, tense meetings Joanne had been in all afternoon at the Scientific Analysis Data offices. Or maybe she was just impatient for a drink. Whatever the reason, Joanne couldn't help overanalyzing the way she walked up to the bar at the Gramercy Park Hotel, held her pocketbook tight to her chest with one arm, and with the other, casually leaned on her elbow so that her hand was slightly open, a few fingers loosely together as if to point behind the bar while looking out the window, as if she had no interest in getting anyone's attention. A bartender walked up to her in less than a minute, and she ordered her martini. The drink ordered, she sat down, looked around a bit more closely at the scattered couples around the very old and inviting cocktail lounge, and started to think about every movement that had just occurred from her walking into the bar and getting her drink. *Message conveyance.* Language, gesture, custom. Yes, she realized, she had a lot of work to do.

Her watch showed 5:10. Twenty minutes early to meet Vivian, who would most likely be twenty minutes late. Perfect. She had planned on having at least one drink alone, perhaps two. Joanne had a lot to go over in her head before dinner with Vivian (a dinner she already planned on keeping short, with the excuse of a headache from flying). When Vivian had left the day's five-hour meeting after only an hour, Joanne was supposed to report to her everything that she had missed, and Joanne needed some time to go over just what she'd tell Vivian she'd missed and what she'd just let her miss. *Message disconveyance? Antimessage conveyance?* Joanne smiled as she sipped at her martini, already feeling the confidence alcohol gave her. *Human interference?* The whole project had begun to seem like some kind of calling for the dislocated poet-in-residence of a midwestern city's "other" university, and she wondered if she really needed any of Vivian's help to carry out the project from here.

Human interference had been the first of many points Joanne and Amy Briggs had argued over that afternoon. Vivian and Joanne had arrived promptly at noon at Scientific Analysis Data (or SAD, as Joanne kept referring to it in her own mind). They were kept waiting in a windowless conference room for close to half an hour until Vivian called things to order.

"Has it occurred to you that your meetings aren't the only reason we might happen to be in New York on such short notice?" Vivian demanded, and the room was soon filled with a half-dozen scientists, all in their thirties (with the exception of one man who looked close to sixty) and all so casually dressed in jeans and open shirts that Joanne felt overdressed in her pinstriped suit.

"I'm Amy Briggs. We spoke on the phone. You must be Vivian."

"Ms. Reape, yes. This is Joanne Mueller."

"I'll briefly attempt to catch you up on our work at this point," Amy had said and proceeded to spend an hour discussing desert terrain, water tables, and geological histories of the mountain for which Joanne was attempting to feel compelled to write a poem. While Joanne managed to be interested in the little she could understand, Vivian constantly shifted in her chair until she finally interrupted to announce she was leaving.

"Joanne will be my eyes and ears. I'm afraid I have an appointment back at the National Institute of Poetry. I'll find my way out. Please don't get up." Vivian made her way out the door as another man in a sport coat and loose tie made his way in. No one bothered to introduce him, and Joanne ignored him, deciding to take advantage of Vivian's exit to stop the apparent stonewalling that was taking place by the team of scientists.

"You've said before that time is of the essence, so why don't I just ask questions, and you answer them," Joanne got in before Amy could determine exactly where she had left off.

Amy looked skeptically at Joanne and slowly shut the thick folder of notes in front of her. The man who had just entered carefully pulled a chair back from the table and sat behind her. None of the scientists would even make eye contact with him, and Joanne couldn't help feeling a kind of kinship with him, as he seemed equally unwanted.

"Why bury it in the ground at all if there are so many concerns about water tables and earthquakes?"

"Space and oceans have been ruled out, Ms. Mueller. Would you care to see the reports?" Amy reached behind her for another telephone book–size folder.

"God, no," Joanne replied, before she was subjected to another lecture. "Where is the stuff now?"

"Temporary aboveground storage, usually located in proximity to nuclear reactors all across the country. You should be able to imagine that a single, centralized burial would be much preferable."

"Out of sight and out of mind?"

Amy sighed an aggravated sigh. She was slightly pretty and younger than Joanne. Her steel blue eyes would fixate when irritated so that she almost looked cross-eyed at whoever caused her annoyance, which in this case was Joanne. She went on. "It is determined that by having such toxic waste spread out with no system of managing it, the risks of exposure from potential weather and human interferences—"

"But isn't it easier to keep an eye on it at ground level? I mean, why spend all this time worrying about Ice Ages and plate shifts if it can just be checked on like I check on my own car?"

"Washington decided that future generations shall not inherit our own waste-management problems." Amy said this with a finality that, by evoking Washington, the reason for all of them meeting here in the first place, indicated the discussion was over. "May I suggest, Ms. Mueller, that you confine yourself to the subject of message conveyance, specifically the literary, as this was the reason you were sent to us?"

"I wasn't the one naming every rock formation north of Las Vegas, Ms. Briggs." Joanne looked down at the endless pages of reports in front of her and saw the phrase "human interference," the exact phrase Amy had just said. It had stuck in her mind like an oxymoron. "You say here, page 131, graph four, that you have ruled out human interference. Can you explain?"

"One of the reasons for choosing the site at Yucca Mountain is its lack of appeal for population growth."

"How long will this waste be buried?"

"Ten thousand years, Ms. Mueller, we've been over this."

"Where exactly did mankind live ten thousand years ago?"

The table was silent, and the older scientist, who had yet to speak, sat forward.

Joanne continued. "What I'm trying to point out is that man, it seems, has advanced the most in the last few hundred years. The Industrial Revolution, rapid-growth technology, the taming of this entire planet. If you tack on another ten thousand years, couldn't man, say, discover a way to turn sand into freshwater? Mountains into fields? Maybe just give up on the earth completely and move whole nations underground?"

"This might be something for you to consider when you write your poem," Amy said dismissively.

"This might be something for you to consider before you recommend burying something this toxic under a world we can know nothing about."

"We can't predict the world ten thousand years from now."

"And you can't look into the future if you can't look into the past."

"Ms. Mueller," the older scientist finally interrupted, "my name is Judd Hailey, executive director of Scientific Analysis Data. Let me first welcome you. I'm afraid we get a bit tribal when strangers come in our midst, and we haven't exactly been polite. I'd like to concede that you bring up very good points. Many points that we have already argued with the federal government and the board of the Yucca Mountain Project. Presently, we are trying to prepare reports as best as we can to rate this site in terms of safety, both scientifically and culturally. We are also preparing data in terms of its economic impact on the state of Nevada. We can only confine ourselves to what knowledge exists, I'm afraid, as I believe you will eventually realize as well."

Joanne let this sink in and stared down at her hands, which were clenching her pen in such a way that it seemed on the verge of breaking. She carefully set it on the table in front of her. "Mr. Hailey, I am grateful you appreciate my concerns. However, don't you feel that working along with a project such as this in any capacity will, in fact, condone it, eventually recommend it, when you may actually disagree with its premise?"

"The problem of nuclear waste won't just go away," Mr. Hailey responded, with a grandfatherly smile. He was entirely bald and slightly pudgy, the kind of man who seemed to enjoy placating

174

ambitious women, the kind of man Joanne was beginning to think waited at the end of every road she ventured down.

"What, may I ask, is your interest in this project, Ms. Mueller?" Amy interjected.

"Bills to pay, Ms. Briggs. Same as yours."

After a break, the meeting went into more specifics of message conveyance, the feasibility of designing a site that could convey a warning of what it contained. Amy continually pointed out that language was thought to be a very weak tool for such an enormous task, and most of the conversation was based on structural concepts.

"You use the pyramids, Stonehenge, and the Parthenon as examples of surviving structures withstanding the test of time," Joanne said. "I would argue that the very awed spectators these sites attract to themselves are against the grain of what you hope Yucca Mountain will be. Surely you don't want families from all over the world traveling to a nuclear burial ground with cameras and picnic lunches."

"We study them because they *have* withstood the test of time," Amy shot back.

"I just think it would be more constructive to study monuments that have *not* withstood the test of time. Though I guess we can't do that, can we."

When it neared five and the energy level in the room had fallen into long silences and uncomfortable scrapings of metal chairs, some type of conclusion was asked for by Judd Hailey.

"I would like to hear a conclusion from Ms. Mueller," Amy suggested, their eyes meeting across the table. "After what you've heard today, have you thought of any useful role you could fill in this operation?"

"Oh yes," Joanne answered, "I'll just cover all the not-so-scientific, not-quite-analyzed data you seem so anxious to leave out."

Joanne stepped out into Washington Square, which appeared peaceful in a cocoon of cold mist. The streetlights did little to light the wet, black pavement, and the sounds of traffic were muffled by the rain.

"Share a cab?" the man who had also seemed unwanted at the meeting called out to Joanne as she crossed the street to walk through the square.

"Louis Cunningham," he said, catching up with her.

"You seemed as welcome as I did in there," Joanne said.

"For opposite reasons actually."

"Really."

The center of the park was quiet with its island of a few trees and lampposts at the heart of the overcrowded neighborhood. Up ahead was the square's famous arch, which made her think of Amy Briggs's monuments to time. What did this arch say? "Greetings. Watch your purse."? She was sure no one around her knew, and, as they got up closer, she saw people taking pictures of it, and she thought of waste, thousands of photos of the arch buried for centuries in the ground.

"I'm a nuclear scientist from Washington hired to oversee evaluations of Yucca Mountain. You see, they dislike you because you question their studies and me because I question nothing."

"Nothing?"

Louis was around Joanne's age, a bit square in his mismatched sport coat and tie and slightly shorter than Joanne, which made her like him.

"I believe the atom will save us."

"From what?" Joanne was smiling flirtatiously.

"Ourselves."

They reached Fifth Avenue, and Joanne turned down his offer to share a cab, explaining that the Gramercy Park Hotel wasn't far and she needed the air. When she reached the hotel, she went straight to the bar and ordered a martini.

"Do you think it will just stop?" Diane Whitestone had asked her the day before in Joanne's office at Lake Bluff College. Diane had

176

met with her to discuss some new poems that had been pouring out from her like a disrupted water table for the past few weeks. Unlike the strained, sweet verse she had turned in for class the previous semester, these poems were studies in emotion, sexually charged, dictating intricate rhythms so confidently it seemed the shy student had invented her own forms. Even the words seemed invented, purposely misused and half-rhymed in ways that only poetry could champion. Not all the poems were good, Joanne conceded. But she found herself wrestling with an envy of the young student, an envy of that moment in youth when love can produce perfect poetic lines as simply as a shopping list. Joanne had written like that when she had first met Jon. Every touch, every smell and environment they had met in had such a profound and significant impact that Joanne could barely keep up with the keys of her father's manual typewriter. When she thought of Jon now, she saw fiction, with its furious, steamrolling sentences that could break the back of any poetic construction.

"Will it stop?" Joanne had had no idea how to answer her student's question. "Don't worry about limits at this point." *Human interference!* She wished she could have warned her instead. *I would only think it would be more constructive to study monuments that have not withstood the test of time.*

Joanne's watch showed Vivian was more than half an hour late, and she finally decided to check at the desk to see if she had been delayed.

"Joanne," came Vivian's command, just as she sent the desk clerk looking for messages. Vivian was at the revolving door in her black raincoat, apparently about to go out without her. "Didn't you get my note?"

"I didn't think to check," Joanne stammered, walking over to her.

Vivian rolled her eyes, amused. "I had to cancel our dinner," she said. "Victor Dornan, that lovely doctor who put out that book of poems last year? *Very* Wallace Stevens of him, you agree? He's at the institute for the night and begged me to dine with him. Do you understand?" This was an order, not a question.

"Of course. I can fill you in on the meeting at breakfast."

"What hoops we have to jump through. I'll ring in the morning." With that, Vivian pushed through the revolving door and was yelling for the doorman to get off his stool and get out in the rain to get her a cab.

As Joanne watched Vivian complain to the doorman that a hotel should have cabs lined up on a night like this, she felt relieved that her evening was not to be spent faking a headache and eating too fast.

"Ms. Mueller," the desk clerk called as she walked to the elevator, "your messages."

Joanne thanked him and took three pink slips from his hand. An older man held the elevator door for her, and she quickly jumped in. The first was Vivian's, which Joanne crumpled up in her pocket. The second was from a Leslie Meyer of *ArtTalk*, wanting Joanne to call her at her office in New York immediately in hopes of having lunch pertaining to some article she was writing. Joanne knew it must be in reference to Jon and pushed the note into her pocket to deal with in the morning. The third was from Louis Cunningham, asking to take her out for dinner. Joanne was alone in the elevator now and fell back for a moment in its corner, the first moment of solitude she'd had since arriving in New York that morning. *I believe in the atom,* she remembered. Perhaps it was a symptom of traveling, Joanne reminded herself as the elevator finally jolted to a stop at her floor. His hair had been as black as the pavement, and he'd smelled like rain.

18

THE FREEDOM OF SPEECH

If the art of chanting ever auditioned a muse, Rose Gluck would be called back. Perhaps one of the more subtle of talents, chanting was not something Rose was born into. As a member of gentility of a distinctly midwestern variety, Rose never took pleasure in demanding what she wanted. Such things were expected, and when such expectations were not met, dismissals and reproach were usually delegated to someone hired explicitly for such unsavory tasks. As a child, Rose resisted the impulses such "spoiling" can create— having everything, but wanting it *now*. It was as an adult that Rose explored this more adolescent side—adolescent because that was one of her own impressions of such political demonstrating. This insight didn't take away from the fact that she enjoyed it immensely.

Fifty to a hundred people stand behind a barricade outside a government, university, or industrial building and shout, in unison, for what they want. A line of policemen surround them, arrest anyone attempting to cross invisible lines of public or private property or displaying anything that could be interpreted as a weapon.

Corralled like this, defiance comes from signs or banners, and, most importantly, voices. Rose always stood out as a member of the chorus. Known as "quiet," "reserved," even "mousy," among her family, at work, and in her rather limited social spheres, Rose took to the regimen and repetition of chanting in demonstrations and parades with such gusto that members of the International Revolutionary Socialists would push her forward, closer to news cameras, to bolster their small group's presence and maintain the right amount of enthusiasm. Perhaps the deep boom of Rose's voice came out of a latent "good child" repression, or perhaps she found a joy among the mass, a chance to be a member of this assembly line of sound. Whatever the source, Rose spent her days after a protest soaking her blistered hands and gargling warm saltwater, acting even more quiet and reserved than usual after such political outbursts.

Walter wasn't late; Rose was early.

The corner of Belmont and Sheffield was deserted, something uncommon for early evening on a Friday night, but the cold wind from the lake blustered around the buildings and tunneled below the elevated train discouraging the usual nightlife. Rose had arrived early because she didn't want any extra time alone in her apartment to change her mind about going. It had been Walter's insistence that had convinced her, the way his face had seemed to open like a room when daylight falls into it when he had looked at her at the meeting earlier that week. She had no idea what to make of it. Walter had always been polite to her, but she couldn't remember him ever really noticing her before. Was it something to do with the whole Nicaraguan Contra mess she had gotten herself into two months earlier? Rose could feel a slight blush push up to the surface of her skin when she thought about it, not going so far as to believe there was anything as complicated as sex or love involved—sex and love being two things Rose had never exactly chanted for.

It was the "Contra mess" that caused her to flee from her apartment, in fear that its recent repercussions were holding her back. Her academic probation had just ended, but the incident seemed to follow her like a shadow from the faculty room, to the classroom, to the lonely stacks of the university library, where she spent the majority of her time maintaining the informational systems. As much as she reminded herself that she was being unjustly scapegoated, the allegations unnerved her, as did the heavy debt she now owed her father for salvaging her job and keeping her from having to appear before disciplinary boards that would have gladly skewered her politics and added even more fuel to the fires the local media had lit around her. "Fascists Have No Right to Speak" was the headline in the campus newspaper, with a photo of Rose being escorted out of the hall in handcuffs. The quote was Rose's own, one of her favorite chants. Though, in retrospect, most of the action was a hazy memory of angry faces and police officers, she remembered being a little overtaken by the phrase as she leapt to her feet to shout at the Contra on the stage. Even her fellow protesting socialists were surprised. They had planned to shout out various accusations as the lecture went on, but now pulled themselves up alongside Rose to shout the speaker down entirely before he could utter a single word.

Rose was held in a damp, well-lit cell for five hours. Her father, over the phone, ordered her to say nothing. The family lawyer, at her side in front of the judge, begged her to say nothing. Her few colleagues at the university library who dared to walk with her through the stacks and hear the taunts from students advised her to say nothing. For a month Rose said nothing and, in the end, felt like the one shouted down, the one with no right to speak.

Keeping so much to herself eventually led her back to the group, despite her father's demand that she forever cut all ties with the International Revolutionary Socialists. Rose felt she would go crazy without them, that nothing in her life was her own. She would have been better off fired, she believed, instead of playing along with her father's connections at the university to the point that the obvious deal she had agreed to looked like an admission of guilt. Her decision to go to the meeting Wednesday came out of her own need to know just how much she had damaged her own reputation with the very people in whose name she had caused all this trouble. And it was Walter who had appeared beside her, reaching out to her, insisting on her inclusion, and even going so far as to defend her. Rose tried not to think about Walter's rugged face as she made up her mind to accept his offer of a ride to the protest in Milwaukee, distracting herself by reading up on the month-old strike at the brewery, where the workers' ranks seemed on the verge of succumbing to the threat of replacement workers.

The sound of a horn made her jump, and Rose saw Walter's Honda pull up to the curb. As she approached the car, she could make out Lydia in the passenger seat smiling at her like she had just made a joke at Rose's expense. If she had, Walter hadn't reacted to it; in fact, he looked as if a bomb could go off behind her and he wouldn't even blink in Rose's direction.

"Walter didn't think you'd come, but I told him you'd be here," Lydia said, opening her door and leaning forward to let Rose in the backseat behind her. *That same bomb that wouldn't make Walter blink will certainly not force Lydia to give up the passenger seat next to Walter,* Rose thought.

"Hello, Carl," Rose said, as she finally fell into the small space in back and found Carl Engstrom, who had cornered her after Wednesday's meeting asking about Professor Wright and the nuclear science department.

"I'm so glad you came, I have a thousand questions," Carl said, wiping his running nose with his mitten.

Before Rose could respond, Walter filled the thin space between the two front seats and stretched out a hand to touch Rose's elbow. "I'm glad, too" was all he said, as if suddenly remembering he didn't know her at all.

"Let's go," Lydia said, pushing her seat an extra inch back so that Rose's knees were almost level to her chin. "Hundreds of striking workers are waiting for their opportunity to meet our Contra warrior."

Walter looked at Lydia with a kind of warning. "What?" Lydia demanded. "Oh, for god's sake, would you just drive?"

The four of them were silent for the twenty minutes it took Walter to maneuver the tiny car off the Chicago streets and onto the expressway, which would get them to Milwaukee in less than an hour if the weather held. Thin sheets of snow blew across the highway in front of them. Already the snow was forming fingerlike drifts from the road's shoulders. Periodically, Rose would look up and find Walter's eyes on her in the rearview mirror, and she forced herself to look away. Lydia lit a cigarette and didn't bother to crack her window, so Walter cracked his own. Rose waited for Lydia to comment, but she fussed with the radio dial instead.

"Have you had a chance to look into the little request I made?" Carl asked. For a moment Rose almost didn't know what Carl was referring to. Some of the longer-term members of the group had extremely paranoiac fears that everything around them was bugged, that the CIA, FBI, and even the KGB recorded everything they said, followed them everywhere they went, and were the cause of every poorly attended protest or even bad static on a telephone line. Rose hadn't realized "Eco-Carl," as the group referred to him, had reached this stage.

"I really don't cross paths with Professor Wright very often," Rose said, too tired to talk in circles.

"You've heard about the school's recent grants to design nuclear waste depositories in Nevada?"

"I've heard of them. What exactly is it you don't know?"

"Don't you see? If the government can make the American people believe that the dangers of nuclear waste stockpiling up all around them are as easy to solve as digging a hole in the desert, they can then turn back all the gains of the environmental movement in stopping the building of nuclear reactors all over the world."

"Wait a minute," Rose said, recognizing the type of controversial stand the group seemd to go for on every issue. Rose remembered the Iranian revolution, when the Independent Revolutionary Socialists supported the fundamentalists. When she questioned their human rights record, the role of women, and Khomeini's fanatic religious tendencies, she was reminded that the group was committed to supporting every government the United States opposed. "Do you believe the government should just do nothing about the nuclear waste they have promised to clean up?"

"Oh, Rose," Lydia said, leaning her head back and blowing smoke at the ceiling. "You don't really believe that's what the government is actually doing."

"Well, I—" Rose nearly admitted it was what she had read in the papers but managed to catch herself from making such a laughable statement considering the present company.

Carl broke in, anxious to continue his theory. "You don't think that a man as power crazed as Joseph Wright hopes to win his next Nobel Prize in science as some kind of nuclear garbageman, do you? The whole thing's a cover to get the American people to believe that nuclear power can actually be safe again. Waste appears to be the only nagging issue here. So Wright is funneling as many funds from the depository as possible into his own studies in weapon technology to make sure this country remains the ultimate power. China's got the bomb; India nearly does as well. It's his job to discover the next worse thing and keep it solely for America."

Rose caught Walter's eyes again in the rearview mirror. If he wanted to defend her, he didn't seem to know how.

"I don't really see what I can do," Rose replied.

"What you can do?" Carl said, turning fully around to look at her, which, in the cramped backseat, resulted in one of his knees landing on Rose's lap. "You have the entire university library at your keyboard! Look at his budget. Cross-check it with the grants. Detail the spending. Hell, tap into his databases and his logs."

"Carl," Walter finally said, "what you're asking Rose to do is illegal. Besides, she's already under heavy scrutiny at the school; don't you think her access to such information is already being monitored?"

"We're all monitored!" Lydia nearly shouted, causing Walter to swerve the car slightly. "Since when are we so afraid of a little heat? Besides, Rose is perfect for such work; her own father could just make one telephone call and—"

"I told you I would not allow you to talk like this!" Walter shouted back at her.

Everyone was quiet for a moment. Carl readjusted himself so his leg was off Rose, and Rose looked nervously out the window at the signs for cheese stores along the highway. They were already in Wisconsin. Reluctantly, she turned back to Carl.

"I promise to look into it; I'm sure there are ways I can monitor Wright without breaching academic confidentiality. I'll just say I'm interested in his department's success if anybody asks; but trust me, no one's going to ask."

"Rose, do you have to pee?" Lydia asked, her face filling the thin space between the two seats in front of her.

"Well, actually—"

"Let's pee," Lydia decided for her. "Turn off at this rest area; the girls have to pee."

Walter did as he was told, and in a minute they were in front of a rest room on the median of the highway. Lydia opened her door and flew out of the car, and Rose noticed Carl zipping up his coat so she pushed herself through the space Lydia had cleared for her to let him out.

"Come on, Rose," Lydia said.

"I'm fine, really; I'll wait out here."

Lydia started to say something, but decided not to, her own bodily functions forcing her to leave Rose and Walter alone together at the car. Rose watched Lydia and Carl run the short distance to the rest rooms and shut the door of the Honda, staying outside to stretch her legs. A second later she heard Walter's door open. Walter propped his elbows on the car's roof and stared at her. "You're not cold?" he asked.

"It's invigorating," Rose replied, jumping up and down in place to keep moving against the wind bearing down from the north.

"I *am* really glad you decided to come."

"The work is important. I've missed it in the last month."

Walter looked at her like this wasn't the right answer. Rose just smiled.

"I have—" Walter looked down in front of him and pulled something out of his pocket. "Here."

He reached his arm across the roof of the car. In his glove was a piece of paper. Rose took it from him, and even though her own hands were uncovered, she unfolded it and started reading it aloud.

"In winter, the bulbs dream of the sun, petals opening like your eyes—"

Rose stopped, too embarrassed to read what followed, and looked at Walter.

"It's a poem," he said. "I wrote it for you. Happy Valentine's Day, Rose."

Rose didn't have to worry about how to reply for, in a second, Lydia was upon them.

19

BE MINE

"We're getting an apartment together for the summer," Diane said too fast once Sink accidentally started to let it slip.

Nervous and freezing, Diane looked good, William realized, as he processed the information that his best friend and ex-lover (one night qualified, in William's heart) were setting up an apartment together. She looked good like William wished he could look. Her ears raw, exposed by a baseball cap that only love could convince someone to wear on a night this cold, her every word so confident that William caught himself following her gaze in hopes of finding the image she was sure to notice for later poetic use, and now a boyfriend, the reward, the impossible catch, whose very name was original but on Diane's lips drew away the attention from him to her by sharing in its uniqueness. Sink was no longer Sink. Sink was Diane's boyfriend.

It was the first time the three of them had been together since the party where Diane had walked one way and William had walked home with Sink, and the first time that night that Diane had let her cool exterior indicate there might be anything strange about the three of them huddled together on the Belmont elevated platform waiting to change trains. Diane had invited Sink and herself along to a University of Chicago party with William a few days before, staring into his eyes in such a determined way she made it seem like she would personally see to it that the evening would go without a hitch. Up to that point the only indication that their relationship had changed was Diane's appearance. Her usual preppy clothing had been disrupted by a subtle mix-and-match: ironed khakis replaced with black, prewashed jeans, and underneath her burgundy cardigan was a white oxford left untucked, doing nothing for her athletic figure, but allowing for a more easygoing attitude that fit with Sink's. The happy couple was now looking at William as if everything depended upon his next few words.

"What are you going to do in Lake Bluff all summer?" William managed.

"As little as possible," Sink replied. "You staying in town?"

William couldn't even imagine something as far away as summer, and before he could try to make up some kind of answer, a train groaned to a stop in front of them, and they fell into the warmth inside.

As the train moved between the second floors of row houses to the tunnel that would carry them beneath downtown and then out again on the South Side, the three of them relaxed as the urban scenery took the place of conversation. Diane sat with William, which he resented, feeling even more like the pitiful outsider of their love affair, and Sink sat in front of them with his back to the window, his feet up on the seat where Diane should have been with a bare knee poking out from his jeans and his arm draped across the seat back so his fingers were inches from William's leg. If the train lights flickered, William could recross his legs and brush Sink's hand with his knee, William thought. If the world came to an end this minute, who would Sink grab onto?

The University of Chicago always seemed to have parties. Red-bulb, keg-on-the-fire-escape kinds of parties like those Lake Bluff had off campus semiannually, though in Hyde Park they seemed to go on every weekend. Acquiring an invitation was not so simple as no invitations were ever used. William had first gotten invited to one six months earlier through a man he had met at a bar in Chicago and had slept with for two weeks. Once William had seen the social opportunities of the party he was taken to and had already realized his relationship would barely survive the night, he smartly made it a point to meet enough students there to ensure his attending more.

Diane had always been curious about these parties, and William had promised to take her to one, had been planning on taking her to one, when Sink moved in on her and she forced her old friend's hand as a last-ditch attempt to smooth over what had become so hopelessly rumpled. The fact that it was Valentine's Day was not lost on any of them.

"Everybody at the university seems to study either library science or communism," Diane remarked, pulling William aside. They had been at the party for only half an hour, and William, upon seeing only a few people he barely knew, had quickly deserted his two friends for these acquaintances in order to engage them in conversations about where the other people were whom he knew much better. Meanwhile, Sink had no trouble sitting himself down on the floor with a group of strangers, instantly drawing out their confidences, something William, who had been regularly attending these parties, could not for the life of him figure out how to do no matter how much of the keg he emptied into himself. Diane, who had been at Sink's side for most of this, had finally spied William watching enviously from across the room and accosted him.

"Are all the parties like this?" she continued. "Communist librarians? Revolution through control of informational services? Deciphering FBI-planted misinformation from actual weapons data? Really, William, I'm fascinated."

William glanced over at the jeans-clad, flannel-shirted students

189

clustered around Sink. "Students here seem to take their majors with ulterior motives," he granted.

"I'll say," Diane said, helping herself to some of William's beer as she had finished her own, and feeling for the pack of cigarettes he kept hidden in his sport coat. "I just had the most insane fight on line for the bathroom with this nuclear physicist who actually believes Marie Curie should have known better and left the atom alone!"

William laughed for what felt like, and actually was, the first time that night. Over Diane's shoulder he could see Sink immersed in a conversation with a pretty woman who kept touching him each time she spoke. William tried to convince himself that he didn't envy Diane's position as his lover.

"So how did you and Sink celebrate Valentine's?" William asked, having some trouble getting out the last few words.

Diane looked at him a little startled, then looked back toward Sink. When she turned back to William, there was no indication on her face that she had seen anything that displeased her, and again William was struck with the feeling that she was somehow better suited for the suitor in question. Very Joanne Mueller, he decided, not without envy.

"We didn't really celebrate," Diane admitted. "It's only been a couple of months, and we don't want to formalize anything that hasn't really happened yet."

"You're moving in with him," William reminded her, and she coughed in her beer, as if she had forgotten this detail.

"I guess we're doing things a little out of order, not your basic narrative. Sink's kind of like that, you know, and I could use a little of it myself."

"So, no flowers, no candy, no card?" William wasn't convinced.

Diane held out William's beer, and he took it back while she dug through her jeans pockets. "Just this," she finally said, and opened her hand. In it was a slightly dirty, pink candy heart that said BE MINE on it. William felt all of the air rush out of the room.

190

Diane was laughing, wondering aloud whether she should just eat it, while William felt his face go flush from a pain at the pit of his stomach. All the resolve he had felt moments earlier that Sink was not meant for him disappeared as he tried not to openly envy the simple candy heart in Diane's hand.

He quickly excused himself to the bathroom and went to the enclosed fire escape instead. After refilling his beer, he could still not imagine going back inside, so he climbed up a flight above the keg, where he could watch the party inside but would not necessarily be seen in the slight shadow. He could see Diane walking back to the group of people Sink was with. She casually slipped off her cardigan and tied it around her waist. A few extra buttons of her white oxford were undone, and her hair spilled out of her simple ponytail. William watched how she just stood for a moment behind Sink, listening, and how Sink, still talking, reached behind him and gripped her calf in such a way that the pretty girl who had not been able to speak without touching Sink obediently inched over to allow Diane to sit. When she did, Diane instantly engaged the girl in conversation, and the girl was soon touching Diane whenever she opened her mouth in reply. William imagined that candy heart as good as a revolver in Diane's pocket as he watched the communists, library scientists, and nuclear physicists argue with his best friend and ex-lover about the world like some equation in their textbooks. Relationships seemed to be just another problem to solve.

William's own problems didn't seem that simple. He looked down at his pleated gray pants, his black shoes, which were an old pair of his father's, and his thrift store black sport coat, which he could never bring home because his mother would throw it away. Everything about him suddenly seemed overcalculated, and nothing worked. Indeed, he decided, he was spending far too much time alone on fire escapes in what were supposed to be his carefree college years.

When Sink came out alone to refill his beer (as well as another, most likely meant for Diane), William didn't hesitate and called out to him.

"What the hell are you doing out here?" Sink asked, walking up a few steps and, always the gentleman, handing William the second cup.

"Needed a breath of fresh air."

"Don't blame you," Sink said, and sat down next to him. "There's some chick in there talking Diane's ear off about some professor of hers who drove some fascist off the campus. I think she's a lesbian."

William smiled at Sink's deduction about the girl presently touching Diane every time she spoke.

"You know," William said, " I think you and Diane are a good thing. She's really—"

Sink suddenly kissed him. He just reached over and placed his hands on each side of William's face and clamped his mouth down on William's. William felt the full cup of beer fall out of his hand and down the stairs, and before he could really think whether or not to kiss back or whether or not he already was, he glanced in the direction of the falling cup and saw Diane coming out the back door.

"Diane," William called out, pulling himself away from Sink and standing up. "We're up here."

"Was that my beer?" Diane asked, walking up to the bottom of the steps and pointing at the empty plastic cup rolling in a circle at her feet.

"Afraid so," Sink said, in a voice so calm that William had to look down at him like he had missed something. Diane picked up the cup and filled it again. "Get one for Will too; I found him out here getting all sober on us."

Diane did as told and started up the steps toward them. If she had seen anything, there was nothing to indicate it. She handed William a beer, which he instantly took a long swallow of, and she smiled at him as if glad to see him talking with Sink. William managed to sit back down, and Sink's leg was now pressed up against his for Sink had made room on his other side for Diane. The three of them were silent. William looked straight up through the center of the stairwell, which gave him a strange feeling of antivertigo, that he wasn't about to fall, but fly up. Had any of this really happened? For a moment, William wasn't exactly sure.

"These people make me feel rather dull," Diane finally said.

"Don't let them," William responded, glad to talk, though a little unsure of what he was saying. "They're as pretentious as we are."

This made Sink laugh and laugh loudly, and William couldn't help thinking Sink was releasing something—but what? Guilt? Fear? Sink had set his beer between his feet and reached his arms behind them, dropping them on both their shoulders. Diane let her head fall toward Sink, and William felt every muscle in his body lock into place like he was in a dentist's chair.

"Did any of your friends show up?" Diane asked, her sentence turning into a yawn.

"No, I guess it's too cold," William replied.

"Well, why the hell are we sitting here two hours from home then?" Sink asked and stood up, extending a hand out to each of them. There was nothing in his expression to say that anything out of the ordinary had occurred. *Perhaps nothing has,* William thought. *Just how many candy hearts did Sink give out this year anyway?*

Diane and William both got up, though William did so without making use of Sink's outstretched hand. He downed the rest of his beer and grabbed Sink's, which was still half-full, and they made their way inside.

"I'd better use the bathroom first," William said, and went into the other room. He did need to go after four beers and with a two-hour train ride ahead of him, but he also needed a moment away from everything that had taken place. William walked through the crowd of people who were sort of dancing, though they could have just been talking, and got in the line for the one bathroom. He leaned his back against the wall and finished Sink's beer. A few of the people he knew from these parties had finally arrived, and he waved over at a group of gay men who were waving at him. He realized that some of them were communists and one was even a library scientist. One stepped away from the group and started walking toward him. He was about William's height, but with jet black hair, large brown eyes, and a clear, perfect kind of complexion. William assumed he was getting in line for the bathroom too, but he was coming straight up to William with a look of intention, and William felt a desire to start kissing him, like Sink had just kissed him, only this time he'd remember to kiss back.

"William Dunning?" the stranger asked, once he had arrived right in front of him. William continued to lean back casually against the wall. The beer had seemed to work, or perhaps it was the kiss, but whatever it was, William didn't have any prescribed answers or feel any need to think up any.

"And you are?" he asked, in his most casual Sink Lewis way.

"My name is Peter Brooks. I've been wanting to meet you for a while now. I think you know my grandmother."

The polite thing to do would have been to excuse himself, tell Sink and Diane to go ahead without him, and return to Oma's grandson. But nothing could make William move from that spot against the wall. The bathroom line moved on without him. If Peter was aware of any intrigue between William and the friends he was with earlier, he didn't seem to care as he leaned in a little closer each time William said something back, and if the world ended that very minute, William felt he could just grab on.

20

MIRAGE

Las Vegas was a gamble, but Vivian could surely afford it. Her commanding view of Caesar's Palace from the Flamingo Hilton reminded her, of all things, of her view of Chicago from the Drake. Nothing in the visible landscape, climate, or people had anything to do with that cold early morning a month before, but the adventure of being alone in a hotel room (something Vivian had known all her life) and the unblemished white tablet perfectly centered on the desk nearby (so white and blank that it hurt Vivian's eyes to look over at it) brought back to her that same expectation of the creative, only this time it was joined with an increasing feeling of uneasiness and frustration. Vivian focused her eyes on the brilliantly sun-lit desert stretched out in front of her, covered by roads, hotels, parking lots, and fountains. What was that sense of memory not inspired by any physical detail of the environment around her, but a memory of pure feeling—the luxurious loneliness of travel, the poem she willed to write itself? Vivian longed to cry out, not what *is* this called, but what should *she* call *it?*

Vivian rushed from the window to the desk and sat down. The

pen was there, the tablet was there, even a glass of spring water sat poised to extinguish any unexpected thirst. Vivian closed her eyes, keeping the pen held close to the page to catch whatever could possibly fall from her mind as it darted along this tangible lead, this potentially inspired idea that would use words only as props, rich, measured, beautiful props. Vivian had been at this for a few hours. She had actually been at this for a solid month, but today felt different, *will be* different, she had decided after an efficient breakfast of fruit and bran cereal (Vivian held a special admiration for hotels that provided menus to order from the night before and punctually delivered at the hour indicated), a quick shower, and a series of phone calls to Boston and New York to take care of her NIP obligations, which were primarily made up of checking in to see if other people were keeping up on their work. Vivian loved the time difference from the East Coast. It was the only time she ever felt in sync with the world, for when she was dressed and ready to take on the day's work (usually before the sun had actually come up), people all over the East Coast were already behind their desks ready to do her bidding.

Memory . . . remembrance . . . displacement . . . markers . . . déjà vu . . . Vivian relaxed every part of her body to allow these words to float in and out of her, waiting for one to catch, to trigger. She let the words collect as one large entity capable of breaking down the impenetrable wall she had found herself pushed up against, that blank, college-ruled, pristine wall with a hundred more pages waiting behind it, layers of bark on a tree, spiral-bound and crisp. If she could just get through the first, if she could find the first word, phrase, the rest would come in a flood, and those pages would fall in an intricate design like dominos reaching out across the room, over the bed, out the door, and down the hall. If she could just—

The phone rang. Vivian's eyes flew open, and like flies caught in a blast of repellent, the words, *her words,* fell down lifeless around her. The room was as sharply outlined and empty as it was before, and on the perfectly blank tablet in front of her was a single black circle where the page had sucked the ink out from her pen like a sponge, penetrating to a half-dozen pages beneath. At the second ring Vivian grabbed the phone from the bedside table next to the desk.

"Yes," Vivian hissed, in a way she had discovered worked quite well with ambitious students, unwelcome poets, and every kind of phone sales solicitation.

"Ms. Reape?" came the terrified reply. "It's Peter, Peter Brooks. I'm returning your call."

Vivian sighed, annoyed with herself for not asking the front desk to hold her calls and knowing it was too late to brush him off as she was too interested in any information he might have.

"Yes," Vivian repeated now, sans hiss. "I'm so glad you called."

"Are you really in Las Vegas?"

"Poetry knows no borders," Vivian replied, making a face at her words.

"Of course not," Peter said, ashamed that he had actually suggested such a thing. He then lowered his voice to such a whisper that Vivian had to press her ear completely against the receiver. "I'm in nuclear science."

"Not at this very moment!" Vivian nearly shouted.

"No, of course not. I'm down the hall, at a pay phone. I'm using the long-distance code you gave me, like you told me to."

Vivian exhaled in relief. She wouldn't put it past Professor Wright to have the phones in his department tapped, as it was something Vivian would do herself if she was in his position. *Know your enemy, know yourself,* she always remembered.

"And what news?"

"Nothing really," Peter said, a little uncertain. "It's my first day, and I'm only doing secretarial duties, filing, typing labels, answering phones."

"Marvelous!" Vivian exclaimed. There was a silence on the other end of the line. "Don't ever underestimate the receptionists and secretaries of this world, my dear; they know all. If somebody calls, they know who called. If they type a letter, they know what's in the letter. You have done better than good, don't you see?"

"I do, I mean, I don't, quite. What I mean is, it would help to know what I'm looking for."

Vivian shifted from the desk to the bed. "Tell me about Joseph Wright."

"Professor Wright? Well, I only met him briefly when I started this morning. He was, well, very nice. He found it a little strange when I told him I had an interest in nuclear science, though he didn't quiz me on it, thank god. I complimented him on his department's famous history and important future role in the continuous development of efficient energy, just like you told me to, and he seemed pleased by that. I made sure to pay a lot of attention to where all his files and mail went when they showed me my responsibilities—oh, and I found a proposal from *you!* Something about a poet-in-residence and some kind of poem for a nuclear waste—"

"Yes, never mind all that," Vivian interrupted. "Go on."

"I must say, Ms. Reape, that a real poet-in-residence at the university is a wonderful idea and—"

"Go *on*, Peter," Vivian commanded, sitting up on the bed. "I'm sorry, I have a lot on my mind today. Where was my proposal anyway?"

"At the bottom of Professor Wright's interdepartmental in-box," Peter carefully replied.

Vivian sank back on the four pillows she had propped up at the headboard. She considered telling him to Xerox it and put it in every in-box in the nuclear science department, but realized she must protect her source. At least for now.

"You're doing very well, Peter," Vivian finally said. "Just remember, pay attention to everything. Who calls, who writes, budgets, official visits. I'll tell you more specifically at some point what you should look out for once you get a feel for the whole department. For now, just absorb and tell me anything you find peculiar or out of the ordinary."

"Of course," Peter rejoined. "Did you get a chance to read any of the poems I sent you last week?"

Vivian tried to remember anything of them but couldn't. "I'm afraid I haven't been to my office for so long they must be on my desk waiting for me. Read everything by Thomas Campion."

"You told me that last week, and I did," Peter reminded her.

"Well, read Campion again. And when you finish, read him again," Vivian was becoming impatient.

"Please write me as soon as you read my new poems; you see, I think I may have fallen in love—I can't believe I'm telling you this—but, you see, I can't stop writing; it's like I've gone through a wall or something—"

"Peter," Vivian interrupted, sitting up again, "now listen very carefully to me; don't ever write poetry when you are in love. You must wait until it has passed, until it has either become so domestic that you hardly notice it or it is lost for good. There is no poetry in love until it is lost."

This completely silenced Peter, and Vivian became slightly alarmed that she was losing him. "I'll look at the poems when I get back to Boston next week, but for now, *absorb*, you understand me? *Absorb.*"

"There was one thing," Peter said, and Vivian did not interrupt. "A woman from the university library requested copies of budgets and security codes for computer archives."

"Do you remember the woman's name?" Vivian asked, already knowing the name.

"Yes, Rose Gluck, the one who got arrested last December at that Contra lecture."

"This request came to you?"

"Well, it came to the department, but I got it."

"And what did you do with it?"

"Nothing, yet. I was going to ask who I should pass it on to."

Vivian paused for a moment, remembering Rose from the board of regents' meeting. Rose's admiration, Rose's strange resemblance . . . "Peter," Vivian said, "don't show this request to anyone. File it, and give her all the copies and codes she requested. Enclose a note telling her to call you directly if there is anything else you can help her with, and sign your name. Do you understand?"

"Yes," Peter Brooks seemed more curious than nervous. "I understand."

Once Vivian was finally off the phone, she stayed on the bed. It was already afternoon, and she felt the loss of the morning, those precious hours that were always so productive for her, as she imagined Peter would someday feel the loss of love and, perhaps, finally write a decent poem. She glanced over at her writing tablet, now soiled with that single ink blot, and made a mental note to find a decent stationery store *somewhere* in this city and start again. She reached down to the floor and pulled up half a dozen folders and reports she had received the day before from the Nuclear Waste Management offices downtown. The reports were poorly Xeroxed, some of the pages dotted with excess ink so that they appeared unreadable, should she ever read them: *Radiation: A Part of Our Lives, Carbon-14 and Our Environment, Site Characterization and How Fluid Moves through Rock.* Vivian decided to do her best.

She had come straight to Las Vegas from New York. By the end of her stay in New York, Vivian had noticed Joanne's growing interest in the whole program. She dutifully attended every meeting, offering Vivian pages of notes at the end of the day, and was dining with various nuclear scientists each night. Faced with returning to Boston to attempt (again) to start the poem, she switched her ticket to Las Vegas when she noticed the address for the Offices of Nuclear Waste Management for Yucca Mountain at the bottom of one of the endless pamphlets Joanne had given her. Naturally Joanne presumed that she was to write this poem and that Vivian, as usual, would play the part of editor and middleman. The grant hadn't been secured officially, and, more importantly, no check had arrived to be cashed. Vivian would figure out how to deal with Joanne's role once everything was in place. Perhaps she could just send Joanne a copy of her poem in a girlish way, pretending she had had a flash of inspiration. Perhaps she could go so far as to flatter Joanne and ask for her valuable imput. Or, if things had gone far enough along, she could just pay her old student off and make up some story about Joseph Wright only wanting to deal with Vivian.

Whatever she'd do, she first needed to produce the poem herself, so, for inspiration, she'd decided to go out and see exactly what was there, this mountain that Native Americans and environmentalists went on and on about, the government land once used for nuclear testing, and now the future home to those very bombs that were never used. Vivian felt that this could provide her with a way into the poem. By seeing what inspired the need, she could, perhaps, inspire herself to write the poem.

Her plan had been to stay a night in Las Vegas, visit the Nuclear Waste Management Office, and set up a tour of the proposed site for the depository at Yucca Mountain. Then, perhaps, she'd stay a few more days to write. But when Vivian had arrived the day before and been told by the woman at the Nuclear Waste Management Office that Yucca Mountain was a two-hour drive away in an area without hotels ("but some very cute motels"), Vivian simply asked them to send over all relevant materials so she could just read about it instead.

She started with radiation: *rays, particles, decay, millirem*—millirem? Vivian adjusted her pillows again and started over. This time she only made it halfway through before setting it aside and picking up another of the poorly Xeroxed reports. She started with the question of groundwater. Groundwater? She nearly laughed. As far as she could see, the only water in the state came from the elaborate man-made waterfalls and fountains surrounding the casinos. Vivian blinked her eyes a few times and kept reading, but the words made no real sense to her and reminded her, oddly, of poetry: *association . . . memory . . . déjà vu . . .*

When Vivian opened her eyes again, the room was half-dark. For a moment she had that wonderfully frightening feeling of not knowing where she was at all, but her eyes were drawn to the windows, where a strange glow rose from the frantic lights of the Strip outside. Without even looking at the time, Vivian leapt out of the bed, ran some water over her face and hands, found her purse and key, and left the room.

At the hotel's revolving door she spun out into the heat, which had drastically dropped in temperature since the sun had started to set. Vivian's favorite part of Las Vegas was the all-encompassing air-conditioning in every building she had need to set foot in. Most of the casinos, in fact, kept huge entrances wide open with a complex series of air-conditioning blasts aimed at keeping the hot air out, sparing no expense at getting the people in. Upon finding the cooler air outside now as well as in, Vivian decided against a cab as the Strip was already bumper-to-bumper, and, as she had discovered last night, walking the Strip had an advantage of getting you there in half the time.

As she walked, Vivian remembered her struggle that morning. She reminded herself that it had been twenty years since she had attempted to write a poem. All the same, she felt let down, so confident was she that form, classical forms, the very ones she had taught, critiqued, and memorized all her life, would carry her through this; but now she was faced with the fact that structure wasn't her problem. Vivian just didn't know the words. This was where she had hoped to trick her own mind. Thinking about it as hard as she had been, the very language of poetry suddenly seemed surreal: Was it made of sentences? Paragraphs? Phrases, narrative, first person or third? Her mind felt like everything she knew, everything she had *controlled* for so long, had been lost; and the sooner she could clear her head completely, the quicker she could start piecing words together again, words into lines, lines into stanzas, until the form would be mere polish on the wood, a pedestal for the statue.

Vivian glanced at the groups of tourists making their way around her. Most of them were in shorts or sweat suits with the kinds of T-shirts that announced destinations Vivian had no intention of ever visiting. Vivian herself was dressed tastefully in a navy skirt and matching jacket. She wore a very simple and elegant purse strapped over her shoulder in contrast to the brightly colored money belts most people wore around their waists. Looking at her watch, she realized she had missed the staged ship battle in front of Treasure Island, though she should arrive in time for the fake volcanic explosion at the Mirage. From her hotel, the Mirage had seemed to be about three blocks away, but she had been walking for nearly twenty minutes, and it seemed like she had at least another fifteen to go. *Perhaps that is the mirage,* she thought. A light dust in the wind had started to gather around her eyes and lips, but the air was still cool as if they had just enclosed the entire city and provided central air, which would be just fine with her.

She had just reached the last block before the hotel when she suddenly saw it. The hotel's structure was a cross, making four perfectly outstretched wings all covered in a kind of golden glass that suddenly seemed to capture the entire sunset and mountain range nearby and reflect them in a way that it seemed you were looking right through the building itself. Each wing of the hotel was also reflected, so that the effect was an outline of a structure with nothing inside. Vivian nearly gasped as she stopped and stared. She was reminded of how certain people could be moved by architecture, how she, herself, was moved by Greek and Roman ruins on trips to Europe, but now, in front of her, was this imposing building designed, it seemed, to make itself nearly disappear and allow the natural environment to replace it. Modern man wholly absorbed in nature. But a mirage, Vivian reminded herself.

After one last look, Vivian hurried across the six-lane street. She saw crowds beginning to form around what she presumed was the volcano, but instead of joining them she kept walking and got on the moving ramp way that would take her directly into the hotel. As she settled herself comfortably against the railing to enjoy the guilty pleasure of the people mover, she thought of Rose Gluck and her strange request for information from Joseph Wright's department. Was Rose, for whatever political reasons, about to do Vivian's work for her? She made a mental note to drop a card to Rose in the morning. Thinking of Rose inevitably led her to think of Joanne, causing Vivian to slightly bristle and look impatiently ahead of her for the entrance to the hotel.

"So good to see you again," Lenny the dealer called out as she approached the blackjack table. Vivian smiled back at him and carefully chose her chair at the end of the table directly on his right, where she would have the best opportunity to control the cards. "A vodka-cranberry for the lady," Lenny called out over Vivian's shoulder, and Vivian smiled and nodded in agreement.

The other players (a young couple, an older man who was safely seated away from Vivian, and two middle-aged Japanese women) all smiled patiently at Vivian as she maneuvered her large bulk into the small chair and pushed five one-hundred-dollar bills across the blackjack table to Lenny, who happily exchanged them into chips.

"High school English teachers must be doing pretty well these days," Lenny remarked, as Vivian quickly eyed the stacks of chips to check his count. Again, Vivian merely smiled, and he dealt out the cards, giving Vivian two jacks while he showed a three. "You know, you shouldn't be back here," Lenny continued, dealing the other players their cards as he continued to talk to her. "With your winnings last night, I had hoped you would take it all home and buy something nice for yourself." Lenny had come to Vivian's hand, and he knew to pause. Stretching out two fingers, Vivian indicated for him to split her winning hand, causing the table to gasp and protest this move. Lenny merely rolled his eyes up and dealt her two more tens and busted his own hand.

"Oh, Lenny," Vivian said, throwing him a tip as he pushed the chips toward her, "I always win."

PART 2

Warmest Summer on Record

*She hadn't a drop of poetry in her, but she had
some of the qualities that create it in others; and
in moments of heat the imagination does not
always feel the difference . . .*

—Edith Wharton,
The Reef

21

FIVE DOLLARS A FOOT

Lake Bluff College Resident Poet Joanne Mueller could not recall when winter ended and summer began. The snow and bitter wind-chills had stretched into April and finally given way to an early spring that allowed plant life to begin its enthusiastic climb toward the sun, only to be knocked down by a late blizzard immediately followed by a kind of heat usually associated with late July and August. Grass grew, and flowers rebloomed, but with an over-ripeness that made such greenery appear like it had been thrown down along the sidewalks and alleys instead of rising up. Pedes-trians walked through this heat in a daze; their steps, which had once moved heavily between drifts and ice, now pushed through equally obstructive layers of humidity trapped within the dense concrete and steel maze of the city. The talk was all about the weather, which became its own repetitious force as there was not much to say about weeks of ninety-degree temperatures coupled with 100 percent humidity, and it appeared the sun was blocked, as it were, by a strange whiteness, as if the sun itself had exploded into a million parts and beamed down from every possible angle.

When it did rain, it came hard and fast, pummeling the hard ground that resisted soaking it in until the quick return of white sky would evaporate the stagnant puddles back into stagnant humidity.

Joanne's bedroom window, which, only months before, could extinguish a match through the glass, had been opened since the last of the snow melted. A match could now be lit, but slowly, as it searched for the proper amount of oxygen to ignite, the cardboard bending in dampness as Louis Cunningham pulled it toward his cigarette, cupping it out of habit though the flame was an equal to the hot air. A patternless, cream curtain hung in the window and rarely moved as it browned from the light it was meant to keep out. Joanne lay right beneath it, covered only at her midsection by a rope of a sheet that also snaked across Louis's midsection as they were lovers too new to do away with this discretion and too hot to even think of touching each other.

"Tell me that part again about the waves," Joanne said, watching the stream of smoke push out of Louis's mouth and spread out in a dull white cloud not unlike the sky outside.

"Tell me that part again about why you can't have an air conditioner," Louis replied, propping himself up against the bare wall, preferring his slight discomfort to the use of one of the hot pillows.

"It would blow the power in the whole building."

"That's crap. Every two-bit row house on this block is cranked up with them. They're just trying to drive you out so they can redo the place into condos."

Joanne smiled at this rather shrewd deduction she hadn't considered before. "I thought you liked my apartment."

Louis looked down at her with the slight annoyance that such heat seems to bring out in everyone. "Let's just say it was more romantic trying to keep warm than it is to stay cool."

Joanne remembered the week he had come out to stay with her in March after she had come back from New York. Their bodies had stayed glued together all night beneath the half-dozen blankets and sheets; and though she had reminded herself that he could be considered anyone, she had made it through five frigid winter months without letting "anyone" in her apartment for the night. The night before, his first in town, they had made love in a bathtub of lukewarm water without candlelight because the flames would feel like an added source of heat. She still felt a small ache in her lower back from the bathtub, and it made her feel cool when she concentrated hard enough on it.

"Why don't we just stay at Joseph's tonight? He really won't mind," Louis asked, referring to the head of the University of Chicago's nuclear science department, who was putting him up while he was in town for the week sitting in on meetings on Yucca Mountain.

Joanne sat up and reached for her blue cotton robe. "I told you, I can't. I'm too involved in all of this to be seen bunking at some U. of C. residence. Don't ask me again." With that Joanne left the stifling bedroom for the stifling hall, which led to the even more stifling kitchen. As she measured coffee, she could feel the hot light coming through the kitchen window, and she knew she was once again at the start of a very long day.

She hadn't meant to be so short with Louis, but everything around Joanne seemed taut and about to snap back in her own face. Everything circled back to the grant: her strange involvement with Jon; her weekly phone conversations with Vivian, who gave her endless letters to write, meetings to sit in on, and literary, historical, and environmental points to research; and, of course, the poem itself, which not only refused to be written, but managed to halt all of Joanne's other creative endeavors. She was aware of some vague deadline in September that a government board had set for a draft of the poem; and though it was close to the end of June, Vivian had just laughed when Joanne had reminded her of it on the phone a few days earlier.

"They must think we're a couple of lovesick teenagers in a college workshop!" Vivian roared. "The *deadline* for the poem is when the poem is done. Timetables haven't exactly been a high priority for them regarding that poor mountain anyway so why torment *us* with them? Besides, no money has been agreed upon to the dollar amount, and until both of us are fully compensated for the work we've done and the years of work ahead of us, not one word will be written—except, perhaps, in the popular press."

"How much are you asking them for?" Joanne finally thought to ask.

"For our services? Standard consulting fees, but on a national scale. The poem? Well, if top prose writers can get five dollars a word, I don't see why we should settle for a cent less than five dollars a foot."

Joanne gasped.

"Leave all of this to me. In the meantime we must surround ourselves with epics. Nothing short of heroic couplets, sextameter, octameter, however many metrical feet can fit across the page!" Though Vivian laughed while saying this, Joanne was definitely reminded that brevity was not exactly welcome on the door to the nuclear waste dump.

The coffee was made, steaming from Joanne's cup and hushed by milk and ice in a tall glass for Louis. Joanne turned and found him leaning in the doorway with his arms folded across his bare chest. His boxer shorts had clocks patterned all around. Louis looked good in boxer shorts, somewhat short but stocky, his thick, hairy chest supported by a slightly sloping waistline, and muscular legs filling out the wide leg openings of the shorts. She had no idea how long he had been standing there.

"Have I mentioned how much I like your apartment?" he asked, and Joanne felt herself blush. They had no common ground for this kind of arguing. They had one weekend in New York, a week in Chicago, and now this hot morning in what seemed to have become the windless city. Joanne returned the apology by walking over to him and handing him the glass of iced coffee, condensation dripping from the sides. He pulled her against him with one hand while he took the glass from her and set it on top of the refrigerator next to him. They stood there limply, pressed together, a slight moistness instantly developing in every place their bodies touched. Joanne thought about the dozens of clocks on his shorts, each one set at a slightly different time, and felt that if she was threaded through a sewing machine she'd come out in the exact same pattern.

"Dinner on me tonight," he said, lifting her heavy hair and lightly blowing on the back of her sweating neck. "Like a date."

Louis was about Joanne's height, and she laid her cheek on his shoulder just in time to watch his wet glass of coffee slide off the top of the refrigerator.

"Café latte, Professor Mueller?" Diane asked, as she did every weekday around two when Joanne came into Coffee Bar to take her favorite table far back in the corner. Joanne glared up at her student.

"I know, Joanne, Joanne, Joanne. By September I'll have it down, and then you'll want me to go back to Professor Mueller in front of the other students."

Diane went back behind the counter to make her drink. Joanne had grown increasingly interested in the girl. First, the wildly sexual poems that seemed to take on forms and imagery with a confidence that was amazing to find in the poetry of a twenty-year-old stuck in the rigors of a small college writing program. The poems weren't all good, but Joanne found them to be a relief from the mathematically metered ones that fulfilled the assignments like pop quizzes making sure a student had read a book. In the four months since she had started showing Joanne these poems, Diane had changed in other, even more remarkable ways. The preppy sweaters and button-down shirts had been replaced with flowing cotton skirts and muscle T-shirts beneath old, long-sleeved oxfords, which were now wrinkled and left open. Her hair had grown long and was left slightly wild, though she kept it in a ponytail with a rubber band while working at the coffeehouse. Joanne knew she had moved in with Sink Lewis, news that at first had made her slightly jealous as she imagined the two of them carefully riding that first roller-coaster hill of love. Joanne worried for her, about what kind of man she imagined Sink to be, and whether Diane would be able to get all the way to graduation with a man like that in her bed encouraging her to go along on whatever joyride he came up with.

"Can you sit a minute?" Joanne asked when Diane returned with her mug. Diane waved an arm toward the nearly empty room and pulled out the facing chair. The emptiness of the place was the reason Joanne came by every afternoon. By fall it would surely be filled with students arguing Jack Kerouac over Nietzsche, and Joanne would have to return to the safe boredom of the faculty lounge.

"I don't think it will kill anyone."

Joanne was pleased at how easily the two of them could talk, unlike her conversations with Vivian, which were always filled with silences while Joanne searched for subjects like coins between seat cushions. Diane's ease with an adult (her own teacher, no less) reminded Joanne of talking to an old friend, someone she didn't quite know everything about anymore, but with whom she shared some kind of important history.

"How's your writing?" Joanne asked, the typical teacher question, though she tried to say it casually while sipping her café latte to encourage Diane to be honest, like a friend.

"Oh, it's there," Diane said, sounding honest. "I guess I've grown sick of all the sex poems. I'm ready for what's next."

"There's nothing next," Joanne replied a little too quickly, and Diane looked over and smiled at this confidence, no matter how depressing, that she was being invited into.

"I guess that's what I'm ready for then," Diane summed up.

"And Sink?"

"I knew that would be the next question."

"I suppose he's *there*, too?"

"Oh, he's *everywhere*." Diane paused to pick at a fingernail, probably sorting through information for the right pieces to give to her teacher. "He doesn't pick up anything, never washes a dish. So I don't either. This is the messiest month of my life. But you know what? I'm not minding it, for right now."

Joanne tried to think of the right thing to ask to get a little more of a view into the home life of her two student poets without being dragged through the window entirely.

"Why don't you tell me all about your nuclear waste grant?" Diane suddenly asked, sitting forward with her elbows on the table and her hands in fists on each side of her head.

"I see word travels fast," Joanne said.

"Dupree and that horrible Professor Drake were in here a week ago screeching about it. You'd think that with all the money the Dupree family has he'd allow someone else to enjoy getting a little."

"Dupree and Drake, having coffee, in here?" Joanne was lost, trying to picture the two of them together outside Sandburg Hall.

Diane leaned even closer until her face was just above Joanne's half-filled cup. "He's got something going on with my boss, or at least he thinks he does." Joanne looked over Diane's shoulder at the nice-looking man who seemed to fall exactly between Diane's age and Joanne's and whom she remembered meeting through Alex at Gianni's. She knew his name was Tom, that he also ran the connecting Book Bar, and that he always treated her with the greatest amount of courtesy and respect but always seemed afraid of bothering her.

"I'm sure Alex didn't mean any harm in what he was saying," Joanne said, sounding like the adult for the first time in their conversation.

"Then tell me about it. I'm fascinated." Diane retreated back to her elbows, her fist back at the side of her head.

"I'm to write a poem warning people thousands of years from now to stay away from a highly toxic dump of waste buried deep in Yucca Mountain in Nevada." Joanne had actually practiced this

215

sentence, but found with this, its first real application, how much she hated saying it. How ridiculous she must seem even to a student who probably thought she could do no wrong. "Hopefully," she felt the need to throw in, which was also practiced, "I can make enough money from it to take a year or two off and finish a novel."

"Shouldn't they just put up one of those signs, you know, that kind of nuclear-looking flower?"

"They're not confident its meaning will transcend time," Joanne replied, reading right from one of the federal documents stacked a foot high by her bed. "Not that my poem can either." She found herself retreating. "It's just a part of a whole package—landscape design, local education, water tables, and fault lines."

Diane looked confused, not used to seeing her teacher explain herself like this, and Joanne felt like she was the student with the mess in her apartment, the man who might not be so good for her, the possibility of never graduating. A loud clamor of teenagers at the door broke the silence, and Diane reluctantly got up.

"I'll be back in tomorrow," Joanne said, wanting her to go so she could regroup.

"I think you'd better," Diane called over her shoulder.

Louis had Joanne meet him at an expensive restaurant downtown, where he insisted they sit outside. The night air was still muggy, and Joanne felt like she could write in it with her finger. Over chilled white wine and cool salads they told each other about their days.

One of the first things Louis had asked her four months ago was "Do you own a car?" after a meeting in which she had challenged the room to be more protective of the environment. His question challenged her and drew her to him as she had always been drawn to men who seemed to know more than she did.

Whenever Joanne would throw some article at him she'd found about fault lines running below Yucca Mountain, possibilities of an Ice Age, or the ever-threatening long, slow drip of groundwater through miles of rock, Louis would calmly look back at her and say something like "So your solution is to leave it all spread out, above ground, where eventually some breach of security will allow it to fall into the wrong hands or the wrong water tables?" Or, his favorite, "So you advocate the continued burning of fossil fuels, which will eventually turn that ozone hole we're hearing so much about over Antarctica into a tear stretching all the way up to North America?"

After dinner they walked along the Chicago River with its spotlights on the sides of the city's skyscrapers, their ornate towers lit up like a birthday cake along the river. He stopped at the front door of Executive Plaza Hotel, one of the first postmodern glass box buildings and eventual scapegoat of the architectural school. Louis pulled a room key from his pocket and handed it to her.

"You're kidding," Joanne said, looking up at the glass front of the hotel as if she could actually pick out the room the key was for.

"One night where we don't have to sleep on opposite sides of the bed," he said, pulling her into the revolving door, both of them packed into one stall like a couple on prom night. "It's on the government. Surely they'd want us to look after our mental health."

Upstairs they stepped into a dark room lit only by the wild skyline, which was so close around them that it seemed like they were in the center of an amusement park. Louis reached over and turned the thermostat all the way down to sixty.

"Quite a waste of energy, I'd say," Joanne said.

"We'll keep the light off," Louis guided her gently to the large bed. Afterward they shared a cigarette, pressed together with the sheet, blanket, and bedspread pulled up to their chins.

"Tell me that part again, about the waves," Joanne said, letting her eyes close, her head in that comfortable position at the indentation between his chest and shoulder. She was asking him to tell the story again about the French nuclear test he had been at a year before in Tahiti. A mile-long hole had been dug straight down through a reef and a hydrogen bomb detonated. She wanted to hear about the way, when the bomb went off, small perfect circles of water began rippling around the small island, eventually growing in size and intensity as the impact of the bomb made its way to the surface.

Louis offered her the cigarette, but she didn't take it. "Are you still looking for a place to start your poem?"

"Of course. Tell me what it felt like."

Louis paused, having to think about this question for a moment. "It felt like the world was an extremely large place where we would forever be floating on the surface."

22

THE NEXT MORNING

Tom McMann had never woken up so comfortable with a hangover. He was in the exact center of the largest platform bed he'd ever seen, with ten pillows all slightly different shapes piled along the simple, bleached wood headboard. A luxurious silk sheet half covered his naked body and made him feel like a very well-paid porn star. Though floor-to-ceiling vertical blinds covered the entire wall facing him to keep out what could only be the ferocious summer sun, Tom could make out that he was in an extremely large and nearly empty room that was entirely white. White walls, white ceiling, white carpeting, white bed, white love seat, white writing table, white dresser—even the overly simple fireplace, which was a mere hole in a wall, appeared to be white on the inside. Tom felt a gratitude for the power of the blinds as he didn't think his dry, smoky eyes could withstand the shock of opening in such a place in broad daylight.

Tom tried to retrace his steps as to how he'd gotten to this place, but did not see any of his clothes indicating some kind of trail he could start following back. He sat up and started further back, before all the drinks that seemed to still slosh behind his heavy eyes. Tom knew he was in Alex Dupree's apartment, and this was, perhaps, the block preventing him from remembering how he got here. Tom had been out with two friends at Prague, a small asexual nightclub on the near-North Side. Chicago was rather famous for these types of clubs, a general mix of gay people, straight people, and neighborhood people, with a few punked-out, political kids who had to show up to give any place credibility. At Prague, Tom and his two friends (Mark, an ex-boyfriend, and his roommate, Steve, whose boyfriend Tom had always longed to be) had a few beers and started to dance. By midnight the small room was filled, and the three of them moved up to a small riser in the back to dance, a stage usually reserved for drag queens, but since it was a Tuesday night, no sideshows had been planned. At this point a bartender started bringing Tom drinks and wouldn't say whom they were from. The drinks were tumbler-size, most likely vodka, but an expensive brand that Tom drank quickly, always receiving another the moment he set down the empty glass still loaded with ice cubes. Once Tom had become curious enough to corner the bartender and demand to know who was buying him all the drinks, he spied Alex Dupree, alone, at the end of the bar, smiling in Tom's direction and still managing to look a little goofy in the sexy, smoky light. Tom remembered pushing through the crowd and talking to him, though he couldn't remember what was said and probably couldn't hear anyway as it was well after midnight and the music had shifted from upbeat dance tracks to more-hard-core bands. He remembered riding in Alex's Mustang down Lake Shore Drive with the top down. He remembered putting his arms up like he was on a roller-coaster and telling Alex to drive faster, while Alex kept reaching over to pull his arms back down. Finally, he remembered being in another large and empty room of the apartment and Alex handing him yet another drink in a tumbler that Tom had a dim memory of spilling and then nothing more.

"You're up," came Alex's cheerful voice, and Tom carefully

220

turned his head to the side to see Alex in the doorway dressed, of course, in white. He presented a small tray, which held more white objects with the exception of a tall wineglass filled with orange juice, a near-riot in contrast to everything else. Tom had the feeling he had landed in an extremely expensive rehab center and turned back to focus on the fine razor blades of light coming through the vertical blinds.

Tom hadn't tried to talk yet and concentrated very hard as he pushed words out of his scorched throat. "What time is it?"

Alex came in and sat on the lower corner of the bed, which seemed a car-length away, and carefully set the tray on the sheet between them. "Not that late really; I thought you'd sleep till noon."

"I have to make a call, about the store," Tom said, as he accepted the glass of orange juice Alex stretched out for him and the small saucer with two (white) aspirin. From what seemed like thin air, Alex pulled out a cordless phone.

"You had a little too much to drink last night," Alex said, smiling, like the straight-A student you get saddled with for a roommate your freshman year.

"I believe it was you doing all the ordering," Tom said, a little too harshly, though his ragged voice was bound to make everything sound harsh.

"Guilty!" Alex exclaimed, loud enough to make Tom's head hurt, and he quickly focused on the (white) phone to keep him quiet another minute. Somehow, by concentrating on the numbers, Tom's fingers were able to dial Diane Whitestone's number from memory. A good sign of recovery, he decided.

"You sound like shit," Diane informed him right off.

"I'm glad I caught you at home." Alex had gotten up and was slowly turning the blinds, looking over at Tom with a playful expression on his face. *This will only hurt a little.*

"Of course I'm home. It's only eight o'clock. Where are you?"

"Tell you later."

221

"Oh, god. Can you really see Lake Bluff from up there?"

"I don't know yet. Would you like me to wave?" Alex was busy straightening things that didn't need to be straightened, playacting like he wasn't listening. "I'm gonna be a little late. Can you open Book Bar, too? You don't have to help people, just tell them to come back."

"There're all of ten people in Lake Bluff, Tom. I think I can handle the early Fourth of July rush."

"See you at noon," he said, and hung up before she could ask any embarrassing questions.

Tom slowly lifted his head up and removed the hand he had used as a visor while Alex opened the blinds. His eyes slightly squinted, but his head didn't pound from the light, and he could hardly see any differentiation between the wall and the sky outside the window. He reached down to exchange the empty wineglass for a cup of dramatically black coffee.

"How high up are we?" Tom asked, as Alex still seemed caught up in pretending not to listen.

"Twenty-eighth floor."

"Is that north?"

"Northwest."

Tom decided not to ask about seeing Lake Bluff; maybe after a shower he'd look for himself. "It's cool in here," Tom said, feeling like a blemish on the perfect surface of Alex's room.

"It's been the same temperature since I moved in five years ago," Alex said, proudly.

Tom took a deep breath. As much as he appreciated waking up in an apartment set at a civilized temperature, he suddenly felt claustrophobic. Alex walked back over to the bed and sat down on the side of it, a little higher up this time, within reaching distance.

"I think you should know," he began, while Tom concentrated on carefully sipping the hot coffee, "nothing happened last night." Tom almost smiled, but looked back at Alex instead, feeling a twinge of tenderness at this confession. "You just slumped over on the couch, and I managed to get you into bed and undress you. I mean we did sleep with each other, but just slept. I don't think you moved an inch the whole night. You snored horribly."

Tom did smile now and reached down for a croissant. He wasn't really hungry, but felt like this would be a good time to keep both his hands and mouth occupied.

"I appreciate your taking care of me," Tom felt he should say, though his mouth was half-filled. "I'm actually not as hungover as I should be. It must have been very good vodka."

"It was gin," Alex corrected him. "A very good drink for June and July." Tom winced a little at the memory of it. "How old are you, Tom?" Alex had swung a leg up on the bed toward him so they faced each other.

"Twenty-nine. Why? How old are you?"

Alex seemed to retreat a little at this. "Forty. But that's not the point." He paused and smoothed his manicured hands on his perfectly pressed pants. "The point is, well, what exactly are you doing?" Tom waited, knowing he was about to be told what. "You kill yourself running a small store that truly wouldn't be missed if you only kept it open two days a week. You live in a two-room cave on a block with no trees. You're a poet who isn't writing. You edit a small review that reflects more than it addresses. I'd guess you have no money in the bank, and you don't own a decent suit."

Alex said all of this very quickly while looking up at the ceiling, and Tom felt his hangover disappear, as if Alex had thrown a bucket of cold water on him.

"You left out no health insurance, no car, and a bank loan for a coffee bar I had the brilliance to open right at the start of the hottest summer ever." He said this calmly, and Alex looked over at him like they were truly on the same track. "I'm sorry if I somehow misled you."

"No, you see, you don't see." Alex was fumbling and finally let his hand fall on Tom's discretely covered knee. "I want you to look around." Tom rolled his eyes side to side across the strange room. "Not just here, I want you to look all around. I have this enormous apartment. There are two more bedrooms, a library, my office, a living room, and dining room. You could have one of those rooms, any room. This room. We could summer in Europe, winter in Mexico. We could write."

Tom felt a slow panic rising out of his stomach, where the croissant floated on what had just been classified as gin. "Alex, I don't think—"

"You're not thinking," Alex interrupted. "I have everything. You have nothing. Think of that."

Tom was starting to get angry, but before he could even begin to say what he felt like saying, a strange bell rang from another room.

"Oh, lord," Alex said, standing up quickly as if caught.

Tom indicated the phone that lay next to him.

"No, it's the door. I'll be right back."

Once Alex was gone, Tom lunged from the bed, rocking a little unsteadily once he was on his feet, but still determined. He opened one white door to find a walk-in closet. The next one was the white bathroom he had anticipated, and he went in and locked the door behind him. Everything was already set out for him: a thick towel on the side of the Jacuzzi-tub-shower, a toothbrush, and what appeared to be a brand-new tube of toothpaste, a razor and shaving cream, and an assortment of shampoos and soaps on a small glass table. Tom immediately turned the shower on hot and started brushing his teeth. The powerful jet stream made it impossible to hear anything from the next room, and he calmed down a little. After lingering in the hot shower, he dried off and wrapped the towel securely around his waist. Now he only had to make it to his clothes and the front door.

When he stepped back out into the bedroom, Alex rushed right up to him looking particularly exasperated.

224

"It's Vivian," he said so fast it came out in a hiss. "Vivian Reape, surely you've heard of her. She's come over for breakfast. I completely forgot."

"You have people over for breakfast?" was all Tom could think to say as he stepped around Alex.

"It was her idea actually. Oh, god, it's all my fault."

"You can give her mine, I hardly touched it."

"No, I already ordered up."

"You can order breakfast?"

"There's a gourmet deli on the first floor—oh, never mind. Look, why don't you just get back in bed. There's a library with a million books in the next room. It will only be an hour."

"I have to get back to that store that's killing me," Tom said, talking twice as loud as Alex.

"All right then." Alex let out a deep breath. "Your clothes are on the couch there, the front door's straight down the hall to the right. I'll come by to see you later this afternoon."

Tom walked over to the couch, where his clothes were nicely folded, and picked up his T-shirt, which was ripped down the middle. "Did I do this?" he asked holding it up to Alex.

"No." Alex put a hand to his forehead. "I'm afraid I did. I got a little carried away putting you to bed." He slightly grinned, and Tom felt a wave of the hangover wash over him again. "Take any shirt of mine; the closet's there." Alex walked back over to him and took both of his hands. "I'm sorry, she's waiting. She doesn't like waiting." He kissed Tom lightly on the forehead, where it hurt the most. "I'll come by later." Alex flew to the door and leaned in one last time. "Think about *everything.*"

Once he was sure Alex had gone, Tom dropped the towel and pulled on his briefs and cut-off jeans, which smelled like the expensive gin he must have spilled on himself the night before. He looked over at the closet but pulled the ripped T-shirt on over his head instead, realizing he couldn't give Alex any more reason to expect anything back from him. He started to look around the

225

couch for his high-top tennis shoes when he remembered the trick he had learned so well he had obviously managed to do it last night. When Tom first began going downtown to bars with a friend in college to have one-night stands, his friend told him to always take off his shoes, shove his wallet into one of them, and hide them under a couch. This way he could avoid being robbed and even keep his identity secret should he find a reason to do so the next morning. Though Tom couldn't remember actually doing it, he was now sure his shoes and wallet were stashed safely under the living room couch he had passed out on last night. Tom made one last quick glance around the empty white room before heading out the door and taking a left where Alex had instructed him to bear right.

He followed the faint sound of voices to the end of the hall where it opened to an extremely large room that seemed to be surrounded by windows on three sides. Peering around the corner, he could see Alex with his back to him in a straight-back chair facing an extremely large woman who sat on the very couch Tom now remembered from the night before. Squatting down a little, he could make out the tip of one of his high-tops beneath the couch right next to the woman he presumed to be Vivian Reape.

"Think of it as a new frontier," Vivian was saying. She held her coffee cup and saucer primly at her chest, though her size made it look almost like a child's tea set. "The University of Chicago needs you. You'd be head of the department. Why, for the first few years at least, you'd *be* the department."

Tom couldn't help listening.

"I'm rather rooted to Lake Bluff these days," Alex said.

"Nonsense," Vivian replied. "That whole program's going to hell with Joanne and her damned fiction. I'd say you're lost at sea up there with your classical forms. I'm throwing you a lifesaver, Alex, and I expect you to grab on and start kicking."

It didn't take Tom long to realize there was no way to get Alex's attention, so he finally just stepped through the door.

"Oh, my god," Vivian exclaimed, her eyes wide and her cup falling with a clatter onto the saucer. Alex spun around and stood up in one quick motion.

"I'm sorry," Tom stuttered, unsuccessfully trying to hold the ripped edges of his shirt together. "I just, well—" The pale expression on Alex's face convinced him just to get it over with; and Tom walked up to Vivian, who gasped as if he were about to put a knife to her throat. Tom bent down between her legs, and pulled his shoes out from beneath the couch. Vivian had put a hand up to her nose, probably smelling the stale smoke and gin that permeated him. He turned quickly back to the door and called "goodbye" over his shoulder as he nearly ran the length of the hall to the front door. He could hear Vivian say, "Alex, *really*," and then he was out.

The boiling air outside felt good once he had made it past the doorman and onto a sidewalk alongside the lake. He didn't see any immediate way to cut across the six lanes of Lake Shore Drive, so he walked north instead. In twenty minutes he was past the downtown and felt significantly better as he approached the small beaches, parks, and rocks that made up the north shore. He even pulled out a cigarette and risked retriggering his hangover. Young men sped by on bicycles and roller blades, some looking expectantly at him, others purposely away. Sweating gin from every pore of his body, Tom finally stopped at a slightly shady spot and looked back at Lake Point Towers, which proudly stood out from the forest of downtown, the only building actually on the lake. He tried counting up twenty-eight floors but couldn't judge where the first floor actually started and the windows just reflected light anyway, like shields. He lay down under a tree and stretched out his arms and legs. The grass felt cool, slightly itchy, and green.

23

SEARCH BY SUBJECT

Rose Gluck stared hard in the mirror and didn't see the difference. Three people had told her how good she looked: "fresh," offered Tammy, the secretary in the university library's main office; "well rested," commented her father when she accidentally ran into him on his way to meet the dean for lunch; and "like the summer has been agreeing with you," said a loyal student who was in the neighborhood and dropped by the library to finish some research for a thesis. Rose twisted her head side to side, picked up her slightly graying hair and held it up, took a few steps back from the mirror, and stood straight in her simple navy skirt and white, high-collared shirt. She noticed a little more color to her face, and her neck looked fuller, less gaunt. Rose undid the top three buttons of her shirt. Yes, she could see, her head didn't seem to stick out from her body like a branch; rather, it bloomed, seeming to gather strength as it lengthened from the exposed curves of her shoulders and hint of cleavage.

She pressed both palms to her cheeks and stared, like Walter would do, holding her face just a few inches from his and staring into her eyes like he was trying to find something. Rose would allow her eyes to widen to say, *Here* or *What about there?* The confident query in his eyes reminded her of the freshmen at the University of Chicago who would come to her without a title or an author, determined there *must* be a book on the subject they wanted and that Rose was the one to put it in their hands. When Walter kissed her, she felt the same thoughtful probing—the way his hands moved lightly over the shape of her body, not yet possessing, just skimming the surface to be sure—*of what?*

Rose jumped back from the mirror at the sound of someone trying the locked bathroom door. She fingered the opened buttons of her shirt but let her hand fall away and stepped back out into the Green Café.

Carl Engstrom had arrived and didn't see Rose until she approached the table from the direction opposite the front door.

"There you are," Carl exclaimed, awkwardly half-standing in the small space where the rickety small table and two chairs were positioned tightly next to other tables in a faux-European clutter. "You look terrific."

Rose's hand instinctively closed up her open shirt as the two of them sat down.

"How?" Rose asked, leaning forward to Carl as if she was asking for a source, holding one finger on the page she was reading and flipping to the back to find the footnote, the reference, a place for the quote to be attributed. "How do I look *terrific?*"

"Gosh, Rose." Carl seemed dumbfounded by the questioning of his compliment. "You just seem opened up or something. Happy."

"Why? I mean it. Why do I suddenly look so different?"

Carl snickered, his thin shoulders rising up and his chin pushing into his small chest. He glanced quickly around the nearly empty room and moved his hand slightly over his mouth as if to stop anyone from lip-reading what he was about to say. "Maybe you should ask your boyfriend. You know, *Walter?*"

Rose snapped back into an upright position. A cold tingling

crawled up her spine and spread up her exposed neck. She knew it; she didn't look any different, she was *perceived* differently. She had a lover, and people had accessed this information, passed it around to use out of context, without permission.

"What have you heard about Walter? About Walter and me?"

"Come on, Rose, it's not like anyone who was with the two of you in Milwaukee four months ago couldn't see what was going on," Carl said, smiling in that way all men smiled, teasing and handling her like she was their common property.

"What exactly did Walter tell you?"

"You're missing the point. Walter hasn't said anything; he's never said anything about the women he's with, especially while he's with them."

Rose dropped her face into her hands and squinted her eyes together like she could just blink and make the entire conversation, the whole past four months of her life, dissolve like an apparition. But when she opened them again, there was a strange face just inches away, a woman's face topped with bright green hair. She was squatting down next to Rose and had an arm around the back of her chair.

"Are you all right, dear?" she asked soothingly, cutting a hard glance at Carl, who was also trying to reach a hand over to her. "You look terrible."

Rose let out a quick breath. "Coffee," she said. "Just coffee."

The waitress stood back up, and Carl asked for the same. She looked at him with a scowl and walked off. They were both relieved no one else was sitting in the immediate vicinity, and they were quiet for a moment, Carl afraid to say anything and Rose with no idea what to say. She watched the pedestrians walking by the café in the direct sunlight. They seemed to move in slow motion. Rose felt violence in the heat that had gripped the city with a mix of irritation and fear all summer. She felt the potential of violence every time she rounded a corner or stepped off a train, that with one false move, one misstep, her own hot body would be put in contact with another, and she imagined entire blocks breaking out into sudden brawls until the police in their uncomfortable uniforms would arrive glad for the chance to pull out their nightsticks and spray their Mace.

"You're taking this wrong," Carl said, carefully setting out each word like cards making a house, and Rose felt that same irritation and fear rise up in her as if Carl had flown out of a train she was waiting to get on and knocked her down. "The group always gossips when this type of thing happens. Really, we're all very happy for you."

"Tell me about the other women," Rose said, stopping herself from making eye contact with the green-haired waitress, who set her coffee cup down so tenderly it made Rose feel like a skittish cat.

Carl let out a long sigh and folded his pale arms across his chest. Rose knew Carl was around her age, yet he somehow looked at least ten years older. Years of smoking, Rose deduced, and strange macrobiotic diets.

"You know about the other women," Carl said. "We all do."

"I was never really a part of the group when it came down to the kind of gossip you refer to."

Carl sighed again. "There was Lydia; I think you know Lydia." Rose turned her head to the side abruptly at the mention of her name. "Most recently?" Carl suddenly sat forward, like he had something. "We never really knew who she was. Walter never brought her to meetings like he did with the others, though I don't think it was because he didn't invite her; something tells me she didn't want to go. Joan, I think the name was. A poet, teaches at Lake Bluff. Or at least that was what Lydia claimed. You should really have this conversation with Lydia; she seems to have kept quite a record."

"Joanne," Rose said. "Joanne Mueller."

"Walter told you about her?"

"Yes, I mean, he did when I asked. We were at his apartment, and she was on the answering machine. It was during that last blizzard in April. I remember it being very cold outside."

"What did he tell you?" Carl had come in close again, half-covering his mouth in that habit of paranoia. Rose suddenly felt she should be doing the same.

"Just that she was a poet, and he had gone out with her for a while during the winter." Carl's eyes seemed to be stroking Rose's, encouraging her memory. Rose leaned in and lowered her voice. "And that she had gotten caught up in the federal grant for the Yucca Mountain Project." Carl closed his eyes and slowly nodded. Rose started talking faster now, having found the thread. "A grant to write poetry as some kind of warning for the waste they're burying there."

"More coffee?" The green-haired waitress was suddenly alongside of them, and they both jumped back in their chairs. Neither of them spoke, and the waitress topped off their nearly full cups and left.

Carl sprung back across the table at Rose the moment she was gone. "What have you found out about Professor Wright?"

"Nothing. Quite a lot, but really nothing."

"Start at the beginning, and don't leave anything out."

Rose looked at Carl impatiently but knew she had no choice except to tell him everything she had learned, no matter what her opinion was in terms of its importance. It was the reason for their lunch in the first place.

"I must say I was surprised by how easy it was to get my hands on this information. When I sent over my initial request for budget data, it was fulfilled the very next day, which made me think there's nothing really there to uncover, or, at least, nothing they are afraid of having uncovered. My reputation around the university kind of gives me away."

"What did the data say?"

"It added up. That is, it added up into extremely large figures for what appears to be very little progress. It's all bogged down in site evaluation, contracts to corporations for research on transporting hazardous materials, developing long-term storage canisters, studies of water tables and Ice Age patterns. It's an amazing balance sheet for very little results, but everything totals out."

Carl clapped his hands together and smiled, causing Rose to jump a little in her seat.

"I really don't see the connection," Rose said, whispering again.

"Rose, it's the oldest connection! It's just what I suspected." Rose stared back at him. "Look. You have a capitalistic society that propels itself on waste, waste, waste. It's reached the end of its own borders, so suddenly we are an international market. Unions have brought workers ahead enough to make a sizable dent into profits. Corporations take their factories to Third World countries to avoid higher wages and costly environmental protection, while at the same time promoting U.S. goods."

"I know all this."

"Wait." Carl was taking very deep breaths, and Rose felt she was the first one to hear him putting this entirely together. "Cheap and abundant energy is a necessity for the success of this scenario. Industry needs it to make goods at the least cost. Industry also needs the consumer to have it in order to operate their cars, their televisions, their fax machines—whatever useless invention they want to come up with next. Nuclear energy fulfills this need. Forests don't have to go down, mountains don't have to be stripped—"

"That all sounds good to me."

"But wait! Society doesn't have to be reeducated to want less, recycle more, *conserve*. Capitalism can just continue its murderous growth, feeding from the bottom to give more money to the top."

"Are you advocating that we should just leave highly toxic waste above ground, spread out all across the county?" Rose had become interested. She drained her coffee and looked around for the green hair of the waitress.

"Nobody is advocating that. What is being advocated is that if they can turn something as deadly and undesirable as spent plutonium into a profit center, then not only can they continue pursuing this highly risky, inexpensive mode of energy to prop up their empire, but they can also encourage even more corporate growth by turning garbagemen into Fortune 500 companies!"

"You still haven't answered my question," Rose said. "What do we do with the waste?"

"And you're still not grasping the larger issue. They can store it all on their golf courses if they're so worried about it."

Rose stared at Carl for a moment. It was typical for some of the more fanatical members of the organization to turn the answer to a simple question into a "larger issue," a loosely wrapped package of economic, historical, and class concepts that always worried more about future results than immediate conflicts. Carl's face was slightly flushed, and his gray eyes seemed to dance around in their sockets. She knew he was about to hand her his ultimate theorem.

"Listen," Carl said, leaning forward again and lowering his voice enough to force Rose to lean in as well. "Nuclear power plants have been paying an annual fee to the government that goes toward the eventual long-term storage of the waste they produce. What if this money was taken, along with god knows how many billions of tax dollars, and handed over to waste management corporations and universities, who would specialize in long drawn-out studies and planning. Universities, mind you, that already have significant departments in nuclear science. Corporations, mind you, that have extensive investments in the very power plants that pay the fee that is eventually reabsorbed into the same company! All with additional American tax dollars for a healthy interest! And all this while social programs are being slashed mercilessly and your average taxpayer is seeing no return on their taxes, with the possible exception of being able to live in a society that promotes energy-guzzling products for him or her to guzzle more energy with."

"Do you have documentation showing links between such companies?"

234

"I have all the information I need."

Rose hated this kind of self-satisfaction, which at times seemed epidemic in the organization. "Then you certainly don't need me anymore."

"Oh yes, I do," Carl said, grabbing onto her hands across the table. How sweaty and small Carl's hands were, Rose noticed. How strange to be used to another man, a man with large hands that always felt cool in the center of the palm. "What could you find out about Joanne?"

"Joanne?" Rose pulled her hands away, wiping them quickly on her skirt beneath the table. "Joanne Mueller?" Rose found that she hated saying the name.

"Yes, the whole cultural program, the Doomsday designs is how I've heard it referred to."

Rose was reminded of the earlier part of their conversation, that cold tingling going up her spine, and she felt a headache coming on. "Nothing. Well, just that the government had approved an undisclosed amount of money to be included in the cultural grants for the purpose of a poem. This seemed to be something that Wright's department had opposed."

"Opposed? That's interesting."

"Wouldn't you guess he'd oppose something as frivolous as that?" Rose shot back, causing Carl to look up at her with a curious expression, and Rose knew she was giving herself away a little, wavering between loyal comrade and jealous girlfriend. Her head throbbed.

"I would guess that Wright and his cronies would understand the government's position on needing to sell this whole thing to the public as well," Carl said. "Not a single nuclear plant has opened in this country for years. If they're unable to convince the public at large that as scary as all that Cold War boogeyman, nuclear holocaust stuff was, nuclear energy is really our friend, then the whole thing will be lost. From what I've heard, in Nevada they've set up a tourist office right on Las Vegas Boulevard, providing tours of the mountain. They want to convince people to care for nuclear waste, like they've convinced people to separate containers into glass, aluminum, and plastic."

"That's crazy," Rose said, waving her hand in front of her face. "How can they expect anyone to incorporate something like nuclear waste into one's day-to-day existence?"

"Why don't you ask Joanne Mueller that?" Carl asked, smiling slyly at her.

"I don't *know* Joanne Mueller," Rose said.

"So ask Walter."

Walter was finally asleep, and Rose slipped noiselessly out of his bed. She had been doing this since March when they first had sex. Rose would lie alongside of him, her head usually tucked right beneath his chin, and stare at the rise and fall of his chest until she could make out the rhythm where the body takes in air less frequently, but more deeply. Once Walter started to do this, Rose would slip out from his arms, find her clothes, carry them into the hallway to put them on, and leave. Walter never asked her about this. Whenever they'd speak next, it was as if it were perfectly natural for a woman not to spend the night with a man she had been having sex with for nearly four months. It even occurred to Rose, as she drove her car south one night on the nearly deserted North Side streets, that Walter was probably awake half the time when she carefully closed his bedroom door, not letting the knob turn until the door was perfectly set in the frame. She wondered if this was love, his letting her go without question. Or perhaps he was just glad she was gone.

Rose wasn't technically a virgin when she met Walter, but she felt as though she might as well have been. When she had first joined the Independent Revolutionary Socialists over ten years ago, she had done so at the urging of Wayne Morris, an English professor at the University of Chicago who was already a member.

Wayne was famous for his Marxist interpretations of early American literature, and Rose had started to attend some of his lectures, curious to understand his theories of capitalistic supremacy taking early root in the novels of James Fenimore Cooper, Mark Twain, and Herman Melville. She admired him for leading literature classes that didn't follow the typical path of a love for literature, demonstrating instead its power to perpetuate racism and oppression. Wayne soon noticed her among his more youthful underclassmen, and when he bumped into her in the library, he asked her out for lunch.

They met for lunch every week for a month before he asked her to come to a political meeting with him. Rose immediately thought of her father, her entire wealthy family, how her own position at the university had been put in place less on her own merits than on her father's money. But her decision to attend the meeting and eventually to become a member herself was ultimately based on the way Wayne made the invitation, his eyes slightly pleading, his fingers gently brushing her sleeve. Rose had never really felt this kind of interest from a man before, and she had definitely never felt her own willingness to need it.

Rose lost her virginity to Wayne at a conference in Ohio in the back of a van in a motel parking lot sometime after midnight. It had been quick and clumsy, and Rose had felt pain more than anything else. They'd avoided each other for the rest of the conference and for a good month back in Chicago. When they did start talking again at meetings or in the library, it was always about politics, both of them trying too hard to agree with the other.

Sex with Walter had been different. Though she was sure he could sense her inexperience, he never showed it, gently moving her body around into positions she'd only imagined; and Rose surprised herself by responding to what his own movements seemed to tell her. She was glad he kept the lights off and that there was always the distant bass of another apartment's music for her to

237

concentrate on. "Rose, Rose, Rose," the thumping sound seemed to say as she let her muscles relax until her limbs seemed to float away from her body.

Afterward she didn't really see how she could spend the night. For the first month, her leaving came from a need for sleep, because she hadn't shared a bed with someone since she was a child and couldn't imagine starting again now. Eventually, as her car found the proper speed to travel close to thirty city blocks without missing a light, she realized that she was more afraid of getting used to Walter's body wrapped around her all night, his hot breath pushing through her hair, his fingers releasing and gripping hers in the strange jerks of sleep.

Rose looked back at Walter as she started gathering up her clothes. All night she had felt like her lunch with Carl had dislodged something inside of her, and when she and Walter had had sex, she noticed her body responding in more dramatic ways, grabbing and biting, wanting to leave a mark. Rose walked over to Walter and sat down near his head. He was definitely asleep, his mouth fallen slightly open and low, nasal sounds beginning to rise in volume. His handsome face had that faraway composure, and his lips seemed to slightly move with—what? A name? A woman's name? Rose stood up again. She's in there, Rose knew, and she ran from the room not remembering until the last possible moment not to slam the door behind her.

24

LIVING TOGETHER

Diane woke up on her futon to find Sink gone. She stretched her arm out on the side of the bed where he usually slept, between her and the wall, and moved her palm along the sheet that was warm from the heat but not from his body. Sink would usually sleep until noon, and Diane would have to call him from the Coffee Bar, letting the phone ring nearly ten times, to make sure he'd get up for his job behind the photo counter at the pharmacy in town.

"I'm up," he'd answer, and Diane had learned not to prolong any conversation as he was always irritable during the first hour of his day.

Diane sat up to examine the room, but there was no way to find any clue as to where he might be. The room, the entire apartment, looked like an earthquake had struck it. Everything leveled to the floor: lamps on the floor, suitcases for drawers, piles of clothes and books; even the couch in the living room was made from an old mattress pushed up against a wall to form a seat and back with an old blanket tucked around it to cover the tears and stains.

Sink had probably not made it home at all last night, Diane realized. She stood up, pushing up with her arms and legs, something she had already begun to hate about sleeping on futons, though it had only been two months. "I suppose he's *there*, too?" Joanne Mueller had said to her the day before. Diane, like most of Joanne's students, always remembered exactly everything Joanne said to her. It was always prophetic, like she was able to see everything going on in her students and form sentences that would cut through all the false layers of what they believed to be their lives and jolt them to attention. *No,* Diane thought, *he's not really* there *anymore.*

Diane wished she hadn't had that third margarita the night before with William and his new boyfriend, Peter. *Where's Sink?* William had asked, as she knew he'd ask when she met them at Lake Bluff's only Mexican restaurant, where they knew one of the waitresses and could always get an extra pitcher of margaritas on the house. The restaurant was air-conditioned, which made it easy to drink too much. Diane did not feel the dehydration until she was home again, moving slowly through the musty air of the basement apartment. Every night Diane opened the small windows near the ceiling to let in what there was of cool night air, and every morning she would shut them to try and keep that air in. It had worked pretty well up until now, but the heat wave persisted, and even basements had lost their natural ability to stay cooler.

"Out somewhere," Diane had answered, and the two gay men had looked at her somewhat sympathetically, projecting all their own insecurities and fears onto her five-month relationship. "It's not like that," Diane told them. "We're not married or anything."

Sink had not left a note for her when she got home from work the night before to shower before meeting William. Sink hadn't left a message when she got home from the restaurant to open all the windows before bed. Sink probably wouldn't even call her or drop in the Coffee Bar that day to let her know where he'd been. He'd either be home when she got off work, or he wouldn't be. It was *that* simple.

Diane didn't mind the arrangement. It was the same arrangement they had had since they'd first started seeing each other during the winter. Moving in together for the summer had been an easy decision because there had been no long discussions about monogamy, no negotiations as to how they each preferred to live, who would clean what, how they would deal with money, people coming over, or bad moods. It seemed like they had just thrown the futon in the corner of the second room and slowly spread out from there. During that first month Sink would sometimes come home with flowers, a loaf of French bread, a package of noodles, and ingredients for a spaghetti sauce. He'd always have forgotten something, and there never seemed to be the right pots or utensils to cook up whatever he'd brought home, so Diane would go out to the small grocery around the corner to fetch the missing ingredients: salt, olive oil, a strainer.

Diane stepped out of the shower. She'd run the water hot for the first half and then turn it cold for the last few minutes so that stepping back into the hot room could almost feel like a relief. She looked up at the ceiling made up of the exposed pipes that fed water to all the apartments above them. When they had first moved in, Sink had swung from the pipes like a monkey, once showing her how he could get all the way from the bed to the bathroom at the opposite side of the apartment without even touching the floor. Diane had almost told him not to, afraid a pipe would break and flood their apartment, but she realized she didn't want to sound *that* way. Her bare skin soon lost its steely chill, and she reached down to pick up the closest shirt and jeans from the floor to wear to work that day.

"I saw your double the other day," Diane told Joanne Mueller as she delivered her café latte.

241

Joanne looked up from the book she was reading with a serious expression.

"At least some woman who looked a lot like you. She came into the café with this tall guy, and I thought it was you at first from behind. Same height, same hair; it just *seemed* like you. I almost walked up to say hello until they turned around."

Joanne turned to look out the window, which was steamed over from the mixture of coffee machines, air-conditioning, and heat outside.

"Who were they?" Joanne asked.

"From some political organization. They were hanging up posters for a meeting downtown. Revolutionary Socialists or something? They introduced themselves to some students, but no one seemed particularly interested in talking to them so they left."

Joanne stared at the wall by the door, which was covered with posters for apartments, clubs, meetings, protests, and pets for adoption, but Diane knew she couldn't read any of the posters from where she was sitting.

"How's your nuclear waste poem going? What's it about?" Diane suddenly thought to ask.

"It's about killing me," Joanne responded.

The day before, Diane had walked home with Tom. He lived a few blocks out of her way, but since neither of them had air-conditioning, they took their time walking along the shaded streets of Lake Bluff.

"Are you and Alex Dupree dating?" Diane surprised herself by being so blunt. She had become terribly forward that summer, which she blamed on drinking too much and trying some drugs. She no longer cared what people thought of her, and when she wanted to know something, she just asked.

Tom stopped walking for a moment. "No, we're not dating."

"It's okay if you are," Diane said, knowing she should just shut up. "He might not be the best teacher, but he's very nice when he comes into the store. And he's way into you."

They had started walking again, which Diane took as a good sign.

"I don't know what I'm doing," Tom said, lighting a cigarette and offering one to Diane. "I know what he wants, but I have no idea what I want. I mean, I'm not in love with him, but I'm starting to wonder just how important that really is."

Diane felt her face get hot. She asked for the cigarette she had turned down a minute before.

"I'm not sure you'd understand," Tom continued. "I think it's a turning thirty thing. Half of me wants to act really young and irresponsible, and the other half of me wants to be very old, set up, fixing up a place I can stay in for the rest of my life."

Two young boys were chasing each other around in a yard. Tom and Diane stopped to watch them play, amazed at how they could move around so quickly in the heat. Diane had grown fond of Tom in the two months she had worked for him. She had never fallen in love with a gay man and didn't exactly think she was in love with Tom, but she found herself thinking that Tom would be the kind of man she'd like to be with. He was honest, laid-back, worked hard, used to write poetry, and didn't seem to mind not writing anymore. He cared for her in ways that Sink couldn't imagine. He'd tell her to take the afternoon off whenever a particularly bad hangover was making her lean her elbows on the counter to hold her head up or notice she had done something different with her hair or matched a shirt and skirt in a way that made them look new.

"It's all very confusing," Tom said, "which isn't a good indication. There should be nothing confusing about falling in love. You should just want nothing more than to do it, right?"

Diane had absolutely no answer to this so she just smiled. They walked the last block to his apartment house and said good-bye.

"How's Sink?" Tom called after her.

"Around," Diane said, turning to walk backward a few steps while she said it.

Sink wasn't around when she got home, and she didn't even bother to look for a note or a message on the answering machine.

"You could have been dead!" was how Diane imagined the fight starting. "You don't carry a wallet, you get fucked up and wander all over the city. You could be unidentified in some hospital, and I'd just sit here until someone bothered to get in touch with somebody to get in touch with somebody to let me know."

"You want us to keep tabs on each other?" Sink would shout back at her. "Call each other every five minutes to say where we are? Not trust each other? Get married?"

"That's not what I said."

"I hate you for having to ask for this."

"And I hate you for making me sound like this! Does our entire relationship have to be based on not asking for anything?"

At the word "relationship" Sink would stop talking and stare at her with a severity that would make his beautifully soft face look old. Then he'd jump up and grab the pipe over their heads and swing himself through the entire apartment and out the door without once touching the ground.

Diane walked into the bathroom to splash cold water on her face. She did this every half hour like smelling salts to keep herself from falling into a kind of stupor from the heat. She walked over to the futon and pulled Sink's guitar on her lap. Since she had stopped writing at the end of spring term, she had started teaching herself chords on the guitar. Sink didn't even seem to know how to play it, claiming someone had left it in his dorm room and he liked having it around. She liked the feel of the wire strings under her thin fingers. She had started to put together songs, making up words as she went, until, by the time she was ready to fall asleep, she'd have a halfway decent set of melody and lyrics. By the next morning she was always unable to remember anything of what she had composed the night before, so she started to record herself on the cheap cassette player that Sink referred to as their home entertainment center.

When Diane woke up the next morning, Sink was there. He was lying on his back between her and the wall, still dressed and sound asleep. She felt a strange disappointment that he had come back just as she had started to think what a good way it would be for their relationship to end, nothing said, nothing moved in or out, no long discussions, and no announcement to friends. "Oh, I saw Sink the other day," William might say to her, "he's living in some warehouse downtown with ten other people." Diane had even started to think that a paint job and a couple of pieces of furniture could make the place a decent apartment. She couldn't imagine doing any of that with Sink there.

She looked him over carefully. He didn't have that innocent look on his face he usually had when he slept. His eyes appeared to be strained shut, and his arm was crossed over his chest, his hands gripping at the sheet he was on top of. Diane guessed he had dropped acid the night before, stayed up all night, made it to work propped up on pot and caffeine, and then gone back to whomever he had done the acid with to either do more or get very drunk and talk about all that had happened while they were tripping. Diane guessed this because she had done this herself with Sink a few times.

After showering she walked back into the bedroom and found Sink rolled over on his stomach so that he took up the entire futon diagonally from one corner to the opposite, reminding Diane of how he used to sleep on top of her in her single bed in the dormitory. They'd open the window partway so that the room would get close to freezing and sleep nearly inside each other. She sat down next to him and tried to memorize every detail of his body, every sensation from the muggy room, the low rumble cars made driving by above her, the stale smell of unwashed clothes piled around them. She knew, over time, her memory would distort all of this, turn the bad worse and the good better, but for now she reveled in this delicate balance: freckles on his shoulders from the sun, his head on the pillow where hers had just been.

25

DECLINING AN INVITATION
TO DINNER, PART 1

Joanne had said no thank you. *Thank you, but no thank you.*
Really, Jon, it's nice of you to think of me, but I don't think it
would be a good idea. Not yet. But thank you. Joanne played this
entire conversation back in her head as the rickety elevator lum-
bered up the twelve stories of Jon Sullivan's apartment building.
She had already prepared herself to find Jon's apartment to be
much more spacious and well insulated than hers, ten blocks south,
which she had nearly frozen in all winter. But Jon, as a man, could
afford to live better in an edgier neighborhood; while Joanne, who
had never lived alone before, felt confined to the better-lit, reno-
vated blocks. "The tallest building in Rogers Park," Jon had told
her after he'd moved out of their house in Lake Bluff, after she
had confronted him with his affair with his student, and after he
had moved in with this student, gotten his grant, and moved again.
"You probably think I have a problem being alone," he had said
in way of confronting the awkwardness of his new living situation,
begun a mere month after leaving a ten-year marriage. "That's

exactly what I think," Joanne had replied and hung up, not speaking to him again for three months.

The elevator finally lurched to a stop at the twelfth floor, and it felt like it had hit the roof. Staring at the retractable cage door between her and the hallway to Jon's apartment, Joanne had no idea where she would find the strength to pull the gate back and step out. It was nearly a hundred degrees in the small compartment, but Joanne hardly noticed. She could just stay there, suspended, as it were, and eventually someone would call the elevator back down, some stranger getting on from another floor, and they would nod at each other, mention the heat, and feel the relief of the door finally opening to the lobby. Outside, the air was just as hot but circulated in a light breeze from the lake a block away.

Joanne, Jon again. Look, my uncle called, and apparently there's some discrepancy regarding the budget Vivian has put in for your consulting fees on Yucca Mountain. I can take care of it, but I think we should go over it. Let's have dinner. Friday, eight o'clock. I'll expect you then.

Joanne had to play the message twice to completely comprehend its meaning. She was not to call back. She was not to check her calendar and call back to say, "Yes, Friday's fine. Can I bring anything?" or "I'm sorry, but Friday's completely impossible. How about next week?" Jon's message was an invitation and a confirmation rolled into one. Placing her hand on the elevator's accordion metal door, she got out.

She wore what she had worn all day, khaki pants and a white T-shirt, which she didn't bother to tuck in. She had looked closely at her face and hair in her car's rearview mirror while she waited for a light to change and modified what she saw with a simple combing with her fingers. When Louis had asked what they were planning for Friday night, she confessed the predicament she was in, and he offered to go along. Joanne considered this. She imagined walking into Jon's apartment with another man, but realized this would only amuse him somehow and give him the opportunity to be charming to a potential rival whom Joanne hadn't even decided was really a rival at all. Jon seemed intent on an intimacy with her life, and until she could get a check—cash a check—she was bound to whatever dinners he could wrangle out of her.

At the apartment door Joanne could hear the muffled sounds of two voices—an argument? She had presumed the girl would be there, had actually hoped she'd be there, as insurance that Jon wouldn't expect any type of romantic evening alone with her.

"I'm Shelly; you must be Joanne," a tall, pretty girl said before the door had entirely opened. Joanne smiled so hard her eyes nearly shut, and she stepped into the cooler, but still warm, apartment.

"Jon didn't ask me to bring anything so I'm afraid I didn't," Joanne said, walking directly to the living room window, which had a surprising view of the Chicago skyline. She was glad for the excuse of looking out a window until she recalled the views from the Cliff Dwellers' Club that night with Vivian, which already seemed like years ago. *And you'd be crazy not to take half,* Vivian had told her when she protested any involvement with her estranged husband to get access to a federal grant. Joanne quickly turned back to Shelly, who still stood at the door, her hands gripped tightly in front of her. Jon was nowhere to be seen.

"I'm a big fan of your work," Shelly said, more to the floor than to Joanne. *Where's "I'm over here"?* Joanne thought she recognized the voice, a floor above her, the darkened hall.

"I'd love a drink." Joanne was still smiling. "Where's Jon?"

Shelly rushed over to the top of a bookshelf, where an ice bucket and assorted bottles of liquor were arranged. "He's just out of the shower; he didn't expect you to be on time."

"I'm always on time," Joanne said, walking toward her. Joanne had considered showing up a good hour late but realized this would somehow translate to Jon as some silly act of wounded ex-wife rebellion. She had decided to treat the entire evening as a business meeting, and punctuality was one of the few things Joanne was good at in business.

Shelly turned to her with a glass of ice in one hand and a bottle of scotch in the other.

"I don't think I asked what you drank," Shelly said, letting out a nervous breath.

"Vodka. On the rocks is fine," Joanne said, picking out the bottle herself. She felt strangely sorry for Shelly, sorrier than she felt for herself. It seemed more hurtful to her than to Joanne, this pursuing the not-yet-ex-wife by having the child you left her for cook dinner. Joanne took the glass of ice from Shelly's hand and poured her drink. "Can I make you one?"

"Yes, please," Shelly said, and Joanne did. "I'm sorry, won't you sit?"

Shelly indicated the couch, and they both sat down. Joanne immediately saw the half-filled pack of Marlboro Lights on the coffee table and pointed to it.

"I know," Shelly said, as if it had been an accusation. "I had quit; it's just when I get nervous, or stressed, I just—"

Joanne leaned close to her and put a hand on her wrist, causing Shelly to slightly jump. "Let's have one together," she whispered, and took two cigarettes out of the pack. It was the first cigarette Joanne had had that month, and something told her it wouldn't be her last. The first drag of it followed by a long swallow of vodka made her head spin, and she fell back into the couch.

"I see the two of you have something in common," Jon said from behind, and Shelly spun around to him, smiling as hard as Joanne had when she'd first entered the apartment.

"What's that?" Joanne asked, rolling her head to the side so she could just see her husband from a corner of her eye. He was dressed in jeans and a short-sleeve oxford shirt. His hair was still wet from the shower, giving off the impression he had just had sex. Joanne was amazed at how well he seemed to have every detail planned out, and she was more intent than ever on throwing him off course.

"He means our smoking," Shelly said. Joanne felt sorrier and sorrier for her by the minute. "I'm gonna check on dinner," Shelly said, like she was asking permission, and stepped backward to the hallway. "Oh," she exclaimed, just before she was out of sight. "You do like fettucine alfredo, don't you?"

"My favorite," Joanne said. "Can I help?"

"No," Jon said from behind her, just as Shelly opened her mouth to say the same. "She has it under control. Let me show you around."

Joanne got up, but not before draining what was left of the vodka from her glass. She held on to her cigarette. Jon stared at her with the familiarity of someone she'd known for years; someone who's known her history, her moods, her opinions, and her body; someone who still believed they knew everything there was to know.

"This is the living room," Joanne said, and took another long drag from her cigarette.

"When did you start smoking again?" Jon asked.

"Just now, actually."

Jon smiled, taking her response to be some type of compliment, and Joanne instantly regretted saying it. He was still handsome, but it had no effect on her. He had become a house she had once loved, furnished, and cleaned, a first house forever coded with sentiment and the memory of being young enough not to notice the deficiencies, a loved house where a few bad years eventually make it easy to leave. Yes, she realized in relief, the roof leaked one too many times, the freeway was finally constructed close by, and somewhere, deep inside of her, someone she had cared for and loved had finally died.

"The bedroom's here," Jon said, motioning to the room he had stepped out of. Joanne knew this was a dare. She casually walked past him and looked in at the small and crowded bedroom. The bed was queen-size, the kind most couples have for the first few years they live together.

"It's charming," Joanne said, making a point to glance at him as she walked back to the center of the living room.

Jon walked past her to the hallway, where Shelly had disappeared a moment ago. "My studio's in here," he said, and Joanne obediently followed. From the kitchen, at the end of the hall, Joanne could smell garlic cooking and heard the nervous rattle of pans. She forced herself into the room Jon had already gone into and smiled when she realized his studio was the largest room in the house, with a corner view of the lake and the now lit-up Chicago skyline.

"Can you believe the view?" he said with his hands on his hips, the city suddenly another mistress he had acquired in her absence. "People pay a million for this in those blue-glass egg cartons downtown. We got this for less than a thousand a month."

"Have you taken up Japanese gardening?" she asked, nodding toward what looked to be different brown shades of canvas lying on the floor and covered with small stones in different patterns.

"Welcome to Yucca Mountain," Jon said, and Joanne realized this had been the true destination of her tour. Looking between the floor and Jon, she indicated her confusion by lifting her brow.

"You're three miles above in a plane, what do you think?"

Joanne looked down again and put a hand over her mouth so she wouldn't laugh. The center canvas, a slight orange color, had the stones arranged in the international symbol for nuclear power, the symbol used on fallout shelters, the strange trinity with a circle in the center and three boxes fanning out from it. To the right, on a more tan canvas, was what looked to be a skull and crossbones, though she had to kind of squint her eyes to make it out. Farther down, on a darker brown canvas, was what appeared to be a high wall of stones in a circle and "Keep Out" written in stones around its circumference. Another canvas was made up of about ten parallel lines of stones, and on the last one the stones were just randomly scattered about.

"The Aztec lines," Joanne finally said, pointing at the one made up of parallel lines.

"That's where I started."

"What's the actual scale?"

"Miles and miles and miles. I'd like to cover the whole mountain if possible."

"Isn't this the work of the architect, the botanist?" Joanne asked, inquiring into the other two approved positions on the arts council.

"Perhaps their ideas won't be as good so they'll just have to hand over their grants to me as well," Jon said, and Joanne looked quickly at him, realizing he wasn't joking. He knelt down and picked up a few rocks from the nuclear symbol. Below it the canvas was pure white against the orange. "We can treat the soil of the entire mountainside. The sun should then rework the chemicals to create the orange everywhere but where these rocks have been put. As thousands of years go by and the rocks are moved or weathered down, the earth below them will do the work by maintaining the difference in color." Jon sat back on his heels and looked up at her. "Which one is your favorite?"

A light cough came from the door behind them, and they both turned to Shelly, who was standing nervously at the threshold.

"Sorry," she said, causing Joanne to instantly stretch her face back into a giant smile. "I just need to know when you'd like to eat."

"Well," Jon said, standing, "perhaps another drink and then we'll—"

"I'm famished," Joanne interrupted. "Why don't I help you? I haven't seen the kitchen yet anyway." Joanne put a hand on Jon's sleeve in an old gesture. "Another vodka on the rocks? My glass is on the coffee table."

Despite Shelly's protests, Joanne stirred the sauce while Shelly cooked the pasta and tossed the salad. Jon brought Joanne's drink, and Joanne demanded he go back and refill Shelly's, which he brought back a moment later and then left the two of them alone. They lit cigarettes while they cooked and drained their drinks at the same time. Shelly strained the pasta, and Joanne poured the sauce over it. They talked about the restaurant where Shelly worked, Joanne's boredom with teaching, Shelly's interest in being either a dancer or a writer, and Joanne's encouragement for her to be both.

They carried their banter to the small kitchen table, reminding Jon to bring a bottle of wine, which Shelly and Joanne kept between them. Through dinner Jon continually tried to ask Joanne about old friends, her family, her fellow faculty at Lake Bluff, but Joanne would always turn the question back to Shelly by explaining to her what Jon was asking about and managing not to answer his questions. Jon seemed to become less cheerful as the meal progressed, and by its end he hardly said anything at all.

When Shelly started gathering up plates, Joanne leapt up to help, waving away her protests.

"Sit down, Joanne," Jon suddenly said. "I think we should talk about the project."

Joanne stared at him for a moment, his command cutting through her comfortable layer of vodka and wine, until Shelly took the plate from her hand and smiled. Joanne did as she was told.

"According to a source of mine at the University of Chicago, your grant looks good," he began. "The only confusion seems to be that there are two of you; that is, you and Vivian."

"What's the confusion?"

"Well, for starters, who exactly is writing this poem?"

Joanne stared suspiciously across the table at Jon. "You know Vivian doesn't write poetry," she said, watching his reaction to her words. "She's a critic and the head of the most important society of poetry and letters in the country."

"And she has asked you to write this poem."

"Yes—well, not exactly, but yes." Joanne stared down at the table. "What are you getting at?"

"They have agreed to divert money for a poet. They are confused as to why there are two of you. Indeed, if you are to write this thing, what exactly are they paying Vivian for?"

Joanne was aware of Shelly quietly putting things away behind her. When Joanne turned around, Shelly handed her cigarettes over without Joanne needing to ask.

"Look," Joanne started again, once the cigarette was lit, "Vivian was the one who set this whole thing up. She saw an opportunity not just for money—" Jon rolled his eyes at this—"well, of course for money, but also, in her capacity as a representative of poetry in this country, as an opportunity to keep the art at the forefront of contemporary politics. Let's just say that poetry could use as much press as possible these days."

"But let me ask you this. What would you imagine Vivian's defense would be if *she* was asked why there are two of you?"

Joanne took a drag on her cigarette and looked past Jon and out the window at the intense blackness that represented where Lake Michigan was. She felt at the very edge of one of the densest metropolitan communities in the world, the place where the city just stopped, constrained by nature, the buildings pressed up against the shoreline looking out.

"You're telling me to beware of Vivian Reape," Joanne said, smiling.

"I'm trying to tell you that Vivian Reape isn't well liked by certain important people at the university, and with one phone call they'd be more than happy to take care of Vivian for you."

Joanne smiled. She would get her check. She would possibly need Jon beyond just getting her check. He was possibly setting her up just for that to happen. Joanne stabbed out her cigarette in a saucer and looked at her watch.

"I appreciate your concern, Jon," she said, standing. " You've been wonderful about this thing."

"There's just one other thing," Jon said, also standing. Somehow Joanne knew there would be, and she steadied herself by placing her hands on the back of her chair. "Have you heard of CHIC-ago, the magazine?"

"I've seen it."

"They want to do a profile on us."

Joanne looked over at Shelly, who was wringing a dishrag in her hands. "Us?"

"You and me. Mr. and Mrs. Yucca Mountain." Jon laughed, and Shelly laughed a little too, which caused Joanne to turn and face her.

"What do you think of this?" Joanne asked Shelly, who looked at Jon, something she had done a lot that evening whenever Joanne asked her a direct question in his presence. "Look at me. I wasn't asking *him* what you thought."

Shelly, a little stunned, looked back at Joanne. "I think you said that poetry could use all the press it could get."

"And you could use a little, too," Jon added.

"Whatever you say," Joanne said, and started moving down the hallway to the door. She remembered Friday nights, married to Jon, cooking dinner or ordering out, the way the evening would weave in and out of being together and drifting apart, turning on the TV, picking up a book, making a phone call. The way he would go to bed first, and how the entire house would then be filled with a solitude that was safe with the thought of him in the bed upstairs sleeping. For Joanne, marriage seemed to be that very negotiation of being alone in the presence of someone else.

"You didn't tell me which one was your favorite," Jon said, stopping her with his hand on her shoulder at the door to his studio.

Joanne stared through the door at the five canvases covered with stones.

"The one with the stones randomly strewn about."

"That's not one of your choices. I haven't worked on it yet," Jon said.

"It's the best one. It draws no attention to itself, and besides, no displaced tribe thousands of years from now would really want to go through all the trouble of removing all those stones to build a city, would they?"

Jon stared down at the rock-strewn canvas debating this idea, unsure whether she was putting him on or had given him the answer to all his questions, and Joanne took advantage of this to make it out the door.

26

FORMS OF LOVE

William Dunning thought it best to say nothing. No one said anything. Peter Brooks was looking at his grandmother in an amused way, which William thought condescending. Oma stared blankly at the table, and William alternated glancing at the two of them. They sat in the lazy embrace of candlelight around Oma's mahogany dining room table, which William had come to know as the heart of Oma's house. The table was usually covered with stacks of magazines and cut-out articles, books, bills, letters, and the phone. Oma would spend most of the day and evening at this, her command post, right in the center of the first floor, with the living room, study, front entry hall, and kitchen opening from it on each side like points on a compass. The table was cleared of Oma's things now, replaced with food crumbs, half-filled water glasses, and half-empty sherry glasses. Oma had just willed her house to her grandson.

Most people, in William's position, would excuse themselves to the kitchen (taking a few leftover plates), wash a few of the dishes, and step out the back door to smoke a cigarette, allowing at least a good half hour for family finances to be gone over. Outside, perhaps, he would consider his own family, his own lack of or promise of inheritance, while staring out across the flat distance separating northern Illinois from southern Wisconsin, basking in a kind of sweet melancholy that the distance of immediate family can particularly provide. But William did none of this. In fact, in the silence following the announcement, William reached over for his cigarettes and lit one right at the mahogany table. He had known his lover's grandmother longer than he had known his lover and felt confident of her desire for him to bear witness to the legacy she was passing around like a plate of after-dinner Italian cookies.

"William Dunning, you're *dunn* for!" Sink Lewis had exclaimed the last time William had phoned to cancel (for the third time in a row) meeting Sink and Diane for a drink. William had smiled back into the phone with the satisfaction of being in love, those first precious months of being in love when the first casualties were engagements with friends. How often William had been faced with canceled Friday nights as his friends fell in love. How it always went unremarked when they showed up again after that first fight or affair, once the love had worn down like the rubber on a tire skidding at high speed or spinning in place should it back up into a snowdrift.

That Sink should be the one to exclaim the obvious was all the more poignant because Sink was one of the few men William had ever felt such emotion for. Love erases love, William realized: writes over it, restages it, improves upon the original. At least this was what William believed as he hung up the phone on Sink to call Peter, as he had done twice before and would happily do again. Around him crops were failing, electrical power companies were burning close to brown-outs, and the elderly and newborn were nearly dying in a summer of weather excess, but William could only give a passing glance to the front pages of newspapers as he commuted the forty-five minutes separating him from the man he loved.

Still, sitting at Oma's dining room table, William became aware of the short amount of time he had known Peter. They had met on Valentine's Day, a fact much celebrated by everyone they knew. By the end of March they had used up every variation of the verb "like." By the end of April they had gone through "attracted," "trust," and "need." May left them with nowhere to go but "love," and they were able to make so much use of this simple yet potentially dangerous word that it wasn't until the end of June that their long phone calls and late-night talks over dinner and in bed left them with "commitment," "monogamy," and "live together."

It was at this point that Oma handed them her house. William counted the minutes of silence going by on the grandfather clock in the next room and already felt directly included in Oma's proposal. The only problem, he realized, was that despite a semester spent learning each other's personal histories and four months of sleeping together, William did not really know Peter at all.

Peter wrote poetry. It was one of the first things he had said in the conversation they had had on the fire escape at the party where Sink had kissed William. *Who are your favorite poets? When did you first start writing? Have you ever gone out with another poet?* Next, it was established that William was the better poet, not so much by a critical assessment of each other's work (by the second week they both claimed the other "better" upon reading their work), but by the fact that William was fortunate to be in a structured writing program under the care of Joanne Mueller. Peter was deemed the intellectual by his attending a school as prestigious and rigorous as the University of Chicago (a school William had actually been rejected by, though he'd never gotten around to confessing this to his lover). Once these roles had been established, a balance of power achieved, it was only the business of sex that waited to be resolved.

"I'm sick of one-night relationships," Peter had said on the fire escape. "It seems backward to try and know someone physically before you can get the chance to meet them mentally."

William desperately tried not to take this as a sign that Peter wasn't attracted to him. "I can't say I've had much luck with that style of relationship either," he answered, feeling like he was in class discussing a form of poetry instead of falling in love.

Peter reassured William with a kiss. A good kiss. A kiss that was better than Sink's (William instantly decided), a long, slow kiss that hinted at everything to come and masked everything they still didn't know. For two weeks they kissed like this, embraced, sat on each other's laps, and slept in the same bed in Peter's dorm on nights when their conversations let time slip away from them and there seemed no way Peter could allow William to brave the streets and train stations of Chicago's South Side at so late an hour to get home. So, with their underwear kept on, they wrapped themselves together in Peter's single bed and slept without really sleeping.

By April, William's concern that Peter wasn't attracted to him grew to panic. Around him, spring had come with streets overflowing in slush and litter, the snow sinking down into black ice piles like the remnants of a bonfire. Cars with their windows down and radios blaring sped along flooded streets, soaking the pedestrians who filled the sidewalks, talking loudly and cursing cars. Even the birds seemed not to chirp so much as scream from the trees, which had been especially damaged by the winter, their branches splayed out on the ground beneath them like a spilled box of matches. But William could hardly partake in the beauty and excitement of the change of season around him, obsessed as he was with the fact that he and Peter had gone out for over a month and had not had sex. It would be his luck that once he found a man who was everything he wanted, *wanting* itself would be the one thing he lacked.

"Young people go at things so slowly these days," Oma had said to him around this time. "All you hear is how compulsive and fast-paced life is for people your age. I think it's the opposite. When I was young, you met a man and got engaged. You chose a profession and started work. You decided on a place to live and bought a house. I've always believed that if you think about something for too long, it never gets done."

William was replacing her storm windows with screens, and she was following him around the house while he did it. It was the end of March, and though the temperature was in the sixties, William wished he had worn gloves because everything he touched seemed frozen, as if winter had just retreated to the sides of the house and the dirty storm windows.

"I guess there are a lot of choices now, different ways to live," William said.

"*Too* many choices," Oma corrected him, steadying the ladder with one of her thin hands as he came down. "It's still the same world. Find someone, start a job, build a home, raise children, settle in. Now people want to wait until their thirties before they face it, and by then they're all used up. They've learned too much about disappointment, are too used to being on their own."

Oma, of course, knew about his relationship with her grandson. It was never discussed, but she knew. He carried the last of the storm windows down to the cellar, and she followed him.

"See that?" Oma pointed to the corner where a small bed was covered with a brightly patterned afghan. "For the forty years we were married, I would come down here about once a week to sleep. I'd slip out of the bed after Douglas had fallen asleep and come down here and be back in the kitchen making breakfast before he'd come down the next morning. It wasn't until the children left that I found out he'd known about it all along. We had been going through a lot of things that summer, giving extra things away to the children, who were starting their own houses, throwing things out we hadn't used for years. He says to me, 'Why don't we throw out that old bed in the cellar?' I said something like, 'It's not bothering anything; just leave it there,' and he smiled at me."

"Why were you coming down here?"

"That's not the point," Oma said. "The point was he knew

about it all those years. I could feel my face blushing, like I had a man stashed away down here or something. I could have said it's cooler down here in the summer and warmer in the winter, but I didn't. It wasn't true anyway. You live with someone all those years, and you get in on all their secrets. You learn not to mention certain things. The order in which he puts his clothes on, the window he stares out of, the dining room chair he always sits in, the times you know not to ask anything. *Those* secrets."

William hadn't exactly seduced Peter; they'd seduced each other. One April night Peter had come up to Lake Bluff and planned to spend the next day with his grandmother. Early in the evening, as they walked around the still-frozen lake, the ice a bruised purple color, William told him he should just spend the night instead of going all the way home in the opposite direction only to come back the next day.

"I was thinking the same thing," Peter replied.

Peter was slightly shorter than William, and his body was in better shape: thicker arms and legs, a more prominent chest, and a waistline that seemed, to William, more masculine with its slight bulge at the top of his pants. William was amazed how well he already knew Peter's body without having made love to it. The coarse hairs on his shoulder blades, which felt like straw, the nest of birthmarks on his upper chest, and the long, discolored scar on his right calf from a childhood injury.

"Oma talked to me about her marriage," William said, at the one Italian restaurant in Lake Bluff where they had dinner. Since Peter had agreed to stay the night, they both seemed nervous and hadn't enjoyed their usual easy flow of conversation.

"Did she tell you she never loved him?" Peter asked. They were well into their second carafe of wine, and William was glad Peter seemed to be drinking as much as he was, which usually wasn't the case.

"What do you mean?"

"It was a marriage of convenience. My grandfather was coming home from the war to start a practice as a doctor and needed a wife. I think he found her exotic, like bringing home a kamikaze sword or something. Oma needed to get out of Europe, though I don't think she ever banked on the fact of Illinois, but she wasn't about to go back."

William was silent for a moment and stared down at his half-empty plate. He could still picture the small bed pressed against the corner of the cellar, the afghan neatly arranged on it, and the single pillow with its light blue case. He had forgotten to ask Oma if she still came down there to sleep even though her husband was dead.

"I'm surprised she hasn't told you that," Peter continued. "She seems to tell you everything else. Perhaps she's getting romantic in her old age."

When they got back to William's dorm room, they didn't bother turning on the light. As they clumsily pushed away each other's clothes, William had the impression they were getting something over with, like they had waited so long that they had to get this first time out of the way in order to balance all they had proclaimed to each other with what they didn't know sexually. It lasted about half an hour and was awkward and distant, not like the times when William had been with strangers, when it seemed all right just to take, to make clear what he wanted and negotiate from there. The whole process with Peter seemed like a test they had studied too hard for, and he knew Peter was as relieved as he was when it was over and they were just lying together in his bed enjoying the simpler intimacy they had proved to be so good at.

"What was your grandfather like?" William asked. He ran his hand down Peter's chest to his stomach to his thigh. He felt more aroused now than he had when they had first pulled each other's clothes off. The next time would be better, he decided, much better.

"Quite a bit stern. Oma had all the life. I would think that after forty years of marriage her energy would have been a good influence on him, opened him up a bit, made him laugh more or something. Instead it was like she absorbed it all out of him to compound with her own."

William couldn't help thinking Peter was probably a lot like his grandfather, in the way he pursued a prelaw degree despite his interest in poetry, and, more telling, in his dismissive attitude toward Oma whenever she acted affectionate or emotional toward her favored grandson.

"You're a good influence on Peter," William remembered Oma telling him a few weeks earlier during one of their conversations about Peter, in which they never exactly discussed the fact that William was his lover. "He's on such a plotted course: college, law school, the bar. I'm afraid he'll grow rigid as he goes through the motions of things he's decided on, were decided for him, so long ago. Take things too seriously. Stop writing poetry. When you act older than you are, what happens to you when you're old?"

The sex did get better. It found its pattern, a type of route to follow that could relax them enough to enjoy it. After a few months, William stopped noticing the quickness of it, the way it reached its conclusion without all the flourishes to draw it out.

By the middle of summer, when William and Peter were walking the two miles back to William's dormitory on the night Oma had willed Peter her house, their sexual relationship had already overcome the shock of not having sex every night, even letting entire weeks pass, and William wondered if, when they got to his room, Peter's hand would grab William's as it reached for the light, pull his body to him in the way William had come to know—one hand palmed at the small of his back while the other reached up to pull down from the back of William's slightly taller shoulder. William enjoyed this familiarity and no longer worried about it being routine or slightly mechanical. There were other things that made up a relationship, he felt. The house they had just left being one.

They walked silently for the first mile through the heavy night air, the humidity teasing the dry cornfields with the moisture it refused to release. Even the stars across the wide sky seemed dull, like they were about to burn out.

"You should have talked to her more about the house," William finally said. "It seemed to mean a great deal to her."

Peter laughed and draped his arm across William's back. "Oh, but I have," he said. "The last three times she brought it up, I talked to her about it at length. She's a broken record now."

William was startled by this.

"You never told me," he said, remembering their long conversations about places to live: New York, San Francisco, a farm in the middle of Wisconsin.

"What's to tell?" Peter took his arm away, and William could feel a slight dampness where it had been. "I've told her a hundred times I'd never live in that house."

27

VIVIAN'S HEADACHE

It started when Alex's hustler walked into the living room and pulled his sneakers out from between her legs. Vivian loathed summer. Everything became exposed and vulnerable to every possible kind of assault on the senses. A civilized person could not count on going anywhere without passing through the inferno of humid, overripe air, and once safely arrived at a properly climate-controlled destination, there was always the further threat of base human acts and urges that the season seemed to bring to a boil. Even in a place as distinguished and refined as Alex's sitting room, with its view superior to that of Vivian's own hotel room at the Drake and its tea served in century-old Meisen cups and saucers, any vagrant in cut-off jeans and a torn T-shirt could yank out his filthy tennis shoes from right behind her legs. All summer Vivian never fully relaxed, knowing far too well that some hideous creature could crawl out from any possible corner at any time.

"Alex, that will not do," Vivian scolded, once they heard the front door slam.

"That was my nephew," Alex unfortunately explained. "He's in from out of town—"

"Oh, Alex, *really,*" Vivian interjected, to stop him from further embarrassing himself. She set her half-spilled tea cup and saucer on the antique coffee table and moved herself slightly down the couch, away from the offensive spot where the shoes had been and closer to Alex so as to take him a bit more into her confidence. "A man of your stature, society, and sensibility must deal with such matters more delicately," she told him, nearly whispering, still unsure they were actually alone. "You need a companion, the kind of man who could be your equal, a man with whom to read aloud, tour Italy, cook, and philosophize. Perhaps a younger apprentice, a vessel, well schooled enough to appreciate the knowledge and experience your classical tastes can bestow. I know such men, Alex. You need such a man."

Alex stood up. "Let me refill your tea. Can I get you anything else?"

Vivian gently rubbed her left temple. "A couple of aspirin if you have it."

With Alex gone Vivian took a moment to examine the room, the porcelainlike bleached wood floor, the minimal placement of simple antiques and modern pieces around the exceptionally large room in order to allow the curve of the windows to command your attention with its views north, east, and south. Vivian calculated the room's worth from maintenance to maid service, the interior decorator and market value, the unobstructed views and family heirlooms. There was no way to even approach a correct figure, and Vivian grew frustrated trying, though she marveled at the man who could own such a place and still pursue a career teaching poetry at a small midwestern college. He was a man still wanting, Vivian realized, whereas she would be happy just to watch the sun rise and set as reflected on the glass towers the room looked down on without another thought to the complex inner workings of academia, the posturings of grants and résumés, the simple business of words.

Vivian's week-long trip to Chicago was entirely made up of such exhausting relationships, and everything came with negotiable price tags. It had been a trying year for the National Institute of Poetry. Patrons had seemed to die off in record numbers, and their wills, though generous, were hardly epic enough to warrant their names bestowed on new wings or awards. As president, Vivian was under pressure to provide the right amount of publicity to encourage future support, while the federal government made it quite clear it was not to be bothered. There was talk of reducing the amount of the society's space in its New York City brownstone in order to sell a few upscale residences. There had been hints of tightening expenses, including Vivian's, which, Vivian knew, once taken away would never be reinstated. The end of an era seemed to be at hand; the mob was about to storm the palace, and Vivian realized she had to act fast. She was putting all her money on one horse, so to speak, the costly grant that would place a poet-in-residence at the University of Chicago. From that she expected the continued funds and publicity of the Yucca Mountain grant to allow her investment to ride long enough for the fruits of further publishing and speaking engagements to encourage more donations.

Everything seemed to be in a tangle; even good news was embroiled in contractual disputes. For instance, the society had finally found interest in establishing its own imprint at a prestigious New York publishing house and wanted Vivian to write a book-length criticism on contemporary poetry and edit a major anthology of formal American verse. On closer inspection, however, Vivian found herself still obligated to produce a book for Silo Press, having received an advance from the house over ten years ago. She had believed they had gone bankrupt when they'd stopped bothering her about it a few years earlier, but her lawyer had found out otherwise a few weeks ago.

Vivian would be sixty in two years. Her retirement hinged on setting the institute up with a successor worthy of the legacy she had established and well connected enough to provide her the proper financial comfort she deserved (she personally had her eye on one of the very apartments the society was considering selling, a brownstone in Gramercy Park). This successor could not be a person overly qualified for the position, for then what possible need would they have to see to it that Vivian was well taken care of once she stepped down. No, this person must be personally sought out, groomed in their career and publishing, and made to feel thoroughly indebted to her for the honor only she could bestow. The successor must also come from the very upper realms of society, the last protector of an art whose era seemed to be passing. That successor had just returned to the room with her freshly refilled cup of tea.

"I want you to listen to me very carefully," Vivian said, once she had received her fresh cup and saucer. "I don't want you to think that the unfortunate incident that happened here this morning in any way affects my choice of you to head up what will surely be the beginning of an extremely prestigious program in poetry at a very prestigious university. On the contrary, it reminds me of what human frailties we all are subject to. Just be a little more careful of what types of people of the evening you allow yourself to step out with."

Alex was silent for a moment, and his face did not flush. Instead, it seemed to bleach like the wood floor beneath his feet as he stared intensely down into his steaming tea. Finally, after carefully setting the saucer and cup down on the side table between them, he let his head fall into his hands.

"Oh, Vivian, he isn't my nephew and he certainly isn't any prostitute," Alex wailed through the fingers clenched over his face. "He's the man I love, and I believe he will never love me."

Vivian looked in the opposite direction of Alex's muffled sobs for as long as she felt was the proper amount of time to give him to stop, but he didn't seem like he would. Finally, she set down her cup in front of her and hesitantly touched his arm. "I see we have more than your appointment at the University of Chicago cut out for us," she said, in way of consoling. "Did you by any chance remember my aspirin?"

By the next day, Vivian's throbbing head had settled into a more muted, overall ache, as if the one main pulsing artery had burst into a hundred. She knew to blame the heat. Usually, in the months of July and August, Vivian would keep to her Boston home, where delivery services and her own air conditioners would insulate her enough from the elements so that spring and fall could almost become one continuous season. It was only the crisis of poetry that convinced her to forego her own comforts for a week in a place as landlocked as the American Midwest in the midst of what was proving to be one of its hottest summers on record. Her itinerary was hectic and sporadic. Vivian knew that her dealings were at a stage when everything was in motion at once, and she too must be prepared to follow whatever lead.

"What a pleasant surprise," a pleasantly surprised Rose Gluck exclaimed when Vivian walked up to her at the Central Information Services desk in the University of Chicago library. "What can I help you locate?"

"You, actually," Vivian replied, dabbing at her forehead with a handkerchief.

Rose seemed slightly troubled by this announcement but rose to the occasion. "Why don't we go back in my office and sit down."

Rose seemed different to Vivian. However much the summer seemed to assault every pore of Vivian's, it made Rose radiate. Her white shirt was free of wrinkles and sweat, daringly open at the neck to reveal more skin than Vivian ever remembered seeing on her. If she had ever resembled Joanne Mueller in the past, she seemed her exact twin now, her long hair pulled casually back behind her head and her movements steady and self-assured. Rose set Vivian up in the most comfortable chair in her small, window-

271

less office, right next to the vent of the building's central air-conditioning, and set a tall glass of ice water beside her without Vivian's having to ask for it.

"Now, what can I do for you?" Rose asked, settling herself behind the desk facing Vivian.

"I'm in town on some rather frustrating business with your university. You must remember my plea to include a poet in the nuclear depository program Professor Wright's department is at work on. I seem to be encouraged and discouraged from so many directions that I've begun to think Professor Wright is truly strapped financially in bringing off the scientific end of the program and that he has no money to spare for developing the more educational and cultural aspects. What I am saying is that I do not want to burden his work in this era of shrinking federal funds should this be the case and I thought, perhaps, you might be able to advise me with whatever you know of his situation."

Rose seemed amused by Vivian's noble predicament and rubbed her mouth with her fingers in a way that seemed to try to remove the small smile that was there.

"You are not alone in your concerns about Wright," Rose began. "The entire project seems plagued by political controversy and possible scandal."

"Political controversy?" Vivian asked, in her most incredulous of voices.

"Certain political organizations are highly suspicious of the corporate interests perpetuating an energy source that appears to make certain people rich at the expense of the environmental and health protection of the greater, less powerful population at large. By solving the crisis of waste, which Wright has set out to do, what's there to stop the continued reliance on such a dangerous energy source?"

Vivian pondered this for a moment, remembering Rose's particular political reputation at the school.

"What did you mean by scandal?" Vivian asked, trying to move her away from any further political speech making and get at any hard figures Rose may have uncovered.

Rose laughed. "Let's just say that I wouldn't worry about burdening any of Wright's budgets with the cost of your poem. Don't get me wrong, Vivian. I find your interest in this whole enterprise, your attempt to protect future generations from the harmful waste they plan to inflict on Native American land, to be wholly pure and admirable. Surely *something* has to be done with the stuff. My only objection is the larger picture, the encouragement of further nuclear development once this Band-Aid has been applied on that poor mountain. We are truly on the same side in this conflict. Your work comes from within, while mine must always remain far outside."

Vivian took a long sip from her water and tried to regroup. She wasn't exactly getting the information she was hoping for and needed to find a better angle.

"Perhaps," Vivian attempted, "you may have uncovered some specifics as to what part of their budget has been promised toward the more humanitarian end of this project and what further moneys could be made available for the work that lies ahead. You see, my partner, Joanne Mueller, and I have already spent considerable time—"

"Joanne Mueller?" Rose repeated and stood.

Vivian looked quickly over her shoulder to see if Joanne had actually come in the door behind them and, seeing it still closed, looked back at Rose. She seemed suddenly changed, more in focus, every line and edge of her face taut and bloodless.

"You know Joanne?" Vivian asked carefully, nearly afraid of saying the name again.

Rose clenched and unclenched her hands a few times in front of her and finally fell back down on her chair in a heap, her head fallen back and her arms dangling from the sides. Vivian sat up on the edge of her chair, quite alarmed by Rose's physical state.

"Rose, what has happened?"

"I have no one to say this to. I have no experience in such matters and don't know where to turn. I take each day as though it will be my last and find myself wishing it would be. Up to this point I have not even allowed myself to say it, but I can no longer hold it in. You see, I have fallen in love."

Vivian sank back in her chair and placed a hand at her pulsing temple. "With Joanne Mueller?"

"No!" Rose nearly screamed, causing Vivian to wince from the sound deflecting off the walls. "With a man who seems completely possessed by her. Why the whole world seems to be possessed by her. Everywhere I turn, she's there, and I've never even met the woman."

It took Vivian over an hour to extract herself from Rose's life story of lack of love and Joanne Mueller, and after repeated assurances from Vivian that Lake Bluff's premier resident poet was truly no cause for such unchecked anguish, she was able to obtain two aspirin from Rose's top desk drawer and head back out to confront what was left of her day.

What is happening to everyone? Vivian wondered, as her cab sped north to the Drake Hotel. She was hard-pressed to remember seeing such shameful confessions of emotion from people whose dedication to work, to Vivian's work, was something she had so counted on. Summer, she reminded herself, staring out at the crowded promenades along the lake, the terrorists on bicycles and roller skates, the fawning couples and self-satisfied families. Had the entire city sent everybody home from their offices to pursue love, to stroll the lakeshore hand in hand, to stare longingly from the top floor of a condominium at the horizon of sky meeting water, to sit behind a desk at the library in search of that most overcatalogued and cross-referenced way into the human heart? Even the once bold and powerful skyscrapers along the lakeshore seemed to blur at the top as waves of heat made every vertical line falter as it fell out of focus.

Back at the hotel there was a single message from Professor

Wright wanting to meet for dinner at the Cliff Dwellers' Club. Vivian decided it was best not to call back, as all her concentration was fixed on removing her drenched clothing, drawing her curtains, and lying on top of the made bed with a moist, cold cloth draped over her forehead. She had been in this position for only five minutes when the phone on the bedside table assaulted her split nerves, and she knew no other way to protect them but to answer it.

"Ms. Reape? It's Peter Brooks. I'm in the lobby."

Vivian had to take a deep breath before deciding what to say. She felt cornered by the entire city, trapped at the top of a tree with people violently shaking the trunk to bring her to the ground.

"Yes?"

"I have information for you. I thought it best to come over to deliver it in person."

Vivian decided not to question any of his youthful methods or dramatic motives. She had, after all, instructed him to do this very work. She told him to wait ten minutes and she'd be down.

After a splash of cold water on her face and changing into a dry, unwrinkled dress, Vivian felt somewhat more spirited as she walked into the lobby and found Peter in a high-backed chair at a small table in the corner. He was dressed in fresh khaki pants and a simple white polo shirt. His hair was neatly parted at the side, and his slightly tan complexion showed no strain of having braved the heat to arrive at her front door. Vivian paused for a moment to look at the young man before he could see her. His legs were crossed casually at the ankles, and he sat back in the chair very straight with his arms folded across his chest. He didn't look remotely out of place in the splendor of the Drake's lobby. He could easily be freshly showered and dressed from a morning tennis match or, perhaps, waiting for a companion to catch a plane for a tour of Italy. Peter Brooks was suddenly beautiful with such possibilities, and Vivian sighed.

"So nice of you to come by; please don't get up," Vivian said, and Peter got up. She sat in the high-backed chair facing him and declined his offer to fetch her anything.

"I know this must seem strange," Peter began, "but when I heard *your* name spoken in the department this morning, and spoken by Professor Wright, I just felt I had to come and deliver the news to you personally."

"*My* name?" Vivian asked, feeling slightly girlish and realizing she most likely had already received the news he was so proud to bring her.

"He's to meet you for dinner to settle the whole business of your application for a poet for his nuclear waste program. It seems the dean himself called from his summerhouse in Michigan to encourage him."

"How did he react to this order?"

"Quite cheerfully. I only heard about it because he was standing outside his office telling someone about it. I'd say your troubles are over."

Vivian forced a smile as she received Peter's good wishes. Her troubles, she knew, were not so easily over, but she would look into it over dinner at the Cliff Dwellers' Club. For now, it was time to change subjects.

"Did you get a chance to do the assignment I gave you?"

Peter looked down at his hands, and Vivian felt encouraged. "You mean the poems, the love poems I sent you in the spring."

"Yes," Vivian said, leaning toward him. "You were to try removing that too personal second person and set them more comfortably in third? *You, me, I*—I felt as if you were making love to me. Do you have the results to show me?"

Peter didn't look up. "I'm afraid the pronouns only became more confusing."

Vivian paused, pretending to think this over. "Could that be because the pronouns in question share the same gender?"

Peter looked up at his mentor and smiled in a nervous relief that brought out all the youth in his blue eyes. Blue like a lake viewed from high above, a lake with a ship that had lost its bearings in search of a siren's call. Vivian felt satisfaction as this new course was started and she went on.

"I'm afraid I'm not the best teacher with such matters. However, there is a man I'd like you to meet, a man I hope will fill that very post of resident poet you so hope will be filled. A man of very distinct civility, taste, passion, and experience. A man, Peter, not unlike yourself."

28

SINK GETS SLAMMED

Earthly Delight had a hit on its hands. Every Friday at midnight in the back dining room hundreds of poets, would-be poets, poetry lovers, and antipoets would pay a five-dollar cover charge to pack around the small tables and bar to hear poetry. Anyone's poetry. If a poet signed in by midnight, he or she would get the chance to read one poem. The trick was getting through the poem. The raucous and usually drunk audience had the right to shout anyone off the stage for any reason. Some poets were not able to make it past their poem's title. One woman, overuniformed in a beret, black turtleneck, and riding pants, whose poem appeared to be written on a parchment scroll, was not even able to make it to the microphone. On some nights the nervous, sensitive poet would be pitied and encouraged to read through his or her entire piece. Other nights, that same poet would be booed off stage at the first tremor in his or her voice. At the end, the poets who had survived their readings (some nights there were only two or three, while on other nights close to twenty) would be voted on by audience applause, and the winner would receive a portion of the cover charge, which could go as high as three hundred dollars.

Shelly was one of three waitresses who worked the tables for the "poetry slams," as they were referred to, those late Friday nights. She had been forced to cover the shift once when they first started the event in the spring; and though only about twenty people showed and her tips could hardly justify the late night, Shelly enjoyed the spectacle of bad poetry being shouted down and the few good poems rising above the unruly bar crowd to silence them with their odd allusions to love and loss. After a month of word of mouth, it seemed the entire city was made up of poets who came armed with what they thought was their best weapon and were usually laughed away from the microphone. Old women, long-haired hippies, college students, local business owners—everyone seemed to have a poem, or what they presumed was a poem, written down on some envelope or in a dream journal. Shelly was always amazed by the good writing of the few winners, many of whom she had seen before in the restaurant. She would never have guessed the depth of their emotion. Soon the Chicago newspapers had written up the event in their "Must Do" and "Must See" columns, and even a few national magazines had sent writers to cover the phenomenon of poetry as spectator sport, a Roman feeding of poets to the lions, as one put it, the first time in years poetry had made a headline anywhere.

With such press coverage, the crowds made the prize money grow enough to encourage established poets to risk the embarrassment of failure. No magazine paid as much for a poem, and Shelly's tips soon became the envy of the other waitresses, who were all now more than willing to cover her shift those late Friday nights. But Shelly never took them up on their offers. Besides, her lover, Jon, liked to stay home Friday nights, and Shelly, much younger, found the poetry slam to be the perfect compromise when faced with the prospect of sitting alone in front of the TV while

Jon locked himself into his studio to move rocks around on canvases.

"I've had enough poetry readings to last my lifetime," Jon had told her when she'd encouraged him to come. "They should all be slammed if you want my real opinion."

Budding poets Sink Lewis, Diane Whitestone, and William Dunning had discovered the contest by accident when they'd dined at Earthly Delight one Friday night. Sink immediately signed up.

"But you don't have anything with you to read," William had said, when Sink came back to the table to tell them.

"It's up here," Sink replied, pointing to his head. "Well, most of it, at least."

It should come as no surprise that Sink stepped out from the group of twenty-five candidates and won the event that night. Diane would later say she always knew the drunken competition was the perfect venue for Sink's career to begin its erratic course, and William would later record the evening in his unpublished memoir as a classic example of a star being born. As for Shelly, who laughed along with everyone else as Sink casually tried to remember the lines of a poem and made some up when his memory failed him, she knew, having witnessed other Fridays at Earthly Delight, that it always helped if the poet was pleasing to look at.

Beauty was something Sink knew a great deal about. As someone who possessed large quantities of it, he had a talent for finding the smallest detail in the ugliest landscape and used this part to transform the whole. He wrote poems for Joanne Mueller out of such details: the relief in the older woman's face as the train approached the station, the tattoo on the arm of a man on a Greyhound bus. "Be specific," Joanne always reminded her students. For Sink, this came naturally. Beauty was always quite specific.

Sink thought Diane was beautiful when she didn't know he was looking at her. For instance, at a party, while she talked to somebody she didn't really know, one of her hands would play with the ends of her hair while her expression tried to stay in beat with the conversation, always threatening to laugh before the joke was told or sigh sympathetically before the story turned sad. She always seemed too smart for the kinds of people they sat on the floor with at dinner parties, talking about books she had already read or movies she'd never want to see; and however much this was something that attracted Sink to her, it occurred to him that he was just another one of those people Diane could listen to on automatic pilot, nodding, agreeing, and laughing at all the right moments without revealing anything about herself.

William was beautiful when he was in love. That is, Sink qualified, when William was in love but not in love with Sink Lewis. William looked better at a bit of a distance, taking a few days to return a call or glancing, preoccupied, out a window while in the middle of saying something. Up close William came apart: too eager to stay included in a conversation and too worried about what would happen next. Now that William was in love with Peter Brooks, Sink felt he could fall in love with William, but only the William who was in love with someone else.

By referring to such matters in his verse, which was spare and embellished with humor, Sink had done what no other poet in Chicago had come near; he won Earthly Delight's poetry slam two weeks in a row. Diane had no idea it was her face referred to as beautiful when engaged with someone else's, and the next week William was deaf to the fact that it was he who was beautiful when kept at a good distance. At the time, William was actually too preoccupied with his own recent humiliation on stage, having only made it to an unfortunate metaphor of love and warm milk when he was literally screamed off the stage.

"There must be some other way for us to pass a Friday night," William complained, once they arrived for Sink's opportunity to make it three in a row.

"You were in excellent company," Diane reminded him. "Only Sink and two other people survived. Besides, Peter has never been to it. In fact, we've hardly ever had a chance to get to know him."

William looked up from the small table he was at with Diane to the bar, where Sink and Peter were getting drinks. He could not imagine what the two of them had to say to each other as Peter had already shown a slight dislike for William's friends and Sink seemed rather uneasy around Peter as well.

"You do like him?" William suddenly asked. "Peter, I mean."

"Of course I do," Diane said, a little too quickly William felt. He stared back at her, urging her to go on. "He seems everything you're looking for: smart, stable. What's his poetry like?"

"Smart and stable," William answered, and Diane laughed. He thought it was time to change the subject. "Why don't you read?"

"Oh, god, I can barely read aloud in class; you know that."

"I guess Sink can support you both if he keeps winning every week."

Diane was looking blankly at the small platform a few tables in front of them, where an extremely thin, long-haired man was set-ting up the microphone. "I guess," she said softly, and kept watch-ing the man who was now testing the sound by tapping his finger on the mike. William felt a sadness that he didn't really know his friend very well anymore. His remark about Sink suddenly seemed inappropriate, and Diane's response made him feel like a stranger politely making small talk while they waited for the others to join them. The man tapping on the mike had achieved the sound level he was looking for and left the stage, but Diane kept staring at the place where he had been.

"A beer for you and a diet Coke for the lady," Sink said, sitting down in the chair next to Diane, who finally turned back to the table. William and Sink exchanged a quick glance. Diane had re-cently stopped drinking when they went out to bars or parties. Initially, she had made a reference to the heat and how alcohol added to her overall dehydration; but it now seemed to be a delib-erate preference, though it didn't affect her ability to keep company with Sink and William, who were both more aware of the amount they were drinking with each of Diane's diet Cokes.

Peter took the chair next to William and sat on the edge of it in a tense way. William realized he would be doing all the work to bridge the conversation between his old friends and his lover.

"What are you reading tonight?" William asked Sink.

"Something new," Sink said, patting the breast pocket of his shirt, in which a folded-up piece of paper was stuck. "I was watching the sun rise from the Belmont rocks a few days ago and tried to describe it. You know how there are all those colors that hit the skyline before the sun ever comes up? There was this split second where it wasn't hot, and all these people started pouring out of their condos to jog along the lake. It was funny."

"When were you at the Belmont rocks watching the sunrise?" Diane asked, more surprised than accusatory. William watched Diane carefully.

"A few days ago," Sink replied, not looking at her. "Last week."

William allowed the four of them to fall into a silence, unable to think of something else to say and a bit resentful that he was the one doing all the work. He slipped a hand on Peter's thigh under the table, and Peter jumped. William knew the four of them wouldn't be doing this too often in the future.

The tables were now filled, and the rest of the crowd was lining up along the sides of the room and in the back at the bar. Shelly and the three other waitresses quickly made another round, taking orders from tables. Though the room was air-conditioned, the capacity crowd and cigarette smoke kept the heat wave present all around. Shelly walked past Sink's table, noticing the college students had gone to the bar to get drinks, most likely afraid she'd card them. She recognized Sink as the man who had won the last two slams and made a note to keep an eye on their drinks. Should he win again, she was bound to get a good tip.

At the back of the room she approached a table with a man and woman and did a double take. When the event had started two months earlier, she had always wondered if Joanne Mueller would turn up, and, since meeting her, she had stopped worrying so much

283

about it and was caught off guard by the woman with long, graying brown hair talking to a tall, rather attractive man. By the time Shelly got to the table to set down bar napkins, she realized it wasn't Joanne after all.

"A Bass ale and a gin and tonic," the man told her.

"Either one of you reading tonight?" Shelly asked, trying to find out a little more from the woman, who looked so much like her lover's wife. The woman smiled in a self-conscious way, nothing like Joanne, and glanced quickly at the man.

"Maybe next time," he said, and Shelly went to the bar.

Walter and Rose had been at an International Revolutionary Socialists meeting at Lydia's apartment a few blocks away. Though the meeting had been short and hadn't erupted in any of the usual long arguments, Rose had felt extremely shy around Lydia, who continually made references to her past relationship with Walter. "Do you like what I did with the floors?" she asked him right in front of Rose, and, "I found some more of your books; I'm keeping them." By the end of the meeting, Rose's dark mood convinced Walter to decline joining the group for drinks and to have dinner alone with Rose at Earthly Delight. Neither of them had heard of the poetry slam before, and they decided to check it out after eating.

"Why won't you read?" Rose asked, after Shelly brought their drinks.

"It's supposed to be pretty brutal," Walter told her. "I think I'm out of practice."

Rose thought about this. "Did you used to be more involved with this whole scene?" she asked. "Going to readings, hanging out with poets?"

Walter looked at her curiously. He was used to Rose asking something without directly asking. She would fold even more into her body, attempting to make her question seem casual, yet bracing herself for something she didn't expect.

"I've never really been *involved* with any kind of *scene,* Rose. What are you asking?"

"I just meant, well, you dated a poet once, recently?"

Walter stared at Rose, feeling strangely guilty as he again noticed the resemblance to Joanne in her cheekbones and eyes. The same color hair at the same length. He wondered if anyone who knew Joanne and had seen him with Rose was thinking he had replaced Lake Bluff's resident poet with a copy. Evidently Rose Gluck might be thinking the same thing.

"Do you know Joanne Mueller?" he asked.

"I know people who know her."

"Joanne and I never went to readings or sat around discussing poetry. She was the poet; I wasn't."

"Why did you break up?" Rose sat up a bit straighter in her chair, and Walter felt this was the first of a hundred questions Rose had been longing to ask him about Joanne. He was about to deflect it when the lights in the room went down and a single spotlight illuminated the small stage, causing the room to burst into shouts and applause. He reached across the table and squeezed Rose's hand as if to say he really wanted to answer all her questions, but obviously couldn't.

The first three poets up were the first three poets down. The first, the woman who had never made it past her poem's title a few weeks earlier, actually made it through what seemed to be an entire stanza before a few people in the back broke in, yelling, "What?" which caused the rest of the room to start laughing. She was followed by an extremely nervous young man, who spoke so softly into the microphone that it wouldn't have mattered what poem he read as nobody could hear it. He seemed relieved to quit once the crowd told him to. The third poet, an older woman, nearly made it to the end of her poem about stray cats, the problem being she should have ended the poem there instead of going into a long description of what seemed to be her childhood bedroom.

When Sink took the stage, his chances could not have been better set up, and his introduction, mentioning his past two wins, drew a hearty round of applause. Sink seemed unstoppable as he took the microphone in hand and flashed a broad smile around the expectant room.

Shelly was behind the bar putting together a large order for a table of ten but decided to wait to hear him read. Like most of the people who had applauded him to victory the past few weeks, Shelly had a crush on him. His poetry wasn't exceptional, but his performance always won over the crowd. He had an ability to read through emotional passages with an eyebrow raised, as if asking the audience to humor his indulgences in love, and a way of slightly questioning declarative statements so his own good looks wouldn't outweigh the vulnerabilities his poems pursued. Still, Shelly started to wonder how much of it was an act, how much his ability to perform surpassed what he truly had to say.

He had been about to start when his eyes hooked onto someone at the back of the room. Sink squinted through the direct spotlight with a faint expression of recognition. Shelly tried to look at where he was staring but could only see the crowds at the back tables and the people lining the wall. An old girlfriend? Someone he didn't like? Someone who didn't like him? The crowd became restless at even this brief pause, which was enough to throw Sink off his usual self-confident course. Sink then did what he had never done before, he started explaining why he wrote what he was about to read, something Shelly always coached people never to do as it made the audience in the hot room impatient, not wanting to hear a poem after it was already described for them. Sink rambled on nervously about watching a sunrise over Chicago and how his apartment was nearly underground, affording him no view of the outside world. Someone up front called for him to get on with it, and Sink, startled, was unable to find a witty comeback, which usually came easily for him when faced with a heckler. Instead, he pulled a sheet of paper from his shirt pocket and, with one more quick glance to whomever it was he had seen at the back of the room, started to read what was in front of him.

After a few lines about the sunrise and the colors it made on

286

the skyline (pretty much the same thing he had already said), a few people started to boo him. Shelly noticed his eyebrow wasn't arched and his expression was more serious than usual, as if he was just trying to get through the chore of reading the words in front of him. More people started banging on their tables, while others shouted, "Next!" Eventually, the sounds from the crowd drowned him out, and he stopped. Without looking back at the crowd, he left the stage and found his way back to his table. Shelly looked at the back of the room, but all she noticed was the man and woman she had thought was Joanne Mueller getting up to leave, and Shelly hurried over to collect their bill before someone else could grab the money.

29

GREENHOUSE EFFECTS

Lake Bluff was at its lowest level in twenty years, but Helen Drake didn't need the local newspaper to tell her this. From her back terrace she could see where the lake had shrunk back nearly five feet from the stony shoreline. Certain weeds, which had always politely grown underwater, now swarmed at the surface, choking entire areas of the shoreline; and motor boats had been restricted due to the number of sandbars within reach of propellers. The water itself had taken on a most unpleasant brown color and sat stagnant most days beneath the powerful sun, secretly stealing more and more of the water with its hungry rays. The *Lake Bluff Star* went on to say that such droughts operated on twenty-year cycles and this one should have reached its peak. Their expert predicted a winter with high precipitation, which would start replenishing the lake, and in a few more years its water level should return to normal. Helen threw the paper down. In her opinion, the lake was already dead.

She picked through the other newspapers at her feet, the *Chicago Tribune*, the *Chicago Sun-Times*, *The New York Times*, until she found *USA Today*. She preferred the large-sized, full-color weather map on the back page of the front section, which gave extended forecasts for cities across the country. With the back page spread out on the table in front of her, Helen studied the large areas of orange and red covering most of the United States. To the west were hotter temperatures, surely heading her way. To the north, the orange band arched up to the edges of Canada, making Helen shudder. She didn't bother looking at anything farther south of Chicago as she had no intention of taking one step closer to the equator. As far as she could tell, she was still a good day's drive from any significantly cooler climate.

It was nearly ten in the morning, and Helen started to gather up her newspapers and coffee to head back into the house where she'd stay until evening. Above her, three air-conditioning units butted out from windows, straining against the quickly rising temperature and dripping from their fans into the perfectly positioned flower boxes.

Helen's three-story, four-bedroom house, "my house of my own," as she liked to refer to it, had seven air conditioners in all, six of which had been running simultaneously since early May. She would take one out of commission every few days to clean its filter and give it a rest. As Helen neared the sliding-glass door leading into her kitchen, she could make out a voice fighting to be heard through the roar of the air-conditioning units.

"Helen," the voice insisted. "Helen, it's Alex Dupree."

Helen turned around and spied Alex's balding head rising above the rosebushes that fenced her terrace.

"So it is Alex Dupree," Helen exclaimed. "Well, come around and take this tray from me so I can get us inside."

Alex glanced around the terrace to find the opening in the hedge. "These roses are excellent," he told her before disappearing around them and coming up to her from the lakeside.

"You're not planning to turn me in," Helen said, as he took the load of newspapers and the tray from her.

"Turn you in?"

"My garden! Pretty well concealed from the front, you must admit; a complete wasteland in the front. Surely you noticed." Helen dropped the volume of her voice and leaned close to Alex as he passed by her into the rather cold house. "We've been banned from watering since mid-June, but I'm not about to let my roses go. None of my neighbors can see into my backyard, and with the lake so dead I don't really have to worry about many recreational boats going by, so I head out every night at ten and water the whole thing. I could always claim there was a natural spring or some such nonsense should anyone think to turn me in. What would they do with an old woman like me anyway? They'd probably blame my poor roses for draining the entire lake."

Alex laughed rather nervously at her confession and folded his arms across his chest in defense against the cold air blasting from air conditioners all around him.

"I'm sorry for barging in on you like this," he said. "I was just driving by."

"Sit down, please," Helen commanded, and Alex moved toward the kitchen table. "Not there, in the sitting room, of course. You've never been to 'my house of my own.' Please, this way."

Helen walked Alex through the living room and library to a sunny, glass-enclosed room with its own air conditioner doing battle against the sun. To say Helen Drake's house was furnished would be an understatement. Every possible corner and tabletop were covered with vases, lamps, throw pillows, empty picture frames, and assorted knickknacks. Alex had the distinct impression she had cleaned out a dozen antique stores the day she bought the house three years ago with the advance from the unfinished Virginia Woolf novel that turned out to be a hoax. He remembered her telling him that it would be more difficult for the publisher to recover any money if that money had been absorbed into physical goods. Alex, who knew a lot about recovering large sums of money, realized this was far from the case; but upon seeing Helen's house he discovered just how much she believed it to be true.

"Tea? Coffee? Perhaps a Bloody Mary?" Helen asked, once she had situated him on a large white wicker chair with the best view of the lake and her gardens.

"Nothing, really, I just wanted your advice on something. I really don't mean to keep you," Alex protested.

"Stay where you are," Helen replied, and darted back toward the kitchen. In a few minutes she returned with another tray, this one with a large pitcher and two tall glasses. She set it in front of him and took the wicker chair at his side. "It's summer vacation, isn't it?" she said, as she poured what could only be a Bloody Mary into a tall glass with a celery stick and handed it to him.

Alex realized she must have had the pitcher already prepared and wondered if this was part of her daily ritual, the coffee service followed by the vodka service. He decided to get on with it.

"I've been offered a job."

"A job!" Helen exclaimed, settling back in her chair with her Bloody Mary perched at her lips. "You know, Alex, I find it endearing how you pursue your career. I mean, it's not like you need money. In fact, we're alike in that, though of course I don't have everything quite paid for yet; but once I do, well, Lake Bluff College will just have to do without their Woolf scholar."

Alex pushed on. "Vivian Reape has offered me the opportunity to head a new creative writing department at the University of Chicago. She'd like me to start as early as the fall."

"How wonderful! Of course, how sad for us. Oh, Alex, we'll never see you, and just as we were becoming such close friends."

Alex noticed she was already halfway through her drink and found himself drinking rather quickly himself. "You see, Helen, I'm actually quite happy at Lake Bluff—"

"Of course you are."

"—and the thought of starting up a creative writing program

291

all on my own at a school as prestigious as the University of Chicago—"

"Completely terrifying; endless potential for failure."

"—it's just that I enjoy the comfort of the job I have now, the limited hours, the routine—"

"In and out and don't take the work home with you."

"—but the opportunity, the honor of being asked to take on such a task—"

"An honor worthy of your family's name."

"—oh, Helen, how I wish such decisions could just be made for me."

"Of course you do. And there's Joanne Mueller to consider."

Alex looked at her, perplexed, and she took the opportunity to take his nearly drained Bloody Mary from his hand and refill both their glasses.

"What does Joanne have to do with this?" Alex asked.

"How would I know? You tell me."

Alex stared out at the lake Helen had proclaimed dead. He had come by to gauge her response to the importance of the position being offered to him. If he could gather enough academic envy, he felt he could find the courage to accept Vivian's proposal and make a success out of it no matter how many hours he'd have to devote to class work. So far, between Helen's fluctuating responses and the Bloody Marys, Alex hadn't heard what he'd expected.

"You and Joanne Mueller have the sweetest of rivalries," Helen started in after Alex had been silent for a few moments. "It's like brother and sister the way you two work together and compete for the modest laurels available for poets in this day and age in this rather artless part of the country. Now, with Joanne receiving that grant, that nuclear waste thing, I can see where an offer like this is impossible for you to turn down no matter what sentimental attachments you have to your old school."

"Really, Helen, I haven't even considered what this might have to do with Joanne."

"Oh, Alex. If it wasn't for what we've all read about in your very beautiful, if slightly shocking, verse, I'd say you were in love with her. Knowing 'about you,' as we all do, I can only say you are rather jealous of her success, or at least you are spurred on by her achievements to attain a few of your own, no matter how little you actually need the work or money."

Alex could only stare back at her. "In love? With Joanne Mueller?" Helen Drake had always seemed slightly off balance to Alex. Up to this summer, however, he had confined his interactions with her to the hallways of the college, where all the professors seemed somewhat eccentric when talking to their peers. The faculty lounge seemed like a classroom filled with oversized and over-educated students competing with each other for attention. But now, in the middle of summer vacation and in her own home, Helen seemed even more out of touch. What was it about Joanne Mueller that could inspire such obsessions in people? Alex wondered. Perhaps Helen was right, that subconsciously Alex himself led his life in service to what effect his actions would have on his fellow poet-in-residence. Or was Helen's behavior caused by something else, Alex speculated, like two Bloody Marys before noon on a Tuesday?

Helen stood up, walked over to the window overlooking the lake, and glanced out. "We live in very dark times, Alex. Nothing is any longer what it has seemed."

"Helen?"

Helen spun around and faced him again. Her expression, which was usually grave, was full of color, and her eyes were wide. Alex was becoming quite alarmed at her overall condition. "Joanne Mueller tends to her garden just as I tend to mine."

"Helen," Alex said, getting up as well, trying to think of something to say to calm her.

"I'll show you," Helen said, grabbing Alex's hand and leading him from the room. She took him back to the kitchen and opened a door to what appeared to be a pantry and pushed him before it.

Alex looked inside and saw endless rows of plastic containers filled with a clear liquid.

"Alcohol?" Alex asked.

"Water, water, water," Helen insisted, sinking down on a chair at the kitchen table. "Surely I don't have to explain all of this to you. The earth's temperature has risen three to five degrees—"

"Since the Industrial Age."

"—and what with holes in the ozone, constant pollutants, greenhouse effects—"

"You've been reading too many newspapers."

"We are doomed. The ice caps *will* melt, the oceans *will* rise, crops *will* fail as rivers and lakes dry up."

"And another hundred years will go by before any of this can possibly come true."

"You must know all this; you must be *consumed* by this."

Alex slowly walked toward her and took a seat opposite her at the table. He realized Helen's strange behavior wasn't the result of an obsession with Joanne, though she used the poet-in-residence as her sounding board, and it wasn't even the alcohol, though it certainly didn't help. Helen suffered from a far more common affliction that was nearly epidemic that summer: the heat.

"I'm heading north. I'm selling 'my house of my own.' I have agents looking for me in Canada. Invest in everything Canadian, Alex; it's the new Eden. Their borders will close the moment too many of us catch on."

"So you're quitting Lake Bluff, too?"

"Not right away. I'll rent a smaller house here when I buy something up north, where at least I can escape for the summers."

They were silent for a moment, and Alex listened to the machinery of the air conditioners. It was a beautiful old house on beautiful property; a bit cluttered, but beautiful. He felt sorry for her and her pantry filled with jugs of water. Had Helen stepped off the edge? Or was she onto something? Alex had not really taken the hot summer all that seriously. In fact, one large facet of the Dupree Corporation was in sheet metal and central air-conditioning, and business was booming. He decided against mentioning this to Helen.

"What did you mean about Joanne? About her tending her garden?" Alex asked.

"She's playing a very dangerous game. This is no time for profiteering."

"It's only a poem."

"Only a poem?" Helen's face lit up again in color. "Alex, you surprise me. Surely a poet of your sophistication sees the danger here. Lowering herself to crawl into bed with such an evil as nuclear energy, to write pretty verses to clear her conscience and monopolize public opinion purely for her own gain, her own self-promotion."

"She's merely received a grant to produce a poem. Nothing more."

"Nothing more? You haven't seen the current issue of CHIC-ago magazine?"

Alex didn't bother to answer as Helen was already rifling through a pile of papers to produce it for him.

"Here," she said, dropping the magazine in front of him. "Just a poem, is it?"

Alex stared down at Joanne looking back up at him. The cover photo was of her and her husband in front of a sign for a nuclear shelter. Large type across them said "Nuclear Family" and below that "Poet Joanne Mueller and Artist Jon Sullivan to Save the Planet." Jon was smiling broadly, and Joanne looked at the camera seriously, as if willing it to be over with. It was a good picture of both of them.

"I can't believe Joanne would do this," Alex said slowly, jealously, knowing he would do it himself in an instant. "It doesn't seem at all like her. And with Jon? I didn't know they were speaking."

"They're speaking all right. How do you think she got this thing in the first place?"

Alex looked up at her. "Through Vivian Reape?"

"Through Jon Sullivan's uncle, some famed nuclear scientist. It's all there in the article. She's ruined, Alex, completely ruined."

Alex looked up at Helen, perplexed by this opinion. The only ruin he could see was that he had wasted his time coming to her for advice when he should have been getting career guidance from Joanne. He couldn't wait a moment longer.

"Could I take this with me?" Alex indicated the magazine.

"Of course, of course. Read all about it." Helen walked with him to the sliding-glass door facing the terrace. "I hope I have been of service in your career plans."

"Yes," Alex lied. "Great help. Thank you."

Alex recalled the two Bloody Marys when he hit the hot air outside and felt a little light-headed. As he rounded the terrace to go back to the street, he paused at Helen's roses and, after a quick glance to make sure she wasn't watching from the kitchen, took out the Swiss army knife attached to his car keys and cut one off. Though he had sworn not to, a quick trip to the Book Bar wasn't a bad idea since he was already in the neighborhood.

30

THE SCREW

"Vivian?" Peter repeated.

"What?" Vivian snapped, turning to him so suddenly that she nearly upset the delicate marble-topped table that sat between them in the lobby of the Drake Hotel.

"I meant," Peter started, as he carefully wiped up the coffee that had spilled from Vivian's cup with the cocktail napkin beneath his Coke, "what do you do when what you want to say doesn't fit?"

Vivian leaned her head against her hand and rubbed vigorously at her temples, like she was trying to push something off of them and out of her head entirely.

"In poetry, I mean, in a prescribed form."

"You don't say it," Vivian said, and picked up her coffee cup. She sat back in her chair and glanced around the hotel lounge. Peter knew this gesture to mean her point had been made and the conversation was over. For six months Vivian had supposedly been tutoring Peter on the mysteries of poetry; but in six months all Peter had received were reading lists made up of obscure masters of meter like Thomas Campion, and when Vivian ran out of titles, she would tell him to read the same list over again. Peter, mean-while, had accessed nearly every file in the University of Chicago's nuclear science department, Xeroxed budgets, memorized internal memos, and listened in on whispered conversations. He thought it was about time he got some return on his hard work, and what better time and place than in the well-appointed lounge of the Drake Hotel?

"But really," he pressed on, "what if you have the perfect line, the perfect emotion, image, and idea, and it just won't fit the prescribed metrical form?"

Vivian sighed, turned back to him, and slammed her cup down on the table. "Then your line is imperfect. Your emotion is wrong. Your image, idea, everything is wrong, wrong, wrong. Does a carpenter force a wrong-sized screw through a nut? No. He searches for the right one. Or it won't hold; it won't even go through. You have the wrong screw, so open your eyes and look for the right one."

They were both silent for a moment as they each pondered the potential brilliance or idiocy of Vivian's comparison.

"But, Vivian," Peter finally said, "have you ever considered that the problem might be the nut?"

Vivian took a long, steady sip of her coffee and stared at her young apprentice. It was a stare that finally made Peter look down at his soft hands neatly folded in his lap. He didn't dare say anything else and regretted having pushed it this far. Vivian made one more glance at the main door, gave her temples one last shove, and leaned close to Peter.

"You want me to teach you how to become a poet. You want me to tell you, 'Do this,' 'Don't do that,' 'Always put this word here,' 'Never put that word there.' Well, I can't. No one can. If it was up to me, all the creative writing programs, instructors, students, seminars, conferences, retreats—what do they call them?— *workshops!* All of it would be outlawed, thrown out, held up to ridicule. Everywhere I go, every lecture I give, every school I visit,

I'm asked why. Why is poetry dying? Why is poetry shrinking the fastest of all the fine arts? Do you know what I long to tell them, what I know I could never tell them but dream to say because it's the truth and no one really wants the truth? That it's these very programs, seminars, teachers, students, conferences, retreats, *workshops* that are killing the fine art of poetry. Can you imagine? Turning out people at the ridiculous age of twenty-two, telling them, 'You're now qualified to be a poet; go do that,' like they were doctors or lawyers? For what good? To create a class of people who do nothing but sit around and read each other's work? American poetry is truly proof that the more poets a society creates, the less poetry anyone bothers to read. You want me to teach you something? I say read the masters, live your life, search yourself for truth, beauty, and whatever else it is you're supposed to search for and then, if you must—only if you absolutely must—put it down on paper properly or just don't bother us with it at all."

"What a charming introduction."

Vivian jerked her head toward the voice behind her and let out an audible gasp. Peter quickly rose to his feet as if a woman had walked up to their table, when in fact it was merely the polished, expensive look of Alex Dupree that caused his confusion in etiquette. Alex's eyes were immediately upon him.

"Allow me," Alex continued, as Vivian attempted to pull herself back together. "I'm Alex Dupree. You must be the U. of C. prodigy Vivian has been telling me about."

Alex extended a hand, and Peter lunged for it, squeezing so hard that Alex looked at him with even more interest. Peter took in the famed classical poet who, according to Vivian, was soon to be his mentor at the university. He felt a slight disappointment at Alex's prominently high hairline and his slightly odd face but remained unable to introduce himself as he felt a wave of importance roll off Alex's perfectly pressed, checkered sport coat and slacks, moisturized skin, and manicured nails. Besides, his body seemed to be in about the best shape he had ever seen on a poet.

"Peter Brooks," Vivian finally said for him. "Oh, won't both of you sit down, I'll break my neck talking to you." Alex and Peter complied, and Vivian resumed her position with one hand at her temple and the other firmly holding onto her cup of coffee.

"Now what exactly were you telling this poor boy?" Alex said, expertly waving at a waiter and ordering himself a martini without taking his eyes off Peter. "Something about poetry being one big bother? Something like, don't bother?" Alex was smiling and winked at him, and Peter worried he had something in his eye.

Vivian neatly drained her coffee and stood up. "Alex Dupree, you are exactly half an hour late. My head is splitting. Peter Brooks is in such dire need of instruction that I have brought you two together in the nick of time. Alex, I am counting on you. As for you, Peter, I am counting on you as well. Mr. Dupree hasn't exactly printed up new business cards yet, despite all of my hard work to secure his appointment, and I expect you to convey to him how important his acceptance is to the likes of poetry-impaired University of Chicago students like yourself. Don't get up. I will check in on both of you next week."

Alex and Peter watched Vivian make her way across the lobby and disappear around a corner of elevator banks. Alex's drink arrived, and they both waited for him to take a long sip before speaking.

"If Vivian has been your only source for poetic inspiration, I can very well imagine your reluctance to speak."

"Ms. Reape has been very good to me."

"And what are you doing for her?"

"Excuse me?"

"What's your end of the deal? Come on, I'm not your teacher yet. Vivian doesn't do anything for anyone without getting something in return. Hence, my reluctance to start ordering office supplies in Hyde Park. I'm still trying to figure out just what my promotion to head of a newly formed writing department can possibly do for her."

Peter looked down at his Coke. There were puzzle pieces scattered about in his head that were not difficult to put together. He just wasn't sure if he should do it aloud. Alex reached over and picked up Peter's Coke and took a careful smell of it.

"Have a drink," Alex said. "Make it lesson one."

"I'm not used to liquor," Peter said.

"Then I have the perfect solution for you," Alex said, waving the waiter over again, hardly taking his eyes from Peter's. "The screwdriver. Think of it as your daily dose of vitamin C."

Peter felt intensely self-conscious walking into Prague with Alex Dupree. After an expensive dinner, where Alex's fine breeding showed off his abilities to order wine without a list, translate a French menu at a glance, and pay the bill without looking at the total, Peter was unsure the night should end up at a bar where youthful looks and thrift-store clothes took the place of impeccable French pronunciation and an American Express gold card. Going to Prague had been Alex's idea. Peter sensed that Alex had picked up on the obvious fact that Peter was not quite ready to go home with the highly respected, middle-aged poet.

"Of course I've been there," Peter had said, as Alex circled his Mustang around the crowded North Side streets. "Not a lot. I don't really enjoy such loud and barbaric kinds of places."

Peter's attempt to reassure his future poet-in-residence seemed about as futile as Alex's attempt to find an appropriately long, well-lit parking space. Finally settling on an extremely well-lit parking garage, charging what Peter thought was an outrageous hourly rate, the strange couple found themselves at the door of Prague, in line with far trendier groups of gay men and straight women. Peter thought the night would end at this awful point. Surely the doorman, who looked like both a model and a rock star, would never wave in a preppy college kid with a man who looked like his father, but the line suddenly surged forward, and Peter instinctively grabbed hold of Alex's luxuriously soft sport coat and stayed so close to the dyed- and gelled-hair group in front of them that the doorman possibly believed they were all part of the same group. Or else he simply didn't want them seen standing in front of the image-conscious club. Either way, they were in.

"I love this song," Alex shouted in Peter's ear, as they began the first nightclub ritual of pushing through the long, crowded bar to get to the coat check. Peter listened for a moment. A groggy male vocalist was whining about someone having blue eyes, green eyes, and gray eyes.

"Who is it?" Peter shouted back.

Alex looked like he hadn't heard the question and then quickly avoided it by dodging through a sudden opening in the crowd, forcing Peter to run behind him. Walking behind Alex, who definitely seemed to know his way around the dark space, Peter took the opportunity to look around him. Lined up, three-deep along the bar, were endless gay men who looked like they were in the middle of photo shoots, the club's lighting a technical marvel in its ability to sharpen cheekbones and create chins while smoothing away every wrinkle and blemish. Height was a benefit if one wanted to see and be seen, something Peter lacked and hated in an environment like this, where he was forced to continually look up just in time to see a taller, more attractive man look purposefully away.

Ahead of him, Alex was patiently making his way through the throng, taking time himself to glance around whenever he came to a standstill, and Peter found himself jealously following Alex's gazes. A tall blond laughing at something the bartender had said to him. Two dark-haired boys, also tall, wearing matching muscle T-shirts. A long-haired boy, who didn't seem that tall, but was dancing on a platform so he managed to tower over the heads of everyone else, making Peter realize the only way to compensate for size in this place was with nerve. Alex's balding, oversized head swayed slightly to the music in a stiff, determined way, and Peter felt a kind of protectiveness for him. He hadn't thought of William Dunning all night.

They finally reached the coat check, where an extremely rude young woman with no hair on exactly half of her head grabbed their coats and threw back their tickets. Somehow her jar of tips was stuffed with one-dollar bills, and Peter quickly put one in it, realizing they might never see their coats again if he didn't.

"Another screwdriver?" Alex shouted, making a drinking motion with his hand and nearly blinding a shaved-headed youth next to him with his elbow.

Peter eagerly nodded, and they began the second nightclub ritual of pushing back toward the bar, getting up to it, and getting the attention of one of the overly butch bartenders, who looked like a Marlboro ad but talked like a Virginia Slims. Halfway there, Alex stopped and, much to Peter's surprise, started waving an arm over his head toward one of the tall boys with good bone structure who lined the opposite wall. After a few awkward moments, a rather good-looking man approached, who looked to be about halfway between Peter and Alex's age.

"Tom, this is Peter," Alex said simply, leaving the younger men looking at each other in hopes of a more significant explanation. After a quick, friendly glance at Tom, Peter looked back at Alex, who seemed obviously more animated by the encounter. The two of them started taking turns shouting into each other's ears while Peter, who stood right next to them, observed them coolly, unable to hear a word said. Peter had always wanted to be the kind of person who could go into a club and run into people he knew, especially good-looking men, while on what was starting to feel like a first date.

The three of them slowly moved into a corner as the traffic between the coat check and the bar continued to push them out of the way. Peter took in Tom's casual plaid shirt and jeans, his slightly mussed hair, and the familiar way he managed to shout words into Alex's ear without having to distort his face the way Peter imagined he did. Peter slightly overheard Alex telling Tom about his offer at the University of Chicago in a way someone would try to impress an ex-lover.

"How do you like U. of C.?" Tom finally shouted at Peter, forcing Peter to lean across Alex to carry on the polite exchange.

"A lot," Peter said, choosing his words carefully, as anything longer than a simple phrase would surely not be understood above the furious bass of what seemed to be the same song Alex had proclaimed he loved when they first arrived. "I have never met anyone quite like you before," the same depressed singer moaned as everyone on the dance floor moved solemnly in place, heads slightly bowed down, some eyes closed. "Are you in school?"

Tom laughed at this, and Peter was immediately ashamed of having revealed his limited, academic point of view of the world.

"I manage a bookstore," Tom yelled back, and though Peter's conversational instinct was to ask what store, where, for how long, etc., the music forced him just to nod his approval.

While leaning in to hear Tom go on to tell him that he, too, used to write poetry, Peter became aware of Alex's body, slightly pressed up against his side. Before he even realized he had done it, Peter let a hand fall on the small of Alex's back, causing Alex to look down at him with surprise and to drop an arm around Peter's shoulders. The three of them stopped talking for a moment, and Peter allowed Alex to move in a little closer so that his mouth was near the side of Peter's face. They both acted like such intimacy was something they did together all the time, looking more like a married couple than a teacher and student contemplating a one-night stand. Alex mumbled something in Peter's ear about how glad he was to have met him, and Peter replied by tightening his hold on the back of Alex's soft belt holding up his well-pressed, pleated pants. Tom was gesturing to someone behind him in the crowd of tall, gay men, and a moment later Diane Whitestone appeared at Tom's side, facing Alex and Peter.

"Alex, you know Diane. This is Peter," Tom shouted at them. Diane and Peter locked eyes and simultaneously smiled at the sound of their names. Peter's instinct was to pull away from Alex, and he wondered if it was Alex's as well, but the two of them remained locked together, leaning all the more on each other for support.

"Oh, it's the last time; oh, it's the last time; oh, it's the last time," the depressed song went on in the silence sitting squarely between them. Peter had the sense that his life was significantly changing and that he didn't have to do anything to cause this. A significant chain reaction had already started, and in a matter of days everything would be different. He remembered that first night on the fire escape with William, how the two of them had talked into the early morning. That anticipation of a first kiss was just how Alex's arm felt upon his shoulders, like a new piece of clothing, exciting and not yet worn in, allowing you the illusion that it made you look different.

"What do you want to do?" Alex mumbled in Peter's ear.

Peter remembered the expensive dinner Alex had paid for. He pictured Alex's red Mustang, the top down, racing south on Lake Shore Drive. He remembered Alex describing his condominium with sweeping views from three sides, and he imagined the perfectly cool air circulating from ducts in every room. Diane pulled Tom out on the dance floor. Diane always seemed to have a way of keeping her life from overlapping with anyone else's. She and Tom moved well together on the dance floor, the way two people are supposed to, and Peter guessed Diane would know the name of the song.

Alex repeated the question.

"I want to see the view," Peter finally replied.

31

NO POETIC JUSTICE
FOR NUCLEAR WASTE

Rose's recurring nightmare would start out ordinary, a scene of her out with her family on an excursion or, one from later in her life, working in the regulated quiet of the university library in the company of fellow workers and students. "It's like the dream is purposely deceiving me, lulling me with a peaceful scenario," she had once told a psychiatrist. "It pulls me firmly into its lair, that deep sleep that is so hard to come out of."

Once Rose was in that deep sleep, violence would break out around her. Passing strangers who, moments ago, had seemed inconspicuous, would pull out guns and knives, curl their fingers into fists, step into the foreground, and attack Rose, her friends, or family, depending on the setting. There would never be blood or gore; Rose would never feel any direct physical pain. What she felt was a thundering in her ears as everything went into a kind of heavy slow motion until she woke up in a sweat, gasping for air in the dark quiet of her bedroom. If she tried to close her eyes again, the horrible scene would instantly come to life, and she had no choice but to get up for a few hours until her mind could thoroughly empty the thoughts from her head.

"It started when I was about twelve," she continued to the psychiatrist, whom she had consulted a few years ago when the dreams returned after an absence of nearly ten years. "I remember having them nearly every other night for a year. I would usually climb in bed with my parents, and my mother would let me sleep next to her for a few hours until I felt like I could return alone to my room."

The psychiatrist had nothing to tell Rose that she hadn't already considered. He spoke of a child's first awareness of a violent world, of seeing violent images on television, and reading of historical events like the Holocaust and Hiroshima. As Rose grew older, the dreams occurred less frequently until they stopped altogether. Rose stopped seeing the psychiatrist once a month passed without having the dreams, though the psychiatrist wished to press on with discussions of Rose's relationships with her family (her father in particular) as well as her lack of relationships with men, going so far as to hint that Rose might actually prefer women.

"I'd say I distrust women as much as I distrust men," Rose responded and promptly canceled all future appointments.

Rose's ongoing complaint with the International Revolutionary Socialists was their refusal to rule out the possibility of violence in order to achieve the necessary revolution to overthrow the capitalist state.

"Remember Russia," Lydia had chided her in front of the group once, in the typical way members liked to use the Russian Revolution as a model for what they hoped to facilitate while, at the same time, always admitting that after a few brief years, the revolution itself had dissolved into an authoritarianism that was no different from what the Russian people had previously lived under. The only tolerated differences of opinion were whether the revolution failed with the death of Trotsky or at the end of Stalin's regime. Rose had no patience for the group's fringe members, who believed Stalin's years of forced labor and executions were necessary for the country to industrialize and defend itself from surrounding hostile nations. "In the years following the overthrow of the czar, there was a need for the workers to enjoy a certain amount of violence to keep the fallen regime in check," Lydia continued. "You can't exactly expect that a complete overthrow of the existing power will be politely accepted like a normal election. When you start a garden, there's a certain amount of weeding and tilling that needs to be done in order for it to grow."

Walter didn't bother to stick up for Rose, something Rose had noticed for the past couple of meetings. She understood that it was partially his reluctance to give opinions that had hidden motives for protecting his girlfriend, but at the same time she worried that his interest in her was truly waning.

With this in mind she agreed to meet Carl again at the Green Café to discuss strategy against the University of Chicago's involvement with the Yucca Mountain Project. Though she had promised her father, the board of regents, and herself not to be involved in any political actions, especially ones involving the university, Rose could feel Walter's skeptical glance whenever she came under attack from Lydia in meetings. She was desperate to rekindle any of the lost intimacy she had noticed.

"Tell me what you know about this nuclear waste poetry reading," Carl whispered, moments after they had seated themselves in a corner a safe distance from the other customers. Rose wrinkled her brow at him even though she knew exactly what he was referring to. "The event the university's announced for the end of the month, a poetry reading with Joanne Mueller and some other woman to brag about their humanitarian interests in saving civilization from the dangers of nuclear waste."

"I've heard of it," she admitted.

"What have you heard?"

"Nothing more than what you just said. It's a press conference masquerading as a literary event. I doubt the university president could really deny that." Rose was tired of Carl continuing to try to use her position at the school to give him information regarding nuclear waste. She was tired of the way he ignored the delicate position she was already in politically and was tired of his ignorance regarding her job as a keeper of information at the library, which involved a certain amount of discretion. Rose was especially tired of the name Joanne Mueller.

Carl leaned closer to her over their steaming espressos. "This is our opportunity. No need for organizing a demonstration and hoping for the media to respond. What does Lydia call it? The media held captive? Let the other side send out the press releases, book the hall, and plan the date. All we have to do is show up and get the stage."

"Are you suggesting we shout down a poetry reading?" Rose asked incredulously. Not only was Carl asking that she, Rose Gluck, infamous campus radical who denies the campus its freedom of speech, should go to a campus event to again shout down a speaker, but that the speaker be Joanne Mueller, the actual rival for her lover's attentions.

"Well, I've been entertaining a few possible scenarios," Carl said.

"Do I need to remind you that I am the only one in the entire chapter, if not the whole national organization, who is even willing to discuss your interest in how nuclear waste affects the working class? Just who do you expect to mass at the brigades?"

Carl looked around nervously, and Rose realized she had let her voice get too loud. There were hardly any customers in the café, as it was an extremely muggy night outside; and despite the air-conditioning, the Green Café was barely able to fight the heat from its own coffee brewers.

"I'm sorry, Carl, I just don't feel like this is the right windmill."

"Then why listen to me at all? Can you honestly tell me that nothing I have told you about this whole corporate welfare energy state means anything to you? Maybe Lydia was right, you *have* bought into what this university tells you."

"Lydia said that?"

"I defended you, Rose; I told her she didn't know what she was talking about. I told her you had already been a great help in giving me information about the university's dealings with the government. I told her you were extremely sympathetic. And I also told her she was just jealous because you were involved with Walter."

"You did not," Rose stammered, feeling her face heat up at the mere mention of the soap opera she had allowed herself to fall into.

"Who's right, then? Lydia or me?" Carl leaned back in his chair and folded his spindly arms across his chest.

Rose felt Walter was slipping away from her. She believed people like Lydia were doing all they could to prove her lack of commitment to the organization, a significant part of Walter's life. By helping Carl, she could answer her critics; and if she refused to be involved, Carl would surely give Lydia all the ammunition she needed to make Rose look weak, foolish, and bourgeois in front of Walter. Rose sensed all her energy fail her as she realized the trap Carl had set. She simultaneously hated and admired him and wondered why, with this kind of manipulation, the group couldn't manage to seize control of the country.

"What do you want me to do?"

"I knew you wouldn't fail me."

"I can't leap on some stage and grab the microphone from Joanne Mueller's hand. My position is already under probation, and with one more incident I'm out, and that will surely be of little use to you in the future."

"Understood. I will need a more detailed itinerary than that ridiculous press release."

"I can do that."

"And I need a map of the auditorium they plan to have this thing in, a map that clearly indicates exits and adjoining rooms."

"I can do that."

"I also need a list of who will be in attendance, VIPs and press being the most important."

"Not a problem."

"And I need a security report outlining exactly what security precautions the university intends to employ. Will they be relying on the Chicago police as well? If so, I need to know what kind of backup they will be providing."

"What scenarios are you considering?"

Carl stared at her, ignoring the question. "Can you handle that?"

"Of course—"

"Good. I haven't determined what kind of demonstration we can pull off. As you pointed out, our manpower is limited. Perhaps just a banner will unroll from the back balcony. Harmless. But a nice visual for the newspapers."

Rose smiled at this idea. "No Poetic Justice for Nuclear Waste!" she imagined it saying. "Joanne Mueller's Elegy for Planet Earth!" She couldn't wait to help Carl paint the words on the bedsheet.

"Tell me what else I can do," she gushed, her energy newly restored.

"Well, that should do it for now. Of course I might need you the day of the reading."

"I wouldn't miss it," Rose replied. "I wouldn't miss it for the world."

The next night Rose showed up at Walter's apartment for their routine Tuesday night of sex. But when he let her in, she noticed he seemed distracted, explaining that he wanted to finish the book he was reading and hoped she had brought along some work herself. She assured him she had but immediately changed her mind. "Come on," she said, walking over to him and taking his hands. "It's so warm out, and I've been cooped up in air-conditioning all day. Let's take a walk by the lake."

Walter glared up at her, his book still open on his lap.

"Oh, please, just half an hour; the exercise will do us both good."

Walter's face relaxed a little as he shut his book and let her pull him up from the chair. Rose had planned to tell him all about her plans with Carl to take on the university's nuclear program, but once they were outside walking along the rocky edge of Lake Michigan, she realized she couldn't. Surely he would rankle at the involvement of Joanne, possibly defend his ex-girlfriend, and go so far as to warn her. But once the protest exposed Joanne Mueller as just another cog in the corporate machine, he would realize how lucky he was to be with someone as like-minded as Rose and how glad he was to have someone like Joanne out of his bed, and on the other side of the barricade where she always belonged.

Rose linked her arm through Walter's, and they walked in silence in the heavy night air.

"When I first arrived in Chicago, I used to take walks along the lake every night," Walter said. Rose had no idea how to respond to this as she had grown up with the lake and had taken it for granted for as long as she could remember. To their right, the lights from the tall condominiums set off the sky with an important glow. On their left, the lake created a black void, broken only by the lights of a few passing boats. "Do you know how it is that we have this park stretching all along the lakeshore in this city?"

Rose knew but decided to let him tell her.

"After the great fire, the city seized all the property along the lakeshore that had previously been owned privately. They decided to take advantage of the catastrophe to plan what would eventually become one of the premier cities in the world. Can you imagine how expensive this property must be? And here it is, available to any citizen to walk along any time he or she chooses to."

Rose smiled at him. She enjoyed pretending to be the one without the necessary historical detail, civic information, or appropriate analysis. She had often looked down upon women who allowed the men in their lives to take on this more masculine, intellectual role, but now she wondered if it wasn't necessary to do it every now and then for the well-being of the relationship. Still, she couldn't help herself.

"But don't you think," she said a bit hesitantly, so as not to sound as if she disagreed with anything he had just told her, "don't you think that the politicians at that time realized the potential property value for the city would be much higher if it was planned with more parks and promenades?"

"Of course," Walter joined in, as Rose had hoped he would. "Just think how much more valuable those condos are with a view of this park than they ever would be if the city had just been allowed to industrialize itself right into the water, polluting everything in the process."

Walter's arm tightened to pull her a bit closer, and he slowed his walk, not noticing that a half hour had already passed and they still had to walk all the way back.

Rose's dream that night started off with her sitting in a grand auditorium with Walter. There was a full orchestra on stage, and she realized they must have gone to a symphony as everyone around them was dressed in tuxedos and gowns. Walter was wearing jeans and an old, bright red wool sweater. Rose was equally comfortable in a long cotton skirt and a loose-fitting T-shirt. Walter was holding Rose's hand; and even though Rose had never seen any classical music in his apartment, he seemed to be enjoying the soothing sound of the orchestra. Slowly the aisles of the theater started to fill with men carrying guns and clubs. They were not policemen. Some were dressed in tuxedos, while others wore what appeared to be fatigues. Walter's hand tightened on Rose's. As Rose's ears thundered, the scene around her collapsed into violence, like a whirlpool churning up the entire theater, and she felt she was holding on to Walter's hand to stay afloat in the storm that had descended.

She woke up, sitting up straight on the bed in a complete sweat, and found she was still holding Walter's hand. She looked over her shoulder and saw him looking up at her from his pillow. "Are you all right?"

Rose realized she was naked and in his apartment. She took a few deep breaths to slow her heart rate down and wiped at the sweat on her face. "Just a nightmare," Rose said, unable to look at him.

"About what?"

Rose sunk back down on her pillow and pulled the sheet back up over her. Walter moved in a little closer and slipped an arm under her neck and pulled her close to his chest. She remembered sleeping next to her mother as a child, how her mother would soothe her by running her fingers through her hair until she was able to sleep again. Her father would stay asleep on the other side of the bed, and Rose was always glad he never woke up to find her there. She pressed her free hand flatly on Walter's hairy chest and let her fingers spread out. She could sense her own heartbeat slowing to the same steady beat of Walter's.

"You stayed the night," Walter said, his voice slightly muffled by her bunched-up hair.

"Yes."

"I'm glad you did."

When Rose shut her eyes, the images in front of her did not break up into chaos. She saw the park built along the lake. Green grass where burnt-out buildings had once stood.

32

THE LAST TIME

"I know," Diane said.

"What do you know?" William asked.

Diane sighed and adjusted the pillow behind her back, which supported her against the wall. They were sitting on her futon, and the sun was coming up, an ominously deep orange sun. William had called around six-thirty. When Diane suggested he come over, William guessed that Sink wouldn't be there.

Diane billowed some air up inside her oversized T-shirt then pulled her long hair out to one side and dropped it over her shoulder. She was stalling. William couldn't believe it. He suddenly had to be prepared to hear the worst from everyone, all starting with Peter Brooks's phone call just an hour earlier.

"I ran into Peter the other night. At Prague. He wasn't alone."

"Why didn't you tell me this?" William's body seemed to fly forward in a kind of relief, almost glad to have his emotions distracted by his best friend's poor judgment so he didn't have to wallow in the empty room of his boyfriend's announcement that they were breaking up.

"I didn't feel it was my business at the time," Diane said, her eyes locking on to William's in a way to prove her concern.

"You're my friend. You're my best friend. What if I had run into Sink with another woman, wouldn't you expect me to—"

"No." Diane's eyes fell down to her hands in her lap, and William had the sensation he was falling with them, down a long fire escape, with Sink and Peter watching from the top. "I wouldn't expect you to tell me such a thing."

They were both silent. Above them were muffled footsteps of their neighbors forcing themselves to start the day. William stared at what he imagined was Sink's side of the bed. The pillow looked untouched, and next to it was a pile of his dirty clothes. He couldn't decide which of their situations was worse: having a boyfriend who would come and go as he pleased or not having one at all. Again, he realized just how little he knew of the woman he claimed as his best friend and felt even worse.

"He called to tell you this at five in the morning?" Diane finally asked, and they both laughed.

"I hadn't heard from him for two days. I had left about ten messages, and I finally said that if he didn't at least call to tell me he was alive, I was going to the police. So he called back three hours later and told me he had met someone and that he was confused and didn't want to be lying to me. Of course I pleaded with him that maybe this other person was just a fling and we could work it out, which made him tell me it wasn't like that and it was totally over. How embarrassing."

Diane sat forward and put her hand on his elbow. William knew she expected him to cry, but he didn't; he hadn't even felt like crying. Everything still seemed like a strange dream, like he was watching himself from a distance.

"Who was he with at Prague anyway?" William finally thought to ask. Diane sunk back on her pillow, and William knew things were going to keep getting worse for a while longer.

Diane forced William to take a shower and come with her to

open the Book Bar and Café. He didn't really like the idea of being out in public, but he knew he did not want to go back to his dormitory room and stare at all the mementos from his six-month relationship. Diane set him up at a corner table with coffee and a Danish and went to work behind the counter with Tom.

From the way Tom kept glancing over at him, William knew Diane had told him what had happened. There had been a time when William had thought Tom was cute. Now William only wanted to run from him and nearly everybody else except Diane, but he had to wait until Diane's morning break because she had promised to go back with him to his dormitory and put everything that reminded him of Peter in a box and store it in his small storage space in the basement. William did not think he could physically do this by himself.

Just as he was starting to mull over the strange news that he had been dumped for his boring, middle-aged poetry teacher, Alex Dupree, Joanne Mueller walked in and came up to his table. At the sight of her William felt like crying for the first time in what was proving to be the longest day of his life.

"You don't look so good," the ever-observant poet-in-residence pointed out after the briefest exchange of greetings.

"I was dumped," William blurted out and, remembering the short stories of Joanne's marriage, added, "for another guy."

Joanne sat down without asking permission and locked her gaze on him the same way Diane had earlier, as if she were holding him to the side of a lifeboat. "This was the poet, right?" Joanne asked carefully, obviously remembering the rather bad poems William had been turning in since last February. "The one at U. of C.?"

"Right. And you won't believe who he dumped me for," William went on, determined to get it all out at once. "Your fellow faculty member Alex Dupree."

William noticed Tom look up at him from across the room while Joanne fell back in her chair, her hands spread flat on the table in front of her.

"Alex? How in the world does he know Alex?"

"I don't know. Maybe your friend Vivian Reape introduced them."

"Vivian?" Joanne exclaimed. William had the feeling he was now the one holding up Joanne alongside the boat. "How did he know Vivian?"

"She was tutoring Peter in poetry. Telling him what to read, critiquing his poems."

"Was he paying her?"

"Of course not. Peter has no money. He's work-study, interns in the nuclear science department five days a week."

Joanne leaned her forehead down on her hand, and William again had the feeling that he was watching a scene play itself out from a distance. He didn't have any idea what either of them would say next.

"Is that all of it?" Joanne asked, glancing up at him again.

William didn't know exactly what she was referring to, but kept talking.

"Actually, no. Diane told me that Alex is starting up a writing program at U. of C. next fall. Some kind of grant through Vivian Reape. So Peter will effectively be dating his teacher."

At this Joanne stood up and slung her bag over her shoulder. "I have to put a stop to this," she said.

"To Alex?"

"No," she called back to him over her shoulder. "Vivian."

Once the door had slammed shut behind her, Diane rushed over. "What did you say to her?"

"I don't know," William said defensively. "Do you think you could take your break early? I really need to get out of here."

Diane sat with William on his single bed once she had finished taking the box she had filled with pictures, letters, assorted trinkets, a cardigan sweater, and even a journal down to the storage space.

318

With so many objects gone, William's cell-like single room looked even more sterile, and Diane decided to extend her break into an early lunch.

"Now what?" William asked, smoothing the light blue comforter with his hand.

"Now nothing," Diane answered. She knew William would expect her to be honest. "Take it day by day, think of every day that passes as another mile past it, and eventually it will be out of sight."

"Maybe I should write him a letter, not call, but a letter."

"Saying what?"

"I don't know, something like, 'Did this really happen?' "

Diane paused before saying what she had been wanting to say all day. "You didn't have any kind of clue that the relationship wasn't going the way you both wanted it to?"

William looked up at her a bit startled. "His grandmother wants to will him her farmhouse. For me, that's exactly what I'd like. For him, it made him feel suffocated. We're majoring in poetry, Diane; aren't you a bit paranoid about what's going to happen once we hand in that last poem?"

Diane laughed. "You mean we're not going to start getting paid for it?"

"I guess I freaked him out."

"I wouldn't be so hard on yourself. Look at this Alex Dupree thing. In my opinion it's Peter who's paranoid and searching for the safe road after graduation. What better way than to sleep with the future head of your writing program, who also happens to have pretty incredible views from his condominium?"

"And what a view of a head it is." They laughed some more until Diane noticeably looked at her watch. William felt the impending loneliness of seeing people go on with their lives as he sat immobile in his small room waiting for his to start up again. "I think about him and Alex and feel like I hardly even knew who he was. That nags at me."

"Do you really think I have a fucking clue who Sink Lewis is?"

William caught her eyes. "Actually, I think you have a pretty good handle on him."

Diane stood up and reached for her bag. "Yes, you're probably right." She leaned over and kissed him lightly on his forehead. Her hair brushed around his face, and the feeling was foreign to him.

William tried to read for a few hours after Diane left, but nothing held his attention. Every time he closed his eyes, he could clearly picture Peter as if his brain were working overtime to create a permanent image he could go back and refer to years from now. Every memory revolved around last times. The last time they had had sex, over a week ago, in Peter's strangely subdivided room in that ruined mansion in Hyde Park. The walls were paper thin so they had to be careful not to make a noise, and this had somehow made it more erotic for William. He hadn't remembered to ask Peter if it turned him on, too. Every memory somehow turned into a specific regret. The last time they had seen each other was exactly three nights ago. They'd met at an Italian restaurant in New Town, exactly halfway between the two of them. Peter hadn't wanted to come all the way up to Lake Bluff, and William hadn't wanted to go all the way down. William tried remembering specific details of their conversation, searching for clues.

"I don't think Vivian's happy with my work," Peter had said. Their meeting had been normal, a brief half-hug, both still bashful about too much public affection. Peter was wearing a very bright, green crew-neck shirt, which made his eyes seem green even though they were blue. He had on his designer jeans, which fit him perfectly, low waisted and not too long at the crotch. At first William couldn't remember what he had been wearing, but then he realized it was an old white oxford and a pair of dirty khakis. They had reached that point where they didn't really pay particular attention to how they dressed when they saw each other, a lazy comfort William relished.

"She keeps telling me to reread the same stupid poets. Minor poets. Thomas Campion, Thomas Campion. Don't ever read him, just ask me; I can just recite whatever it is you want to hear."

William tried to remember if he had mentioned that Alex Dupree had forced them to read Thomas Campion for the few weeks Joanne Mueller was out of class leaving her husband. He tried to remember every time he had ever mentioned Alex Dupree. He had surely brought him up with disdain, telling amusing stories about what a dull teacher he was and how his only critique of his students' poems was a literal counting out of metrical feet and end words slashed with his red pen because they were half-rhymed or didn't rhyme at all.

"I'm definitely applying to law school next year," Peter had said. "I don't want to be a lawyer; I would just like to get school over with all at once and have it to fall back on."

William hated this conversation. They had it often, and William just let Peter talk, not wanting to say what he really thought. Peter probably knew. Whenever he asked William about his plans beyond Lake Bluff, all William could come up with was wanting to move to the North Side of Chicago.

"And do what?"

"Rent an apartment."

"I mean what kind of work?"

"Something that will hopefully not take up too much of my time."

At this point William would get the idea that Peter was letting him talk, not really saying what he thought.

After dinner they had both stood on opposite sides of the elevated Belmont train track. William remembered looking around and, when he was sure no one was looking, doing a little dance to make Peter laugh. He did a soft shoe, a tap, even a few ballet poses. Peter smiled and looked around him anxiously, afraid someone would see. William remembered that Peter's train had arrived first. The last time he saw him, Peter was looking for an open seat on the el car as the train pulled away. *How embarrassing,* William thought, *dancing like an idiot, while he was figuring out how to break up with me.*

The phone rang, and William grabbed it on its first ring.

"Is that you?" came Oma's raspy voice. William didn't bother with disappointment that it wasn't Peter. This was just as interesting.

"Hello, how are you?" Did she know? Was she calling to console him? Perhaps she had some ideas about how to bring her grandson around?

"Fine, fine." Oma hated the phone and always barked into it, trying to bring the conversation quickly to its point and hang up. "I wanted to know if you are still coming over for dinner tomorrow. Peter called and says he can't. I told him fine; I still wanted you. So are you?"

William fell back flat on his bed and stared up at the ceiling. Oma had talked to Peter, and he hadn't told her? Peter had not even objected to her inviting William over anyway? Again, he felt far away, watching himself lying flat on the bed holding the phone to his ear, wondering what he could possibly say.

"Hello? William! Are you there?"

"Yes."

"Yes, you'll come?"

"Yes."

"Good. I'll see you at seven. And don't bring wine. That stuff you brought last time was just terrible. I'll save it for cooking or something. If you must bring something, bring bread. And maybe some brie. You figure it out."

Oma hung up, and William just let the phone sit on his shoulder for a few minutes. When the recorded operator started repeating that a phone was off the hook, he finally sat up and hung it back up. He decided not to think about having dinner with Oma until tomorrow.

Diane called twice that night to make sure he was all right. Each

322

time he tried not to let his disappointment come through his voice when she said hello, though he was sure she knew it was there anyway. She told him he could come over if he wanted and that Sink was there. But Sink was probably the last person he wanted to see outside of Alex Dupree, and he graciously declined. He promised her he would be fine, that he was taking a sleeping pill and would call her in the morning.

Another few hours went by before he thought to sit down at his typewriter. Was it Joanne Mueller who had said never to write when you're in love? No, she had been quoting Vivian Reape, using various bits of her wisdom as examples for never saying never with regard to the subjects of poetry. Still, William had felt singled out by the comment. He decided Vivian had been right. He also realized she had been right about another thing. Peter was most definitely a lousy poet.

33

DECLINING AN INVITATION
TO DINNER, PART II

One good thing about Alex's address was that you could find it without using street numbers or directions in case a time came when you desperately needed to see him. For Joanne, that time had finally arrived. When she left William at the Book Bar and Café, she went straight to Sandburg Hall and knocked on Alex's office door. She then went to her own office and tried his home number. With all that William had just told her about his new lover, Joanne decided he was there and not picking up so she hung up on the answering machine and got in her car to find out. Joanne had never been to Alex's well-appointed home. He had often talked of throwing some kind of faculty party but had never followed through despite Helen Drake's endless inquiries. Joanne had always been curious to see the kind of place she could only see pictures of in interior design magazines, and, in a way, her impulsive decision to arrive at his door to find out firsthand about Vivian's alleged job offer was partially motivated by a curiosity to see just how better-off the better-off Alex Dupree lived.

Joanne aimed her compact car squarely at the sleekly curved tower of Lake Point as she sped south on Lake Shore Drive.

"Alex Dupree," Joanne told the doorman, using as much authority in her voice as possible. The old man smiled and picked up a phone. After what must have been a few rings, he glanced at her and asked if he was expecting her.

"Of course he is," Joanne lied. "Tell him it's Joanne Mueller."

The doorman repeated this into the phone and, after an excruciating pause, hung up and instructed her to the elevator bank and told her the floor.

"Joanne, what on earth?" Alex was standing in his open door in a black silk robe that came down to his knees. Joanne had the feeling he was literally blocking her way into the condominium and knew she would have to plead her case. "I hate dropping in on you like this, but I really don't know who to turn to."

Alex looked over his shoulder and, aiming his voice down the long hall behind him, said, "Of course, Joanne, do come in."

He literally steered her to the end of the hallway to a sitting room filled with light from three sides. Joanne politely kept her eyes straight in front of her until she was safely seated on an ornately carved, needlepoint chair.

"Alex, really, this is lovely."

"I know," Alex said impatiently, definitely not in the mood to provide a tour. He now stood blocking the door Joanne had just come through. "Can I get you coffee? A drink?"

"No, please, nothing. I just wanted to talk to you for a moment."

Alex relaxed a little and sat down in the matching antique chair next to her, careful to keep his robe from flying open as he crossed his legs. To her right Joanne could see the route her car had just taken down Lake Shore Drive. She wondered if Alex ever sat and watched for someone who was running late or kept guard for anyone he didn't want to see. Outside the temperature had gone well over ninety, but Joanne's skin shivered in the abundance of air-conditioning swirling around her.

"Is it true? You're going to U. of C.?"

Alex jerked his head back at this question and seemed unable to reply.

"Don't ask how I heard. Trust me, no one else knows a thing, though I think you should call Douglas Skidmore soon so the school has enough time to replace you."

"I have received an offer," Alex said, and Joanne noticed his slight smile. He had probably been looking forward to telling her of his success.

"Vivian procured this for you?"

Again Alex's head jerked out of his temporary self-satisfied smile, and he looked alarmed.

"Don't get me wrong, I'm very happy for you. It's a good opportunity, and I can't think of a better poet for the job. I'll miss you, you've been there for me when I've needed you; and I hope you think the same of me." Joanne said all of this with the utmost of sincerity, and Alex's expression softened a bit, touched by this coming from his old rival. "It's Vivian I've come to talk to you about. As you know, I've been rather reluctantly involved with her in this whole Yucca Mountain Project. I can certainly use the money, but I'm a bit confused by her intentions. To be blunt, the fact that she never mentioned to me her appointing a poet-in-residence at the University of Chicago makes me suspicious. Not to take anything away from you; I just wonder now what else there is I don't know involving her dealings with the school, dealings that involve my own role in the grant money they're providing for the damned poem I'm supposed to be writing."

Alex took all of this well, a bit confused himself by what she was not exactly telling him.

"I myself would like to know her intentions," he finally said. "I'd like to know them before I call Douglas and set something in motion that I might be unable to stop."

326

"So there's nothing you can tell me," Joanne said.

"No. Perhaps you should drop in on her."

Joanne sunk back in the rather uncomfortable chair and gazed up Lake Shore Drive as if she could possibly see Vivian from where she sat. "I would, Alex, but she's back in Boston by now, and I'd rather ask her these questions in person."

"You can; she's still here," a voice said from the doorway to the hall. Alex flew out of his chair, and Joanne had to lean to the side to see around him. Standing in the door was a young man wearing another black silk robe, though his came down closer to his ankles as he was significantly shorter than Alex. He was good-looking, in a prep school way, and Joanne realized she needed no introduction.

"This is a friend of mine," Alex said, attempting one anyway.

"Do you know where I can find her?" Joanne asked the boy, ignoring Alex's large body, which still tried to block him from her.

"Right now?" he replied, stepping hesitantly into the room so Joanne wouldn't have to stretch her body so far to see him. "No, not at the moment."

Joanne sat back again, disappointed.

"But I do know where she'll be tonight." Both Alex and Joanne looked at him, surprised by this information. "She's dining at the Cliff Dwellers' Club, with Joseph Wright, the head of the Nuclear Science Program, at 8:00 P.M."

Joanne stood up and approached Peter. She towered over him, and he seemed a little afraid of her.

"What is the meeting about?"

Peter looked at Alex, whose expression seemed just as interested in the answer to Joanne's question. "I imagine it's about the poem she's writing."

"The poem?" Joanne repeated. "The poem *she's* writing?"

Joanne pushed between the two of them and started down the long hallway to the front door. She felt dizzy as she passed all the rooms of Alex's apartment and focused her eyes on the front door just as she had when she'd steered her car to Lake Point Tower minutes ago. She was aware of both of them running behind her, but she didn't look back.

"Joanne, what are you going to do?" she heard Alex call to her as she opened the door.

"Ms. Mueller," Peter said, "it was a pleasure to meet you. I've always looked forward to the day when—"

She slammed the door behind her and banged on the elevator button with the heel of her hand. She could hear the muffled voices of Alex and Peter, but neither one of them seemed to have the courage to pursue her any farther.

Joanne spent the rest of the day in her apartment, screening her phone calls and trying to decide her next step. At one point she picked up the phone and started dialing Jon's number but quickly slammed it down before pressing the last digit. The heat was unbearable, but she hardly noticed it. Around five, she sat down at her typewriter and started madly typing out a poem for the first time in nearly a year. It was a strange mix of emotional imagery and life questions. She pushed through a dozen lines without any real idea of what the poem was about and paid no attention to any formal structures. Joanne had not made a career writing poetry in this fashion. She usually chose her subjects and forms well in advance of sitting down at her typewriter. Today, however, as the hot sun was finally obstructed by the buildings west of her, she felt like she was behind the wheel of her car as she wrote, her mind bombarded with ideas, and she dutifully recorded them as fast as she could. At one point she wondered if this was the poem, the poem she'd presumed she was to have been writing for the past six months, the poem she had learned to dread, had researched like a science report, and now, it seemed, the poem she was to lose.

At six she dragged herself from her typewriter and took a hot shower. As she stood beneath the spray of water, she found herself going over finances; how much was in her savings, how much was in her checking, how much was in her purse. She thought about her car. She tried to calculate what needed to be done to it, how much that would cost, and finally, just where she was expecting to drive it to that would justify such expensive work.

She realized she had no outstanding invoice for any of her short stories and no stories were currently in the mail to bring in any extra income. Her initial check for the Yucca Mountain Project had been cashed and already figured in her slim totals for her checking and savings accounts. As she lightly toweled herself off, she knew she had to proceed extremely carefully. She at least needed one more check equal to the amount of the one she and Vivian had already split; that is, she had presumed Vivian had divided it equally between them.

She pulled out her thin wool suit, the same one Vivian had complimented her on at the Cliff Dwellers' Club last winter when the whole thing began. It was obviously too warm for an August night in the middle of a heat wave, but Joanne had no choice. Besides, something in Joanne's determination seemed to keep every pore of her body tightly sealed against the heat. It also occurred to her that even though her name would not be present on one of the half a dozen lists she needed to get by to go up to the restaurant, perhaps someone would remember her in that suit. She doubted this, but would take any help she could get.

While she was brushing out her hair, her machine picked up, and Louis's voice came on, wondering how she was, pointing out that he hadn't heard from her for a while. Joanne frowned at the thought of talking to him. She remembered William's puffy face as he told her about Peter. She thought about how her own students were of the age to go through the same adult disappointments she had and how there seemed to be a cycle that, like the heat, wouldn't seem to break. Louis had hinted at the idea of Joanne living with him in a large Georgetown town house in Washington. Perhaps a separate studio out back where she could write, in the vicinity of many well-known and well-endowed universities. No more depressing thoughts about the totals in her savings and checking accounts, no more bad dreams about what could possibly be going on under the hood of her gasping compact car, no more niceties to people who gave out money, no more dinners at Jon's or lunches with Vivian. She pictured Alex Dupree in his black silk robe standing at the window overlooking Lake Shore Drive, impatient for someone to arrive. Louis Cunningham suddenly seemed poised on the same perch, but Joanne decided to head in the opposite direction.

The front desk of Root Tower, which held the Cliff Dwellers' Club aloft, was not a problem.

"I think I left my credit card upstairs," Joanne said with urgency, hardly bothering to stop moving as she passed by. The guard nodded with a look of concern, and she made it to the elevator bank. She told the elevator operator the same thing, remembering that there were at least two elevators to the top. Naturally, she had taken the other one up and down just hours previously.

The front desk waiting for her at the top floor was another matter altogether. It was an elegant mahogany desk, giving the impression that you were there to attend an important board meeting, with leather-bound member lists and guest lists stacked neatly on each side of the stately old woman behind it. Fortunately, two people were standing at the desk blocking the woman's view of the elevator, which made a soft "ding" as the doors opened. Joanne immediately walked to the heavy door that was the entrance to the club and, once she had her hand on the doorknob, turned back around and called out, "Oh, excuse me, which is the door for the rest room?"

The elderly woman looked up a bit confused, but politely instructed her that it was the next door down, inside the club, which Joanne had remembered from being there six months ago. She quickly smiled and pulled open the door and was inside.

"Good evening, ma'am, you are joining someone?" Joanne recognized the same maître d' who had seemed like the first friendly face she had encountered when she had come with her name on the proper list last winter. Joanne was relieved to see him and even thought he still recognized her.

"Yes," Joanne said. "Vivian Reape's table."

The maître d' smiled and lightly touched her sleeve. Joanne couldn't remember when she had last dry-cleaned the suit and tried to keep as much distance from him as possible as he ushered her through the handsome room to a table with excellent views.

Vivian saw Joanne when she was just a table away. She didn't gasp or drop her menu, as Joanne had imagined she would. She politely smiled and nodded to the empty chair facing her, though this time Joanne's chair looked out at all the sparkling lights of the office towers around them—surely this chair had been designated for Prof. Joseph Wright. Vivian most definitely had something very important to ask of him.

Joanne sat down and joined Vivian in silence as the maître d' pushed in her chair and left.

"I take it this isn't just a happy coincidence," Vivian said, picking up her martini.

Joanne just stared at her, realizing she didn't have to ask Vivian anything. A waiter moved by offering her a drink, but Joanne remembered the drunken state she had been in when Vivian had so rudely advised her to stay close to Jon Sullivan, to take any money she could get her hands on, and to stop using so much slang in her verse. She politely declined.

"How long were you planning on stringing me on?" Joanne asked.

"You have the wrong idea."

"I finally got the idea."

Vivian wrinkled her brow at her, and Joanne knew she was trying to guess who had told Joanne whatever it was she knew.

"You just involved me to get to Jon."

"That's ridiculous. It was a nice foot in the door, but your husband's silly rock piles are hardly what could bring about all that I am bringing about."

"Then why? Why make me your secretary for six months? Is the National Institute of Poetry so short staffed?"

"You are a young, headstrong woman. This project is beyond you."

Joanne laughed. "What, exactly, are your credentials in the art of *writing* poetry?"

"My credentials are based on a lot more than turning journal entries into short stories and posting them up in any rag that will take them."

Joanne's face didn't move. Despite the attack and despite the view, Joanne's eyes stayed directly on Vivian's, wanting her to go on.

"Do you remember coming to me over ten years ago with your silly yearbook verses? Do you remember pleading with me to take you in, to guide you, to move you through a career in a field not exactly known for a plethora of entry-level positions? How dare you sit here now, uninvited, I might add, and so rudely try to compare whatever credentials I may have been stupid enough to hand over to you so that you can throw them back in my face in comparison to my own lifetime of work. Has anyone, ever, had the opportunity to say, 'How dare you, Joanne Mueller?' I'd say not. I'm happy to be the first."

Vivian drained what was left in her martini glass and set it down with enough show that a waiter quickly ran over to replace it. Joanne's face still bore no expression as she stared back, though her cheeks felt a slight tingle, as if they had just been slapped. She could feel herself teetering on the edge of something. On one side was the young girl faced with her powerful instructor, and on the other was the woman she had somehow become. She knew the routine of playing the student. She had done it for all the years she had known Vivian. As for that strangely formless woman outside the windows, beyond the majestic towers, and out in the empty black space where Lake Michigan seemed ready to catch her, Joanne had no clear idea who she really was. She let go of

Vivian's gaze and looked down at her wrinkled lap. What was in-between? What had she really come here for in the first place?

"Why then?" she found herself repeating. "Why string me along?"

Vivian's face suddenly flushed as she looked beyond Joanne's shoulder. As Vivian clumsily stood up, Joanne looked back at a rather poorly dressed, middle-aged man, who must surely have been the head of the nuclear science department at the University of Chicago.

"Vivian, sorry I'm late," he said, looking anxiously at Joanne as the maître d' did too, wondering how a table for two had been set for a party of three in a place that had probably not made such a mistake in its hundred-year history.

"I'm Joseph Wright," he said, extending a hand to Joanne, as Vivian seemed reluctant to introduce them herself.

"Joanne Mueller," Joanne replied, not really caring anymore what would happen.

"Joanne Mueller? I have looked so forward to the opportunity of meeting you. Just the other day the dean and I were remarking on how elusive you have been throughout this entire process, and what with the reading only a month away, we had hoped, by now, to have the opportunity of meeting you and expressing our admi-ration for your work. We're both looking forward to seeing any rough drafts of the poem you are planning to read from to an-nounce the poetry grant."

Vivian fell back into her chair with what sounded like a crash.

"I must apologize," the maître d' said to her. "I have no idea how this could have happened. If you would all like to wait at the bar while I—"

"No need," Joanne said, rising from her chair. "I just dropped by to say hello. There is nothing wrong with the reservation."

"You will not be joining us for dinner?" Professor Wright asked.

Everyone now looked at Joanne, and she no longer felt like she was teetering on an edge. She smoothed out the wrinkles on the front of her suit with a flourish and touched the maître d's arm to request his guidance in getting out of the place she had gone through so much trouble to get into.

"It was a pleasure to meet you, Professor Wright. I, too, look forward to the reading."

With that the maître d' led her back to the door. He still seemed confused by what had occurred, as Joanne imagined Joseph Wright and Vivian Reape were as well, but Joanne remembered Vivian's quick glance before Joanne turned away. It was a look that seemed to dare her. And after all no one, it seemed, had ever said, "How dare you, Joanne Mueller!"

At the elevator bank she saw a pay phone and didn't waste time punching in the numbers.

"Jon?" Joanne said, signaling the elevator operator who had just opened the doors to take her back down to wait for her. "Do you remember what you told me about Vivian? About calling you? Well, I'm calling you. Let's lose her."

34

CHECKED OUT

Rose wasn't a big magazine reader. Although she subscribed to the *Socialist News,* which she had mailed to her home, and *Library Science Monthly,* which she received at school, and occasionally settled down to a few stray issues of some East Coast intellectual magazines with occasional stories of interest to her, she found herself in an endless dispute between the students at the university and her own desire to strip the periodical wing of the library of everything but the few magazines "without pictures," as she liked to gauge the difference. One of Rose's most time-consuming tasks was to balance the library's budget. As costs for newer and more sophisticated computer systems mounted, the school continually lowered the amount of money she had to play with, and faced with the terrible possibility of reducing the number of titles the library could feasibly procure, she turned her attentions to the periodical room, where, in her opinion, too many students lounged around looking at fashion advertisements to avoid studying. Her plan to reduce the number of titles from close to five hundred to a little more than one hundred was met with more resistance than she had seen any political event cause in the ten years she had been working at the university.

"It is our opinion," the memo from the board of regents informed her, "that consumer periodicals provide not only well-deserved leisure reading for the student body, but also help keep our hard-working young people in touch with mass consumerism in a world that, through recent technologies, has become more and more linked with popular culture."

Defeated, Rose still managed to do her best to eliminate whatever she could from this den of mass consumerism. She quietly weeded out titles that were overlooked by students. Sometimes, she would purposely fail to renew a subscription and pretend the current issue had been checked out should a student inquire about it. She demanded that all new issues of magazines be placed on her desk so she could scan them for anything too inflammatory (a provision she had discovered in researching the small print of university guidelines for the library), and whenever she saw an opportunity, she would cancel an entire subscription based on one single racist, pornographic, or sexist remark in a given article. It was while doing this daily task that Rose happened upon what would be, for her, the most inflammatory of all such potential materials, and she didn't need to go further than the front cover.

"Nuclear Family," the cover line screamed at her as Rose stared into the eyes of Joanne Mueller. She could feel her whole body tighten up as she clutched the latest issue of CHIC-ago magazine. Rose had no trouble finding the article; it seemed the entire feature well was devoted to the story and photographs of Joanne with her husband, Jon Sullivan. Unable to even think of reading the thousands of words, she relied on pull-quotes to get the gist. " 'It's not about being pronuclear or antinuclear,' says the poet. 'The waste is all around us, and something has to be done. I can only hope that the arts might be a way for people to learn more about the energy that runs their world and decide collectively if and how they would like to change it.' " Above a more casual shot of Joanne and her husband, both of them appearing to be laughing at something one of them had said, were the words: "Married for ten years, the couple is surprised by the reaction of friends and colleagues to their work. 'It's as if I'm suddenly radioactive just by explaining it,' Joanne remarks. 'This is an issue nobody wants to hear about.' "

A few pages later were some smaller photographs of Joanne; a yearbook shot, a wedding outtake, all carefully chosen, Rose decided, to show off every inch of beauty the woman had. "I do not have a martyr complex," more display type proclaimed. "I do not imagine that anything that comes out of my typewriter can truly protect a world as large and complex as ours against something as large and complex as the storage of nuclear waste."

The magazine seemed to be in love with Joanne Mueller, spreading her face and words across the pages as naturally as those of a Hollywood actress or a seasoned politician. Rose imagined dozens of more magazine covers following. Photo shoots in artistic black and white, location setups at the top of Yucca Mountain, paparazzi photos of Joanne attending premieres and exclusive parties on the gossip pages, and Walter clipping out each one of them and keeping them in a special scrapbook underneath his bed.

"I thought it was you when I first saw it," her secretary, Lynn, said, breaking Rose's thoughts. She stood on the other side of Rose's desk and indicated the cover of *CHIC-ago* magazine, which Rose had just flung down. "Isn't that funny?"

Rose stared at Lynn and considered firing her on the spot.

"Can I take this?" Lynn asked, a bit nervously as she removed all the other magazines and correspondence from Rose's outbox and reached for *CHIC-ago*.

"No," Rose said, pulling the magazine away from her and causing Lynn to step back. "Do you really think we can just display a story like this at a school that has the most famous Department of Nuclear Science in the entire country?"

Lynn stared at her, not comprehending the severity of Rose's tone.

"It is my duty to take this straight to Professor Wright. I'm sure *he* won't have such a high opinion of it."

With that, Rose pushed past her assistant and headed for the nuclear science department, located on the opposite side of campus. When she entered the office, a young intern looked up at her curiously, and Rose quickly hid the cover of the magazine she had folded in her arms against her chest.

"I must see Professor Wright," she announced.

"Could I have your name?"

"Rose Gluck."

The intern paused again and stopped from going back to announce her arrival. "Ms. Gluck, I hope all the material you have requested has been of help to you."

At first Rose didn't understand what he was referring to. Then she suddenly remembered the hundreds of reports and budgets she had received without question from the department for her work with Carl.

"Yes," she nearly whispered. "Just updating files."

"I'm trying to get you everything regarding the reading as quickly as I can," the young man went on. "The guest list should be finalized by tomorrow."

"Tomorrow."

"Professor Wright's office is this way."

Rose followed the intern reluctantly, now wishing she had never come.

"Rose Gluck," Joseph Wright exclaimed, once she was presented at his door. "Now this *is* a surprise. What can I do for you?"

Rose realized she hadn't seen the famous department head since the last board of regents meeting. He was one of the many board members who had looked at her with a kind of amused tolerance ever since the incident with the Contra that had led to her probation. She knew exactly what men like Joseph Wright thought of her and also knew they wouldn't dare say it to her face due to her father's financial position with the university. Rose felt like her body was moving so fast her mind couldn't keep up. Like the computer search at the library, one wrong key punched and an entire subject would appear before her on the screen, making her forget what it was she had been looking for in the first place. Rose felt like she was punching at keys wildly and stared at Joseph Wright like he was some strange list of titles she had not meant to request.

"You seem agitated," Joseph said, coming around from his large desk. "Is something the matter?"

Rose *was* agitated, but more annoyed that Joanne Mueller continually had the power to break through her professional armor and leave her visibly shaking in front of someone like Joseph Wright.

"Here," Rose said, thrusting the copy of the magazine out from her. "I thought you should see this."

He took the magazine from her hand and examined the cover featuring Joanne Mueller.

"Actually," he said with a smile, "I already have a copy. But I do appreciate you bringing it to my attention."

"Do you mean to tell me you approve of this?"

Joseph sat back down behind his desk and studied Rose for a moment.

"We're the ones *paying* for it," he told her. "In fact, I just met Joanne last night for the first time. She'll be doing a reading here in a few weeks."

Rose had nothing to say. She felt the urge to run, like everything around her was radioactive and she had voluntarily walked into the very nucleus of the atom.

"As I'm sure you'd know," he continued, "someone with your experience in politics and the media, we've decided not to avoid the press in regard to Yucca Mountain but to work with them instead. That way we can control our image directly and not sit around waiting to be ambushed."

"But why Joanne Mueller?" Rose pleaded, her voice rising at

the name. "Surely somebody more respected, like Vivian Reape—"

"Vivian Reape is no longer working on the project," Joseph Wright said, and smiled. As shocked as Rose was by the news, she felt like this was the first time he had said this to someone and that he relished the words. "There was apparently some confusion on Vivian's part as to who was writing the poem. Last night, over dinner, she even went so far as to tell me she was firing Joanne from the project and planned to write the poem herself! Now, as far as we know, Vivian is not a poet, but more important is the fact that we had already done press on Joanne." He nodded at the magazine Rose still held between them. "We surely cannot afford to suddenly announce a change in poets and make ourselves look like we don't know what we're doing when there is so much more politically sensitive work ahead of us. Anyway, you can imagine how relieved I was to talk to other, high-ranked people in the program and find out that they had their own issues with Vivian. I just got off the phone with them now, and if you'll excuse me, I must now deliver the sad news to Vivian herself."

Professor Wright picked up the phone between them, and Rose, unable to respond to any of the information she had just absorbed, turned to go.

"Rose," Joseph called from behind her. Rose looked back. He had one hand over the mouth of the phone and was pointing at the magazine Rose had rolled up in her fists. "There's quite a resemblance. Any relation? Yes, hello. Vivian Reape's room, please."

Rose took it upon herself to shut his door behind her and leaned back against it for support. Despite whatever tactics she had resorted to in her years of political work, Rose was not a woman to listen in on private conversations. But as she heard the muffled voice of Joseph Wright come through the door behind her, she was truly paralyzed by what was taking place, as if, once again, Joanne Mueller had broken through all of her well-kept professional mannerisms and put her at risk.

"Vivian, Joseph Wright here. . . . Yes, dinner was lovely. . . .

Yes, it was nice to finally get a chance to talk things over. . . . Well, actually, Joanne Mueller is the reason I'm calling. Look, Vivian, I'm just going to come out with it. After much discussion with my colleagues both here and in Washington, I'm afraid we no longer have need for your services. . . ."

Even though it wasn't one of their usual nights, Rose drove straight to Walter's once she left work. Ever since she had spent the night with him, there was a bit more openness to their relationship, and Walter didn't seem surprised when he answered his door.

"You look tired," Walter said, after a brief kiss.

"I had a bad day," Rose replied.

Rose couldn't exactly recall how she had gotten through the rest of her day. She'd shut herself up in her office and found the most simplistic work available: data entry of new titles, purchase orders for requested books, internal memos regarding vacation schedules and new student tours. None of the work seemed to make any sense to her, but she had done it long enough that she was able to fill the day without having to think about anything. The cancellation of the library's subscription to *CHIC-ago* was the one task she did that caused her body to recoil into the knot it had been in all morning.

"I'm glad to see you," Walter said, and Rose sat down on his worn-out couch.

"What were you doing?" Rose asked, a little too shrilly.

"Thinking about dinner," Walter said. "Reading. Did you drop by to find out how I spend a Wednesday evening?"

"What were you reading?"

Walter folded his arms across his chest and leaned on the door frame to the kitchen. He still smiled, but a few wrinkles of concern had crossed his forehead. Rose had no idea what she wanted to say. She felt like she was punching keys again without any knowledge of what she wanted to find, and she couldn't stop herself.

"Why don't you tell me what this is all about?" Walter said, in a way that reminded Rose of her father talking to her. She jumped off the couch and started pacing around the room.

"That magazine," she yelled, "*CHIC-ago!*" She started lifting up stacks of papers and books, looked around his reading chair, and nearly overturned the coffee table. "You know what I'm talking about, *Joanne.*"

Walter finally stepped up and grabbed her by the hands. His grip was tight, and Rose was panting.

"It's in the bedroom," he said. "What is this all about?"

Rose dropped her head so her chin was resting on her chest. She imagined Joanne lying in Walter's bed, on Rose's side of the bed. When she closed her eyes, a thundering pounded her ears. She tried pulling her hands away from Walter, but he wouldn't let go.

"Why don't you just admit it," she said, jerking her head back up. "You're in love with her."

Walter thought for a moment then let go of her hands, causing Rose to fall back a step. "This is crazy."

"I knew it."

"You don't know anything about it."

"Oh, god," Rose stepped farther away. "You've been seeing her?"

"Of course not!" Walter shouted at her. His eyes were glaring at her now, and Rose wanted to take back everything she had said. "Why do you have to be so preoccupied with this? It was a long time ago. For god's sake, you obviously saw the article. It looks like she's back to being happily married anyway."

An invisible wall seemed to have collapsed. Walter sat down in his large, overstuffed chair and continued to glare at her. Rose felt like a complete stranger, like a certain illusion had been destroyed, an illusion *she* had destroyed, and he would never look at her with anything but irritation again. He would now see who she was, not who he had pretended she could be.

"I should go," Rose said.

Walter looked away from her, and she knew he was pondering whether or not to stop her.

"It was during the winter," he said, still looking away. "Last winter, you remember how terrible last winter was. We never really had a relationship. It was just sex. She lives nearby, you know, though I haven't seen her since. Anyway, she has this crappy apartment without storm windows or insulation. You know how cool the bedroom is here? In the winter it's hot, very hot; I have to keep a window open. Anyway, I guess she was cold so she would come over and sleep with me. It was over by the time spring came."

Rose had stepped all the way back to the front door.

"She actually told you this?"

Walter looked back at her again and smiled. "Well, no. I read it about a month ago, in one of her short stories."

When Rose got back to her apartment, her body felt a fatigue she hadn't felt in years, but she knew it was futile to get in bed. Her mind still raced with everything that had happened. She didn't know how long she had stood there with her back against Walter's door. It had felt like hours. She had finally repeated that she should go, and Walter merely nodded at her. She drove home very slowly, pulling over to let cars pass at times, knowing she was avoiding being home alone with her thoughts. The air coming in through the open car windows seemed even more humid than it had been all summer, air so thick she could feel it coating the inside of her throat as she breathed, heavy with exhaust, so moist it felt like the hot temperature had finally evaporated the entire lake and was pushing it down on the city.

When she got in, her answering machine indicated there was a message. She didn't bother to hope it would be Walter, and when Carl's voice came on, reminding her of the "things" he had asked her to get for him, she remembered the intern telling her "tomorrow."

Not turning on any lights, she sat down in a chair she had arranged right in front of the only window that gave her a decent view down the street to the green trees of the university campus. And then it finally started to rain.

35

DECLINING AN INVITATION TO DINNER, PART III

Joanne had said to Diane, "How kind. How kind of you to think of me." She didn't go so far as accepting the invitation to a dinner party at Sink and Diane's apartment ("With this reading coming up I really can't commit to anything definite, you understand.") and left it that she would show up if possible. The dinner was a celebration of the reprieve from the heat. Diane said she only hoped the cooler weather would hold out until the weekend; and though the forecast promised it would, it also warned of a return to hot weather by Monday with, again, no end in sight. Joanne had about as much faith in the forecast as she had any intention of attending her students' party, so she found herself mildly surprised driving all the way to Lake Bluff on a Friday night, enjoying a cool breeze naturally styling her hair, which had for so long been overinflated by humidity.

The fact was, Resident Poet Joanne Mueller was looking forward to the opportunity of being just that: Resident Poet Joanne Mueller. All summer she had been Vivian's secretary, Jon's wife, and, now, poet laureate of a highly toxic dumping ground. Since

Vivian's removal from the project, which had occurred at such speed and with such silence that Joanne had hardly slept in five days, Joanne had been on the phone with endless political, academic, and scientific bureaucrats, arguing everything from Native American protests to the very clothes she was to wear when she took the stage in a week to address press, corporate executives, and nuclear scientists to remind them of the importance of a few well-chosen words. That morning, as Joanne got out of bed from another sleepless night, she herself no longer believed how important those words actually were.

Besides, she didn't have the words. What had started out as a poetic frenzy on her typewriter the night she'd gotten Vivian fired had, in daylight, appeared too vague and misdirected, derived more from Joanne's own fear of what was ahead of her than what was to be buried in a mountain in Nevada.

"Perhaps I should go out there," she mentioned to Amy Briggs, whom she had not spoken to since the meetings in New York, as she was now in the midst of an endless discussion of the changes in the Nevadan economy, which had turned a once helpful state legislature into one determined not to bring an ounce of waste into the state. When the government had first scouted sites, Nevada had been interested in the potential millions attached to the project, but as California's property values fell and Nevada's rose, moods changed.

"And do what?" Amy nearly laughed.

"See the site, talk to people—people working there as well as the locals. Get more of a feel for what exactly I'm supposed to be writing about."

Amy sighed heavily into the phone. Joanne had come to expect this response any time Amy was presented with a request that couldn't be run through an analytical formula. "I don't see that as being an appropriate action," she finally replied.

A month ago she could have called Louis Cunningham and enlisted his help in dealing with Amy, but Joanne had broken off their relationship, feeling she was already too much "in bed" with Yucca Mountain once *CHIC-ago* magazine stared back at her from newsstands at every street corner, Jon's arm around her shoulder, literally holding her in front of the camera. As for asking Jon for any more favors, the very thought made Joanne shudder.

"She was firing you while you were firing her!" Jon had told her over the phone the day after she had stormed the Cliff Dwellers' Club. Jon seemed pleased with himself, proud to show off his powerful connections and protect his lawful wife. It made Joanne's stomach sink.

"I know what you're thinking," he continued, after Joanne had not responded. "You're feeling sorry for her. You're thinking about all the things she's done for you and how you have now repaid her by getting her publicly humiliated. Well, I wouldn't worry about it. She'll get even with you somehow. I wouldn't keep my back turned on Vivian Reape for a moment if I were you."

Joanne sighed and quickly got off the phone. Jon was right. She *was* feeling sorry for Vivian, and she took a strange comfort in the thought that Vivian would get back at her some day for all of this. But she wasn't feeling guilty about whatever possible things Vivian had done for her over the past ten years. The reason why Joanne Mueller, true resident poet of the heart, was feeling sorry for Vivian Reape was because she knew her old teacher, critic, and partner had only wished for one thing. No matter whatever money, prestige, or retirement bonus was involved, Vivian had only wished to write a decent poem.

At least Joanne was off the hook for reading anything of the "poem" at the University of Chicago in a week's time. In a brief appearance before the board of regents, Joanne had charmed the dean sufficiently to explain her reluctance to commit to any specific work-in-progress at this point, especially as the project itself had recently delayed any possible acceptance of nuclear waste for another five years, due to further studies of the depths of water tables and the remote possibility of a fault line being active. "I, too, would like more time to run some worst-case scenarios, as most writers would," Joanne told the board.

All of this drove her out of her apartment and literally all the way to Lake Bluff rather than face a Friday night at home with her five-year-delayed poem. She had been promised another check next week, Joanne remembered, and turned the radio up. She had forgotten to ask Diane who else would be attending the dinner party.

Tom McMann was the first to arrive, which was ironic because he had spent the day thinking there was no way he could possibly attend a social function after what he had been through. That morning it had been decided that the coffee bar half of Book Bar and Café would close at the end of the month, as Tom had missed two consecutive payments on his loan. This had actually been decided by his bank, but Tom only felt relief at having the decision made for him. High costs and low profits were sufficient reason for any loan to be called; and after three months hunched over a steaming espresso machine, Tom looked forward to the solitude of books. Still, it was a failure, and, financially, it meant he still owed money that he would have to generate from the bookstore's bottom line. The holiday shopping season started in three months, and he knew the bank had more optimism than he did regarding what kind of sales his eccentric store could generate. On top of all this, Book Inc. was opening a block away, and would surely arrive with high discounts and heavy advertising just in time for the return of Lake Bluff's students and the Christmas season. Finally, Tom knew he would have to find a way to tell his hostess that she would no longer have a job in a few short weeks.

Still, Tom couldn't imagine spending Friday night in his small apartment going over all this for the hundredth time. The rain earlier in the week had brought in temperatures that were humane and drew people away from their air conditioners or, as in Tom's case, electric fans, and out into the world again. It was a kind of spring after the sameness of a season like winter.

"I knew you wouldn't let me down," Diane said, answering the door, and Tom's enthusiasm dipped as he realized he was going to anyway. Sink shouted hello from the kitchen, where he seemed to be cooking some kind of pasta dish on every available pot, pan, and surface. He refused to allow anyone in, including Diane, who busied herself arranging pillows on the floor around a coffee table set up with a strange mixture of different styles of plates, glasses, and silverware. He had never been in Sink and Diane's apartment before, and it looked just how he'd imagined it would, knowing the breezy qualities of their relationship: no furniture, no organizing principles, and an overall temporary mood to the decor, which said more about their plans than their age.

"Diane, there's something I should tell you," he said, once comfortable on a pillow with a glass of sweetly cheap red wine.

"Is it bad?"

"Yes."

"Then don't tell me now." Diane smiled reassuringly and placed a hand on his shoulder. "Too much bad news has been going around lately, and I don't want dinner spoiled." Hearing this, Tom realized he really didn't have to tell her anything.

When Joanne Mueller arrived, even Sink leaned out from the kitchen in surprise. After Diane had given her the brief tour, Joanne sat down next to Tom with her own glass of red wine, and Diane forced her way into the kitchen to make sure that whatever Sink was attempting would at least be edible.

"I didn't know you were coming," Tom said, a bit nervous in the presence of someone he so admired.

"I didn't either," Joanne replied. "But a dinner party and a lot of red wine seem like the best idea I've heard in a long time."

As they talked about the weather and the long summer, Tom realized that he was as close to a contemporary of the famous poet as anyone else there and relaxed. He mentioned his troubles with the store and the fact that Joanne would have to find another place for her daily dose of espresso.

"I'm sorry to hear it," she told him in that sincere way he had always heard her students compliment. "I've really enjoyed the space, though I must admit my enjoyment was due to the very small amount of business you were doing. I'm not sure I would have enjoyed it as much in a crowd."

"I'm not that depressed about it myself. Do you know how you can suddenly find yourself doing things you really don't like to do and have no idea how you got involved in the first place?"

Joanne's face seemed stuck on Tom's remark, like a record needle unable to jump the groove.

"What it is you want to do?" she finally said.

"Downsize," Tom replied, and Joanne laughed. "I mean everything. The store, my possessions, the time I spend doing about everything I do right now. I'd like my life to resemble this apartment a little more. Nothing nailed down, nothing worth stealing, everything capable of fitting in a car at a moment's notice so I can start over somewhere else."

Joanne clinked the jelly jar she was drinking from on Tom's glass.

"I'm so glad I'm finally getting the chance to talk with you," she said.

William Dunning had also not expected to be attending Sink and Diane's dinner. Since Peter's phone call, he hadn't attended anything at all. But Diane had been right. Somehow, as each day passed, everything about the breakup hurt a little less, and he started to show more and more interest in simple things like eating and exercise. Actually, when he had woken up from a nap an hour earlier, it was hunger itself that caused him to shower and pick out something clean to wear and show up at Diane's door.

"To new beginnings," Joanne proclaimed upon seeing William.

He quickly helped himself to a glass of wine and allowed Joanne to steer him to a pillow by her side. His own problems were quickly kept company by Tom's news of the café's failure and Joanne's admissions of her ongoing divorce procedures and inability to write a decent word all summer. William found himself studying the failed businessman as Joanne orchestrated the conversation between the two of them. Tom was dressed in his usual jeans and T-shirt, and his unkempt hair had grown enough to be hooked behind his ears now to keep out of his wineglass. When Tom caught William's eyes a few times, William began to suspect Diane's true intentions in throwing a dinner party—of course, it was for *him*, he believed, still at that age where vanity can actually reveal a bit of truth.

"Did you talk to Alex?" William ventured, once he had taken a proper dose of wine.

Joanne paused, and William knew she didn't want to tell him everything. "Let's just say that Lake Bluff is sorely in need of another resident poet," Joanne replied, causing cheers from Sink and Diane in the kitchen. "No, that's not fair," Joanne interrupted. "Alex Dupree may not be someone you'd ever imagine turning to, but never rule out anyone in this strange, strange, small town."

"To Alex Dupree," Tom said, lifting his glass toward William.

A lock of hair had fallen from behind Tom's ear, and William happily crashed his glass against Tom's.

Sink had finally mastered the lasagna and had safely put it in the oven for forty-five minutes when Joanne came in. "I'd say you won," Joanne remarked, indicating the mess Sink had made all around him.

"It put up a bit of a fight."

Joanne looked more relaxed with the wine, Sink realized. He quickly offered her a cigarette to complete the effect.

"I read that article about you," Sink said, lighting it for her. "I thought you and Jon were getting back together."

Joanne started to laugh, but it turned into a cough. "We couldn't be further apart," she said, taking a sip of wine. "You'd be amazed what you'll do for money, especially when you're older. It traps you. You'd like to think, 'Oh, I could just pack up the car and leave,' but with what? For what? So I'm trying some rather humiliating tactics, which I guess is what everyone eventually has to do."

"Where do you want to go?"

"I have absolutely no idea."

Sink stared at her. She seemed less and less like the teacher who had sat at the head of the table in class, critiquing their poems, encouraging the shyest students to talk, and producing at least one good thing out of everyone. Truth and love, he remembered. Joanne seemed to have misplaced both of them.

"Where would you go?" Joanne asked.

"Oh, I know exactly where," Sink said. "I've been thinking about it for years, and as everything I hope will happen seems to become less of a possibility, this one place gets more and more definite in my mind."

Joanne smiled and turned toward the conversation in the other room, indicating that they should join it. But before going, she looked one more time at Sink. "Do you know how to get there?"

Diane reveled in success. Spread out in front of her were the few remains of what had turned out to be a very good vegetable lasagna, and around her were her slightly drunken guests paired off in conversation. Tom and William talked favorite books and writers in that flirtatious way that could only mean there was a possibility of romance, while Sink was explaining blackjack with a deck of cards to a surprisingly interested Joanne Mueller. Diane felt a little left out from what was going on around her but didn't mind. She knew that Alex leaving Lake Bluff and Peter leaving William for Alex Dupree and Tom closing the café were still only the beginning of some major changes, and after a long, hot summer living on the floor, she was excited by whatever was going to happen.

Diane refused everyone's requests to help clean up, and, finally, after midnight and a dozen cups of coffee, the guests headed out, and Diane looked around at the mess that had spilled out from the kitchen all over the living room. She knew Sink wouldn't want to touch any of it, at least not tonight, and would probably fall asleep in front of the small black-and-white TV at the foot of their bed. Diane also decided against cleaning anything up for now and pulled out the guitar.

"I want to make a copy of some of those tapes you've made," Sink said, leaning in the door to the bedroom.

"Feel free," Diane said.

Living with a beautiful person for three months is, perhaps, the best way to conquer their beauty, Diane realized. Sink still looked good, leaning in the doorway in a way that could be an advertisement for jeans, cologne, for anything really, but in the end remained an advertisement for himself. He broke the pose and walked over to her and sat down. He didn't swing himself across the room from the pipes as he had liked to do so much when they'd first moved in; he just walked across the room filled with dirty dishes and empty wine bottles. His presence suddenly aroused her.

Sink started kissing her lips. She reached out a hand to the back of his neck and pulled him on top of her, pushing the guitar out of the way with her foot.

"I'm glad we did this," he whispered in her ear. "I'll always be glad we did this."

"I know," Diane said, and her eyes opened to the maze of pipes on the ceiling. "I will, too."

36

NEW YORK OR SAN FRANCISCO?

Tom hoped the noise from the air conditioner would help. The roar of the oversized unit over the front door of the Book Bar, which continually dripped onto the same stained spot on the carpet, did obliterate the sounds next door; but Tom could not stop thinking about what caused them. A work crew and various moving companies were disassembling the bankrupt coffee annex. At one point, while Tom smoked a cigarette outside and glanced through the now unsteamed windows, there were nearly a dozen men packing up the equipment, removing permanent fixtures, and stacking up chairs and tables. Probably the most people he had seen in the place at one time, he realized, hurrying back inside the empty bookstore.

The accountant and loan officer had figured everything out. With the sale of all the equipment and with the majority of profits from the books from now through Christmas, the bank expected to recoup its investment with interest. Tom would basically work for nothing for the next six months and then start to pay off debt incurred from those months with the meager postholiday shopping in what would surely be another bad winter of weather.

"Of course there's another option for January," his accountant reminded him.

Tom didn't bother asking because he already knew it: close the store, sell the stock, pay the bills, and come out with, at best, a couple hundred extra. Ten years out of college and a couple of hundred dollars to his name. Tom smiled at a middle-aged woman who had just come into the store and hoped she wouldn't corner him with the usual conversation about how she had always wanted to run a bookstore.

Even if Tom could find the enthusiasm to get through the next six months, pay back what he owed the bank, and hope for enough left over to start the winter, there was the other factor that made such a fantasy all the more unreal. Book Inc. planned to open its new megabookstore in Lake Bluff by September. Tom could only hope to make enough of the bank's money back by then before the chain took all the rest.

Smiling politely, Tom rang up the endangered species greeting card the middle-aged woman had settled on for her purchase and wished her a good day. He thought of calling home. Was William the kind of lover who would answer his phone? Tom smiled at the reminder of one part of his life that was not owned, owed, or borrowed against.

William stared at the phone next to Tom's single bed and debated calling the bookstore.

"Lock the door behind you, and call me later," Tom had said, dropping a key in William's hand when he'd left a few hours ago.

William decided to follow the directions precisely: leave first, call later. He had already stayed in his bed a few extra hours. What if Tom came home for lunch and found him still there? What if he became annoyed by this and asked William to leave? Propping the pillows up behind him, William sat up and helped himself to one of Tom's cigarettes. What if this was just a one-night stand and whatever he did at this point was really no big deal, he wondered, and inhaled.

But he had felt a sense of trust when Tom put the key in his hand. They had been up past midnight, and William had woken up to find Tom fully clothed and sitting on the edge of the bed. Now, glancing around the small apartment, William realized there wasn't that much to steal; but still, Tom had trusted him with the key, and he didn't say to drop it off at the store, just to call him at the store. Suddenly the entire room started to tremble.

Tom's apartment was in the back of a dilapidated yellow row house that faced the elevated train. William had hardly noticed the trains going by the night before, and now the sound seemed romantic to him, something European or from an old movie. It felt strange being with another body after six months of being with the same person. When Tom asked if he could kiss him good night and did, William had wrapped his arms around him and hadn't let go until morning.

What amazed William was how much he had underestimated good sex in relation to love. Peter wasn't the worst lover William had been with, but the moment Tom had started moving his hands from William's shoulders to his chest, he noticed a choreography that had not been as complex in its possibilities with Peter.

"I don't know when I'll be ready for another relationship," he had stupidly said over dinner. Had Tom taken that for a sign that a one-night stand was all there was to get? Was William taking the simple gesture of being handed the key to his apartment as far too symbolic an act?

"I'm about the worst kind of person you should hang out with," Tom had said far past midnight, as they stretched out on the single bed, facing each other. "You have your best year of college ahead of you. There's nothing you can't do. I've just lost half my business and the other half will probably go in six months. I have absolutely no idea what's going to happen."

"Is that it?"

"I haven't written a poem in five years."

William winced in the darkness, unable to conceive of this final admission.

"I might have my best year in front of me, but I don't know what's going to happen after that."

Tom was silent, and William knew it wasn't the same thing, that nothing he could offer up would compare with Tom's experience and pull them any closer together on the impossibly small bed.

"So where would you like to go? San Francisco?" Tom asked.

"New York."

"New York? What's in New York?"

"Everything. I once told somebody that I always wanted to visit New York, and they said I would have to move there if I really expected to experience anything."

When Tom fell asleep, William stayed awake another hour and imagined the two of them in the city he had never even visited. He pictured their entire apartment to be smaller than Tom's bedroom, the window with even less of a view than Tom's of the empty parking lot under the track, and cockroaches like he had never seen before darting between the shadows. They would have to get rid of more than half of their belongings, expect to spend a few months living in sublets, cook every meal, and never take a taxi anywhere until they were able to readjust to the higher costs.

With Tom he would explore every part of the city. They would furnish the apartment from what they could find on the streets. Tom would help William manage money, find a job, open a bank account, forget about his college friends, and enjoy life not being a student. William would remind Tom how to write.

When Tom was William's age, he'd had a boyfriend who was also a poet. As their senior year together at Lake Bluff came to an end, they didn't sign up for interviews at the job placement office, and they didn't once consider moving back home. Together they found a small apartment on the North Side of Chicago, where they spent what seemed to be the best three months of their lives. There was hardly any money, they barely held on to their jobs, they didn't own any real furniture, and they stole utensils from restaurants. But for three months they reveled in the childlike game of playing house together, cooking meals, drinking coffee together in bed, inviting friends over for drinks, and watching television from the five stations they could barely reach with the crooked antenna on their small black-and-white TV. They also wrote poetry and tried to give each other honest critiques of each other's work.

By the time fall arrived, the excitement of not having to write any more papers or study for tests had worn out, and the lack of money and plentiful amount of jobs that went nowhere seemed to crowd into the small apartment like bad houseguests. They had their first fight, which was quickly followed by a second and third. By January, Tom found brochures for graduate schools hidden in his lover's sock drawer, schools that were so far from the Midwest that Tom reacted as if they were love letters.

"Were you just planning on packing up and leaving once you were accepted?" Tom demanded.

"How do I know I'd get accepted? Why not just try to find out?"

"Why not ask if I might like to apply with you? I thought staying together was the plan."

"Staying together is what we're doing. We don't have any plans."

His name was Paul, and he had the silkiest blond hair Tom had ever seen.

The rest of the winter was spent accommodating each other as roommates who shared the same futon. Tom tried going out at night to meet someone else, while Paul stayed up late at the card table they used to eat on in the kitchen, filling out applications and reworking his poetry without Tom's help. By the time spring came, they had actually gotten used to the routine enough to be friendly and occasionally have sex. Then Paul announced he was leaving in one month for New York.

"What if I came with you?" Tom asked, after making love to him so hard he had hoped Paul would be moved to ask this on his own.

Paul's cigarette tip intensified as he took a drag, and Tom could see his serious expression in the brief glow. "I think I should go out there first, make sure it's everything it's supposed to be. Why should both of us go all the hell out there then come back?"

Tom really wanted to hit him but let his hand fall lightly on Paul's hairless chest to caress the smooth valley right where the rib cage ended and the stomach swelled out.

"What if I said I didn't care how many times we had to move and how many places we went to, as long as I was with you?"

Tom always wondered what could have happened if he had ever said that.

New York was apparently everything it was supposed to be for Paul, at least for six years. Tom then got a letter with a new address in Tucson, where Paul was getting another kind of creative writing degree and had matured enough to be able to make fun of his endless academic career. They told each other about their disastrous attempts at relationships, though they would each emphasize a positive possibility just so the other would never think they were desperate or permanently wounded by what had happened between them.

Just a year ago, Paul had called Tom from Chicago's O'Hare on an unexpected three-hour layover. It took Tom half an hour to get there.

"I'm visiting a university in western New York, they have a scholarship Ph.D. program, and the head of the department likes me."

Tom appreciated the soft light in the airport bar. When they'd first met at the United Airlines ticket desk, Tom could only imagine how old he looked by how old Paul did.

Tom talked about his plans to expand the bookstore into a coffee bar and even lied, claiming he was working on a novel. "Always tell old lovers you're working on a novel; it keeps them on their best behavior," an old lover once told him.

"Why didn't you ever come to New York?" Paul asked, looking even older as he drank his scotch and water. His silky blond hair was cut very short, and Tom noticed how it receded on the sides, making his hairline look like a W. "I always wonder what might have happened if you had come to New York."

"Did you ever think I was happy staying here in Chicago?"

"No," Paul said. "I never thought you did either."

When Paul left, he put his arms behind his back and told Tom to pick a hand. Tom hit him on the right arm, a little harder than he'd meant to, causing Paul to widen his eyes in a way that suddenly made him look younger, or perhaps the liquor had something to do with it. Paul handed Tom a fork, spoon, and knife, each with the United Airlines logo.

"I thought you might still need these," he said. "I'll get a set for myself on the connection."

"I've seen Douglas a few times since he died," Oma said, referring to her dead husband as simply as if he had moved to a warmer climate for his health.

All day William had worried about how to explain to Oma why he was no longer seeing her grandson. Had Peter already told her? Would William have to break the news? He even considered calling Peter for advice but knew no matter how sensible the call would be, it would still have the ulterior motive of an excuse to hear the sound of his voice begging for forgiveness, which William would be more than happy to grant after a good month of pleading. It was only two days since Peter had called it off and weeks before William would wake up in Tom's bed. After a three-hour dinner with Oma, William was relieved she had not mentioned her grandson once and seemed to encourage William not to either.

"You're saying you've seen his ghost?" William refilled Oma's sherry glass as she had long ago instructed him to do whenever she had emptied it.

"No," Oma snapped. "He's made his presence *known*. Moved things. One morning I came out to find a box of letters from a childhood lover scattered all over the dining room table. Another morning I woke up, and my wedding dress was carefully laid out on the floor by the bed."

William was careful not to change expression while she said this, careful not to look at her skeptically or sympathetically as she revealed how her seventy-year-old mind wandered, dragging out memorabilia late at night and blaming it on her husband's ghost when she woke up the next morning.

"What do you think he was trying to tell you?"

"That he's still here. That you can't spend half your life with someone and think they'll just disappear. For better or for worse, right? The heart's a stubborn muscle."

William was glad the living room was dark, alive with the flickering of candles, while shadows blanketed all the antique details he knew he would never see again.

"You think I'm crazy."

"No."

"You think, 'Oma's seeing ghosts! Put her away!' "

"Oma—"

"I'll show you."

Oma stood up and walked through the living room. William stood and waited for her to turn on a light as he hadn't lived fifty years in this house and couldn't find his way by memory.

"See!" Oma announced triumphantly once William had entered the lit room. He followed her pointing finger and saw the large mahogany chest she had told him about last winter sitting in the middle of the room. William looked back at Oma, who stood next

to it, her arms folded tightly across her thin chest. "I came downstairs a week ago and nearly tripped over it. I guess he could only
get it this far."

William followed Oma's finger again and saw a brightly colored
square in the corner. He walked over to it and stared down at
what appeared to be a frozen image of what the room's Oriental
carpet used to be, an intricate design of vibrant colors with a bright
burgundy background all held like a photograph in the perfect
indented square where the chest had sat for years.

"Will you move it back for me?"

William wrestled with the chest and maneuvered it across the
room, while Oma looked on grinning. It was as heavy as a large
air conditioner, and William was relieved when it seemed to jump
into place like a final puzzle piece into its old spot on the carpet.

"Now you don't really think an old woman like me could move
something like that across the room, do you?"

William looked up at her and smiled. *Yes,* he thought, while
shaking his head in visual agreement. *Yes, I think you could.*

"If you want to call him, call him," Diane told William, when he
couldn't decide whether to call Tom at the bookstore and called
Diane instead.

"But won't it look a little too serious if I call him while I'm still
here at his apartment?"

"Go home and call him."

"You're not being helpful."

Diane sighed into the phone. "You want my advice? Don't play
games. If you feel like doing something with Tom, just do it. He's
twenty-nine years old. If he minds, he'll tell you. He won't hold it
against you; he'll just be honest."

William could hear Sink saying something in the background
and remembered the old adage that the type of advice you got
depended on the type of person you asked. Sink and Diane were
splitting up at the end of the month; that is, Diane was moving

back to a dormitory, and Sink didn't know what he wanted to do. They weren't necessarily breaking up. William guessed they were just being honest.

"It sounds like you're in the middle of something," William said.

"Actually, Joanne's here."

"Joanne Mueller?" William sat up in Tom's bed. "Why's she over there?"

"We don't really know yet. She just got here. But I think it has something to do with nuclear waste."

37

HELEN DRAKE HAS HER VISION

"Ladies and Gentlemen. I stand before you as a humble professor, a mere messenger with news from the far northern reaches of small-town academia. I bring news to the heart of this hallowed institution called a university, Chicago's university. What makes a university? A group of colleges. Perhaps someday this great academic state of nations will swallow up my own humble college, Lake Bluff College, for today I bring you news of the recruitment of two of Lake Bluff's finest to do work for your university. It is with sorrow and joy I deliver this message as I'm sure it is with sorrow and joy that your two new messengers arrive."

Helen Drake paused. Brooks Auditorium at the center of the University of Chicago's Hyde Park campus was only half-full, and those who filled it seemed not to notice Helen had taken the podium and begun her opening remarks. The first few rows, filled with cameras and reporters, continued to slowly set up their equipment and dig for pens in their bags. People wandered aimlessly up and down the aisles, and the back doors stayed open. As she was about to reprimand the audience for their poor manners, a rather nervous-looking man with large headphones on his ears began waving his arms over his head from the side of the stage. Once he had Helen's attention, he pointed at his ears and shook his head. With some reluctance, Helen looked down at her microphone and calmly pushed the switch to the "on" position.

Helen did not consider herself well prepared for this task. Her phone had rung just two days ago with a representative of the University of Chicago requesting her to introduce their program announcing the new poet-in-residency of Alex Dupree and the Yucca Mountain Project grant in poetry for a poem by Joanne Mueller.

"Two days?" she had shouted into the phone.

"We realize it's short notice," the representative replied. "There was a last-minute cancellation, and Mr. Dupree was kind enough to recommend your services."

"Cancellation?" Helen's mind raced. "Vivian Reape canceled?"

"I am not at liberty to discuss the particulars of the previous speaker. I am only asking you to fill in."

"Do you realize who you are talking to? If you think you can just call me two days before an event such as this to ask me to take the time to—"

"There is, of course, the matter of an honorarium."

"Ladies and Gentlemen," Helen repeated, her microphone now on, causing the half-filled auditorium to look up at her in anticipation. As she went on with her speech, which she had spent the majority of the time during the two previous days writing, revising, and memorizing, the crowd slowly resumed the same lack of interest they had shown when her microphone was still off. Such a response was not uncommon to Helen whenever she had the honor—and honorarium—of making a speech. Still, she had expected that this event would have to have a bit more significance, and in her role as the maker of the opening remarks, she drew a poor opinion of a school as important as the University of Chicago in regard to the proper etiquette for such events. Wasn't this the same school that had shouted down some sort of Central American speaker last year? As Helen read off her remarks praising the important contributions of Alex Dupree to the world of letters, she felt a shudder creep up her back as she recalled reading about the political fiasco. Had they dumped pig's blood on the speaker as well? Rioted in the aisles? She glanced around in suspicion of each person who came down the aisle and took a seat.

Helen's spine had actually begun to shudder earlier that morning as she read the morning papers. The editorial pages were filled with news of the event she was to introduce; and though this flattered her immensely, she began to grow concerned as a few of the editorials started to question the appropriateness of a university officially taking sides on an issue as divisive as nuclear waste, especially a school with a famed nuclear science department that obviously had much to gain from such a supportive position. Her concern turned to panic as a few of the news stories wondered if the school's student body, which had in the past resorted to extreme forms of political demonstration, would try to disrupt the proceedings that day. Switching from coffee to a Bloody Mary, Helen wasted no time dialing Alex Dupree's home phone number.

"Helen, I can assure you, the utmost in security has been put in place," Alex assured her.

"I'm sure the school said the same thing all the other times such an event turned into political chaos."

"What other times?"

"You know what I'm talking about. Last year, some Central American leader was run off the campus before he could even get a word out."

Alex sighed into the phone. "Central American dictators are a much different matter than grants to poets. You are jumping to conclusions."

"Vivian Reape apparently jumped to those same conclusions."

"Vivian? What on earth are you talking about?"

"Her mysterious cancellation. Don't try to tell me she would go through all the trouble of securing a post as important as yours and then miss a flight or something so she couldn't be the one to hand it to you personally."

"Helen, really. I'm sure there's a perfectly good reason why Vivian couldn't make it. In fact, I believe it has something to do with Joanne, some type of rift in their working relationship on this whole nuclear waste issue."

Helen drained her Bloody Mary. "Exactly. Just what *is* Joanne's interest in this whole thing? You must admit she doesn't exactly seem to be the kind of woman who would jump on a bandwagon like this. Exactly what is her *agenda?*"

"The same as yours."

"What?"

"Money!" Alex sounded truly exasperated, but Helen wasn't about to stop. She felt like she was on to something.

"Surely the woman gets enough money from those diaries she calls short stories. Why, I didn't even think she wrote poetry anymore. What exactly is she up to taking such a grant?"

"Helen, I have to get going. Look, have a drink, relax, read your speech, and leave if you feel this way. If anything political occurs, I'm sure it will wait for Joanne anyway."

Helen got off the phone and took Alex's advice, pouring herself another healthy amount of vodka with just enough tomato juice to color it red. She barely had time to finish it and brush her teeth before the car she had insisted upon arrived at her house to take her to the event.

Naturally, the weather had returned to the prolonged heat wave that had already taken two entire months of the summer. Despite the brief reprieve, it again looked like no end in sight for temperatures climbing well over ninety, and the rain that had seemed like such a relief now only seemed to add to the dense humidity.

"Could you turn up the air?" Helen asked in way of greeting the driver of the black sedan taking her to Hyde Park. *How could Alex be so foolish?* Helen thought as the car made its way down

Lake Shore Drive. Surely extreme environmentalists would make a connection between nuclear waste and global warming, and with heat like this on the very day of the event, well, Helen was amazed that the sedan made it to Brooks Auditorium without having to go through any throngs of demonstrators.

"I've had the pleasure of working intimately with both the poets you honor here today," Helen told the audience. She realized she was rushing, but given the audience's inattentiveness they would probably appreciate her finishing up as soon as possible. She imagined a lot of them were also concerned about political outbursts and was certain that the reporters were counting on such a thing to fill up their notebooks and film to lead the evening news. She hadn't seen either Alex or Joanne and wondered if they were both being kept in some undisclosed room, surrounded by security. Certainly Joanne was. Helen couldn't believe the story she had seen in *CHIC-ago* magazine, where Joanne had literally flaunted her involvement in such an inflammatory activity, believing a poem, *her poem,* could somehow explore the horrific realities of burying something as highly toxic and politically sensitive as nuclear waste, turning the whole thing into some kind of platform for her own career. *Platform for her own career.* Helen stopped speaking for a moment, almost saying the phrase out loud. *Truth and love,* Helen remembered hearing a student reporting to a committee that had investigated Joanne's teaching methods when this student had complained of Joanne's rather personal interests in her students' lives. The man with the headphones at the side of the stage looked up at Helen in the same nervous way he had when her microphone was off. "As I was saying," Helen finally went on, "as glad as I am to see your university take an interest in the art of poetry, it is with regret that I see one of Lake Bluff's poetic leaders taken from us to pursue it."

As Helen kept on with her carefully memorized speech, her mind kept working. *What do morals like truth and love have to do with supporting an industry intent on destroying the very planet it claims to serve? Why, exactly, has Vivian Reape dropped out of the grant? What kind of rift is there between the teacher and her prize pupil?* The auditorium was nearly filled by now, and sensing her speech coming to an end, most of the audience listened somewhat attentively as Helen wrapped things up.

"As a Virginia Woolf scholar, I am reminded of her words when introducing the words of the two poets you honor here today. It is fitting that it should be the rather dull housewife, Mrs. Ramsey, in *To the Lighthouse* who comes to mind as I see our rather humble poets step forth on this great stage at this great university. To summarize, and to quote, as Mrs. Ramsey stared at her blank canvas at the end of this great novel: 'It would be hung in attics, she thought; it would be destroyed. But what did that matter? she asked herself, taking up her brush again. She looked at the steps; they were empty; she looked at her canvas; it was blurred. With a sudden intensity, as if she saw it clear for a second, she drew a line there, in the centre. It was done; it was finished. Yes, she thought, laying down her brush in extreme fatigue, I have had my vision.' "

The auditorium burst into applause as Helen stepped away from the podium, causing her to jump at the roar. When she got to the side of the stage, she still saw no sign of either Alex or Joanne. The man with the headphones indicated a side staircase she could use to take a seat among the audience for the rest of the event. Helen shot a quick smile at him and went down the stairs. She had no intention of hanging around to see what would transpire.

"Ladies and gentlemen, I am Prof. Joseph Wright, head of the nuclear science department." Helen paused along the side wall, halfway to the back of the auditorium, curious to see what kind of reception this man would receive. "Five years ago, when our university first started working with the government to find a suitable site for the safekeeping of nuclear waste, I would have been the first to laugh at the idea of poetry having anything to do with the work needing to be done. I am not laughing today. As has already been so eloquently pointed out, we are faced with a great task here. The future of our very civilization depends on how we solve a problem as complex as providing energy to our ever-growing world, and at the same time, how to protect this world from some of the unsolved aspects of that very energy. It is only through government-supported programs like the Yucca Mountain Project that we will be able to continue our studies of the disposal of nuclear waste while continuing to provide our country with cost-effective and abundant energy for each and every one of us to pursue our own American dreams. In my department we deal in numbers and experiments, numbers far too complex to explain to the common man and woman about the importance of the task asked of us. We are fortunate that a poet with the emotion and talent of Joanne Mueller should help us bridge the chasm between science and society, the analytical mind and the human heart, the mountain and the message."

Helen nearly scoffed aloud at this. She looked around at the crowd. Nobody seemed incensed by this propaganda, and as eager as she was to escape any potentially violent demonstrations, she found herself somewhat disappointed by the sheeplike attitude of the crowd. Nothing seemed real about the proceedings. She was certain something much darker was waiting to erupt.

Truth and love, she imagined Joanne preaching to her cultlike following of students. *Truth* so intensely worshipped she used her own short stories to discuss the scandalous embarrassment of her divorce. Helen could not imagine Joanne walking up to that podium to read something in praise of the destructive forces Professor Wright so arrogantly praised. *A platform for her career,* Helen remembered. *A platform for truth.*

As Helen turned to go, she saw Joanne, just down the center aisle, about to take a seat. She could not see her face but recognized her shoulder-length hair, her long, thin neck, her rather imposing height. In her hand was an odd-looking briefcase. It was thicker than most briefcases and not at all like the simple backpack Joanne used to carry her students' poems back and forth in between classes. Joanne took a seat on the aisle about ten rows in front of Helen. What was she doing in the audience? How like her to desire the melodrama of being called up to the stage from the crowd to take the platform for her career.

Professor Wright did not seem to notice that the very woman he was praising had walked down the center aisle and taken her seat. Perhaps he, too, did not expect this.

"It is also with great pleasure that I announce the National Institute of Poetry's gracious grant to the University of Chicago for a residency in poetry," Professor Wright went on. "I would now like to introduce the recipient of that grant, a colleague of Ms. Mueller's, Alex Dupree."

The roar from the audience again startled Helen. Her instinct was to leave. *Leave now,* her mind told her. But as she turned to go, she saw Joanne again. Joanne walking back down the center aisle from which she had just minutes ago come up. But something was missing. As the crowd kept applauding, Alex (dressed extremely well, Helen noticed) walked out onto the stage to shake hands with Joseph Wright. Helen, despite the voice in her head telling her to leave, *leave now,* made her way toward the stage along the wall. She found the aisle Joanne had sat in. She saw the empty seat on the main aisle she had just vacated. She looked back to the doors and saw Joanne disappear through them. And then she saw the briefcase, left in front of the empty seat, slightly sticking out into the aisle, aimed directly at the podium Helen herself had been speaking from moments ago.

"Ladies and gentlemen, it is with great honor that I address you today," Alex's voice rang from that podium, "to accept your request for a poet who—"

"Alex!" Helen screamed, causing him to stop speaking and look in her direction. The sea of heads in the audience also turned toward her. She was backed up against the wall, her arms spread out to brace herself. "Alex, stop!"

Alex's face went from an expression of alarm to annoyance as he caught Helen's eye.

"Joanne!" she screamed, pointing to the back of the auditorium. "A bomb!" she continued, now pointing toward the briefcase twelve seats from where she stood. "I tell you, it's a bomb!"

38

ORIGINAL SIN

"I didn't think you'd come," Lydia said to Walter as he sat down in the chair facing her at the Green Café.

"You said it was urgent; I always come if a member of the organization says it's urgent," Walter replied, shaking his head at the waitress who'd started to approach the table.

Lydia allowed this with a long drag on her cigarette. Walter knew it wasn't urgent.

"I imagined you would be busy today, with Rose."

Walter considered walking out. Not only was it not urgent, but it appeared Lydia only wanted to take up his time insulting Rose, who, as Walter perceived things, he was no longer involved with anyway.

"Why would you imagine that?"

"A big day for her," Lydia said, widening her eyes in mock surprise that Walter would even need to ask. "Her return to political activism, and at her father's university, no less. I told Carl, when he called to ask if I would provide backup should any arrests take place, that *this* I had to see for myself."

"Would you please tell me what you're talking about?"

Lydia smiled, somewhat triumphantly, and pulled out a flier from her bag. Taking it from her, Walter read: "Yucca Mountain Project in Poetry Presents Joanne Mueller." His eyes flew back to Lydia. "Just what are you trying to pull here?"

"What am *I* trying to pull? I merely thought you might want to join me as backup for your girlfriend's demonstration at an event featuring your former girlfriend—do I have that straight?"

"Demonstration?" Walter let his voice betray some panic.

"Nuclear waste. You know, Carl's pet project of abundant energy for the First World destroying the Third World. Really, Walter, I would have thought Rose would have kept you up on all of this, though I guess she realized it could have been awkward, considering Joanne what's-her-name's role in it."

Walter stood up. "What are they planning?"

"How would I know? As far as I know, Rose is just driving the getaway car, her very *comfortable* getaway car. I just volunteered to sit here drinking coffee until the whole thing was over, and if I saw any disturbances, to get Carl and your girlfriend out of jail if it came to that. Where are you going?"

"I have to get over there," Walter said, the flier in his fist.

Lydia glanced out the large picture window facing the center of campus. "I think you're too late."

Walter followed Lydia's gaze. Across the street, the doors of Brooks Auditorium had flung open, and it seemed everyone was stampeding out at once.

When Rose stepped out of Brooks Auditorium and felt the wall of heat, she stopped sweating. In front of her was a serene college campus on an ordinary late summer day. Some students walked along the sidewalks while a few others sat on the brown grass in the few patches of shade. A couple of policemen in their impossibly warm uniforms leaned against patrol cars talking, and the blue police barricades lay discarded in a pile in a corner of the plaza, unneeded for a poetry reading that had apparently remained poetic. Rose started to walk across the plaza, and no one even looked at her.

"I told you I can't go in," Rose had told Carl an hour earlier as she leaned against the door of her car in the parking lot behind Brooks Auditorium. "I'll pick you up in front, like you said."

"You need an invitation or university ID," Carl said, pacing in front of her. "If I had known that, I would have figured something else out." Rose took the sting of this calmly. Despite all the information she had passed along to him about the event, this one detail had somehow been overlooked, and it was all Rose's fault.

"What about Lydia?"

"She's across the street keeping watch in the unlikely event that we're arrested. She's still under a thousand-dollar bond for last month's ROTC protest anyway. She'd do this if she could."

Rose looked down at the attaché case on the ground between them. "What's in the case, Carl?"

"Rose, I knew you could be counted on."

"What's in the case?"

Carl sighed and looked up at the cloudless sky. Despite the season, his skin was still a pale white, and he had started sweating from the intense heat. Rose, on the other hand, felt chilled by the turn of events she felt powerless to control, and she rubbed her bare arms, which were folded defensively in front of her.

"It's not what you think," Carl said, lowering his voice and stepping closer to her so the attaché case was between his legs. "You think I'm crazy or something? It's an audiotape, connected to two internal speakers, which will state our message for all the media, students, and officials to hear. You're the one who's so good at chanting; well, you'll love this. Disruption without anyone getting dragged out. Freedom of speech, right?"

Rose met Carl's intent eyes. "Open it, and show me."

Carl held her gaze. "It took me four hours to lock and seal it

374

just so it can make it through the full speech before anyone can tamper with it."

Rose looked sharply away, toward the auditorium where she could see people starting to go in.

"Take an aisle seat toward the front," he continued. "Put it under your seat. As you put it there, take this chain and secure it to the metal part of the chair; make sure it's the part that is bolted to the floor. Sit for another five minutes, and then calmly leave the auditorium, looking like you're simply in search of a rest room and intend to return."

"Carl." Rose kept her arms folded across her chest as he picked up the brown attaché and held it in front of her.

"No one's getting hurt. I promise you."

She had taken the attaché. She had taken an aisle seat and put it under it. As she'd started to reach into her coat pocket for the chain, three students pointed at the seats next to her, and Rose twisted her knees to the side by way of telling them they weren't taken. After they pushed by and sat down, Rose did not take the chain out and secure it to the metal part of the seat that was bolted to the floor. She stood up and glanced around the auditorium as if she was looking for the rest room. "Do you know where the rest room is?" she almost considered asking the young woman in the seat next to her, but she wanted no interaction with her. "Don't give them the opportunity to be human," Lydia had once screamed at Rose in Indianapolis as they counterdemonstrated the Klu Klux Klan. Rose had stopped to speak to an older woman who held a Confederate flag and had been trying to explain to her why the Confederate flag could possibly offend black people. Rose walked up the aisle of Brooks Auditorium, keeping her eyes on the back door, the hundred faces on each side of her blurred into one single mass.

She wished she had demanded to see what was in the case.

Outside she kept her steady pace across the plaza, knowing that in just a few more steps her car would be in sight, and then she would be locked in it and could drive as far as Canada if need be. Ten hours to Canada. That was something else Lydia would say during the worst moments of a demonstration, the moments when they would start to physically press up against the barricades, elbow a few scabs, or block the path of a cop. Rose imagined Canada to be a place filled with Americans suffering the consequences of demonstrations gone wrong.

A pigeon hopped across the pavement in front of Rose, and eyed her with its head sideways, hoping for food. Without any reaction from Rose, the pigeon suddenly flew away.

From where Rose stood at the center of the plaza, she could have heard the doors of Brooks Auditorium fly open and the hysterical cries of people shoving against each other to get out. She could have also heard the sounds of the police cars on the opposite side start their engines and the footsteps of some of the cops as they ran toward her. Instead, Rose could only hear that thundering in her ears as everything around her turned into slow-motion: the startled police, the students who had so peacefully been sitting in the shade standing up to stare, the pigeons flying up. Rose kept walking. "There must be a rest room around here somewhere," her face and movements instinctively said.

When Alex heard Joanne's name, he looked to the side of the stage where she had just been standing. "I think we need a drink," Joanne had said to him, when they announced his name to summon him to the podium. When he didn't see her there, his eyes flew back to Helen, and his instinct was to duck down behind the podium. The crowd by now had started that nervous movement and intake of breath he had seen on airplanes during a rough landing. As Alex watched a security man talking to Helen and noticed another one starting to walk toward him across the stage, he knew there was nothing he could do as he gripped the sides of the podium and realized he couldn't physically move.

By the time the security man had reached him, the crowd had started to swell. As more policemen and brown-shirted campus police attempted to come down the center and side aisles, reporters, students, corporate donors, and faculty had started to push in the opposite direction toward the doors. People were screaming now, and Alex distinctly heard the word "bomb." The younger students were avoiding the crowded aisles by jumping over the seats like hurdles. Somebody blew a whistle.

The security man with the name tag "Stan" reached the podium and gently put his hands on Alex's shoulders to move him away. The terrified look on Alex's face must have convinced him that this was not going to be easy to do, and Stan finally twisted the microphone toward him so he could speak into it while Alex held on to the podium for dear life.

"Ladies and gentlemen," Stan said, just as Alex had said a few minutes earlier. "Please leave the auditorium in a calm and orderly fashion. Leave your personal items where they are."

Alex looked out at the mass of people pushing toward the back, oblivious to the instructions Stan gave. By now the people backstage had run out and joined the throng of people in the aisles. Alex saw Joseph Wright using the seats as hurdles as the students had. Helen was long gone, and Joanne was nowhere in sight.

Stan was behind Alex now, his thick arms on top of Alex's and his fingers slowly working on Alex's tight grip to the sides of the podium. "It's gonna be all right," Stan whispered in Alex's ear as a lover would, and Alex let himself fall back into Stan's strong embrace.

Joanne didn't need to use the rest room, she needed to be in it. As she watched Alex walk out onto the stage to give his speech, she knew she had at least ten minutes if not half an hour, and she slipped back through the curtains and electronic equipment and found the bathroom she had noticed when she'd arrived half an hour earlier.

Joanne was not wearing her pinstripe wool suit. After her phone call to Jon her message machine and mailbox filled with official letters and information from the Yucca Mountain Project, including another check that was nearly three times what she had received initially, making her believe that Vivian had purposely miscalculated her previous fifty-fifty breakdown of the grant. Paying off every outstanding bill (with the exception of deciding whether or not to do further repair work on her ailing car or just buy a new one) left the resident poet flush; and though she deposited the rest of the money, she went straight to Michigan Avenue to find a summer version of her old wool suit. She settled on an off-white linen skirt and jacket, livened up with a pink, low-neck silk shirt. Even Joseph Wright noticed.

"So good to see you," he said, grabbing onto her elbow when she arrived at the auditorium that morning, "and looking so well."

The rest of their conversation was not as polite. "I read your speech," he told her, still holding on to her so she could not get away.

"How did you manage that? I only sent copies to members of the arts board who would not be able to attend."

"Let's be straight about all this," Joseph had said, with a smile that made Joanne instantly know never to trust a word he said. "I oversee everything regarding this project. I have been doing that for years. You already had your fun spreading liberal misinformation in that magazine article, which was a lesson to us on maintaining control of this project. I'm afraid we won't allow you to talk so candidly with the media in the future. You're one of us now. Though we have decided upon an actual site and things are to be, well, more public, I am still to be cc'd on everything in relation to the depository before its public release. Including your poetry."

"I see," Joanne said, smiling back as fiercely as he smiled at her. "I hope I won't bore you today repeating myself then."

"Actually, there are a few changes you could make that would be a pleasure to hear."

Joanne didn't reply.

"All the stuff about the Native American tribes and their sacred lands, the need to carefully include them in surveying potential disturbances, blah-blah-blah. There is truly no need for you to concern yourself with this as we already have a separate committee addressing those nonproblems."

Joanne knitted her brow together and nodded her head at him in mock agreement.

"As for all that Oppenheimer stuff—"

"A historic figure in nuclear development," Joanne interrupted. "I'd thought you'd be pleased by my interest in the science of all this."

"Science, yes; conscience, no. You went a little wild quoting him."

"Is it not true that he called the bombing of Japan the original sin? Is it not true he mounted a campaign of fellow scientists to stop the U.S. government from using their science for further military purposes?"

"That science was paid for by the U.S. government, in service to the U.S. government, to save countless American lives. We wouldn't be standing here today without the aid of the U.S. government in all of our fine, if you'll allow the expression, emperor's new clothes."

Joseph reached out and brushed a stray hair off the lapel of Joanne's new linen coat.

"Let's not ruin any more of this great occasion with such talk," he continued. "I was more than happy to get rid of Vivian for you when she tried to get rid of you, and I want you to know how much I still want you involved in this program. So why not just say thank you and read a few poems. I think you'd sleep better tonight."

Joanne cupped her hands in the cold water in the rest room and splashed it on her face. She couldn't hear anything from the auditorium in the small bathroom and worried she was on and couldn't be found. Taking a paper towel she dabbed at her face and smoothed her expensive linen jacket. She had no idea what she would say to the audience.

When she opened the door, she heard a low thundering, which was mixed with the hysteria of high-pitched voices. She ran through the empty backstage and out onto the stage, where the first thing she noticed was Alex being literally carried up a side aisle by a large security officer. All the rows were empty, and a large crowd massed by the three back doors desperately trying to get out.

"Lady, come down from there!" a security officer yelled at her.

What, Joanne thought, *did Alex say?*

When Walter reached the plaza, it was already filled with the people who had poured out from the auditorium. They all talked in that excited way Americans use to greet any catastrophe they have survived, and he knew it wouldn't be long before news cameras arrived to relieve them of their need to tell their stories. As he pushed through the crowds, he overheard the word "bomb" quite frequently, and as he got closer to the doors, he started hearing Joanne's name as frequently as the word "bomb," and Walter soon realized they were being used in the same sentence. Walter finally stopped at the front of one of the main doors, which was jammed with people coming out, and listened to a woman hysterically talk to a policeman.

"Of course I would recognize her again if I saw her. It was Joanne Mueller. I believe she was to speak after Alex, oh, poor Alex. She just left the attaché case under her seat and walked out."

Walter finally saw a small opening in the doorway and plunged through as policemen ordered him to stop. Eluding them, he made

it all the way through the second set of doors and into the auditorium, where just a few dozen people were still running out.

"Lady!" he heard a security man shout, and Walter looked toward the stage and saw her. She was dressed in white and seemed
frozen, like an ice sculpture. Walter knew he shouldn't shout her
name, so he just started running down the center aisle.

"Don't move!" Walter commanded, once she had seen him and
started walking to the edge of the stage. Walter swung himself up
on the stage and grabbed her arms. Joanne still looked up the
center aisle, where a half-dozen police officers were running toward
them.

"Is there a back way out?" Walter asked, grabbing her face
roughly with one hand so she'd look at him.

"Through there."

Walter spun around and started running backstage, with one
hand gripping Joanne's arm. He heard her half-falling behind him
as he dragged her back through the curtains toward the glow of
an exit sign.

"What's happening? Where are we going?" Joanne pleaded, trying to keep up.

Before Walter could possibly answer, they were outside on a
quiet side street on campus. At the far end was the roar of the
crowd and sirens in the plaza. Walter dragged Joanne in the opposite direction and started waving frantically at a light blue car.
He didn't really have much choice for a getaway vehicle, and when
the blue car stopped in front of them, he opened the passenger
door and threw Joanne in it.

"Where's Carl?"

"I'm on my way to pick him up in front of the Green Café."

"I'll get him. Just get her out of here."

As the car drove off, Walter paused to see the two heads at the
same height with the same hair color turn toward each other. He
tried to imagine what Joanne Mueller and Rose Gluck would possibly talk about as he raced back to the plaza.

39

THE GETAWAY

Diane had been able to establish the following: While Joanne
Mueller was in the rest room at Brooks Auditorium at the University of Chicago waiting to give a speech outlining her plans as the
designated poet for the Yucca Mountain Project in Nuclear Waste
Management, fellow Lake Bluff professor Helen Drake had
shouted something from the audience to recently former fellow
Lake Bluff professor Alex Dupree, who was on the stage about to
start his own speech accepting a grant from the National Institute
of Poetry headed by Vivian Reape, establishing him as sole resident
poet at the University of Chicago. What Helen shouted had something to do with Joanne not being in the rest room behind the
stage but in the audience, where she had just vacated her seat and
walked out of the auditorium in the back. What caused Helen to
shout was that the woman she presumed to be Joanne had left
behind a briefcase beneath her aisle seat, which Helen presumed
to be a bomb.

After Brooks Auditorium was nearly evacuated, a man entered
the auditorium and walked to the stage, where a security officer

saw a woman who later fit the description of Joanne provided by Helen and Alex. A University of Chicago professor in nuclear science, Joseph Wright, was also helpful to authorities in regard to a description of what Joanne was wearing that day. The unknown man and Joanne were pursued backstage, where they managed to exit and not be seen again.

Moments before a police bomb squad unit was to enter Brooks Auditorium, the briefcase went off, releasing a high-volume audio speech condemning the government's continued reliance upon nuclear energy and alleged business with corporations and universities who profit from the continued research of nuclear energy and the long-term storage of its waste. After the ten-minute audio ended, the police bomb squad opened the briefcase to find the tape player and a chain that they presumed was to have been used to secure the briefcase to the leg of the bolted-down auditorium seat.

Diane was able to establish these facts from Joanne herself as well as the local news, which had interrupted regular programming. Diane did not know how Joanne had gotten from Hyde Park to Diane's Lake Bluff apartment or why she had chosen this destination. She also did not know if Joanne had actually been involved in planting the audio-equipped briefcase.

Presently, Joanne was lying down in the other room on Diane's side of the futon, sipping a glass of cheap white wine on ice and resting her forearm over her eyes. She had helped herself to Sink's cigarettes as well as a Valium, which Sink kept a good supply of thanks to a friend of his whose work-study job was at the college health center.

The only other thing Diane knew was that her friend William had slept with her ex-employer Tom and didn't know whether or not to call him. She also knew she would move into a dormitory in a few weeks, and that Sink had not decided whether to get a room on campus or move to the city. Joanne had mentioned something about getting out of town, but Diane wasn't sure if she was serious or just making light of the situation.

• • •

Before the phone rang, Alex wasn't sure of anything. Somehow, after being physically removed from Brooks Auditorium and answering a half an hour of police questions regarding Joanne Mueller, he had been driven home by a university-hired car.

"When did you last see Joanne Mueller?" the officer had asked.

"Right before I went on the stage; she mentioned something about having a drink."

"What do you know of Joanne Mueller's political affiliations?"

"I didn't realize she had any."

"How reliable a witness do you consider Helen Drake to be?"

"Helen's been a bit bothered by the heat this summer."

"If for any reason Joanne Mueller tries to contact you, please contact us immediately."

Alex sat in his living room with views of the north, east, and south and stared at the floor. Did he have a job at the University of Chicago? Did he want it if he did? Could he still go back to his job at Lake Bluff? Why was he bothering to teach anyway?

When the phone rang, Alex presumed it to be Peter Brooks, whose very name now made Alex jump. Was Peter related to some kind of alum at the university who'd built that damned auditorium in the first place? What exactly were Peter's political affiliations?

"Alex, it's Joanne."

Alex wished it was Peter.

"I'm instructed to call the police if I hear from you."

"Please don't."

"Did you plant that bomb?"

"It wasn't a bomb, Alex, turn on your television."

Alex glanced south from his living room and saw no rising cloud of smoke from the area of the University of Chicago.

"Where are you then?" he asked.

"I'll tell you in a moment. In fact, I need you to come here; but before I tell you where I am, I need to know that you will not call the police and that you will come alone."

"This is crazy. I thought you said it wasn't a bomb."

"I haven't done anything wrong, Alex. Please. I am asking one favor from you, and when you get here, I will grant you a favor in return that should settle everything."

"I just got home."

"Trust me, you will not regret taking an hour to come here. It will be one of the best things you could ever dream of doing for your career."

Alex took a deep breath. "Where are you?"

"Nineteen-hundred Danner, in Lake Bluff. I'll watch for you to pull up. Oh, and make sure you drive the Mustang."

Sink was packing. He had pulled out an oversized U.S. Army duffel and decided that whatever he could fit inside of it he was meant to have with him. Everything else he had acquired in his life up to that moment Diane could keep, sell, or throw away.

The three shirts, two pairs of jeans, assorted socks and underwear, and one sweater only filled half the duffel, and Sink looked frantically around the bedroom. Joanne had made a phone call and gone outside to sit on the front step. Both he and Diane knew not to ask her who she had called and why she had decided to sit outside. A journal, a battered copy of James Joyce's *Ulysses*, which he had been reading for nearly three years, and a few items from the medicine cabinet didn't do much to fill the duffel. Sink was considering finding a smaller bag when Diane walked in.

"Now what?" she asked, sitting cross-legged on the futon.

"I think I should go with her."

"Where's she going?"

"I don't think she knows."

Diane looked around at the piles of books and clothing that lined the walls of the room.

"What am I supposed to do with all this stuff?"

"Keep what you want; just leave the rest, I don't care. It's not important."

Diane didn't look particularly sad or bothered by his decision to leave. She seemed more threatened by the amount of things he was leaving behind with her; she kept glancing around with her eyes slightly squinting, in a way Sink had come to recognize as Diane problem solving. How many times had she looked at him with that expression? He'd miss it.

"I don't really know what to say," Diane finally said, and Sink sat down next to her and put an arm around her.

"This isn't like we're never going to see each other again," he whispered, becoming more unsure of it as he said it.

Diane looked at him sharply. "From the first time I saw you I never counted on the next time. Why should this be any different?" Diane didn't say this angrily. She was smiling, and Sink loved her smile when she told him things that most people would say only hoping to hurt him.

"Nothing's different."

Diane glanced around the room again. "Did Joanne ask you to go with her?"

Sink smiled. "Of course not. But she's had two glasses of wine and a Valium. I have to at least get her out of the state. If she wants me out at that point, I'll take a bus back."

Alex had no problem finding Joanne once he reached the street she had directed him to. She waved to him from the sidewalk, and he pulled over as if it was any normal day during the school year and he was offering her a ride to campus. He turned off the ignition and got out of the car.

"Don't you think we should go inside somewhere?" Alex asked, nervously looking up and down the sweltering tree-lined street.

"I'm not a fugitive," Joanne said, laughing. "There was no bomb. I didn't do anything."

"Well, I would sure like you to explain that to the police officer who questioned me for half an hour."

Joanne still wore the cream-colored linen suit and didn't seem affected by the one-hundred-degree temperature, while Alex continually wiped his sweating brow. In fact, Joanne looked better than he had seen her in months. Her face and posture, which had recently seemed clenched and distracted, now appeared completely calm and cheerful as if she had just returned from a two-week vacation instead of fleeing the scene of a riot.

"What is this all about?"

Joanne took a deep breath. "I need your car."

"My car?"

"I need to borrow it. Actually, I need you to give it to me. I don't know when I'll get it back to you, but I promise the moment I come back to Chicago I'll return it."

"You're leaving?" Alex stepped back and protectively leaned against his precious red Mustang.

"I have to."

"Where are you going?"

"I'm not sure. But if I knew I don't think I'd tell you."

"What's wrong with your car?"

"It's not going to get me very far."

"Joanne, what you're asking is a great deal. No less the fact that I will be involved in something criminal."

"There's nothing criminal going on. Besides, should anything happen, I'll say I stole it. You can say I stole it. Just don't press charges." Joanne was smiling again, smiling and not sweating. As much as Alex cursed the day he had ever met her, he couldn't help admiring her intensely.

Before he could attempt to convince her to give up this crazy scheme, Sink walked out of the apartment building behind her carrying a large duffel bag. He waved at Alex like it was any normal day on campus.

"Give us a few more minutes," Joanne said to him over her shoulder, and Sink, after taking an appreciative look at Alex's car, obe-diently went back inside, leaving the duffel bag on the front step.

"He's going with you?" Alex whispered, even though there was nobody in sight.

"I guess he is."

Alex started to protest this new development, but realized he couldn't exactly lecture Joanne on the impropriety of sleeping with students. He had reached the point of just wanting to hand her the keys and be done with it, but Joanne wasn't finished.

"As I said on the phone, I want to make this worth your while." Alex couldn't help being reminded of Vivian on the afternoon she had come to Alex's apartment to convince him to leave Lake Bluff College for the University of Chicago. The very self-assured way Vivian had sat down in his living room and taken charge of his career, using the same tone of voice Joanne spoke with now. Alex leaned forward a little, not wanting to miss a single word.

"Where are you taking me?" Joanne had asked.

"Home," Rose had replied.

They were both silent while Rose skillfully maneuvered the car away from campus, both of them staring intently at the police cars and television vans racing toward them.

"How do you know where I live?" Joanne finally asked, and Rose glanced over at her with a look of exasperation, like everything was completely obvious, though Joanne didn't even know the woman's name who had just turned the car onto Lake Shore Drive, skillfully crossing three lanes of traffic with one glance over her shoulder, just like Joanne did every day when she headed to Lake Bluff.

"Could you at least tell me what happened in there?" Joanne looked out across the lake, which was a brilliant blue. She couldn't remember the last time she had been a passenger in a car, and her mind started making images out of the city rushing by, an old habit she hadn't felt for months.

"I planted a briefcase in the auditorium, which someone mistook for a bomb."

"A bomb?" Joanne stopped looking for poetry on the lakeshore and turned back to Rose.

"It was just some kind of audio, protesting the use of nuclear power and the profiteering of corporations through the university."

"You set up a bomb scare at a nuclear waste poetry reading?" Joanne started laughing. Her body, which had felt so tense for the past few weeks, suddenly seemed to release like a deep intake of breath she had held in underwater.

"This isn't exactly funny," Rose said.

"I know," Joanne said, still laughing. She looked over at Rose to try encourage her to see the humor in the situation, but this wasn't going to be possible. The woman driving was actually starting to cry.

"Why don't you pull over and let me drive," Joanne said, putting a hand on her shoulder. "I'm good at it."

They didn't speak again until Joanne had driven to the corner of her block, and they saw the police car sitting in front of Joanne's apartment building.

"Just keep going," Rose said, and Joanne cast her an exasperated look like she was the one now stating the obvious, and Joanne maneuvered them back onto Lake Shore Drive heading north to Lake Bluff. As the freeway emptied back into the north of the city, she had the feeling she was leaving something behind, like this was her last chance to notice details like the elevated train crossing above her, and she would have to rely on memory to make sense of it all later. Sheridan Road seemed to cut between the condominium towers like a mountain pass.

"I'm getting the feeling they think I was the one who planted the bomb," Joanne said.

"It wasn't a bomb."

"If it *had* been me, I think it would have been one."

"You don't have to worry; I'll explain everything. You can just go back to that poem of yours and forget about it."

"Why should either of us worry? What's to explain? Haven't you ever had the feeling that there's no going back?" Joanne looked over at Rose, who stared down intently at her hands in her lap. "What I mean is, have you ever had the feeling of waking up and not being in love with someone anymore? Whether it's a person, a city, or even a job, you suddenly notice it doesn't have control of you, and you expected to be sad, to mourn the loss, but instead you feel liberated, like your actions can be pure again, and if something else comes along, you won't let it pass by. Or maybe you have to be the one to go out and find it. I've always prided myself as someone who doesn't run away from things. Now I feel like someone has literally put a bomb under my chair to tell me to start running for a change. I guess I have you to thank."

Rose looked over at her. The city thinned out on the outskirts, and Joanne found the rhythm of the traffic, making every light. Joanne wanted to keep talking, but her mind was occupied with driving. It was early afternoon on a weekday, and the farther they got from Chicago the more open the roads became until there wasn't a car in front of her or behind her, and it felt like she arrived at Sink and Diane's apartment too quickly. Joanne reluctantly put the car in park and started removing her seat belt.

"I feel like I've met you before," Joanne said, unlatching her door.

"We know people in common," Rose said.

Joanne thought of Walter but decided not to bring him up.

"I don't believe I caught your name."

"It's Rose."

"Well, thank you Rose for getting me out of there. You have a very comfortable car." Rose smiled for the first time, and Joanne got out. She waited on the sidewalk and watched Rose shift over to the driver's side and make a quick U-turn, going back the way they had come.

. . .

Last spring when Sink and Diane had lived apart but slept together nearly every night, Joanne had put them through a poem-a-day class exercise that lasted two weeks. Ten poems in two weeks. And not just random poems, but particular assignments she'd announce in class and that would be due the next day. The assignments specified form (a sonnet, ten heroic couplets, blank verse, a villanelle) as well as subject (retell a fairy tale, choose and extend a metaphor for an entire poem, argue two opposing issues). No one was expected to write ten perfect poems; and though Joanne admitted the two weeks to be tedious, she hoped the rigor of the work would inspire things deeply hidden in their subconscious. William and Diane had joked that she had already emptied out all the emotional conflict that could possibly exist in their twenty-year-old heads and had resorted to this exercise in hopes of uncovering whatever was left.

Whatever Joanne's intentions, Sink, Diane, and William took to the assignments with hopes to write ten perfect poems. By the end of the first week they realized this wasn't possible. Different assignments brought success from different students. While some assignments were complete failures for everyone, no assignment brought equally good poems from the class as a whole. Joanne took delight in reading aloud the poems she considered to be the best each day, always making sure to include everyone at some point in order to encourage everyone to do their best in hopes of hearing Joanne's authoritative voice read their words aloud the next day.

The second week, Joanne assigned them short meter, very short rhymed quatrains, with a subject of "an ending that is somehow a beginning." Diane stayed up nearly all night following extremely elaborate leads: leaving California for Chicago, the loss of her mother—subjects that could not be contained in the short lines, and, by the next morning, she chose the four best stanzas and strung them together in a way that made no real sense but completed the assignment.

In class, after Joanne had spent twenty minutes silently reading through their work, she looked up at her students in mock consternation.

"I think we're all getting a little tired," she said. "But you all get As for effort. Too much effort, I believe. There's one poem I want to read that succeeds. Pay attention to its simplicity, and don't forget there's always room for simplicity in poetry."

She read Sink's poem aloud, read it twice as it was so short: three stanzas about making the bed after spending the night with someone and not knowing if they'd ever return to spend the night again. The poem took place in the winter, and Diane couldn't help realizing it was probably about her, but she refused to look over at Sink.

"What did you think?" Sink asked Diane after class.

"I think it was wonderful."

Sink smiled his really big smile, the one that seemed to wrap around his entire face.

Diane was remembering all this because once she had heard Alex's car start up with Joanne and Sink in it, she had found it impossible to sit still in the empty apartment and had started pulling boxes out of the closet to pack. As she sorted through the piles of notebooks and textbooks around the room, she found Sink's folder of poetry and pulled that poem out. She worried that Sink had forgotten the folder, but guessed he probably had most of his poems memorized. Upon rereading, she realized it wasn't a great poem, that somehow in the six months since he had written it, six months since they had moved in together and split up, the poem had somehow lost some of its power over her. Diane remembered sitting in the classroom that early spring afternoon listening to Joanne read it, the windows wide open even though it was only fifty degrees outside, with the excitement of spring making everyone immune to the cold. Most of all, Diane remembered how well Joanne Mueller's voice wrapped around Sink's simple words and made them great.

392

40

THE MINOR POETS OF CHICAGO

September 1, 1989

Dear Joanne,

I'm sure you never expected to be hearing from me so I will be brief. My trip back to Boston a month ago was uneventful. It's mercifully cooler here, still hot, but nothing like the Midwest. A breeze comes from the ocean, and I didn't even run my air conditioner last night. I realize our parting was not the most civil. Still, we both have our work to do, and so I am writing you now. I am finishing up a publishing obligation and wish to compile an anthology of Chicago poets. Naturally, I would like you to be included. I have looked through clippings of poems of yours from the past several years and think "The Divorce Duet" and "Monday Comes Weekly" would fit into the anthology I have in mind most perfectly. There is, of course, an abysmally small fee to be paid, but I think the exposure, which would include a healthy biography, would be good for your fictional ventures. Of course all copyright reverts to you, so there is really no reason for you to find anything disagreeable about the enterprise. In fact, there is no need for you to contact me at all. If, for some reason, you have a problem with the poems I have chosen or do not wish to take advantage of this free publicity for your talents, let me hear from you by the end of the month. Despite everything, I hope that will not be the case. You could say, I look forward to not hearing from you, though that would be too unpleasant, so I'll just say good luck, and I'm sure our paths will continue to cross in this business of rhyming words.

Most Sincerely,
Vivian Reape

September 2, 1989

Dear Ms. Vivian Reape:

Alex Dupree was kind enough to pass on your request, and I am happy to oblige you. Thank for the kind words you passed along through him about the small literary publication *Rose Is a Rose,* which I coedit and hope to secure proper financing to start up again. I am thrilled to assist you in finding "up-and-coming" Chicago-area poets for your planned anthology. Enclosed you'll find a dozen poems from poets I have already published, a few of whom I personally know and all of whom I think might be on par with the type of poet you hope to include. I am thrilled to hear that Joanne Mueller will be included in this book, though I must say it makes my work harder to find writers who would be able to share such a stage with her. I can only do my best. Please contact me at any time to instruct me further.

Yours Sincerely,
Thomas McMann

September 7, 1989

Dear Mr. Dupree:

As acting director of the University of Chicago Nuclear Waste Commission, I am glad to have you on board as our official poet. Joanne Mueller was kind enough to complete her work with us by recommending you in a letter received this week. Your recent appointment as resident poet for this university makes your role with this project all the more appropriate—we consider ourselves here in the Nuclear Science Department to be a tight-knit family and are glad to have you on board.

Due to the rather dramatic events that have recently occurred with our announcement of a poet for the project, I must inform you that we will not be planning any formal announcements or readings regarding your appointment. A press release will go out upon your assuming the position, and we hope you can meet a rather short deadline for writing your poem. That deadline is November 1.

I would recommend brevity in your writing. Of course I do not want to guide you in any way with your words, but I do want to emphasize the rather controversial environment this "Art for Yucca Mountain" has landed us in after the unfortunate incident at our university last month. I think you will agree that completing the work quickly and keeping a low profile is the best course to take at this point.

Should you have any questions as to what your poem should convey, I suggest you contact Jon Sullivan at the enclosed phone and address. He is the official artist for the project and has already completed a miniature "Rock Chaos," which we plan to start work on once all the necessary studies and building are completed at the Yucca Mountain site. At this point we have targeted a completion date for the site to start receiving nuclear waste by January 2001. I must remind you that this date is subject to change due to the extremely sensitive nature of the project, and as you may have guessed, any further incidents like the one involving Ms. Mueller last month will only further postpone this completion date.

Congratulations on your appointment, and I look forward to reading your poem upon completion. Best wishes to your mother; she has been kind enough to inquire about future scholarships for the university's Nuclear Science Department. She must be very proud of you.

Sincerely,
Professor Joseph Wright
Department of Nuclear Science
The University of Chicago

Date: September 10, 1989
Attn: Dean Griffith
         The University of Chicago
From: Rose Gluck
         Department of Library Science

I regret to inform you of my plans to leave my position at the University of Chicago effective upon your receipt of this memo. I would like to thank you for all your support in my ten-year career at this fine university and regret giving such short notice of my decision. I am confident that the remaining faculty in my department can take on my work until you are able to find a successor. My reasons are my own.

September 12, 1989

Dear Mr. McMann:

What a pleasure it was to read the wonderful poems you sent me this week. I was up all night rereading them and made not a mark on any page. I woke with the sun to call my editor at Silo Press to inform her that I see no reason why we can't make a deadline for the first week of October if you can only continue to find me more of the same. There are about sixty more pages to fill out, and I am putting myself in your hands to help me complete this task. You are the center of this geographic literary tradition, while I am a mere observer hoping to facilitate bringing the words of your fellow conjurers to a larger public.

You will be paid generously for your work, perhaps not with the unfortunately small check that will arrive through me from Silo Press, but in terms of the doors this should open for your future career in letters. I have already mentioned to Daniel Kirby of *Poem* the unfortunate financial problems of your esteemed publication *Rose Is a Rose,* and he is looking into possible benefactors to bring your magazine back to life. But not before you complete the work at hand.

Though my name shall appear on the title page and at the end of a brief foreword to your work, you will be graciously mentioned throughout. I hope to see at least another dozen poems by the week's end, so comb every coffeehouse and bring me more of these blossoms waiting to bloom.

Yours,

Vivian Reape

P.S. As for your concern over Joanne Mueller's inclusion in this anthology, please do not let the "quality" of her work hinder your own. As I'm sure you know, Ms. Mueller is truly an artist of fiction, and I am confident that with a rereading of her verse you will agree that poetry has only served her as a road map to her true destination of prose.

P.S.S. Mr. Dupree mentioned your own past work as a poet, and I was sorry not to see any of your work included in what you sent me. Dust off those poems immediately. I expect a healthy sampling of them in your next batch.

September 14, 1989

Dear William:

It feels strange writing to you. I realize your not returning my phone calls in the past few weeks is a sign that you are not quite ready to hear from me, but I want you to know how sorry I am for the rather abrupt end to our relationship last month. It is hard for me to explain, but I feel like we had different ideas as to our future together and that perhaps mine was a bit more ambitious than yours. I feel very young when I think of the six months we spent together. What was it Evelyn Waugh described? That small door at the base of a tower—where love was? It was all very beautiful.

I'm sure you know about my relationship with Alex Dupree, and though we have decided to spend the month apart so he can concentrate on his poem for the Yucca Mountain Project, I want you to know that if we resume a relationship it will in no way affect the friendship you and I will always share.

Finally, there is one thing: A wool green cardigan with pockets, in particular. I realize I gave that to you for your birthday last June, but I want to remind you that it is nearly forty years old and one of the only things I have left of my grandfather's. We can arrange getting it back to me in whatever way would be most comfortable for you. Perhaps you could just leave it over the back of a chair at Earthly Delight at a certain time, and I could pick it up when I see you leave.

Still fondly,
Peter Brooks

P.S. Oma speaks highly of you, and it doesn't bother me at all that you have continued your friendship with her.

19 September 1989

Whomever It May Concern:

As cosigner of Joanne Mueller's lease at 42 Bradley Place, #2, I have enclosed a check to cover her last two months' rent, which, I understand from your letters dated August 1 and August 31, she has not paid. I am also writing to inform you that Ms. Mueller has unexpectedly left the city, and as cosigner, I have taken over her apartment. I am providing a new tenant, Shelly Milter, who will move in next week after I have finished moving and storing Ms. Mueller's personal items. The enclosed check should cover Ms. Milter's first three months of rent, and I shall remain cosigner on the lease until you feel she has established proper credit with your real estate company. She has asked me to inquire about the garage behind the house. Should there be additional rent for a garage space, please bill me for that.

Sincerely,
Jon Sullivan

22 September 1989

Dear Rose:

Lydia and Carl informed me of your decision to leave your job at the University of Chicago, both of them feeling somewhat responsible as last month's incident may have put undue pressure on you in terms of your role and position at the school. When I called the school and found out you had left the day of your notice, a young woman was kind enough to give me this forwarding address for you in Berlin.

How I envy you, Rose! The East German borders are breaking down; it seems mere minutes until the Wall will come down, and there you will be in the true center of history, East and West fighting to the finish, the possibilities of a true socialist state rising from the rubble of a propped-up Soviet republic. It makes all of our work here seem like an endless assembly line of Xeroxing and chanting—how good you were at chanting. I can only imagine how easily you've taken up the various dialects of class and region in German.

You should see Lydia when your name comes up now. All of us so envious of you, all of us so eager for you to return to tell us what you've seen, all you will see. Even Carl has put aside his eco-crap to devote more of his time to reading accounts from Eastern Europe of socialism picking itself up from the oppressive state the Soviets enforced. You are the Independent Revolutionary Socialists' eyes and ears, Rose. These are your days to shake the world.

I myself am hoping to take a trip to Berlin this fall to meet with some of our European members and would like to see you. In fact, I would prefer to stay with you if you are comfortable with that. Chicago already seems so far away.

Your friend,
Walter

24 September 1989

Dear Mrs. Lewis:

Our records indicate that your son, Sink Lewis, has failed to register for fall classes and has not notified the student housing office of his need for dormitory space. As of the date of this letter, his delinquency in complying with Lake Bluff College's rules of admission forfeits his rights in being a student at the college for the fall semester. Should he be able to show just cause for missing these deadlines by October 1, his situation will be reevaluated. Our recommendation is for him to complete the enclosed form and rejoin the college at the start of the second semester, January 13, 1990. I need to warn you that his scholarship is in jeopardy and that the financial aid office may ask for him to reapply for loans he has already been approved for. If you have any questions about these conditions or can provide information as to your son's plans, please contact our office at the above phone and address.

Sincerely,
Carla Roth
Lake Bluff College Personnel Office

September 25, 1989

Dear Alex:

Forgive the postcard, I will write you a lengthier letter once I am fully situated and have more to tell. For now, Alaska is wonderful. I have a very efficient cabin and three large dogs. My nearest neighbor is five miles away, and I am busy stocking up for what I'm promised will be a long winter. I am reading westerns and pulpy historical novels (the local library—twelve miles south— has not even *heard* of Virginia Woolf). I hear rumor of the advance of the glaciers, but I try to put that out of my head. What news of Joanne Mueller? I'm afraid *North American*s are hard to come by in these parts, so I can't keep up.

Yours,

Helen Drake

September 29, 1989

Dear Joanne (and Sink!—wherever you are),

I am writing to you care of Lake Bluff College in hopes they have a forwarding address. I have no way of knowing if this will ever reach you, so I will pretend it will.

Everything has changed to the point that I feel I am attending another school. Alex Dupree is gone, you are gone, Sink, even that funny Prof. Helen Drake has run off, and no one asks where or seems worried. William and Tom have somehow found each other in all the confusion, and though Book Bar looks done for, it seems to be a relief to Tom, who is full of plans for next year. William hopes to be joining him wherever they end up. Perhaps it will be close to where you are—where are you?

I miss our morning talks at the Coffee Bar, which is now a crystal goddess something-or-other kind of store. I cannot believe the amount that has changed in a few short weeks after three years with what seemed like no change. It makes me sad, but hopeful. I know I will be seeing you and Sink again someday. Didn't you always say it's a big, *big* life?

I'm afraid I'm not writing any poetry. I don't think too much of the temporary poets-in-residence they came up with to fill yours and Alex's positions. They don't seem to have the same expertise, and the classes, I hear, are somewhat of a free-for-all. But I've been writing more and more music, and next month, if I can actually convince myself, I'm to perform at Earthly Delight. Just me, my guitar, and a microphone. Sink always told me to just turn around and perform with my back to the audience, which is exactly what I did for the audition, and I got it. I hope they assume it's part of my act.

If you are in touch with Sink, would you send him all my love and tell him to contact me at the enclosed phone and address at any time? I have also given Tom some of his poems to publish in some anthology that, apparently, you are also in, Joanne. Vivian Reape's behind it, of all people. I sometimes wonder if poems can eventually outgrow the people they are attached to. This anthology makes me think so.

The weather has finally turned cooler, and I take long walks around Lake Bluff in the evenings when the wind feels like the beginning of winter. I already miss the heat, the basement apartment, the drawers and cupboards that refused to close because the wood became so bloated with humidity. It all seems like a kind of feverish dream, Sink and I, Alex and Peter, William and Tom. You drinking wine on my futon. The back of Sink's head driving you away. I hope, wherever you are, that you are warm.

Love,
Diane

1 October 1989

Dear Ms. Reape:

This letter confirms our receipt of your manuscript *The Minor Poets of Chicago* and, as you point out in the accompanying letter, releases you from further contractual obligations to Silo Press. You are right to assume that we find the selection of poets to be a bit random and are somewhat uncomfortable with the inclusion of Joanne Mueller in an anthology bearing the title you have provided. To be blunt, we don't like the title at all. Though you have attempted to explain in your introduction how schools of "minor poets" have made serious contributions to the very survival of poetry, and, as your accompanying letter reminds us, your contract grants you editorial control of such decisions, we must ask you to reconsider before we ask our own legal department to go over such terms in your contract.

We are, however, pleased to have a name as prominent as Ms. Mueller's to help promote the book. Thank you for your further promotional notes regarding Daniel Kirby at *Poem* and Thomas McMann at Book Bar. We have passed this information on to our publicity department and we will certainly call on them in promotion of the book. We agree that the print run for the title should be no more than five thousand and that its distribution should be limited to the five-state region. Upon publication (tentatively set for January 1990) we will send you ten copies of the book along with a check for five hundred dollars that will release Silo Press from all other contractual obligations between us.

Sincerely,
Dominique Riggs
Silo Press

P.S. We are having difficulty getting in touch with Joanne Mueller. Could you please give us a current address or phone number for her?

PART 3

September

A Story of Yucca Mountain
by Joanne Mueller

I snap the sheet above the bed,
  a quick suspended yawn,
an apparition as it falls
  of our two bodies gone.

A draft descends upon the bed,
  brings in the distant hum
of shovels scraping away the snow
  I never knew had come.

I smooth the wrinkled, drifted sheet
  and wonder if and when
our imprints blurred together will
  return and sleep again.

—Sink Lewis

I have never been the type of person to sentimentalize places I've left. Still, the desert is not a cornfield, mountain ranges are hardly the Chicago skyline, and most of the people here are from somewhere else. I was once told that New York was that way—city of immigrants, artistic hopefuls, and bored adolescents who somehow find just the right amount of money and guts to get in and, once in, never leave. I imagine Las Vegas to be the kind of place such small-town dreamers end up in someday to die. I should know. I have already met quite a few of them.

Frank is one. He moved out here from West Seventy-fifth Street in New York when his wife died two years ago. Frank tends a garden in a strange triangle of space created by an intersection and a right-turn lane that is just in front of my house and is about the size of my kitchen. Somehow, despite the heat, he manages to grow strawberries, rhubarb, lettuce, basil, and tomato plants. After I'd lived in Nevada for a few weeks, he started waving at me every time I drove by so I finally walked over to say hello.

"Ya wanna strawberry?" he shouts in his thick East Coast monotone, as I approach. I am always charmed by the way older men flirt with me, the way they know not to touch.

"I think it's great the city is doing this," I say, bending down to run my fingers over the lush bows of lettuce.

"City? *What* city?" I look up at his white, bony legs. His sunglasses stick out about two inches from each side of his rather shriveled, sweating, bald head. "All the city's done is give me tickets and threaten to arrest me. I told them I'd take it to the front page of every paper in town. Go ahead! Arrest an old man for planting a garden. I have to water it three times a day. Four when it's really bad."

I can't stop staring at the edible green of the vegetable plants and stand back up. Frank tells me he lives in the complex on the other side of the street facing my house. It's one of those retirement complexes where apartments eventually turn into hospital rooms. He tells me the pamphlet they'd first sent him had shown beautifully landscaped grounds, a footbridge over a stream, plans for a nine-hole golf course. We both look over at Cactus Village, which seems to be entirely surrounded by asphalt except for one fenced area with a pool.

"That's terrible," I say, which is something I find myself saying a lot when I get into conversations with the elderly, which is most of the time now that I'm out here. It only seems to encourage more stories, and I keep reminding myself to come up with another response.

Frank, encouraged, explains how the move from New York had exhausted him so that he didn't have the energy to "tell them to shove it" and find another place. He hadn't moved in over fifty years and never any farther than twenty miles. I tell him I'm late for work but I'll stop by again.

"Your boy helps me carry buckets of water sometimes," Frank says, in way of good-bye. "He's a good boy."

I take the strawberry he hands me, consider the amount of car exhaust that has probably settled on it, and plop it in my mouth, pulling the stem out between my teeth. I widen my eyes to say it's good and walk quickly across the right-turn lane. I have no idea how to tell him that the "boy" he refers to is really my lover.

The egg-drop contest was my idea. I volunteered at the Yucca Mountain Waste Project the first week I arrived. They never questioned my interest in helping to promote public acceptance of the geological studies going on to make Yucca Mountain the first in-ground, long-term storage facility for nuclear waste. They never asked to see any ID. When they found out I could type sixty words a minute, they set me up with a desk and a database, and I started working an hour a day, which in a few weeks became a few hours a day, which a month later became a full-time salaried position. The egg-drop contest had a lot to do with my promotion.

Peg asked me to think about ways to promote the eventual opening of Yucca Mountain for the acceptance of nuclear waste, specifically with young people. I admitted to having been a teacher once, and she interpreted that to mean I had worked with young people—young being elementary school, something I actually have no experience with. Peg Logan is a senior board member for the project. Peg is also a volunteer. Peg is also president of a large chemical company that hopes to expand into mining and large-scale industrial operations. Yucca Mountain is about the largest mining and industrial operation Nevada has seen for some time.

"Draw your own conclusions," I often hear her say into her phone in the office next to my desk. I imagine her saying this to everyone from reporters to federal officials. If she slams the phone down shortly after saying this, I guess it was a journalist or an environmental group. If she laughs or talks more about the project or her business, I guess it's the government.

Peg is a quintessential Western woman, divorced, successful, and hard to miss, unless she's in the company of a lot of other women like her. Her hair is big and done, blonde, though her physical features give the impression that she has never been blonde natu-

409

rally, and her skin is dark and weathered. She wears pantsuits and skirts that always emphasize her thin waist in relation to her hips and low necklines emphasizing her jewelry and breasts. Everything Peg does seems in service of drawing attention to something else. From a distance Peg looks considerably younger than me. Up close she looks significantly older. We are, in fact, the same age.

"My god, Rose, so am *I*," she whispers across the table at Sand Devil, the restaurant in Fashion Square Mall where she took me to lunch the day she asked me to think about young people incorporating nuclear waste into their lives. "I assumed younger," she continues. "Lord, I envy you all those years in a colder climate. You're *preserved*."

I had not told anyone at the project where I'd lived the thirty-five years before I walked into their office. They never asked. I never fooled myself that an enterprise so large and controversial as this would not run routine background checks on anyone who just walked in off the street and volunteered, *especially* anyone who just walked in off the street and volunteered. Still, I feel like a fool when Peg makes reference to my past, and I take a long sip of my margarita to let it pass.

"Age is how you feel," I think I should say, and say.

"Damn right," Peg shoots back, clicking my margarita with the base of hers as she joins me in a long sip. "I'm only surprised they didn't card me!" Peg is the kind of woman who will tell a joke, stare right at the person she said it to for exactly ten seconds, and then scream in laughter. Like she isn't used to being around people who are afraid she might not be joking. As if there are times when she isn't.

"So what brings you to nuclear waste?" Peg finally gets around to as casually as that, one and a half margaritas later in broad daylight in a shopping mall with slot machines. I had volunteered for close to three weeks. I had moved from basic data imput to drafting letters and copyediting press releases. No one has ever thought to ask me this before, but I have really only made friends with the office workers who were there for their paychecks. The board members and consultants seem to avoid me as I avoid them. I realize that most people in the office are under the impression that I am paid something as well and decide it's time to give Peg the answer I had prepared way back the first day I walked into the office.

"Whenever I'm new to a community, I find it beneficial to volunteer at a local organization that is involved in something timely and unique to the city I just moved to."

Peg stares at me for ten seconds as if she's waiting for me to burst into screaming laughter. After half a minute goes by, she refills my margarita glass from the pitcher instead.

"Nevada could use more of you," she says as she does this. "Let's hope it's a sign."

Twenty-one is a round number. Nick told me that the first night we had sex. We had just moved from the first cheap motel we had seen when we drove into town and into the one-bedroom house across from the retirement home. For two weeks we had been the only people we knew, and after the week-long drive from the Midwest he didn't seem like a student of mine anymore. Nick was only supposed to drive me to the Illinois border because I had been in no shape to drive after two Valiums washed down with red wine, but I knew without asking that he planned on going the distance. After five motels along the interstate and an entire week in another motel off the Strip, I presumed we'd never sleep together—we even shared a bed a couple of times, once in Nebraska and again in Utah, but the first night in the rented house changed all that.

"Like we're married now, or something," Nick said. I was already trying to rewrite in my mind the fact that I had made the first move as I watched him get off the mattress and look out at cars turning right from the window.

"Please don't say that," I said, pulling the sheet to my neck as I stared at the perfectly smooth, fluid sculpture of his backside illuminated by the light left on in the next room.

A bottle of red wine to celebrate the empty house we'd rented had led to all this. I can remember my hand falling onto his thigh as we sat on the horrible sofa the previous renter had left. I can remember not taking my hand away and how he just continued talking about how everyone he met our first week in Nevada was from California. I found it harder to keep up my end of the conversation and just let my other hand fall on the back of his neck and started combing his silky, blond hair with my fingers as I had imagined doing for the thousands of miles we had driven together. I couldn't remember ever making the first moves before in my life. A minute later we were kissing and struggling with the dusty sofa before I finally suggested moving to the new mattress we had had delivered that day. Nick had ordered it and had only ordered one. Perhaps that was the first move, I thought to myself, as he ran to the bedroom in front of me, kicking off his tennis shoes and pants along the way.

I had never talked so much during sex in my life. We'd kiss and roll around and start something that normally would build up to a conclusion, and he'd suddenly ask a question like, "Do you think it gets boring with the same person after a period of time?" or laugh about some day-old experience or suddenly spring up and announce, "I have to pee."

Two hours of this had gone by before he finally asked if I was ready.

"Ready for what?"

"You know," he smiled, actually embarrassed, and looked back at me so that I understood. My hands were flat on his hairless chest where I found it hard to remove them. I kissed him. I knew.

When I was twenty-one, I was into my second year of having sex with the man who, a year later, would become my husband, and it would be twelve years before I ever slept with a different man. Then a different man. Then a twenty-one-year-old.

412

"You think too hard about stuff," Nick said, rolling back on top of me in the same spirit he had during what I considered to be extended foreplay but what he obviously considered to be the essential two hours of sex. I decided to remind him of my exact age before daylight could beat me to it.

"I've known your age for two weeks; I looked at your driver's license."

"You looked at my driver's license?" I asked, a little too hysterically to the twenty-one-year-old who had just left college to accompany me to Las Vegas and order a single mattress for a house I had rented in my name.

"We were in a car together for a hundred hours. I looked at everything in your damned purse by the time we hit Des Moines. Here," he leapt from the bed again. I had started to notice how often his conversation would give him an excuse to jump up and do something or get something while my own tended to settle me deeper and deeper into whatever I was sitting on. "Look at mine, if you already haven't."

I looked down at the boyish photo, which looked more like a Boy Scout ID, and ended up staring at the strange numbers of his birth date. I had known his age, but seeing it spelled out numerically left me cold.

"Oh, god," I said, handing it back to him, burying my face in the pillow, which still didn't have a case.

He wrapped his body around mine in concern, his one hand pushing my graying hair from my eyes and the other rubbing my arm up and down as if to warm me. He kissed the side of my face softly, telling me everything would be all right, telling me to just shut my eyes and get some sleep, telling me there was absolutely nothing to worry about, and he was hard again.

"An egg," I tell the twenty expectant faces of the Los Prados Elementary School third-grade class and hold the egg straight out in front of me. Like a bad magician I open my fingers and let the egg

413

splatter on the floor. The class gasps, half of them looking back at their teacher, who stares down at the egg like it's a bomb, and the other half still staring at me in complete delight. I stare straight at Peg Logan, who stands next to the furious teacher, beaming. I know what she's thinking. I *have* them.

For my next act I put an egg in an egg carton and drop it in front of me.

"Now," I continue after showing them the egg has not broken, "how many of you think this carton can keep this egg from breaking if I drop it off a ten-story building?"

Half the class obediently raise their hands, while the other half shake their heads furiously. For a moment I have to think if there even *is* a ten-story building in the twenty-block radius. Then I remember the Strip. I wink at Peg. *You like this? You're gonna love it,* I tell her with my eyes.

"What would you say if I told you that in exactly one week we'll all find out," I say and receive the cheers I expected. "But you all have to help me. You all have to do a little work yourselves. I want each of you to go home and build something to put an egg in that you can drop from that building when I drop mine. You can use anything but an egg carton. You can build it, or you can just use something already made. But I'm sending you home with a letter to your parents so they'll know what you're up to, so don't even think of using something without their permission. Can you do that?"

After a few questions regarding what the prize will be, the teacher dismisses the class for recess, and Peg walks up with a roll of paper towels.

"The safety canisters for the transport of nuclear waste. Rose, you're brilliant," she says, waving me off as she kneels down to clean the floor.

"Oh, it's better than that," I say. In the few short weeks I have known Peg I have already learned how to speak her language. It's exactly like dealing with any editor or dean; just talk press and

414

money, and they'll eat right out of your hand. Peg pitches the rest of the paper towel roll to the scowling teacher, making no effort to include her in the conversation. "I'm not talking about some industrial park in the middle of nowhere with a bunch of kids hurling eggs off a ledge. What would you say to Caesar's Palace and every local news team in town?"

At the pool area at the Flamingo Hilton the palm trees spray mist from hoses wrapped around their trunks. Nick and I get here every Wednesday before noon, before the best lounge chairs are taken, the ones directly under these trees. The first few times we came (after a week inspecting pool areas at other hotels along the Strip), we would first go to the casino and casually drop quarters in slots before separately going to the rest room, where we'd change into swimsuits and walk out to the pool as if we were hotel guests. The first few times we never ordered drinks and spent a lot of the afternoon worried someone would demand to see our hotel key, but Nick eventually fixed all that.

"What shall it be today?" Nick asks me as the white-uniformed waiter grins down at us. "Blue drinks? Red drinks? White drinks?" Nick parks cars at Caesar's five nights a week, right across the street from the Flamingo. It only took him a few weeks to start meeting other people in the hotel/casino industry with whom he could swap favors. Roger, the weekday Flamingo pool manager, enjoys free valet service at Caesar's whenever he wants to impress a girlfriend. Caesar's has the best entrance by car, usually limousine, a long driveway with lighted fountains leading to a grand entrance, where a few tourists always stand watching the well-dressed men and women get in and out of expensive cars. In return for the parking, Roger not only allows us to spend our Wednesdays at the Flamingo pool area, but has also given us a fake room number to use to order whatever drinks and food we want, a room number that doesn't exist in the pink-glass towers of the hotel around us. Using the room number always makes me feel slightly dangerous, like I've slipped back in time to the older, romanticized Las Vegas when expensive things were never paid for, when money was replaced with toy chips, drinks on the house, men in white suits smiling down at you as you picked the color of your cocktail that day.

Wednesdays at the pool make me extremely aware of the difference in our ages. Barely covered by a bikini and sunglasses, my thin body looks all of its thirty-five years no matter how much the sun colors it and no matter how much lotion I apply to make it glisten. Nick's body looks like the protective plastic wrapping just came off. Adult stress, a poor diet, and sporadic exercise haven't shown up on his arms or legs, waist or forehead. He wears baggy shorts that come down to his knees and hang low from his navel, shorts that are very much in style at the time, while my simple navy suit has been chosen for its simplicity, not too skimpy and not too conservative, thirty-five being an age when too much of one extreme immediately becomes too extreme. Not to mention a twenty-one-year-old boyfriend. I never refer to him that way out loud. It's too exact a description for me to ever say out loud.

Nick's arrangement with Roger is another thing that scores the difference in our ages. When you're young, you can get free things, free drinks, free entry to clubs, free parking. Your friends are waitresses and bartenders, valet parkers and doormen. Your social life is made up of restaurants and bars where someone you know works and will get you the best table and no bill. Later, when your friends become real estate agents, teachers, and executive secretaries, the free stuff stops. No one is ever going to offer you a free house, and it's not like you're going to ask them to pinch you a stapler or a computer keyboard.

Despite my hyperawareness of our age difference as we shift the position of our chairs to follow the sun, I don't mind it when Nick kisses me or sits at my side running his hands up and down my colored, glistening legs. That's another good part about Las Vegas, at least the Las Vegas made up of resort hotels, water fountains,

416

large casinos, and palm trees spitting water. The sight of a very young-looking man kissing a very thirty-five-year-old-looking woman is not something that necessarily catches anyone's attention.

"I can tell right off what a good storyteller you are," Donna Black says, gripping my hand with both of hers with that overenthusiastic condescension that makes me realize why Westerners loathe tourists. "I can just tell you're a woman made up of stories, stories I look forward to hearing sometime. But for now our story is Yucca Mountain, and like your own life, it is a story made up of many different stories."

I nearly fall backward a step when she finally releases my hand and turns to the three other tour guides in training. Peg Logan leans against the front desk, and though she has kept on her sunglasses and stays a good ten feet from the high-pitched chatter of Donna Black, I can tell she's winking and grinning at me, hoping I won't bolt.

It's my first day at the year-old Yucca Mountain Visitors' Center, a one-story building about the size of a Gap store and actually located in a small strip mall. The center is not for the employees of the Yucca Mountain Project but for the people of Nevada and tourists from around the world who want to learn more about the first underground, long-term nuclear waste storage facility. As Donna Black continues telling the other trainees about the stories she's confident they possess, I glance around the single room that serves as a science center made up of maps, photographs, Native American artifacts, and small-scale models of the mountain, the proposed storage facility, and the methods of transportation under consideration to bring nuclear waste to the mountain.

"You'll hate her," Peg told me as she drove us to the center. It had been Peg's idea for me to train as a guide. I had always expressed my desire to go to the site and see for myself the place where it was hoped toxic waste could be safely sealed and left

417

alone for ten thousand years. Once the center opened, it was announced that tours of the site for the public would be conducted one Saturday every month. After the success of the egg-dropping event made the front page of all the local papers and even papers as far away as *The New York Times* featured photos of laughing children learning the important work of transporting deadly waste into their own backyard, Peg wanted me to move out of data entry and train for an eventual position in management. Becoming a tour guide seemed to be a good next step, and with my background in teaching, Peg saw it as a natural fit.

"She's one of those overpaid corporate therapists who treats everyone like toddlers when it comes to environmental impact adjustment."

"You mean she whitewashes everything," I say, letting Peg's convertible Miata blow-dry my hair with dust.

"I mean she's a bitch."

"You are the faces of Yucca Mountain," Donna Black tells us, after convincing us to all sit cross-legged on the industrial carpeting in a circle. "There are no issues. There are no politics. There is no right, there is no wrong, and above all, there is no danger." She wears an expensive white business suit that looks Italian, and her red hair is cut in an asymmetrical bob so that her thin face always seems to be at a slight angle, perfectly posed for a camera. I guess her to be younger than me, and I settle down comfortably on the floor in my jeans and T-shirt to enjoy hating her.

"What that leaves us with are stories. A nonjudgmental narrative to tell people what they're seeing and what isn't there to be seen. For example, Bob here," Donna indicates a thin, bearded man who looks like a graduate student in something you can't see the need to graduate in. "Bob is training as a botanist at the site. He will tell people the story of plant life at Yucca Mountain. After showing people the variety of desert life, he will finish his story by explaining how the government plans on restoring exactly all the desert environment that is temporarily being used by workers and machinery. He will show diagrams and timetables explaining how this will be accomplished. Bob has already had extensive training on-site and is, perhaps, a little further along in knowing what kinds of questions to expect from visitors to Yucca Mountain. Let me show you. So, Bob," Donna drops her voice down to mimic a man's, causing nervous laughter from the rest of us. I see Peg walk out the door with a quick hand wave over her shoulder. "Why spend all this money restoring plant life when all that nuclear stuff they're burying here will just kill it all anyway?"

Bob clears his voice and speaks directly to Donna. "There really is no threat to the environment from the proposed storage facility. Evaluations are continuing, and if any potential for leakage is found, the site will be ruled out. The story of plant life at Yucca Mountain will continue with the return of normal desert life once construction is finished."

"Notice his use of *proposed*," Donna says, back in her high-pitched hostess voice. "Though the digging of the tunnel is under-way, this is the only method for continued tests on the suitability of the mountain. When all tests have been concluded to favorably show the safety of the site, then storage will start. This is important because we want our visitors not to feel the story has been con-cluded without them. We are all a part of the story of Yucca Mountain, and by stressing that you will gain the trust of the group. Also, notice how Bob did not resort to words like *nuclear* and *waste*. Avoid these words at all costs. What's that kind of cactus where the needles literally fly out at you when you get too close?" She looks at Bob, who seems caught off guard, unsure whether or not this is one of the potentially sensitive questions he's in training for. "Well, I think those words are like that kind of cactus; get too close and you get pricked."

"You're taking a field trip to a nuclear test site? I think you're going a little bit too far with this job thing," Nick says.

I'm thrilled to be chastised by someone half my age.

"It's not to the test site; it's to the proposed depository at Yucca Mountain, which happens to be within the borders of the test site, which is about the size of Rhode Island. I'm training to be a guide."

"A guide for what?"

"For the general public interested in the fact of nuclear waste in their lives." I am washing dishes and staring out at the traffic triangle where Frank's tomato plants are browning in the intense sun.

"It sounds dangerous."

"It's not."

"How do you know?"

"It's not any more dangerous than sitting in the sun at the Flamingo once a week or working at the front door of Caesar's and breathing in exhaust all night."

"So it's just *low-level* radiation?"

The phone rings, and I reach for the dish towel with a cactus pattern.

"It's for me!" Nick yells, sounding more like my teenage son than lover. He talks with his back turned away from me, and I wonder if it's a girl—actually, I wonder about my wondering if it's a girl and what exactly my life has turned into: weekend getaways to contaminated mountains and weeknights alone waiting for Nick to come home any time from midnight to 6:00 A.M. The dishes finished, I pull out a pail and fill it with water for Frank's garden. I haven't seen him for a week.

"I'm going early to meet friends," Nick says, brushing by me and kissing the back of my neck without stopping. My eyes manage to hold him at the open door. "Are you okay?" he asks. I told myself I would end it when he started asking me questions like that. "I worry about you and this whole nuclear stuff."

"Come along."

"Sure. How do I do that?"

"We have to get you cleared."

Nick laughs. "They're actually afraid of people bringing bombs to a bomb site?"

"It's a party," Peg whispers to me through her teeth. "Mingle, meet men, get drunk."

Peg's entire adobe house seems to be an afterthought of the back patio, which has a spectacular view of a western mountain range and borders a golf course so she can count on the view staying unobstructed. Her company has officially been awarded a lucrative contract for some kind of construction at Yucca Mountain, and she is having a cocktail party to celebrate. The fifty people who fill her patio hardly look at the explosion of color setting over the mountains, which I can't take my eyes off of. I'm still not used to seeing it. The food consists of mini-everything: burritos, pizzas, sandwiches, anything that can be put in your mouth whole.

"Go, have a good time," I protest to Peg, as she drags me from the fence where I've been staring at the sky. "Why do you worry about me so much?"

"I told you to bring a date. You didn't, so now I have to find you one. Ray!" I stop walking when Peg calls out this name, and Peg is yanked to a halt next to me, her arm still through mine. Before I can say anything, a rather burly, sunburned man in his forties approaches us.

"Rose, Ray; Ray, Rose. I've just been dying for you two to meet. Rose here is about the best worker at the project I've ever seen, and Ray, well you'll have to tell her, but Ray has been heading the team boring through the mountain for the past three months. Take her to the bar, and get her something."

Peg leaves with that, giving us both the opportunity to laugh at her and start off with something in common—being embarrassed.

"You look like a woman who drinks wine," Ray says. I have

grown used to the way men in the West make declarative statements about women and are usually right.

"White," I say, as we move to the bar. "Zinfandel if they have it."

I settle for rosé, and Ray takes more scotch. I convince him to go to the fence with me so I can keep watching the sunset, which has greatly changed from oranges and yellows to purples and reds in the five minutes I've taken my eyes off of it.

"The Midwest has a big sky," Ray says, when I explain my interest.

"But nothing to obstruct it. See how the mountains and the sky make those incredible colors? In the Midwest it's usually just one flat color when the sun goes down."

"Actually," Rays says, turning his back on the spectacle so he can lean against the fence. "It's the smog that does it out here."

Ray knows more about things out here than I do, and I encourage him to tell me about his work at Yucca Mountain. He resists at first, accusing me of being a polite midwesterner, but I badger him enough for him to believe my real interest.

"It's quite a machine. You'll see it when you come out. We're making a loop through the mountain so we can set up tracks to bring in the waste without having to turn around to get back out. A lot of dust and rock. What else can I tell you?"

"Do you think it's a good idea? Putting it all in this mountain?"

"The way I see it, this mountain has less of a chance of going anywhere than everything else in the world. But it's not really about how safe that mountain is from water tables and fault lines. Nevada actively bid for this years ago when the government first announced plans to build something like this, back when California was still the more popular kid and Las Vegas was the eyesore. Nevada back then needed the jobs and government money. Testing had pretty much ground to a halt, and here's the government with this big chunk of land already so why not turn it into a graveyard for the weapons they'd been testing there for so long? The only problem was the bottom fell out of California. Earthquakes, brush fires, crime, smog. I'll bet you half the people driving by you every day are from California. Well, you can imagine what all happened when those Californians moved the hell out here and turned Las Vegas into a respectable town, only to find out it would soon be the burial ground for the country's nuclear waste. But it was too late by then. All this crap about a *proposed* nuclear depository. You think that after all the money they've spent there's any chance some tiny piece of data will convince them to say, 'Oh well, back to the drawing board'? They're just buying time until the California contingent gets a little more used to the idea and quits thinking the stuff is somehow going to mutate the greens on their golf courses. You not married?"

Ray extends his pinkie finger from his empty scotch glass to point at my bare ring finger curled around my empty wineglass.

"Are you asking to marry me?" I've always known how to talk to men like Ray.

"Not yet." The sunset is pretty much over, so we go back to the bar, where Ray convinces the bartender just to hand over the bottles of scotch and rosé so we can stay comfortable at the fence away from the rest of Peg's friends, who are quite loud and seem like the Californians Ray was just describing.

"I'm seeing someone," I think to explain. Ray hasn't said much since the marriage comment. "He's living with me, but it's nothing formal. He's a lot younger than I am, and it bothers me." I can't believe I'm saying any of this and gulp at my wine. I haven't talked to anyone about Nick, and suddenly I'm afraid that once I've started I won't be able to shut up.

"Just how casual is nothing formal, and how young is younger?" Ray asks, with an *aw shucks* kind of laugh, and pours me some more wine. It is suddenly very dark, with stars and house lights mixed up on the horizon, and I figure what the hell.

"He's twenty-one, Ray, and I'm thirty-five. He helped move me out here a month ago and stuck around. We sleep with each other and have sex occasionally but don't talk about any kind of relationship. I'm hoping he'll get bored and go back east."

Ray turns around to look over the fence at the black mountains and sky. The slight chill in the air has sent a lot of Peg's guests into the house. I see Peg holding her sides as she talks to three men. She's laughing that hard.

"You sure you really hope that?" Ray asks, without looking at me, and I suddenly wish he'd just kiss me. His face is rough with a slight beard, and though he must have showered before coming to Peg's from work, I'm sure that dust has worked its way deep beneath his fingernails, into the wrinkles around his eyes, along the roots of his thinning hair. Some time goes by as I think about wanting him to kiss me and not about what he just asked me.

"You know," Ray finally says, looking at me, his face slightly illuminated from the fires in Peg's Mexican stoves at each corner of the patio. "Ten thousand years isn't such a long time. Look out there. Can you really believe any of that rock is going anywhere?"

I'm on a tour bus in the middle of a desert, and two armed soldiers in camouflage are walking down the aisle toward me. I feel singled out even though I successfully went through all the clearances necessary to put me on this bus with Donna Black, the three other Yucca Mountain tour-guides-in-training, two certified tour guides, and a couple of dozen displaced Californians (with a few genuine Nevadans) heading to Yucca Mountain with their minds already made up. The soldiers look on the floor between rows of seats and above us in the overhead compartments. They also try to look each of us in the eye as they pass, as if they can determine a potential terrorist from the terrified looks on our faces. The tour guides didn't warn us this would happen once we reached the boundary of the U.S. Testing Site, a literal state within the state of Nevada; and even Donna Black, who has been here before, looks taken aback by this Soviet-style checkpoint. I can already imagine her making mental notes to try and downplay this scenario on future tours. Perhaps the soldiers could wear khaki shorts and Yucca Mountain T-shirts to make them look more like ticket takers at Disneyland. I force myself not to look at Donna (who is across the aisle from me) as I am already nervous enough that they will randomly start questioning me.

"Name?" I imagine the soldier barking at me, the one who looks to be Nick's age and better suited for parking cars than operating an automatic rifle on a tourist bus.

"What's your interest in Yucca Mountain?"

"Whenever I'm new to a community, I find it beneficial to volunteer at a local organization that is involved in something timely and unique to the city I just moved to."

"What's your position on nuclear waste?" I'd look over at Donna at this, unprepared to respond to a question using the exact two words we were trained to avoid. Donna would stare straight in front of her as if she had never seen me before in her life.

"Don't we all have an interest?" I'd answer, careful to avoid repeating those words while at the same time attempting to personalize the hostile exchange.

"It's my job; what's *your* story?"

"It's my job, too."

This, of course, would not appease him, and he would begin dragging me off the bus. I would immediately realize my error and start to think of how to tell him the *story* of my job for Yucca Mountain, the *story* of Nick and me running off to Las Vegas, the *story* of my being left in the middle of the desert at the gate to the U.S. Testing Site.

The soldiers finally get off the bus, and we enter the testing site. Though the barren landscape hasn't changed one bit on the other side of the fence, the tourists are all pushing themselves toward the windows, wide-awake after this brush with the military. I catch

425

Donna's eye, and she too quickly slaps on a smile as if to say well, that was one of those cactus I was warning you about. Get too close, and the needles just fly out at you.

Donna instructed me and the other three tour-guides-in-training to act like normal tourists today, to carefully observe the interactions of the real tourists with the trained guides. We are allowed to ask questions like the tourists; in fact, she has encouraged us to do so; that way we won't look suspicious. Donna has even gone to the trouble of providing us with some sample questions to ask. "How far is the nearest population center to Yucca Mountain?" "What wildlife, if any, make Yucca Mountain their habitat?" "How long would it take a drop of rain to reach the water table below the mountain?" From what I've heard on the first hour of the bus ride, asking such a question would be a bigger giveaway of my training than wearing a name tag. So far the questions have been more like declarative statements. "Why can't they store the stuff in outer space?" "Nevada doesn't even use nuclear power, so why do we have to deal with it?" "If it's so safe, why do they have to drag it all the way out here to bury it?"

The tour guides have done exactly as Donna would do. They calmly answer these questions with the most unthreatening and scientific responses possible. They avoid saying it's absolutely determined that the waste will end up in Yucca Mountain and that's why we're all out here, to see how suitable the site is. No one seems to believe this. I listen more to the murmuring between passengers than the textbook responses of the guides. There is a general distrust of the military, the government, and the East Coast as being responsible for the stuff in the first place, and everyone reacts in that Western way I've gotten used to. In the minds of people in the West, Washington, D.C. is as far away as China, and the government's only interest in the West is to strip it of its minerals and use it as a garbage heap for illegal immigrants, weapons, and waste. The guides try to make a game out of the difference of opinion with the more vocal opposition (a couple of middle-aged men who say they served in the military and, thus, claim to know a lot about anything nuclear). The guides don't do a very good job and sound like camp counselors coaxing children away from their homes on their first camping experience. "On the ride back we'll see if our stories of Yucca Mountain haven't convinced some of you of the careful and important work being done out here." From what I can see, nothing in the barren landscape surrounding us will give the skeptics' stories any surprise endings.

Suddenly the right side of the bus is clamoring to look out the windows on the left side of the bus, and I too strain my neck to see around Donna and find out what's out there. It appears to be an exceptionally tall flagpole in the center of a flat canyon. The tourists talk excitably, and the tour guides pretend not to notice the abrupt change in landscape.

"That pole you see is actually a tower," the male guide finally says, once the bus is nearly past it. "It is as tall as the Empire State Building and was used many years ago as part of the military testing."

Testing what? The tourist bus is suddenly any tourist bus winding through Hollywood homes or pulling up to an ancient city. *What was it for?*

I start to understand the people around me. Their interest is not Yucca Mountain; their minds are made up about the potential storage of nuclear waste in a state developing housing projects and golf courses faster than any other. Their interest is in the nuclear testing site, the chance to pass through the wall and see the devastated landscape they've been taught to fear for forty years. Even I stand up a little to get a glimpse of this tower. Donna is back to staring straight in front of her.

"It was used for recording temperatures at different altitudes during detonations."

"It measured how quickly bodies could burn in a nuclear bombing," I imagine myself telling the group once I'm certified as a guide. I stare at the Empire State Building flagpole and find myself

427

trying to memorize every detail of it, like I had tried memorizing every feature of Nick's face that morning when I kissed him good-bye.

Two days before the trip to Yucca Mountain, Peg convinced me to leave work an hour early to play some slots at the Golden Nugget.

"I'm really not much of a gambler," Peg claims, playing the maximum three dollars on her dollar slot. "I've lived in this town for twenty years. Trust me, the excitement fades. It just helps me relax every now and then."

I only play one quarter at a time on my Flaming Sevens machine and always prefer pulling the lever and not pushing the "spin" button like Peg, as I believe the button is all part of a computerized conspiracy to make you lose. Not that I've ever won. I'm not much of a gambler either, and the little slots I play have always been a matter of how long I can make a twenty-dollar bill last.

"You gotta put in to take out," Peg coaches. "Everyone eventually gets a payout. But it's like stocks; you have to expect to put a lot in to get even more out."

I don't buy any of this but enjoy relaxing with Peg (who does manage to keep hitting up on her maximum bets, while my twenty quickly turns into a ten), and we order a second round of Coronas.

"Ray was pretty taken with you," Peg says, once her streak has run out and she's back to manually feeding in new coins.

"I probably scared him away."

"Why?"

"Just talking too much."

Peg spins on her stool so she's facing me. She wears very tight designer jeans and a low-neck, silk shirt. A lot of people might say I'm prettier, but at the Golden Nugget, Peg gets all the glances.

"When are you going to tell me about this son or lover who's living with you?" she asks just like that. I would be accused of generalizing if I claimed people in the Midwest never had the nerve to pry like that, but Peg's nerve was definitely something I'd had little experience with and greatly admired. Except this time.

"I'll tell you about it when I'm ready to and he's neither," I say, keeping my eyes firmly on the mess of sevens, cherries, and blank spaces in front of me.

"Neither? Is he gay?"

"No." I finally spin around on my stool to have this out with her. Not only does Peg have the nerve to ask such questions, but she has no patience with getting no answers. "It's complicated. He's an old friend, and he just came out to help me settle in."

"There's nothing wrong with sleeping with him."

"No, there isn't. I just don't think I want to do it anymore."

Peg smiles at me as if to remind me we're friends here and there's no reason for raising my voice.

"Ray told you all this?"

Peg's smile falls off her face, and she starts loading dollars into the slot again. "Ray wouldn't tell me something like that."

I wait.

"Rose, we're an agency of the Department of Energy, which reports to Congress. We run checks on about everyone. For clearance to set foot on the nuclear test site there are a lot of checks. When your report came across my desk, I thought I'd look so I could talk anybody out of persuing something about you that didn't amount to anything in the first place. Like your roommate."

Strangely, I'm not angry or humiliated. I believe Peg was only looking to protect me and was also a little curious about my past, something I have taken too long to discuss with her.

"What else was there?" I start putting quarters in again too, deciding to max my bets like Peg.

"Pretty basic. You divorced your husband and came here. Your friend was a student of yours at the small college you taught at. Nobody knows the exact order all of this happened in, and nobody needs to know. You're clean."

"Is that what you think?" My voice wavers a little on the last word. It always comes as a surprise to me when I realize I've made a new friend, that moment when I realize I really care about what they think of me.

Peg laughs and hits her Corona against mine. "You want to know what I think? I think the West is made up of people like you, always has been, always will. Get divorced, lose your job, get bored, turn thirty, whatever ails you, just head west and start over. You're clean all right, clean as a new car."

"Hello, how are you?" Frank says. "Sit down over here." He indicates the only chair in the room right next to his hospital bed. It isn't until I sit down that I realize he has no idea who I am.

After two weeks of not seeing Frank tending his garden and not having the time to do too much to help save his vegetables from the relentless desert terrain, I finally walked right up to the front desk at Cactus Village, and, after mentioning the garden, the receptionist was able to check her computer and send me to the hospital wing kept discreetly in the back.

"He had a pretty bad stroke," a nurse named Gloria tells me. "His daughter and grandson were here last week, but he didn't seem to remember them so they went back east. Are you a relative? It doesn't really matter, go on in."

Frank has about six tubes coming out of him, and he looks like they are sucking life right out of him. His skin appears fragile, bruised around the areas punctured by IVs, and his eyes are glassy, either from medication or merely reflecting the gray boredom of the sterile hospital environment. There is a plant on the bedside table next to him.

"Who sent you the flowers?" I ask, hoping for the best.

Frank thinks for a moment and glances at them. "You did."

"No, I'm afraid I didn't, but I've been watering your garden, you remember, by the highway?"

Frank keeps smiling at me. He lies on top of his sheet in a thin hospital gown that keeps revealing parts of his sides and thighs when he shifts his legs. I force myself not to be embarrassed.

"Do you know who I am?"

"My daughter."

"No, she was here last week."

"Are you my wife?" Frank starts sitting up, trying to get a better look at me.

"No, why don't you tell me about her."

"She's gone." Frank sinks back on his pillows and stares up at the ceiling. I notice there's another empty bed in the room near the window, and I wonder why Frank can't be in that bed. "I don't know where she went; she's just gone."

Gloria walks in and starts writing things on a felt-tip marker chart on the wall next to him.

"Hello, Frank, can you tell me where you are?"

Gloria winks at me in a girlish way, like we're playing a joke on someone. I usually hate it when young doctors or nurses talk to elderly patients in childish ways, but in Frank's condition, it seems appropriate, and he smiles up at her.

"New York?"

Gloria bends down over him and speaks directly into his face. "You're in Las Vegas. You're in a hospital."

"Did I have an accident?"

I feel a knot tighten in my throat. I see myself in that bed someday, I see Gloria there, Peg, Nick.

"Not really an accident, you're just sick, but getting better." Gloria stands back up and starts checking levels in the tubes coming out of him. "Do you know what year it is?"

Frank looks up at her with a blank expression and glances at me like he hopes I can tell him.

"How about the month?"

"September," he says, and smiles.

I catch Gloria's eye, hopeful.

"Don't get excited. He thinks every month is September. His birthday, last month, next month." She doesn't bother to lower her voice when speaking to me, and somehow Frank knows when he isn't included in the conversation and waits patiently. "When's Christmas?"

"September," Frank says, and smiles again.

"I think you should come with me to California."

This is Nick's response to my suggestion that he should go back to the Midwest in time for the start of fall classes on Monday. I woke up early for the tour of Yucca Mountain, and when I looked back in the bedroom after showering, Nick was still asleep. I presumed he wasn't planning to accompany me on the tour, and I thought it was as good a time as any to address the question of his living with me. We haven't had sex in over a week, most likely due to his coming home late and my getting up early, but the break in our sexual relationship after a month of living together has made me feel very old. I can't stop thinking about how attractive I felt with Ray when the sun went down, putting us both in shadow. With Nick it seems the lights are always on, and I'm constantly reaching for a robe the moment I let the bedsheet fall away.

Nick is propped up on pillows with the sheet barely covering his crotch, and his hairless chest and shapely legs remind me of Frank's feeble body falling out of his hospital gown, his stroke making him just as unselfconscious of his body as Nick is of his. I'm between the two extremes, confident in jeans and a T-shirt, freshly showered and lotioned. I can smell from Nick's breath that he had a lot to drink the night before, but his face weathers the hangover well; only his eyes seem puffy and actually make him look younger than that round number of twenty-one.

"I like it here," I say, glancing quickly around the rather ugly and barren bedroom, furnished only with the box spring and mattress. "I'm making friends."

"Nuclear friends?"

"Yes." I smile and let this pass.

"I don't get your whole interest in this mountain thing; what's so great about it?"

I rub my palms down my thighs. After spending ten years watching teenagers get to Nick's age and go on to other cities and careers, I enjoy the feeling of a job involved in the world, the whole world, it seems, not just teaching the same four years' worth of the world to students. I appreciate the people I work with who are just there for paychecks; I appreciate people like Peg who are there for ulterior motives involving their own businesses; and I especially enjoy not really knowing if what I'm doing is what I'll always be doing. There's no way to explain any of this to Nick, who has reached that age when he needs to graduate and move on without me. Getting someone Nick's age to graduate is something I'm very good at.

"What's in California?"

"This guy at Caesar's goes out there a lot for auditions—TV work, commercials, some extra work on films. He says they'd love me and I should go with him and see."

I frown down at my lap at this but know not to lecture. There are years of disappointment ahead of him, after which he'll suddenly find himself working in something he never anticipated and not minding it so much. He'll fall in love, settle down. My watch tells me I'm running late.

"Promise me if that doesn't work out, you'll finish the year of school. Finish it out there at least." I stand up and reach for my bag.

"You think I'm not ready to settle down, to have a relationship, right? Maybe you're all wrong about that."

I lean over and hold his face close to mine. His blue eyes literally dance around when I look into them this closely, and his slight beard is soft in my palms, hardly noticeable it's so blond. I kiss him the way I've kissed every man I've said good-bye to, not too lightly and not too long, just a closed-mouth, firm kiss that feels

433

like it's enough to leave an imprint so years from now he might be reminded that I was here before.

"I know you might be ready," I say, remembering to memorize everything about the face in front of me. "But I'm not."

Reaching a mountaintop is somewhat of a disappointment. I remember a trip to Arizona with my parents when I was young. All day we hiked to the top of a mountain. The hike itself was a disappointment to me as there were no sheer vertical cliffs of rock, only a steady climb that at times seemed like we weren't even going up. Then at the top there was no single rock to stand on, no point to place a flag, just a meandering flat area that tricked your eye and made it impossible to find the highest point of elevation. Yucca Mountain is exactly the same. As I step back from the tour group gathered around a guide who explains glaciers and volcanic activity thousands of years ago, I look around hopefully for that right place to stand. I think I see it and turn to go there.

"What do you think so far?" Donna Black whispers to me, grabbing my elbow just as I start my escape. She glances back to the group, which looks like a scout troop seated around the guide, afraid they might hear her and blow our cover.

"I don't like the guide on our van as much as the other one," I say. We have broken up into four groups to fit in four vans for the dirt road climb to the top of Yucca Mountain. I have no problem with the guide in my van; it's Donna's presence I am trying to avoid. She has decided to keep close to me throughout the day, and I'm afraid she might want to end it over dinner. "I think I'll go down in his van," I whisper, indicating the guide speaking to the group. "I think I'd get more out of it."

"Good idea," Donna whispers. "Just be careful to get in the van discreetly; pretend you missed the van you came in. I'll see you at lunch."

Donna makes her way back to the group, and I wait a few minutes before moving away. She obviously expects to eat lunch with me at the Visitors' Center, which resembles a junior high school. There we will be fed our box lunches, which we ordered the week before, a choice between two sandwiches, beverage, and salad. Though I've hardly eaten a thing all day, the thought of food makes me nauseous. "Altitude might have a strange effect on some of you," I remember the tour guide saying as the van lurched over rocks and around sharp corners coming up. I take this as a suggestion.

Walking backward a few yards, I finally turn around and casually cross the road where the vans are parked and head to the mountain's opposite side. I look back and decide no one's really noticed that I've broken from the group, so I go down the slope just far enough so I can sit down and not be seen. Stretching out in front of me are endless mountain ranges at the edges of the blurry desert. There is a slight breeze, and the horizon is hazy. I try to use the sun to determine direction, but as it's noon I cannot place it. Ray told me that you can't get the bearings of a mountain with one visit, you have to go many times and see it at different angles before you can start to differentiate its location from the environment around it. I see his point. I had imagined just being able to look down and see Ray and his men drilling their tunnel, follow the road we arrived on out to the horizon toward Las Vegas, look over my shoulder, and see California. Nothing like that will happen on this trip, I realize, and hope Ray or Peg will bring me back a few times as I know I'll never be able to go through with becoming a guide, smiling my way through the annoying questions and angry comments from displaced Californians still in search of open land they can own.

I pick up a few rocks and examine them. I wonder how much fallout they've endured over the past forty years and put them in my pocket. I'm not the kind of person who collects rocks from mountains or shells from oceans, but these particular rocks seem to be the real story; surely a scientist could cut them open and read histories of heat and explosions, both from man and nature. Even

Ray talked with a certain respect for the rock his machine bores out from the tunnel. "Ten thousand years isn't such a long time," he told me. "Look out there. Can you really believe any of that rock is going anywhere?"

Nick said he'd probably be gone by the time I got back. He said this in that adolescent way that seemed to beg me to tell him not to go, that I'd go with him, that we'd figure something out. I told him that would be fine and looked at him for a moment in thanks for getting me out here. Nick is beautiful, and I discover I have forgotten beauty: the intoxicating simplicity of beauty that walks out of a pool toward me, dripping dry in the dangerous sun, his sleeping face clenched in wrinkles too weightless to leave an imprint, and his genuine interest in every detail of the world passing by, each road sign a destination not an end.

I hear the vans start up and doors slam shut above me. Soon the wheels crunch on the gravel of the road and fade down the other side of the mountain. This is what I wanted. This feeling of being on the top alone, not fear but a kind of loneliness, the kind that's impossible to find in the world. The ability to imagine yourself alone, the only one left, a lone explorer thousands of years in the past or future. I'm confident that I only have about an hour before there's a head count with the boxed lunches and a van is sent out after me.

I go back to the top and wait. I wonder if anyone's thought to make some kind of plaque, some way of telling someone ten thousand years from now the date when it will be safe again, the day when someone can build a house, plant a garden, dig down without any worry about what might spring up. I look back to the mountain range I presume to be California and wonder if Nick is going there, if that's where he'll stay, and I breathe in that sweet relief of not always being the one who's leaving, that wholly imagined state of being left.